Cathy Williams can rem[...] Mills & Boon books as a [...] she's writing them she re[...] her, there is nothing like creating romantic stories and engaging plots, and each and every book is a new adventure. Cathy lives in London. Her three daughters—Charlotte, Olivia and Emma—have always been, and continue to be, the greatest inspirations in her life.

Louise Fuller was once a tomboy who hated pink and always wanted to be the Prince—not the Princess! Now she enjoys creating heroines who aren't pretty push-overs but strong, believable women. Before writing for Mills & Boon she studied literature and philosophy at university, and then worked as a reporter on her local newspaper. She lives in Tunbridge Wells with her impossibly handsome husband Patrick and their six children.

BOUND BY HER BABY REVELATION

CATHY WILLIAMS

ONE FORBIDDEN NIGHT IN PARADISE

LOUISE FULLER

MILLS & BOON

First published in Great Britain 2023
by Mills & Boon, an imprint of HarperCollins*Publishers* Ltd,
1 London Bridge Street, London, SE1 9GF

www.harpercollins.co.uk

HarperCollins*Publishers*, Macken House, 39/40 Mayor Street Upper,
Dublin 1, D01 C9W8, Ireland

Bound by Her Baby Revelation © 2023 Cathy Williams

One Forbidden Night in Paradise © 2023 Louise Fuller

ISBN: 978-0-263-30704-7

12/23

BOUND BY HER BABY REVELATION

CATHY WILLIAMS

MILLS & BOON

CHAPTER ONE

KAYA QUIETLY LET herself into the house. Frankly, she didn't have the energy to be anything *but* quiet, because she was dead on her feet and brutally cold.

She could feel the February freeze seeping through the layers and pinching her fingers and toes through her boots and gloves. Her cheeks were stinging. She hadn't slept in twenty-four hours and all she wanted to do now was throw herself into her bed and sleep for a hundred years.

The hall light was on. Why was the hall light on? Had she left it on? She'd done a checklist before she'd left Canada for New Zealand two months ago. Would she have written, "remember to switch hall light off"? Unlikely. But Mrs Simpson, who was her nearest neighbour, had keys to the house. Maybe she'd come in to check and forgotten to switch it off.

None of that mattered.

What mattered was sleep.

She dumped the suitcases on the ground along with her coat and shoes, flexed her sore muscles and padded up the stairs.

Kaya knew this house like the back of her hand because this had been her home for the past three years, all thanks to Julie Anne's kindness and generosity. She'd just about managed to make ends meet at university, picking up part-time jobs wherever she could find them to cover her accommodation and her expenses. Then she'd returned back home, clutching her well-earned degree, to find the cost of renting somewhere without much money in the bank and a job yet to materialise beyond her grasp.

Had her mother still been renting their apartment in town, things would have been just fine, but Katherine Hunter had decamped to New Zealand six years ago with her newly acquired husband. Going to her with a begging bowl had been out of the question, the sort of last resort that hadn't even featured on Kaya's radar.

Her mother had finally found her Mr Right, after a lifetime of disappointing relationships with rich guys who'd had no real interest in her, and there was no way Kaya was going to test the marriage by asking for favours. It wasn't as though her mother had any money of her own to throw around and her flamboyant, adorable husband—kind and lovely as he was—simply wouldn't have the means, or probably the inclination, to help out a stepdaughter he barely knew.

So the offer from Julie Anne to lodge with her rent-free had been manna from heaven and Kaya had never, not once, stopped thanking her lucky stars for the older woman's kindly intervention.

Heading upstairs, she paused and took a moment to think about Julie Anne, pushing away the tears pricking the back of her eyes. How could someone so fit, so vibrant, so healthy...so *good*...have died without warning?

Kaya had been working when she'd got the call from the halfway house that Julie Anne had been rushed to hospital—and not the small, local hospital but the one in Vancouver that was over an hour away.

Julie Anne had been talking to Louise, the manager, chatting and laughing, doing the round at the halfway house as she always did on a Friday, when she'd suddenly collapsed. Just like that. Louise had barely been able to talk through her hysteria and tears.

Kaya had rushed to the hospital and had just about made it there to hold her friend's hand and tell her how much she loved her before the life force that had inspired so many over the years had been snuffed out. She had barely taken in the details: an aneurysm…nothing could have been done…a genetic time-bomb waiting to go off… In the end, what had the details mattered when Julie Anne was no longer there, whatever the reason?

She felt as if she'd spent so long crying. There'd been weeks of tears as Julie Anne's death had sunk in, tears for the friend she'd lost—and, as she'd discovered to her confusion and shock, the friend she had not known half as well as she'd thought she did.

So many disclosures and revelations had come in the wake of her untimely death, disclosures she had accepted because there had been no option *but* to accept them. And, anyway, how well did she ever know anyone when she got right down to it? She had resigned herself to the sadness of knowing that Julie Anne had not been the open book she had thought and had focused on all the good she had brought with her instead—focused on the wonderful woman she had been.

In truth, Julie Anne had been her mentor and best friend, despite the age gap. Kaya had known her since she and her mother had moved to this part of the country north of Vancouver and close to Whistler, where her mother had worked. She could barely remember the distant mists of time before that, because she'd been very young, not quite six. She and her parents had lived in Alaska, her father's homeland.

When he had died, they had migrated here, and Julie Anne had become part of both their lives. She had babysat a young Kaya and then, later, taken her under her wing and covered all those times when Katherine Hunter had been out and about with her rich suitor. Katherine had always been more of a pal to Kaya than a mother and never one to curtail her social life to accommodate a child.

Within minutes of decamping to Canada, to this part of the world where she had grown up, Katherine had vigorously contacted all her old connections—not that there had been that many after more than a decade's absence. With single-minded focus, she'd caught up with the town news in record time and concluded that, if help was needed with her young child, then Julie Anne—well known, active in the community and with no ties of her own—would be a very handy babysitter indeed. And so she had been: cheerful, obliging and happy to pick up the slack.

In a lot of ways, their lives had been entwined for so long and in so many ways that she'd been more like a mother to Kaya than Kaya's own mother had been.

Kaya fought back surging memories.

As she quickly and quietly headed to her bedroom on autopilot, she removed layers of clothing. She'd dumped the thick waterproof coat and her fur-lined boots in the hall, and now she wriggled out of the chunky cardigan and slung it over the banister, then the thin, long-sleeved top she wore underneath.

This just left her in a tee-shirt and the baggy, comfy jogging bottoms she had donned for the flight over from

New Zealand. Being cooped up in cattle class on a fourteen-hour flight required the sort of clothes that allowed for a lot of body contortions in a confined space, especially when she was as tall as she was.

It was warmer in here than she'd expected. She had returned to freak weather conditions that had dumped inordinate amounts of snow from Alaska down to Florida. The hour and a half that it should have taken the coach from Vancouver had stretched to three, battling blizzard conditions for much of it. But at least she wasn't half-freezing to death in here, and she wasn't going to think too hard about that one.

With thoughts of bed, and forgetting about the shower because that could wait until morning, Kaya pushed open the door, yawning and rubbing her eyes and not bothering to switch on the light. All she wanted to do was fall onto the mattress, pull the duvet over her and close her eyes.

She wasn't expecting anything to be amiss, so it was with delayed reactions that she realised that someone else was in the darkened bedroom…that someone else was sleeping *in her bed*…and that that someone else was a man…

What the hell was a man doing in her house, in her room, in her bed? Flight or fight?

No question. Fight.

Leo hadn't heard the soft opening of the front door or the swift gust of wind that momentarily blew through it but he *had* heard the sound of footsteps stealthily approaching the bedroom along the carpeted corridor that hived off into various rooms, including one that was locked for reasons unbeknown to him.

What the hell…?

Thirty-six hours! He'd been here, in the town that time forgot, for *thirty-six hours* and he was already deeply regretting the journey he'd made.

Hell, he could have wrapped up all the paperwork from the comfortable, warm, luxurious surroundings of his New York offices. Instead, what had he chosen to do? Come here.

Driven by what, exactly? A thirst to discover the joys of small-town living in the heart of British Columbia? A sudden need for vast amounts of space? The scenery—the little he had managed to glimpse—was eye-wateringly majestic, but he was a city guy, someone who thrived in the jungle of streets and skyscrapers, at home where big money was made, and the cut and thrust of deals being done had a heartbeat of its own.

No, he'd come because he'd been curious.

A private jet and the solid four-wheel drive waiting for him at the airstrip had brought him here, and no sooner had he arrived when the weather had decided to make an appearance. The snow had begun and it was obviously here for the long haul. He'd just about managed to make it to the local shops to stock up on food and drink, and since then he'd been holed up here, without Internet connection and plenty of time to rue yielding to the temptation of seeing a past that had been denied to him.

The last thing Leo needed in the early hours of the morning was the tedium of having to dispose of someone who'd broken in in the hope of escaping the snow storm swirling outside.

He'd remained where he was, waiting for developments. The development that opened the door was not one he had expected. He'd figured on a guy, maybe a teenager or a couple of teenagers out and about in the dead of night, doing whatever they shouldn't have been doing in a small town where everyone probably knew everyone else—smoking or drinking and then suddenly realising that, if they didn't find shelter, they stood a good chance of dying of hypothermia. They probably knew that the house had been lying vacant and hadn't thought twice about breaking and entering.

A couple of drunk teenagers? He could have dealt with that. He could deal with anyone, if he was to be honest. A tough upbringing in foster care had served as sterling preparation for pretty much anything. From the minute he'd been able to walk, he had learnt how to handle himself and, the older he had got, the better he had become at it. Nothing scared him. The only scary thing he had ever faced had been the dawning realisation that he had been abandoned as a baby and that nobody would be coming to rescue him—ever. When faced with that, something as hard as granite settled in the soul and nothing, however frightening, could ever compete.

Every muscle in his body was primed for action as he sat up. His senses were on full alert and he was as still as a predator waiting for its prey to make the first move.

The door was pushed open. No lights were on, but still, there was no need for a light for him to realise instantly that his intruder was a woman.

'Who the *hell* are you and what are you doing in this house?'

That from the figure framed in the doorway, giving Leo no time at all to frame his own question, which would have replicated what she had just hurled at him, word for word.

The overhead light was slammed on, and for a couple

of seconds he was rendered speechless at the sight of the furious avenging angel glaring at him.

She was tall, at least five ten, slender with very long, dark hair trailing from underneath a woolly hat and she was olive-skinned. And she was exotically and unusually beautiful.

'Well?' she demanded, folding her arms, making sure to stay right where she was within easy reach of backing out of the room and slamming the door shut just in case he tried to reach her.

Smart move, Leo thought, although the last thing he wanted to do was frighten her. His instinct was to push aside the duvet and get out of the bed but he remained where he was so that he didn't spook her.

'I could ask you the same thing,' he threw back at her.

'How did you get into this house?'

'The legitimate way.'

'I know for a fact that that's a lie! I don't know who you are, or what you're doing here, but I want you out!'

Curiouser and curiouser, Leo thought, driven to stare at her because she was so physically compelling to look at and he hated the feeling of being caught on the back foot.

'You would toss a poor guy out in a blizzard?' he asked, blatantly sidestepping the fury on her face.

'Without a second thought!'

'I'm thinking that we need to have a little chat.' He pushed aside the duvet to slide off the bed.

'Don't take another step!'

'Or else what?'

'Or else…'

They stared at one another. Kaya's heart was thudding so hard that she found it hard to breathe.

There was a man in her bed—and not just *any* man.

This was the most spectacularly beautiful man she had ever seen in her life. His skin was burnished gold, his hair as dark as hers and his features were so classically perfect that he could have been a lovingly sculpted statue into which life had been breathed.

A spectacularly beautiful *half-naked* man, and heaven only knew what was happening underneath the duvet. Was he *completely naked*?

Her mouth went dry.

His clothes were strewn on the ground. Glancing quickly at the scattered pile, she got the impression that they weren't off-the-shelf cheap. From where she stood, primed for flight if need be, the coat dumped on the ground looked very much like cashmere.

Gripped with sudden confusion, she remained dithering, her empty threat dangling in the air between them.

'Well?' Leo prompted. 'No, scrap that. I have no idea what's happening here, but I think it's worth a discussion, not least because I have no intention of stepping out into that blizzard and taking my chances because you've decided to point me in that direction.' He flipped back the duvet, stood up and Kaya…stared.

She was tall, taller than a lot of the guys she knew, but this man was considerably taller. He stood well over six feet…and he was all muscle, sinew and six pack.

Black boxers were slung low, revealing a flat stomach and a spiral of dark hair going down to…

She licked her lips and looked away hastily but she was burning up.

She was also at a loss as to what to do. The man was right—there was no way she could chuck him out into that snow storm. The taxi she'd taken to get here had been fully equipped with all the necessary fittings to deal with severe weather, but even so it had struggled. She hadn't seen any car out the front, so what was he supposed to do—walk until he could no longer fight the weather?

'It's late and I'm tired,' she said tersely. 'You're in my bedroom and I want you to get out of it. I don't care where that takes you.'

'*Your* bedroom?'

'I can't make you leave it, because you're bigger than me and stronger than me, but don't for a minute think you scare me because *you don't*.'

'You think I would *ever*…? No… I can't believe I'm hearing this! And what do you mean by *your* bedroom?'

'I just want to sleep.' Tears of frustration, disbelief, confusion and sheer rage threatened her composure.

Leo shook his head, raked his fingers through his hair and stared at her for a few long, silent seconds.

'Okay,' he conceded slowly. 'I'll decamp and let you have the room, although I have no idea why, considering you've broken into my house. Call me a sucker for a damsel appearing to be in distress.'

Kaya's mouth fell open.

'Broken into *your house*?' But already the wheels were turning in her head as shock and panic slowly began to give way to a creeping sense of dread. No! Surely not…? *It can't be, not yet…*

Leo didn't answer.

'We can discuss this in the morning.' He began reaching for the clothes he had discarded: the tee-shirt on the ground, the jeans slung over the back of the chair and his computer because he might write a few reports even though with no connection he couldn't send them anywhere.

'In the *morning*?'

'I believe you said you just want to sleep.' He vanished into the *en suite* bathroom, leaving her to stew. In his experience, silence could be a man's best friend when it came to getting someone else to talk, and whatever the hell was going on here a talk was needed. He grabbed the towel he had been using and returned to find her barring his exit from the room, the very essence of feminine fury.

'This is where I live and I want to know why you're here!' Kaya shouted at him, but her head began to throb as they stared at one another, and she could detect a creeping hesitancy in her voice. Those piercing dark eyes pinned to her face made her think that he could read every thought in her head.

He'd said he'd entered 'the legitimate way'. All the signs were pointing in one direction, but she didn't want to read those signs, and the destination to which they led was one she had resolved never to visit.

She'd disappeared off to New Zealand to see her mum and stepfather, to escape the cloying misery and sadness she had felt when Julie Anne had died. She hadn't been able to focus, hadn't been able to get past her feeling of drift—she had just needed to *get out*.

Of course, she'd worked remotely from New Zealand, doing the accounts for a range of local and not so local businesses, but aside from that she had just taken time off.

Having spent her youth making sure her mum was all right, supervising her relationships and being the shoulder to cry on, for the first time she had gone to her mother for support. With oceans and continents separating her from her woes, she had allowed herself to forget the reality of what might be happening back in Canada.

It was enough that she had had to deal with the secrets Julie Anne had carried with her so once she'd left

Canada she had turned her back on all of that, swept it under the carpet.

'Where have you been?' Leo asked, tiptoeing around her with the delicacy of a hunter well aware that the beautiful, snarling cheetah might attack at the slightest provocation. 'No, perhaps I should ask you first of all what your name is.'

'Kaya.'

'I'm Leo. I'm happy to continue this conversation in the morning, but with every passing second I'm getting the impression that there is a lot of ground we need to cover.'

'You said you got in through legitimate means…'

'I give you…' He reached into his jeans pocket for a key, which he proceeded to dangle in front of her. There was a tag on it. 'Key to the kingdom.'

'I need to sit down.'

'You look as though you need more than a chair. Why don't we head down to the kitchen and I can give you something stiff to drink?' He held both hands up in a gesture of surrender. 'And I assure you that you have absolutely nothing to fear from me. We can cover some basic ground, because you're not the only one with questions, and then you can have the bedroom, lock the door and go to sleep.'

Kaya nodded, in a daze.

'Are you going to pass out on me?'

'No,' she whispered. 'I'm not the passing out kind.'

'Glad to hear it.'

He stood aside, waiting for her, and she had to control a shiver as she preceded him out of the bedroom and down to the kitchen. She felt like a convict being escorted back to prison, her gaoler behind her making sure she didn't try and pull a fast one. It was colder out here in the hall and she bent to grab the jumper she had discarded earlier and pulled it over her without looking around, without wanting to see the guy walking behind her.

He had a key.

The legitimate way...

Of course, she knew who he was. He wasn't some random stranger she had found sleeping in her bed. He hadn't trudged in from the cold, dumped his cashmere coat on the ground, kicked off his hand-made shoes and fallen asleep in her bedroom.

Because he didn't look like Julie Anne didn't mean that he wasn't connected to her, wasn't related to her. The guy the lawyers had told her would be coming wasn't supposed to be here yet; they had said it would be a long time, not until everything had been sorted out. And the ins and outs of a tricky probate could take up to a year... more than enough time for her to gather herself and find alternative accommodation.

Those lawyers had been very sympathetic.

They had understood the level of her shock when they had called her in to their posh office in the heart of Vancouver and advised her that the house she had been living in, the place she'd called *home*, would be under new ownership.

Julie Anne had left a will and everything would be going to her son.

'Julie Anne doesn't have a son,' Kaya had told them without batting an eyelid. She hadn't had a clue as to what her friend had decided to do with her house and the land, not to mention the halfway house in the middle of town. She had vaguely figured that the halfway house would be kept and the house and land might be sold, with the proceeds going towards the charitable organisation Julie Anne had founded decades ago.

But a son?

She had been frankly incredulous until they had explained, very slowly and very gently, that they had all the documentation to prove his legitimacy. They had explained it to her in three different ways, had brought her innumerable cups of tea and had told her that she could remain where she was, looking after the place, until the legal work was done and every detail sorted. She would have warning to vacate, they had said.

On top of everything else, that single revelation had hit Kaya for six. To know someone and yet not to know them… To discover that there were secrets lurking beneath the surface, secrets never divulged even to her…

She knew that she had escaped more than just her misery when she'd fled to New Zealand. She'd also been running from her confusion and bewilderment at what Julie Anne had held close to herself her entire lifetime. For reasons Kaya respected, of course, but still…

At any rate, she had returned to Canada, ready to pick up the threads, safe in the knowledge that she would be long gone before anyone rocked up to take over the house.

It seemed that fate had had other things in store for her. Thinking about what was happening now made her feel sick, because it raised a host of issues she didn't feel equipped to deal with, not just yet.

She hadn't wanted to meet the son. She'd pushed his existence to the back of her mind, had barely entertained any curiosity about the man. Who was he? What had he been doing for all those years? Had he been a down and out, forced into a life of penury because of circumstances beyond his control? Drifting this way and that before discovering himself to be the lucky recipient of a fortune he hadn't banked on? She'd parked all those questions and focused instead on making sure she wouldn't be around when she got that call from a lawyer telling her that the son would be heading to the house to claim what was rightfully his.

Glancing back at her as he pushed open the kitchen door, Leo noted the wariness on her face and something else—something he couldn't quite put his finger on.

'We're here,' he advised brusquely. 'The snow's falling thicker and harder with every passing second. I think it's fair to say that we're going to have to trust one another, because we're going to be cooped up in this house for a least the next few hours, if not days, and I don't see either of us having much success if we try to make it into town. Or even to the nearest neighbour who lives… where, exactly? I didn't drive past too many houses on the way here.'

Kaya nodded.

What was his plan? Was he really who she thought he was? How could he *not* be? She felt his eyes on her, darkly intrusive and assessing.

Of course he would be curious about her.

More than that, he was right insofar as they were stuck here together in a snow storm and would have to work around one another, however much neither of them might want that. So wouldn't it be wise to keep her counsel? Give herself time to find out what she was dealing with— *who* she was dealing with? Give herself time to adjust to this unwelcome situation?

He didn't look like a down-and-out lucky enough to have landed himself a house and land. There was something smart and sharp about him, something undeniably refined, but she wasn't going to be an idiot and trust first impressions.

She was briefly reminded of the way time and again her mother had fallen for first impressions, for the rich guy, the smooth talk and the easy charm.

Kaya was too streetwise when it came to stuff like that ever to trust what her eyes saw rather than what her brain said. Right now, her brain was telling her to get the lay of the land.

She duly made something and nothing noises about neighbours before falling silent.

'Talk to me,' Leo urged. 'You're tired and confused, but one thing you shouldn't be is afraid. Where have you been? Have you been away on holiday? Work? Visiting family—a boyfriend?'

They had begun to walk out into the hall and down the stairs, then back on themselves to the spacious, warm kitchen that faced extensive fields and land behind.

Kaya pushed open the kitchen door, switched on the light and looked around at a space that was no longer hers. She watched as he moved with confidence to one of the cupboards and reached for a couple of squat glasses to pour them both something amber-coloured and neat.

'I went to New Zealand to visit my mother,' Kaya said, backing away as he approached and sitting on one of the chairs at the kitchen table. Her voice was level and polite, her dark eyes watchful and guarded, noting everything about him—from the way he moved to the rich, golden colouring of his skin and the hard, cool contours of his extraordinarily handsome face. 'She moved there a few years ago when she remarried. I...needed to get away after Julie Anne's sudden death.'

'Julie Anne…' Leo murmured, shielding his dark gaze. 'And you returned to this house because…?'

'Because this is where I happen to have been living for the past three-and-a-half years.'

'Living here? You've been *living* here?'

'That's right.'

Leo hadn't seen *that* coming, but then again from a million miles away the situation had seemed pretty straightforward.

A letter had come from nowhere and it had blown a hole in his extremely controlled and highly regulated life. A buried past had resurfaced in the form of an inheritance from the woman who had dumped him into foster care at birth.

Leo had sat back and read the contents of that letter with bitterness, tempted to shred it and dispose of it in the bin. He had gazed around him, taken in the opulence of his New York penthouse apartment, one of several uber-luxurious apartments he owned in the various cities where his companies were based, and pondered the life he had conquered without the help of his flesh and blood, who had seen fit to get rid of him as a baby.

Memories he had locked away had resurfaced. He thought back to his young self, getting older in the nice enough foster home outside Brooklyn where he had been a number amongst other unwanted numbers. He'd thought back to the hopes and dreams of being rescued by his mum or dad gradually fading away, until steel had settled in his soul as he'd accepted the permanence of his surroundings.

He'd get out. He'd rule the world. He would become invulnerable.

And he had. He had worked longer, harder and with

more determination than everyone else. He'd got into Harvard a year younger than everyone else and had breezed through a first in law, then moved on to get an MBA, and thereafter the world had been at his fingertips. He had joined a failing company with potential, bargained his way into being paid in shares and made a fortune when he had helped it go public.

He had been twenty-four.

He was thirty-one now and his fortune had multiplied so many times in the ensuing years that he was where he had always planned to be—on top of the world, occupying a place where he was untouchable.

Yet all of that success had faded in the face of that unexpected letter. His mother was dead and he was the beneficiary of everything she possessed, left to him by the woman who had given him up—some kind of token gesture to buy her way past the pearly gates. He had no time for that. It had been way too late for a guilty conscience.

'So you were saying…?' he drawled, shaking himself free from inconvenient trips down memory lane. 'You lived here with Julie Anne…'

'I did.'

Kaya heard the cold cynicism in his voice and stiffened, because whatever secrets her friend had concealed there could be no denying her warmth and generosity of spirit.

'How did that come about?'

Kaya shrugged. 'I returned from university, had nowhere to stay and couldn't afford the rent, at least not to start with. It's expensive here, with it being so close to Whistler.'

'And so this woman decided to step in and fill the gap, no questions asked?'

'I had known her since I was a kid so, yes, there were no questions asked. There were no strings attached to the offer. I wasn't made to rise at five and sweep floors until I collapsed.'

'Very generous of her.'

'She was a generous person,' Kaya said quietly. 'She was kind and sympathetic.'

Leo looked at her in silence for such a long time that she had to resist the temptation to squirm.

He was here to claim his inheritance but what was he going to do with it?

She was gripped by a sudden urgency to find out. Julie Anne had spent her life building up the halfway house, a place for women with nowhere left to turn. Was he here to demolish that legacy?

The lawyers had told her, briefly and as a courtesy, that he had been given up for adoption. That had been shocking in itself, but there would have been reasons behind that, even though Kaya had no idea what those reasons might be and had thought would never find out. Actions always spoke louder than words and Julie Anne's actions had been those of someone with a big heart and a generous spirit.

But now she could feel the tide shifting, and anxiety clawed through her, because this guy was hard as nails. Exhaustion was beginning to catch up with her.

'You're asking a lot of questions,' she said coolly. It was hard to keep her eyes trained on him, because he made her feel uncomfortable, but she managed to maintain a level stare, not that he looked fazed by that.

'I have a right to. You asked me how I got into this house…'

'And now I know.'

Leo's eyebrows shot up and Kaya tilted her chin at a belligerent angle.

'You're the son, aren't you? You're the son who's come to get rid of all of this.'

CHAPTER TWO

KAYA SURFACED THE following morning, groggy and disoriented. For a few seconds, blinking in the darkness like an owl, she half-expected to glance to her left and see the landscape of pastoral Kiwi paradise through the bank of windows—rolling green fields undulating like gentle ocean waves, dotted with grazing sheep. Instead, what she saw was the steady fall of snow, fat, white flakes, and the dull, leaden skies of an unusually bleak Canadian winter.

And events of the night before came rushing back with the force of a freight train, barrelling into her at full pelt. The not-so-prodigal son had returned ahead of schedule, a hand grenade thrown through the window before she'd had time to batten down the hatches.

He'd been startled that she knew who he was and had wanted to pursue the conversation, but she had suddenly been overwhelmed. Overwhelmed by the shock of finding Julie Anne's son in the house. Overwhelmed by a future she hadn't got round to making provisions for suddenly slamming into her with the ferocity of a freight train. As much as anything else, overwhelmed by sheer exhaustion, hours and hours without sleep and everything catching up with her in one fell swoop. She'd had to get away from his stifling presence and, in fairness, he hadn't tried to stop her.

'Morning's as good a time to pick up this conversation,' he had ground out, watching her with an expression she had found disturbing for lots of reasons, and on cue she had fled.

She sat up and closed her eyes for a moment.

What the heck was going to happen now?

While she'd been busy sorting her crazy thoughts out on the other side of the world, trying to come to terms with Julie Anne's sudden death, the legacy of truths she had withheld and the secrets she had concealed, Kaya had spared little time for the practicalities of having to vacate a house.

The lawyers had told her that these things could take a very long time to conclude and somehow she had mentally translated that as 'no need to rush…no need to start looking for somewhere else to live immediately…'

She was someone who had spent a lifetime being sensible and now it felt as though she was being punished for this one time when her common sense had temporarily deserted her. Her mind had been in a different place when she'd escaped to New Zealand, and the consequences of taking her eye off the ball had come home to roost. Now she felt exposed and vulnerable, two things she absolutely hated feeling.

She got dressed at speed, flinging on some jeans, a tee-shirt, a thick jumper and some winter socks. It was after ten in the morning although, as she yanked back the curtains, she thought anyone would be forgiven for thinking that it was still early because the skies were thick and dark with driving snow, and the placid spread of open land, stretching out to the majestic backdrop of mountains, was barely visible through the rapidly falling sheet of white.

She walked into the kitchen in under half an hour to find Leo already there, and she screeched to a halt in the doorway and felt her pulse speed up.

She'd somehow conveniently blanked out the sheer physicality of the man but she couldn't blank it out now.

He turned to look at her and their eyes met and held, tangled in a tense stretching silence. In the cold, thin, unforgiving light pouring through the bay windows that gave onto the front lawns, he was as sinfully beautiful as she now remembered. Long, lean, muscular, and in black jeans and black polo-neck, he looked every inch...
Every inch what?

Every inch some kind of tycoon. Was that what he was—a tycoon? Or had he already started spending his unexpected inheritance?

'Slept well? Refreshed and ready to resume where we left off?'

Silence broken. Pulses racing all over the place, Kaya dragged her eyes away from the guy who had now unhurriedly turned to pour her a mug of coffee, making her feel like a stranger in her own home. Not that this was her home.

Kaya warily moved to one of the kitchen chairs. Out of the corner of her eye, she watched in thickening silence as he took his time with the coffee before bringing it to her and then sitting within touching distance. For a big man, he moved with an easy, stealthy grace that was compelling.

'Two sugars—plenty of milk. No idea how you take your coffee, but I feel it better to make it sweet just in case your blood sugar levels have dropped after last night.

'So, you knew who I was.'

'When did you get here?'

'Irrelevant. I'm thinking that your hysterical reaction to my presence in the bedroom was feigned, considering you were expecting me.'

'The lawyers contacted me. They said that Julie Anne had left everything to you.' Kaya lowered her eyes and felt the familiar clammy feel of bewilderment and betrayal at events she hadn't expected.

'Must have come as a body blow, considering you were living here with her.'

Kaya's mouth tightened and she flashed him an icy, hostile glare. 'I had no expectations.'

'Excellent news.'

'They told me that it would take a while for everything to get processed.'

'Why didn't you say anything? Why didn't you tell me that you knew who I was?'

'I wanted to wait and see what you had to say.'

For a couple of seconds, Leo was stuck for a response, because that would have been very much what he would have done if the boot had been on the other foot—waited and seen, and in the meantime have given nothing away.

He felt a tug of curiosity because a woman who gave nothing away was as rare as hen's teeth in his experience. Disconcerted, he frowned and then carried on, his voice as smooth as silk.

'To get back to what you just said...'

She wanted to wait to see what he had to say...

Leo sidelined his momentary lapse of self-control and focused. 'Under normal circumstances, I expect that would be the case. However...' He dealt her a slow, slashing smile that brought hectic colour to her cheeks.

'Money talks, and I have a lot of it. I wanted to get this situation wrapped up as soon as possible and they fast-tracked the procedure.'

'This situation…'

Leo shrugged. 'Came as much of a shock to me as it did to you. I never expected to be sitting here trying to sort out an inheritance that came from nowhere. You asked me when I got here? Less than two days ago so, as it turns out, it was just a matter of bad luck that you arrived shortly after I did, and even worse luck that we're snow bound. I'm sure you don't want to be here with me any more than I want to be here with you. Truth is, I could have got my people to deal with this but I felt it would probably be more suitable for me to handle it, given the circumstances.'

With every cold, passing word, Kaya could feel her tension building. The picture was slowly coming together in her head. The baby Julie Anne had given up for adoption had gone on to make a fortune and had returned as beneficiary of her estate, to dismantle it.

The prospect of that made her go cold.

Never mind *her*. What was going to happen to the halfway house? The halfway house which had been a godsend to so many young, pregnant girls over the years and was part of the community. It had seen girls come, go and move on to bigger, brighter futures. It had sheltered them from storms that had blown away, given them a springboard to move on with their lives.

Kaya had done the books for the lodgings ever since she had graduated. She'd done voluntary work there since she'd been a teenager. Now this stranger was here, a dark intruder however entitled he was to Julie Anne's holdings, and what was he going to do with…with *everything*?

'I think I need something to eat.' She stood up but for the first time she hesitated, aware that this was no longer her house. He wasn't the stranger. *She* was.

'Feel free.'

He made an expansive gesture and then relaxed back to sip his coffee, watching her over the rim of the cup and sensing her uncertainty, although he had no intention of easing it. He wasn't here to make friends and influence people. He was here to get rid of whatever he'd inherited. He didn't expect to find answers to anything and he was mystified by the tug of curiosity that had brought him here in the first place.

'I haven't moved anything,' he drawled. 'The usual stuff is in the usual places.'

'Are you *enjoying* this?' Kaya moved to stand directly in front of him, hands on her hips, but almost immediately regretted it, because the sheer force of his presence and his ridiculous good looks made her feel unsteady.

'I'm here to do a job. Enjoyment doesn't enter into it.'

She had dressed in a hurry in some faded blue jeans, an equally faded jumper with no make-up, and her hair looked as though she had hurriedly run her fingers through it.

And yet her beauty transcended the lack of effort to promote it.

This was a sight to which Leo was unaccustomed. Cut to the chase: maybe he was enjoying a *tiny* part of it. The part of a red-blooded man appreciating the sight of a beautiful woman.

Not that he hadn't had his fair share of beautiful women. He had. Sexy women who aimed to please and were excellent when it came to stroking his ego. In a high-octane life, who didn't enjoy the calming influence of a soothing, agreeable woman?

This particular woman was scowling. He wondered if she was ever soothing and agreeable but then concluded that she probably was, just not with him. And who in his right mind could blame her?

He watched as she stalked off to the cupboard and fridge, but there was a self-conscious hesitancy as she fetched out whatever she wanted and, as much as that wasn't his concern, he actually felt a twinge of sympathy for the woman because this was not what she had expected.

'I could do something for you,' Kaya said grudgingly and Leo's eyebrows shot up.

'You make the offer sound so tempting.'

'I'm here, and I don't suppose it's any extra effort. It's just bread and jam.'

'Thank you but I'll make do with the coffee. I'm a guy who doesn't need breakfast on a daily basis.'

Kaya shrugged. She wasn't looking at him but his image was lodged in her head, and she was conscious of his eyes on her as she did some toast for herself, using the butter and jam he had bought and resenting him for crashing into her space without giving her the time or opportunity to take evasive action.

When she sat down, she made sure to position herself squarely in the chair furthest from him.

'What do you intend to do with the house and the land and…everything else?'

'"Highest bidder" are the two words that come to mind.'

'Why?' Kaya bit down on a piece of toast and resisted the temptation to launch into an argument with him because, if she faced it, she was in a weak position. How could she angle the conversation in a direction that might persuade him to think otherwise?

'Why would I hang on to all of this?' Leo stretched out his long legs and settled further into the chair to look at her over the rim of his cup as she sipped her coffee.

'You don't need the money,' she returned bluntly.

'Where are you going with this?'

'You said that you've got enough money of your own so why does it matter whether you sell this or not?'

'Are you suggesting that I hand the lot over to you?' Leo burst out laughing. 'Don't get me wrong, I understand that you're taken aback by my premature arrival on the scene, but I've never believed in Father Christmas and I definitely won't be auditioning for the role now. I have no use for any of the stuff my erstwhile birth mother decided to leave me for reasons I can't begin to fathom, but I won't be handing it over to you as a gesture of good will.'

'You're really not a very nice person, are you?' Kaya said through gritted teeth and, when he met her impotent fury with a grin, she had to clench her fists to stop herself from flinging her plate at his handsome head. 'I'm not interested in trying to persuade you to give me this house!'

'Good. Then we're on the same page.'

'There's more to Julie Anne's inheritance than bricks and mortar.' She pushed the plate away. The toast tasted like cardboard and there was a tight knot in her stomach because the guy sitting opposite her was as implacable as granite. Yet more than anything she wanted him to at least try and see her point of view.

Leo stilled.

Did he want to talk about the woman who had given birth to him and then promptly seen fit to dump him in foster care? No.

'Why did you bother to come here?'

'Come again?' His voice, though silky smooth, was laced with warning. Leo was a guy who had always been very clear when it came to boundaries. They were not meant to be stepped over—not by anyone. He was outraged at the open defiance in her dark eyes as she stared at him, her head tilted to one side, not backing down and certainly not intimidated.

'You're not interested in any of this, so why are you here? You said you could have sorted it out long-distance, so why didn't you? I mean, you made the effort to trek all the way here from your billionaire pad, or wherever, so the least you could is…is…'

The ground in front of her shimmered. She knew from the hard, cold expression on his face that she was entering no-go territory, and yet how would she be able to express her point of view if she backed away? If she took Julie Anne out of the equation, then this legacy went beyond her—it was bigger than her and bigger than both of them, and she was determined to let him know that—however it was clear that he just wasn't interested.

She would never forgive herself if the halfway house was dismantled, sold to the highest bidder and to heck with all the young girls who depended on it—the girls who had come and gone and who would come and go in the future.

'You're treading on thin ice here,' Leo said with menacing softness.

In response, Kaya stuck her chin out with more defiance, although she felt a whoosh inside her, a tingle of excitement as she met the cool challenge in his eyes.

This guy was like no one she had ever met in her life before but, then again, how many men had she met before? When it came to the opposite sex, she employed a strict 'hands off' policy because it was important for her to get to know a guy before she even thought about committing to anything like a relationship with him.

She'd learnt from experience, from watching the heartbreaking fallout of her mother's attempts to find love, that throwing oneself into relationships without the benefit of due diligence beforehand never worked.

Unfortunately, it was uneasy to acknowledge that the result of all that caution over the years had resulted in no relationship to speak of. No one had ever quite managed to get through Kaya's checklist.

She wasn't being fussy, she always told herself, she was simply *being careful*. But having had no men left gaping holes in her experience and right now, confronted with this guy, she was at a loss as to how to manoeuvre.

He was a powerful, mesmerising force of nature for which she felt lamentably ill-prepared. There was knowing experience in his dark eyes that made her horribly self-conscious and the way he smiled, the brooding intensity of his gaze, brought her out in goose bumps.

And worst of all was the simmering excitement that accompanied those goose bumps, a titillating sensation of stepping a little too close to an open flame that might be beautiful but was also lethally dangerous.

'Why?' She couldn't meet his stare full-on and she briefly lowered her eyes and licked her lips. She breathed in deeply and looked at him once again but her heart was thumping like a sledgehammer inside her. 'I just want to find out why you bothered to come if you're so uninterested in finding out a bit more about your mother's legacy.'

'I don't believe I'm hearing this!' Leo said with outraged incredulity. 'Are you actually questioning my motives? What business is it of yours, exactly, what I intend to do about my so-called mother's legacy?'

'Because it matters.'

Leo vaulted upright. He was hanging onto his control with difficulty. His normal cool, calm composure had deserted him; but were her questions really so astonishing given the fact that, yes, he had made the choice to come here personally when there had been no real need? He was rich and he didn't need to accumulate any property from anyone to add to his portfolio so, that being the case, why bother with the formalities?

He knew that he hadn't lost his composure because she'd asked one or two reasonable questions. He'd lost his composure because she'd ignored his *Do Not Trespass* sign. The truth was that he had his rules and they were intractable. He had worked hard to be in control of his destiny and there was a core of ruthless steel inside him that had propelled him over obstacles and barriers that would have brought most other men to their knees.

In return, he had come to accept a level of untouchability that was never questioned, and the mere fact that it was being questioned now left him speechless.

Why did Julie Anne's legacy matter? What difference would it make to this life? Would it answer any questions, send his thoughts about his past in another direction? No.

'She had plans for this house.'

'What are you talking about?'

If it had been seven in the evening, he would have helped himself to something stiff and potent but, as alcohol wasn't on the cards, he instead made himself another cup of coffee, black and strong.

When he eventually looked at Kaya, when their eyes

met, he knew that his expression was as unrevealing as it always was and that his thoughts were hidden from view.

'You know about the halfway house…?'

'It's included in the paperwork. But forget about that. You need to give this one up.'

'I can't.'

'What do you mean you *can't*?'

'Julie Anne…'

'Just for the record, dumped me in a foster home so I'm just going to put it out there that that's not exactly the behaviour of someone deserving of admiration. So why are you fighting her corner now?'

'Because I knew her.'

Leo was silenced by those four words. This was a woman who had known his mother, the very mother who had wanted nothing to do with him. A tangle of emotion surged through him and he scowled.

'Really…? You sure about that…?'

Kaya flushed but stood her ground. 'She…kept things from me, yes. Things from all of us, from everyone who knew her.'

'Everyone who thought they knew her,' Leo clarified politely.

'But that doesn't mean that the person we knew wasn't kind and generous and incredibly *good*. Because she was.'

'That's touchingly loyal, but where are you going with it?'

'If you've read through the stuff they sent you, then you'll have read something about the place she set up a long time ago. The halfway house.'

'I got rudimentary information,' Leo said on a sigh. 'I didn't get a book with chapters and paragraphs.'

'Well,' Kaya said stoutly, 'If you'll let me explain—'

'Right now, I don't think I can stand another round of chit chat about a woman I didn't know from Adam.'

He stood up and moved to the window to look outside at sky that remained ominously dark as it continued to shed its burden of thick, white snow across an alien landscape.

It snowed in Manhattan—the winters could be as brutal as this—but there was an essential difference. In Manhattan, the streets and roads were cleared because people had to get to work. The glass towers remained open for business. Broadband continued to do its thing so communications weren't brought to a crashing stop because of the weather. And from his penthouse apartment, with its far-reaching three-hundred-and-sixty-degree views, he could survey the city he felt he owned with a drink in his hand, knowing that the weather would seldom prove too much of an inconvenience.

He spun round to look at her.

'The Internet's down.'

'Is it?' Kaya frowned and was momentarily disconcerted by the abrupt change of topic, but then why should she be surprised if he didn't want to dwell on anything she had to say? 'I don't suppose it's that surprising. Look at what's happening outside.'

'Some snow,' Leo remarked wryly. 'It's hardly Armageddon. It snows in New York as well, believe it or not, and yet against all odds the Internet keeps working.'

'The Internet will be up and running in the town,' Kaya told him. 'Out here, it tends to be a little more erratic when the weather's like this.'

Leo looked at her and for the first time wondered what the hell a young woman like the one glaring at him, a young and incredibly striking young woman, was doing here holed up in a house she didn't own. Weren't bright lights beckoning? Was there a boyfriend on the scene? Some significant other tying her to a place anyone might have thought she would have left a long time ago? Especially considering her mother had upped sticks and moved halfway across the world.

She was asking him about New York, as though curiosity had staged a battle against hostile silence and lost, and for the first time he felt a flare of amusement.

It was satisfying to know that he wasn't the only one who was curious. Where he lived was no big secret. She could look him up on the Internet and find out pretty fast that he was rich beyond words and lived in the centre of Manhattan in an apartment in the most prestigious post code. It was no big deal to tell her about his place as he compared it to the house in which he now found himself.

'I enjoy city life,' he murmured. 'I like looking out my floor-to-ceiling windows and observing what's going on down below—the hustle and the bustle, a living, breathing city alive with possibilities. I don't find it claustrophobic. Now this?' He nodded to his surroundings without taking his eyes off her face. '*This* I find claustrophobic, which leads me to wonder how it is that you don't as well.'

How had he done that? Kaya wondered. How had he managed to reveal nothing about himself, really, while steering the conversation neatly in her direction, asking a question that was flagrantly nosy under the pretext of expressing the sort of anodyne interest *she* had expressed?

How had he made her suddenly think about her life and the paths she had chosen to take? Had she planned to stay put after her mother had disappeared to New Zealand? Or had she simply followed the path of least resistance, liking the peace of being grounded after a lifetime being the grown-up and practically taking care of her mother, who had treated her more as a pal than a daughter?

She had settled into a routine, especially after she had moved in with Julie Anne. She had relished normality and perhaps even found a place in life where, for once, she had someone she looked on as a mother figure, for Julie Anne had been far more of a mother to her than her own had ever been.

It had been easy to drift along without having to make any monumental decisions. And when it came to men…

Had it been easier from that point of view as well? Had it been easier just to stick with what she knew— guys she had more or less grown up with? A crowd she was comfortable in? Had it been easier just to delay the whole business of dealing with her singledom? No one had come along who fitted the bill and that had been fine.

Leo's blunt question dredged all this up and she wished she hadn't opened the door to his curiosity.

As if to remind her of their confinement, she saw the snow through the window and shivered.

How long were they going to be cooped up here? Surely they couldn't tiptoe around one another indefinitely? She would have to use their enforced captivity to at least try and get him to see another point of view, to have some insight into the inheritance he had unexpectedly come into, but how?

Kaya shivered. When she looked at him, she could feel hot colour creeping into her cheeks, depriving her of her ability to talk, sucking the oxygen from the air and leaving her hot and bothered.

The last thing she wanted was to get into some kind of confession mode with this guy, yet there was a dangerous charisma about him that she found difficult to deal with.

'I mean,' he drawled lazily, 'Maybe there's someone else here pinning you down?'

'What are you talking about?' Kaya blinked and surfaced from her meandering, uncomfortable thoughts.

'Well…' he spread his hands wide '…your mother's left for the opposite side of the world, so I guess you would have been free to get out of here and explore what else was on offer. Unless, of course, there's a boyfriend somewhere in the background keeping you tied to the kitchen sink, so to speak? Why else would you bury yourself out here, in the middle of nowhere with only an old woman for company?'

Kaya gasped because she found every single word he had just said offensive but, when she opened her mouth to tell him exactly what she thought of his commentary on her life, he burst out laughing.

'My apologies,' he said, although he was still grinning, 'I'm not that much of a dinosaur to think that the role of any woman is tied to a kitchen sink…but my curiosity was genuine. What has kept you here?'

And just like that Kaya realised that he was the first person ever to have posed that question. Not even her mother had asked her and neither had Julie Anne nor any of her friends. None had ever wondered out loud how it was that she had decided to stay put when she had all the qualifications to forge a different, more adventurous life for herself somewhere else.

'You okay?'

'Of course. Why shouldn't I be?' She shot him a stiff, remote smile but her heart was pounding and there was something a lot like self-pity welling up inside her. And, alongside that self-pity, sheer frustration that a simple question from a guy she didn't even like had managed to raise questions she didn't particularly want to answer, had thrown her into a stupid tailspin.

She gathered herself.

'I like open spaces,' she said, thankful that her voice sounded normal. At any rate, that wasn't a lie, although it did jostle uncomfortably close to truths she didn't care to confront. 'I grew up in Alaska until I was six before moving here. I would go mad if I had to live somewhere like New York.'

'You lived in Alaska? So—'

'So there's Internet in the town,' Kaya cut in before he could embark on another line of questioning. She stood up and moved towards the old-fashioned sink and then stood there, facing him, her hand firmly placed on the counter behind her. 'It must be inconvenient for you, being here and cut off from your work. If we clear the snow, you should be able to make it into town. Once you get to the main road, it'll be a lot more passable.'

And in the meantime, she thought, she wasn't going to let him get under her skin. *In the meantime*, she was going to engineer the conversation in the direction *she* wanted. She didn't have time on her side when it came to ramming her point of view down his throat, and she had no intention of wasting it by breaking out in a hot sweat every time he looked at her.

She was pleased to be back in command of herself. 'If we get a head start, then it can be all systems go when this snow decides to ease off.'

CHAPTER THREE

THE LEADEN GREY skies of the day before were now a washed out, denim blue and the snow had collected everywhere and on everything even though it seemed to be giving up the fight, diminishing to whipping flurries.

There were no houses around, nothing to interrupt an unbroken vista of white. Leo looked at the woman who had started attacking the build-up of snow with even, rhythmic movements—spade in, flick, spade out—at home clearing a path, accustomed to doing this year in and year out.

No boyfriend... No family, he assumed... No ties except those bred through familiarity, old friends and maybe from her school days. A comfortable, unchallenging life, which sounded pretty good if you happened to be retired.

Frankly, he didn't get it.

Her back story didn't matter, and it certainly didn't make a scrap of difference when it came to doing what he had come to do, but it was certainly adding a little vim and vigour to the situation, stuck out here.

'You were telling me about Alaska.'

'Are you going to help shovel snow or are you going to stand there, leaning on the spade and doing nothing?'

Leo grinned. He didn't know many women who would be out in these conditions clearing snow and he didn't think it was a crime to appreciate the sight of one now.

She had changed into her thickest winter gear—jumpers, waterproof jacket and waterproof trousers tucked into serviceable knee-high wellies. Her woolly hat was pulled low over her ears and her gloves were thick enough to withstand snow storms with no threat of frostbitten fingers.

'I'm appreciating the scenery.'

About to plunge her shovel into the snow, Kaya paused to look at him and her heart skipped a beat. He was staring straight at her and she felt heat begin to spread through her, a lick of fire racing through her veins and turning on a switch she'd never known existed.

He had come prepared for the cold. He wore thick, dark layers, serviceable waterproof, fur-lined boots, a black waterproof oilskin coat and a black woolly hat. He looked sexy and dangerous and the way he was looking at her made her wonder whether there had been something flirtatious behind that innocent remark. No, surely not? Had there been? He didn't like her! She was taking up space in his house and she was an encumbrance to be rid of. So why would he flirt with her?

Panic flared, reminding her how innocent she was when it came to games like this. She just wasn't used to it, wasn't used to a man like the one staring at her, his dark eyes guarded and assessing.

She had never cut her teeth on all those youthful make-up and break-up teenage games her friends used to play. She had spent those years learning how pointless those games were, thanks to the example set by her mother. In many ways, she had felt smugly superior at the tears shed when boys had come and gone. She was saving herself for something serious and lasting, for the guy who wouldn't mess her around and break her heart. Except, she realised now, those gaps in her knowledge had made her vulnerable.

She stared at him, frozen and tongue-tied, then belatedly decided to take what he had said at face value and launched into a monologue about the countryside, the tourists that flocked to their pretty little town, an overspill from Whistler, and its skiing industry.

She knew that she was babbling and she could feel herself getting hotter and hotter under the collar. She could barely have a conversation with the man without breaking out in a sweat and she was infuriated with herself for her weakness. She'd always considered herself pretty strong, able to withstand anything and anyone, toughened by a background that had foisted responsibilities onto her shoulders at a young age. Yet right at this moment…

She needed to get a grip. She needed to be that cool, controlled person who could make a case for him not to throw Julie Anne's life work down the tubes because he had an axe to grind with the woman who had given him up for adoption.

Because that was what it came to, wasn't it? He was bitter and she couldn't blame him.

There was also a part of her that could be bitter, that could look back at her dear friend and harbour a grudge against her for keeping this huge secret to herself. But she didn't because she had the benefit of having known her for who she was, whatever secrets she had kept to herself.

He hadn't.

Calmed by that, Kaya resumed shovelling, and out of the corner of her eye saw that he was working at it as well, except in his case he was getting an awful lot more done with a lot less effort.

Her eyes drifted to the flex of muscle just about discernible under the layers and she was riveted when he shrugged off the waterproof jacket and shoved up the sleeves of his dark jumper.

'Hot work,' he said without looking at her. 'Or maybe I'm just not used to a bit of honest manual labour.'

He glanced at her with amusement.

She was flushed, her cheeks pink, her mouth half-parted, as though he'd caught her on the verge of saying something.

'How long did you think you'd have here before I came on the scene?' he asked. Her eyes flew to his and widened.

'A couple of months,' Kaya admitted, looking away. 'If I thought you'd show up as soon as you did, I wouldn't have taken all that time out in New Zealand. I would have returned earlier so that I could sort myself out.'

'I don't plan on hanging on to any of this,' Leo said shortly. 'But I won't chuck you out without at least some notice.'

Kaya thought of the halfway house and the vulnerable girls who walked through those doors with nothing much aside from some hope for temporary respite. For many, it was a last resort. She was honour-bound to protect those girls. She had formed links with many of them over the years, just as Julie Anne had.

There was no place for emotions when it came to trying to save the place. She needed to get him on side. They needed to call a truce and, in fairness, she was the one who couldn't relax.

She hadn't noticed a car when she had arrived the evening before but, as they made inroads into the snow, she saw that he had indeed driven. There was a shiny, black, solid four-wheel drive parked at the side of the house alongside her old, reliable car which had survived many a heavy-duty winter.

'What do you do?' she asked.

'What do I do about what?'

'In life. I mean, what's your job?'

Leo followed her eyes, saw her clock his car and wondered whether he'd been mistaken when he'd spotted a look of something on her face, something fleeting that told him that the spectacle of something so obviously expensive didn't impress her. She was contemptuous of it.

'I own things.'

'What does that mean?'

'It means I built a life for myself without help from anyone.' He stuck the shovel into the snow and rubbed his gloved hands together. 'It means I pulled myself up by my boot straps and sorted my life out without the guiding hand of the friend you're so intent on defending. I buried my head in books, studied until I knew more than anyone else and battled against prejudice to make it to the top.

'I took risks without the benefit of any cushions lying around to break a fall. I gambled for high stakes and, every time I threw the dice, I knew that life could go one way or the other. All I had was faith in my own intelligence, instinct and knowledge of every market I decided to play. Now, I own the world. I have the freedom to do whatever I want and all of that was acquired without help.'

'I can't blame you for being bitter.'

'That's very generous of you.'

He shook his head and half-laughed at himself, because he wasn't given to self-pitying diatribes, but at least it should sound an alarm bell against any more forays into sermons about Julie Anne and the properties he really couldn't care less about.

'I think we've done enough to warrant a cup of coffee,' he said, moving to get his jacket but not bothering to put it on. 'Snow's stopped, at any rate. Augurs well for life returning to normal.'

'You're not the only one who's had it hard,' Kaya said, keeping up with him but only just as they headed to the front door. She could feel her good intentions slipping through her fingers. How did she get through to someone who was so intransigent?

Watching him as he strode into the house and slung his jacket over one of the coat hooks by the front door brought home to her his ownership of this and of everything else that came with it.

'Did I ever say that I was?'

He glanced over his shoulder but he was back in control, a small, amused smile curving his mouth and not a trace of bitterness in evidence. He held her gaze for a few seconds, head tilted thoughtfully to one side.

'What have you got against rich guys?'

This came from nowhere and Kaya's mouth fell open as she stared at him.

'What are you talking about?' She began stripping off, because it was baking in the house, heating full-blast. She yanked off the woolly hat and shook her hair free, not looking at him as her waterproof joined his on the coat hook by the door and her boots got dumped underneath.

'I saw the way you looked at my car, Kaya. Same way I've caught you looking at me. So what's the problem here—is it just me? Is it me because I'm rich? Or is it rich guys in general? Can't be that you have a thing against money because...' he looked around him as he began strolling towards the kitchen '...this place and everything else that came as part of the package deal all point to a woman who had more than enough to keep going.'

'I—I don't know what y-you're talking about,' Kaya

spluttered in response and he laughed and turned away, moving towards the kettle, flicking it on then getting out coffee, mugs and milk.

He owned the space around him. She wondered whether that was just who he was: a guy in charge, the sort of person who would have been as at home here if he'd walked in from the cold to find shelter. A man who was so utterly self-confident that he could have been dumped on another planet and he'd have started working out how he could make it his.

'Sure you do. Milk? Sugar? You know exactly what I'm talking about.'

'You think you're so observant.'

'I don't think. I *know*. Trust me, when you grow up in a foster home you learn how to look after yourself. You learn how to have eyes at the back of your head and how to hear through walls, because nobody in charge is going to be there twenty-four-seven doing that job on your behalf. And you learn fast how to watch people and work out what makes them tick. So, what's it about rich guys you don't like?'

He dumped a mug of hot coffee in front of her and then sat on the very same chair he'd been sitting on before they'd gone outside to deal with the snow.

He had stripped off the black jumper and was down to a long-sleeved, close-fitting tee shirt, also black, that emphasised the muscular body she had surreptitiously stared at when he'd been shovelling the snow.

'You don't look like her,' she said impulsively and Leo frowned, disconcerted. 'Julie Anne—you don't look like her. She was very blonde, very attractive. Blue eyes.' Her words dropped into the silence between them, spreading ripples of restless discomfort through her. He didn't like what she was saying. He'd come here to sort things out but he was happy to leave without knowing anything about his mother, without making any effort to try and understand the good woman she had been, whatever she had done all those years ago when she had been very young.

'I have pictures, if you want to see—on my phone. She hated having her photo taken but I sometimes managed to capture her when she wasn't looking, or else just told her that she had no choice. But in the house…you'd be hard pressed to find any. She just wasn't interested in seeing herself in photo frames on shelves. That's what she used to say—made me smile.'

'I'll pass.'

'Aren't you curious at all?'

'Let's park this,' Leo ground out, eyes cool. 'If I was interested in seeing pictures of Julie Anne, I'm pretty sure I would have been able to get hold of some by now.'

'You were asking me about rich guys,' Kaya said, her eyes as cool as his. 'And you're right. I don't have any time for men with money because they're all…arrogant and full of themselves. They swan around thinking they can do whatever they like, and enjoy snapping their fingers and watching people jump to their command.' She allowed a significant pause and his eyebrows shot up, not in anger, but in amusement.

'I'm guessing that's a dig at me.' He grinned. 'Is that what you think I've been doing? Swanning around and snapping my fingers so that I can watch you jump to my command? If that was my ploy, then I've failed miserably, because so far I haven't seen you doing a lot of jumping at my command. Anyway, isn't that all a bit of a generalisation? Or is your attitude something to do with the tough upbringing you were going to tell me about?'

He remembered...remembered she'd vaguely mentioned that he wasn't the only one who'd had it hard. The conversation hadn't been continued but her throwaway remark had lodged in his head, waiting for the right moment to be pulled out and examined further.

Of course, this was how he had got where he'd got, she thought. He was smart and she could believe it when he'd said that he'd had to work hard and take risks. But there would have been more to it than that because lots of people worked hard and took risks. He would have had that added edge to him of being street wise. He would have been the guy who stored things in his head, who knew how to hold on to information until an opportunity came for him to take advantage of what he knew.

'You really want to know?' Kaya was willing to drop her guard for a bit, to let him see a side of her she didn't normally share with anyone, because to get him at least to listen to her he surely had to see her for more than just a nuisance who kept asking questions he didn't want to answer? He had to see her as a three-dimensional person with a story to tell, something to engage his interest and make him look beyond what was on the surface.

'Try me.'

'My mother,' she said bluntly. She thought of her mother and was taken back through time to when she had become old enough to understand that their relationship was not at all like the relationship her other friends had with their mums.

'My mum,' she said softly. 'My dad died when I was very young. You know...they were crazy about one another. I can't remember much about him, because I was only six when he died, but I remember them laughing a lot. She was always the extrovert. He was very quiet, very serious. She once told me that he was a complete nerd until he met her, said that she made him light-hearted and he anchored her.'

'How did he die?'

'He fell through what should have been solid ice while he was trying to install a system for tracking hibernating sea life under the ice. He was a marine biologist, and he specialised in icy water, because he'd grown up surrounded by it in Alaska. My mother was devastated. He hadn't been good with money, hadn't taken out any kind of life insurance, and without any property or possessions to speak of she was left with very little and a young child to look after. We moved here because this was my mother's home before she left it to go to Alaska with my father. She still had connections here, although no family.'

'And your learning curve…' Leo said slowly. 'She had no money and she…what?'

Their eyes met and she shot him a wry smile.

'You can maybe guess.'

'How did you deal with that?'

'You mean the ever-changing revolving door of cute rich men my mother hoped would put a ring on her finger and money in her bank account? It's like she went off the rails when she lost the love of her life. Every time one relationship ended, she would start looking for his replacement, and it was always easy to find one because she was so beautiful. No…my mum never had a problem finding guys. It was the keeping them that eluded her. The guys who used her were always rich and good-looking.'

'And you're lumping me in the same category? A rich guy who uses women?'

Kaya didn't say anything. She was surprised at how much she had confided and astonished at how heartfelt her confession had been. Had she been deluded into thinking that he was some sort of kindred spirit? Or had she become so accustomed to never opening up that opening up now was like releasing a dam? Perhaps the fact that he was a stranger helped. He would be in her life for ten minutes and then he would be gone for ever, so what was the danger in handing him some confidences?

'I don't see a wedding ring on your finger any more than you see one on mine,' she pointed out, ignoring his look of utter incredulity at the sheer brazen cheek of her having told him what she thought. Indeed she was tempted to laugh out loud at his expression.

'Is there someone lurking in the background?' She pulled the tail of the tiger and felt a rush of forbidden excitement, a stirring in her blood that was heady. 'I'm only saying what you said to me. Is there a girlfriend waiting for you in Manhattan? Maybe not tied to the kitchen sink because, like you told me, you're no dinosaur...'

'No, as a matter of fact!'

Leo raked his fingers through his hair and sat back to stare at her with an expression of outrage underscored with grudging admiration.

'You're a rich guy who plays the field because he can.'

'I can't believe I'm hearing this!'

Kaya wanted to tell him that his very reaction was proof positive of everything she had just said. He was the rich guy who pulled strings and never thought that he had to answer to anyone.

'I'm honest with the women I choose to go out with.' Leo slanted her a darkly brooding look from under his lashes, and Kaya shivered in automatic response to a stretching tension that felt oddly sensual. She knew that this was her inexperience coming to the surface again, undermining her composure and throwing her off-balance. Her one serious relationship, which had fizzled out over a year ago into a something and nothing kind of friendship, had definitely not prepared her for this assault on her emotions. Thoughtful, sensitive and considerate, whilst lovely on paper, had ended up being frustrating in reality and certainly hadn't come close to what this stranger evoked in her, which felt wild and reckless.

'What does that mean?' Her voice was low and breathy.

'It means I don't play games with them—with anyone. I don't string them along, and I wouldn't dream of using any woman. I'm sorry your formative years were spent witnessing your mother's mistakes but, whoever those guys were, they were nothing like me. Believe it or not, I pride myself on being a man of honour!'

'But not a man who's willing to listen to what other people have to say!'

'Meaning?'

'You've written off Julie Anne. You don't even want to know what she looked like, never mind what she was all about. You probably wouldn't care to know that she hoped to turn part of this house into select accommodation for girls from the halfway house when there's overspill. There's acres of land attached to this house. She was going to invest in some horses, something that could provide therapeutic enjoyment for girls who might feel that life is hopeless as they come to terms with pregnancies they're not equipped to handle. Surely you can see that maybe, just maybe, your mother was trying to atone for what she did?'

'Not this again!' He vaulted upright and moved to stand directly in front of her before leaning down, hands splayed on the arms of the chair on which she sat, his expression angry and impatient as he stared at her. He was so close that she could see the flecks of gold in his dark eyes and could breathe in the scent of him, musky and masculine.

'I haven't come here to rescue anything or anyone,' he snarled through gritted teeth. 'I'm going to sell the lot and return to Manhattan where I live, and the sooner the better. So all those bleeding-heart stories about your saintly friend? The very same saintly friend who dumped me thirty-two years ago? Not going to work. Atonement doesn't make up for crimes committed! Atonement is just a pointless, self-serving afterthought!'

He straightened but there was a sudden urgent restlessness in him that made the atmosphere between them electric. Kaya couldn't peel her eyes away from him. She could *feel* his energy, feel his impatience and ferocious disapproval of the way she had pushed back against him, but she refused to be cowed.

She stubbornly met his angry dark eyes until he rasped, 'I have to get out of here.'

'And go where?'

'You said there's Internet in the town somewhere. I need to work.'

'Are you going to *drive* in?'

'I'll walk. I damn well need the exercise.'

He spun round on his heels and jerkily prowled to the window to look through at the fields at the back of the house.

Tension radiated from his body in waves. She'd made no headway at all. All that rage and anger at a past he couldn't change would always stand in the way of him seeing beyond it to the good his mother had done.

By harping on, she had probably done the opposite of

what she had intended, and she could feel defeat settle on her shoulders. There didn't seem anything left to say, so she was silent when he eventually turned to look at her.

'I'll be back when I'm back,' he told curtly. 'We'll discuss formal arrangements then—set a date for when you think you'll be able to vacate the property. If needs be, I can instruct my people to assist in finding you somewhere to live.'

'I'll manage,' Kaya said tautly. 'I'll make sure to start packing my things while you're gone.'

Their eyes clashed and she was the first to look away.

She didn't move but she heard the sound of his footsteps in the hall and then the slam of the front door.

She would start clearing her stuff. The snow had stopped and the sooner she cleared off, the better.

It was a while before Kaya peeped over the parapet. Her head was raging with helpless, fist-clenching, teeth-grinding frustration as she attacked her bedroom, sorting things into piles and discovering that there was a hell of a lot more stored in nooks and crannies than she'd expected.

That damn man was impossible!

His bitterness was insurmountable. He might have made his fortune and found his freedom, he might have had everything he'd ever wanted within his grasp, but none of that, obviously, had given him peace of mind.

He still seethed, and he would seethe for ever, because he would never find the answers to the questions he had probably asked himself over the years.

Why?

Why had he been given up?

Sitting back on her haunches amidst the chaos of

clothes dragged from drawers and cupboards, Kaya lost herself in contemplation of what he must have spent his lifetime going through and what he would be going through now. For it would surely have been rammed in his face that, whatever thoughts he had nurtured about his mother, they had not revolved around her being a decent, middle class, well-off do-gooder. That wasn't the stereotype of any woman who handed her baby up for adoption.

But did he imagine that he was alone in his bewilderment and hurt? Didn't he realise that she, as well, had questions that would now never be answered? Couldn't he see that she had been winded and knocked for six when she'd been told of his existence?

She didn't notice the passing of time until she glanced at her mobile to realise that it had gone five-thirty and he had been out of the house for *hours*. On foot and in unfamiliar territory.

She uneasily debated what to do. She didn't have his mobile number. How was she to contact him? Should she have tried to dissuade him from his crazy decision to walk into town? It was doable, she thought, chewing her lip, but was it doable when he didn't have the foggiest idea where he was going?

The snow had completely stopped, which was a good thing, but there were still piles of it everywhere, great, white drifts pale against the darkness. Piles of treacherous snow lying in wait for an unwary stranger.

Had he even made it to the town in one piece or was he lying somewhere in a ditch, waiting for help to show up? It would be easy to get lost in a place like this, where the snowy fields in winter could become a bewildering maze, and the stretching white mountains a series of lethal ledges and drops.

The man might get under her skin until she wanted to scream but she would never forgive herself if he ended up injured, or worse, because she had driven him to the end of his tether, forcing him to escape on a dangerous walk in unknown terrain.

She flew downstairs, slung on all the warm layers she had earlier discarded and felt the sharp cold on her as she let herself out of the house and headed to her car.

She knew this drive to town and could have done it blindfolded, but she was still forced to creep along at a snail's pace, because of the snow and because she was peering into the pools of darkness for an inert Leo at the side of the road.

The only up side to the tortuous trip was that there was no traffic at all. Only a lunatic would have been out in this part of the country on a night like this. As she edged towards the town, things picked up. Most of the shops were open. Lights glittered and there were people around, picking up groceries, stocking up on water just in case.

The town was a meandering network of charming streets that encircled a little park, now white and empty, and a church that was used throughout the year for all sorts of things. Retail parks and mega-stores still had to make it there and the atmosphere was of a place waiting for modern life to happen. But scratch the surface and, yes, there were Icafés with Wi-Fi, a gleaming shop that sold the most up-to-the minute ski equipment and boutiques where the rich and famous would not have felt uncomfortable.

And on the outskirts of the town, but within walking distance, were all sorts of houses, large and small, bordered with sloping front lawns that lazed under huge, sprawling trees. Settling snow would not have affected anyone living here.

Kaya found parking easily.

She hadn't been here since she'd left to see her mother two months ago and now she looked and appreciated what she'd left behind—the laid-back bustle, the spectacle of the snow on the roofs of the shops which turned the picturesque town into a postcard. The old-fashioned street lights that hadn't been changed in decades cast shadows across the pavements as groups walked by, soaking up the atmosphere and the beauty of thick snow.

She hit the first café at speed. She had no idea what she would do if she couldn't find Leo. Her thoughts were tangled and panicked, and underscored with guilt when she spotted him through the broad planes of glass that opened to a brightly lit space inside.

The first place! Whilst she had been wracked with fears of him wandering in a lost daze in a confusing white landscape, he had gaily made his way to the first café he had come across and set up camp!

There he sat, larger than life and cool as a cucumber! He was sprawled back on one of the low sofas, surrounded by a bevy of men and women, all young and all beautiful and, in the case of the women—five of them, to be precise—all agog with open admiration at whatever he was saying.

Panic turned to rage with supersonic speed. She forced herself to breathe slowly and evenly. She neared the window and peered inside. Should she just do an about turn and walk away, leaving him to make his own merry way back to the house? After all, hadn't he told her that he would be back when he was back? He hadn't asked her to start her own one-woman search party for him! And, besides, in record time he had found himself a fan club. One of them would no doubt snap up the opportunity to deliver him back to the house in one piece. They all looked as though they wanted to gobble him up!

She was swinging away when their eyes met.

His dark eyes pinned her to the spot through the laughing group and Kaya froze. She watched, resigned, as he slowly stood up, while his circle of groupies leapt to its feet in an apparent attempt to detain him. She decided that it was a very unedifying sight.

His eyes never left her face, even when he was making a song and dance of ruefully taking his departure.

She should never have let guilt get the better of common sense. She should have remembered the way he had stormed out, immune to listening to anything she had had to say. Did he have any scruples when it came to saying exactly what he thought? No. He did as he pleased, and behaved exactly how he wanted to behave without the slightest need to obey common rules of courtesy and listen to her.

He wasn't interested in the case she was making for the sake of the retreat Julie Anne had set up, and he didn't see any reason why he had to pretend to show interest. He was the very epitome of the guy he claimed not to be—so rich that he could do as he pleased and then make pointless excuses for his bad behaviour.

The closer he got, the angrier she became and, by the time the glass door to the café swung open and he sauntered towards her, she was ready to combust.

CHAPTER FOUR

HE HADN'T EXPECTED to see her. He'd left the house more wired than he'd ever been in his life.

She'd wanted to open up his eyes to an uplifting vision of all the good work Julie Anne had spent her life doing. She'd wanted him to get past the annoying technicality of his abandonment and look beyond it, to the woman who had decided to seek atonement doing whatever it was she'd done, paving the way for young girls who needed shelter.

She'd wanted him to forgive and forget.

Never had he felt such a surge of bitterness as the old feelings he'd thought he'd laid to rest had returned with devastating force.

He'd had to leave.

Unaccustomed to any loss of control, the rush of emotions overwhelming him, threatening to take him back to a dark place he'd left behind, had been too much. But, even as he'd fought against the snow to make his way into town, with the silence of the night a calming companion, he'd recognised that the woman hadn't said any of the things to rile him.

More than that, he'd been forced to concede that he wasn't the only one with unresolved issues on the subject of his mother.

Yes, he'd had years living with what she'd done, but she'd also seemed to have done a number on Kaya, a person who had loved and trusted her. She'd kept him a secret—surely that would eat away at the memories she had of her friend? Yet, somehow, she had transcended any disappointment or disillusionment and had been determined to give Julie Anne the benefit of the doubt.

He, on the other hand, could not be quite so forgiving.

He'd been glad of the arduous, freezing walk, which had calmed him, and he'd found the café without any trouble. By the time he'd reached civilisation, he'd been more than happy to ditch the work he had resolved to do and immerse himself in the sort of superficial laughter and bonhomie that came as second nature to him.

That he could handle. It was easy to weave that magnetic spell over people, easy to join in, seemingly charming and mesmerising while deep inside he held himself back, always watching from the outside, participating but only so much and no more.

With Kaya and her questions and searching dark eyes...? Well, it seemed ridiculously difficult and he wondered whether it was because of a connection throbbing between them, one he hadn't instigated but one that was there nevertheless.

The connection of his mother.

Kaya made a mockery of his self-control and that, as much as anything else, he had wanted to escape.

But he hadn't expected to look through those panes of glass out into a lamp-lit street to see her standing there looking, it had to be said, livid.

The sharp satisfaction he had felt the minute he had spotted her defied common sense. Just like that, earlier frustrations vanished and his equanimity returned, stabilising him and bringing a small smile to his lips as he joined her outside in the freezing cold.

'This is unexpected,' he drawled. 'To what do I owe the pleasure?' Next to Kaya, scowling and glaring, all those attractive young women he had just been chatting with faded into oblivion.

Under the street lamps, her exotic beauty was thrown into sharp relief. He felt a kick of sexual awareness and drew in a sharp breath.

'You were gone for hours,' Kaya said through gritted teeth, stalking towards her car, not sparing him a glance and absolutely regretting every guilt-ridden twinge that had propelled her into getting behind the wheel to seek him out.

When she thought of the way she had anxiously peered left and right, scouring the verges *just in case*, only to spot him flirting away with a bunch of women in the café, she wanted to grind her teeth in frustration.

'My apologies if you were worried.'

'Who said anything about being worried?'

As she yanked open the car door, he could see the tinge of colour in her cheeks. She tugged her hair and he noted the slight trembling of her fingers. And she was *still* studiously avoiding his eyes.

Because…what?

Because she was *aware* of him? Because underneath her annoyance she was as aware of him on a basic, primal level as he was of her?

Leo didn't get it. This wave of incomprehensible attraction he felt when he was near her was so unusual for him.

Was it down to the extraordinary nature of their meeting? Or was it because she was just so different from the sort of women he went out with, dated and slept with? She demanded, she ignored his barriers, she challenged him and then stuck to her guns even when he signalled to her to back off. He shouldn't have found any of that alluring but, against all odds, he did.

Was it the pull of novelty? The truth was that he had never sought out a woman like Kaya. He wasn't and never had been interested in cultivating long-term relationships with anyone. He didn't do love because he didn't believe in it. What examples had he ever had of a loving relationship? His own flesh and blood had not been able to love him and surely that should be love in its purest form? Surely that should be love that lacked self-concern, the most selfless love of all? And if he had never experienced that, if that had been too tough for a couple of feckless parents to master, then what hope for the complicated, gruelling business of love that was based on attraction, hope and belief in fairy-tale nonsense about happy-ever-afters?

No; in his head, love was pain and loss and in ways that he couldn't put his finger on. He had come to accept that it was an emotion he would never allow himself to feel.

So, if he went for relationships that were transitory and superficial, then that was just fine with him because he wasn't interested in anything beyond that.

Part of him acknowledged that in going for a certain type of woman, for laying down boundaries that he insisted be adhered to, he was taking the route he knew to be safe, the route that would protect his heart.

He had never envisaged feeling any sort of sexual pull to a woman who demanded more from him than what was straightforward.

So Kaya? It was baffling.

But right now, as that telling colour remained staining her cheeks, there was certainly something about this inexplicable tug, something that made his blood hot and suffused him with a sort of keen, restless craving that was utterly novel and disturbing.

But also quite exciting.

'If you weren't worried, you wouldn't have bothered,' Leo pointed out reasonably. 'If I recall, you weren't exactly the height of warm and friendly when I decided to head to town.'

'Can you blame me?'

'Really want to go down this road again? Because I don't.'

Kaya slanted a glance at him and bristled. The man could not have got on her nerves more and yet she was still so aware of him next to her as they bounced along back to the house, driving back to it slightly faster than she had come from it.

He'd left the house with an angry slam of the front door but he couldn't be in a more chipper mood now. That was what a fan club of pretty young things could do for a guy, she thought sourly, and then was immediately impatient with herself for the thought.

Fact was, she was the only one fuming here. He was cool, calm and collected. He'd made up his mind and he wasn't going to start having second thoughts. If she ventured into that slice of forbidden territory again, then there was no telling how hard he would slam the door in her face.

And the truth was that she still had a load of clearing out to do, including Julie Anne's quarters, which she had left as was when she'd disappeared off to New Zealand.

At the time, she'd been far too shaken to undertake that heart-wrenching task.

They were going to be sharing space for at least another twenty-four hours and low-level sniping was going to be exhausting.

Thinking rationally was one thing, though. Putting it into practice was quite another when the guy sitting next to her was making her feel as though she were on the verge of going up in flames.

'I had no idea whether you'd become disoriented out there,' she said in a driven undertone. 'You don't know this part of the world and I wanted to make sure you hadn't fallen in a ditch.'

'I've always been very good at navigating my way in places I don't know.'

'So I've seen,' Kaya muttered. 'You certainly managed to navigate your way to a jolly crowd of friends in no time at all.'

'What can I say? People like me.' He paused. 'With one or two exceptions.'

'Do you think this is funny?'

'What?'

Kaya's head was bursting. Everything was rushing at her all at once. Seeing him there in that café, laughing and joking… Somehow it had brought home to her the life she led—a careful, responsible life; the life of someone who didn't hang out in cafés laughing and giggling with the cute new guy in town.

He had swept in on a blizzard of snow and everything was upside down now. She had been forced to face limitations within herself that she hadn't faced before. How entrenched had she become in a life that held few surprises and stretched ahead of her without the excitement of anything unknown?

If her mother had been the 'naughty one', then how easy had it been for her to over-compensate by being the good girl?

And did *good girls* have fun?

Somewhere along the line, had she ended up equating fun with being like her mother—irresponsible, throwing herself into untenable relationships…getting hurt over and over again?

She resented the fact that Leo had opened her eyes to all this murky stuff. But more than that she resented the fact that, despite it all, she still couldn't stop her body from responding to him. She still couldn't sit next to him in a banged-up old four-by-four without this electric thread of sexual awareness running through her veins.

Because that was what this was. It wasn't just an objective appreciation of a guy who was sinfully good-looking. This was the sort of attraction that she had never before felt in her safe, guarded, carefully thought-out life.

And there he sat, refreshed after socialising at the café, not a care in the world.

She pulled into the still snowy drive that wound its way up to the house with reckless abandon, barely aware of the slide of the four-wheel drive as it shuddered to an uneven stop.

'Everything!' she said. 'None of this is funny.' She stared at him and there was a stretching silence. It went on and on and on. She could feel her temples begin to throb.

'No. None of it is.'

Kaya stared at him. It was dark out here and she could feel the cold collecting around them, trying to find a way past her layers. His eyes were dark and glittering and he was looking at her with deadly seriousness. Suddenly the confines of the car felt very, very oppressive and the atmosphere had become electric.

Her eyes widened. When she drew in a sharp breath, she almost couldn't release it, and when she did it was on a wrenched shudder.

'You don't understand,' she whispered. 'I don't know what to do. This is all I've ever known. Okay, I knew I'd have to leave the house—I accepted that. But I just thought I'd have time to come to deal with it.'

'I told you, I'm not going to force you to pack your bags and leave first thing.'

'I still have so much clearing left to do. I never realised how much could accumulate in the space of a handful of years, and I haven't even begun to go through Julie Anne's rooms yet.'

'That's the locked room?'

'She has a suite. She liked pottering there—watching telly and doing admin. It's cluttered. I still have to go through her things, and it's going to be awful.'

She broke eye contact but her heart thudded painfully inside her and she gripped the steering wheel for dear life.

For the first time since he'd appeared in her life, changing *everything*, Kaya felt the prick of tears behind her eyes. All the arguments, all the determination to try and get him to appreciate the legacy he had inherited, had leeched out of her and she was left feeling hollow inside.

She felt his hand cover hers and heat washed over her. She looked down at his hand and then at him. She didn't want to move because she didn't want him to take his hand away. She liked the heat of it burning through her jacket, jumper and the million and one layers underneath.

It was a shameful acknowledgement and it left her feeling weak. It left her feeling…as if she wanted more. More than just his consoling hand on hers, more than just his kindness because he could see that she was all over the place.

She wanted him to touch her properly. She wanted him to sweep her into his arms, to kiss her, hold her close and whisper heaven only knew what in her ear. Not sweet nothings, because she was sure that wasn't something he did.

Confused and out of her depth, Kaya tried to work out what it was, exactly, she wanted this man to do. Did she want the one thing she had always promised herself she would never want—sex for the sake of sex? For them to be two ships passing in the night with no love involved and no plans for a future? It was horrifying and scary to think that she could jettison her hard-held beliefs for someone who couldn't have been less appropriate.

Frankly, it beggared belief.

But she was still sitting still and she still hadn't asked him to move his hand, and when she did finally find her voice, she barely recognised it.

'We should go in. It's getting cold out here.'

'We should.'

'You're looking at me,' Kaya heard herself whisper and her heart skipped a beat when he smiled at her. It was the sort of smile she imagined he would deliver when he was with a woman and wasn't busy arguing with her. A slow, toe-curling, sexy smile that made the world stop turning.

'It's no hardship.'

Kaya had no idea what would have happened next if he hadn't been the first to pull back, to rake his fingers through his hair and then glance outside briefly, taking hold of a situation that had felt dangerously out of control.

She jerked back, all in a fluster. Her breath was rapid, as if she'd been running a marathon, and when she opened her mouth nothing emerged.

It was a relief when he let himself out of the car, moving round to her side to open the door. Out here the snow was still thick and deep in the places where it hadn't been cleared.

The tyres had left skid marks through the snow like slanting exclamation marks where she had screeched to a stop, dark and muddy against the pristine white.

Kaya didn't notice any of this. She was just aware of the beating of her heart, the racing of her pulse and the guy opening the car door.

That would be why she lost her footing. Why else? She clambered out of her four-wheel drive, and didn't pay a scrap of attention to the deep furrow of snow banked up at the side. She didn't trip over anything, she just tumbled into a fall—an awkward, clumsy fall—and his lunge to catch her was as clumsy because of the impediment of the snow.

But catch her he did, and he swept her up in one easy movement.

For a millisecond, Kaya luxuriated in the feel of him, his hardness against her, the strength of his arms around her. A millisecond of stolen, treacherous pleasure.

'Put me down!'

'Just as soon as we're inside. Don't lock the car. I'll come back to fetch my computer.'

'I don't need you carrying me!'

'I don't need you stumbling to the front door and doing more damage to your ankle.'

'My ankle is just fine.'

'I'll give you my verdict once I've checked it over.'

'You are *the* most arrogant guy I've ever met in my entire life!'

'I know. Is that a bad thing?'

Kaya shivered, every bit of her body tingling in response to his proximity and to the husky teasing in his voice.

They were in the house, which was blessedly warm, and she gave up the fight and subsided into him as he headed to the sitting room and deposited her on the sofa, as gently as if she were a piece of priceless china.

Her instinct had been to repel the act of kindness. It was something she wasn't used to. She was tall, strong and accustomed to looking out for herself.

His sudden tenderness was disconcerting, as was his gentleness as he eased off her boot, followed by her thick, insulated socks. He was kneeling at her feet and she was absorbed in the moment as she watched his dark head. She had to resist the temptation to sift her fingers through his hair.

'Tell me if this hurts.'

'It hurts!'

'Sprain. Nothing serious. Is there a first-aid kit in the kitchen? Bathroom? You just need it to be contained with a compress and keep the weight off it for a day or two.'

'Suddenly you're a doctor? There's a first-aid kit in the kitchen. It's in the cupboard next to the sink.'

'I'm a man of many talents.' He glanced up at her, and their eyes met and remained locked long enough for Kaya to lick her lips as nervous tension ratcheted up a couple of notches.

She suddenly found that considerate and gentle Leo

was a lot more difficult to handle than arrogant and infuriating Leo.

'Don't move a muscle. I'll be back in a minute.'

Move a muscle? Kaya felt as weak as a kitten as she watched him vanish. Her eyes drifted to the coat he'd dumped on one of the chairs in the sitting room and her mind drifted to the look in his eyes in the car, the huskiness of his voice when he'd told her that looking at her was no hardship...

She was doing a balancing act on uneven ground and... wow...quicksand had never felt so good.

She tensed when he re-entered the room less than a minute later, and her breath hitched in her throat as he began to wind the compress around her ankle. She'd never thought that big hands could be so delicate.

'Where did you learn how to do that?' she asked gruffly, to break the stifling silence.

There was a smile when he replied.

'Foster care wasn't all bad. There was a rota when you got to a certain age—first-aid cover. We had some basic training over a two-day period. Plenty of opportunity for kids of eleven to fool around with medical equipment and ask stupid questions. I can't imagine what the guy who came in to instruct us would have thought of all the horseplay—maybe he expected it. At any rate, he did a good job...and I can tell you that if you suddenly choke on a fish bone tonight, I should be able to see you through.'

'I can't picture you as a kid.'

Leo rested back on his haunches to look at her with a crooked smile. 'Sometimes, neither can I. You need to have a bath. I'm going to carry you upstairs and run a bath for you.'

'No, I'm fine!'

'Nonsense. You wouldn't make it up the stairs without a lot of discomfort. I've already broken the ice by bringing you into the house…'

Kaya nodded jerkily. Did she mind him carrying her up the stairs? No. She wanted him to. She wanted a repeat performance of her body melting surreptitiously against his while her mind took off in all sorts of forbidden directions.

She wanted to have time out from being careful.

There was no danger when it came to this guy because he wasn't her type. She might be madly attracted to him, but she could never really fall for someone who had a commitment-phobia, someone who probably enjoyed relationships that lasted five minutes and then disappeared. She was just too serious when it came to the heavy stuff.

But this wasn't heavy. This was superficial, illicit enjoyment, the sort of stuff her teenage self might have got up to if that teenage girl hadn't been so busy taking care of the person who should have been taking care of her.

'That's true. And I really do feel a bit grubby. If you wouldn't mind running a bath for me, then yes, that would be helpful.'

'Does this mean that you're not going to argue with me about it?'

'Why would I?'

'Because you're argumentative?'

'Weirdly, I'm not at all.' But she didn't want to return to the subject of *why* she was so argumentative when she was with him. She didn't want to get bogged down, yet again, in the business of trying to get him to understand her point of view. That ship had sailed. He'd made that patently clear and she would just have to deal with the fallout of his decision.

This brief truce between them felt too good to endanger. She reached for him as he leant to scoop her up and relaxed as he carried her up the stairs. She was five-ten, but he made her feel petite and light as a feather.

'I'll run a bath for you.' He stood back, having settled her on the comfy chair by the window. 'Try not to get the compress wet, but it might be tricky.'

'I'll manage,' Kaya told him gruffly. 'I can drape my leg over the side of the bath and it'll be no problem wriggling my way out. I'm pretty athletic.'

Leo grunted.

Did she have any idea what images she was generating in his head? He pictured her naked in the water, bubbles not quite covering her belly and her breasts... Her legs apart with one resting on the lip of the bath...

If he wasn't careful he'd be having a cold shower at roughly the same time as she was having her hot bath.

Leo had never been turned on by pursuit of the inaccessible. He had built his life around work with everything falling into place around it. And that included the relationships he had. They came and went and they never interfered with his work. When it came to pursuit, he was really only interested in the kind that involved the acquisition of power and money. Neither was essential, per se, but having lived his life deprived of both they certainly held quite a bit of appeal.

Certainly for him.

As far as he was concerned, time involved chasing a woman made no sense. Bed was the final destination and sooner or later boredom was the eventual outcome. So why waste time on courtship?

Maybe he was lazy when it came to the opposite sex. Maybe all his considerable energies were held in reserve for his primary focus. That was something Leo didn't dwell on.

What surprised him was just how much air time he was giving Kaya, a woman he had only just met. More than that, she was definitely inaccessible, yet he couldn't stop himself from wanting her. What was that all about?

He finished running the bath and then backed out, leaving her to her own devices, muttering something about preparing food for her.

Watching him edge hurriedly out of the bedroom, making sure to shut the door behind him, Kaya wondered whether he could be more obvious in his sudden desire to be rid of her company.

She debated whether to lock the bedroom door but why? She didn't know. He wasn't going to barge in on a tide of lust, that was for sure.

The bath was perfect. He'd managed to get the temperature just right and she took her time getting all her clothes off, manoeuvring slowly to avoid jarring her ankle, which felt better with the compress.

When she was naked, she stood, balancing on one foot, and looked at her own nakedness in the mirror. It wasn't something she usually did. What she saw was a tall and slender woman with small, high breasts and a neat waist. A strong, toned body.

When she examined herself through a guy's eyes, though, the picture was different. Too tall…too flat-chested…too boyish and athletic. Did men like strong women? At a push she could probably lift up a lot of the guys she knew. Was that sexy?

She took her time in the bath because she was thinking, while the time passed by. Thinking about Leo and this curling desire inside her that was so alien, so exciting and so difficult to deal with.

She feverishly turned over in her head the way he had backed out of the bathroom earlier, as though the hounds of hell had been snapping at his heels.

In her mind, she played over every word spoken that evening, every look exchanged, and wondered whether she was reading meaning into things that had been insignificant.

She cursed her own inexperience, which was crazy, because there was no way she could go back in time and adjust her life to fit this one moment.

What shocked and unsettled her too was the fact that Julie Anne and the huge secret she had kept to herself, which had preyed on her mind for all the time she'd been in New Zealand, had somehow ended up taking second place to Leo. How could that be? She was terrified to think that she could be like her mother—drawn to a rich guy who knew how to talk the talk and walk the walk but would always be as unreliable as the day was long.

She *needed* reliability. It was part of her emotional foundations.

Only when the water was getting tepid did Kaya realise just how long she'd been in the bath. She made to move and winced as her ankle took the brunt of her weight as she levered herself up.

The water sloshed around her as she gripped the sides of the bath. Every ounce of effort was focused on the time-consuming business of getting out and protecting her sore ankle at the same time, and the chill of the air on her skin was bringing her out in goose pimples.

She didn't hear the soft push of the bathroom door. She was frowning and concentrating hard, and it was only when she glanced across that she saw Leo's hand on the door, his shadow on the tiled floor.

'You okay in there?'

Kaya's head went blank. She felt heat pour through her body, and she knew she should say something, but her vocal cords had seized up and all she could manage was an inaudible croak.

And then the door was pushed open and there he was, the guy she'd spent the last forty minutes thinking about while the bath water had gone cold, her skin had puckered and he...*what*?

He'd left her to have a bath and she'd taken so long that he'd understandably become worried—just as she'd understandably been worried when he'd headed into town on foot in the snow...

'Leo!'

'Kaya...'

They spoke at the same time.

'Get out!'

The words seemed to hit Leo from a long way away. He'd done his best to clear his head in the kitchen, and had taken his time making them both something to eat. But when he'd glanced at the clock on the wall, and seen just how long it had been since he'd run that bath, he'd felt a little tendril of worry begin to curl inside him.

He'd left the food in the kitchen and headed up the stairs, and then he'd listened by the door and heard nothing. He'd knocked softly and then increasingly harder but had heard nothing. And then, with his hand on the bathroom door, he'd heard something that had sounded very much like a cry of pain and gut instinct had taken over.

He stared.

Her body... How long had he been fantasising about

her body without realising it? How long had he been telling himself that this woman was out of bounds? That whatever attraction he felt was rooted in nothing more than the kick of novelty and the strangeness of the bond between them in the form of his mother?

She was beyond beautiful. Her body was a golden olive. Her glaring eyes were bright and dark and her long, soaking wet hair streamed over her body, clinging to her shoulders and falling in strands to partially cover small, perfect breasts.

She was supporting herself on the bath. He could see the strain of sinew in her arms, and beyond that the length of slender legs and the dark thatch between them.

Their eyes met, she yelled at him again and the spell was broken. Leo reddened, averting his eyes as he backed away.

For the first time in his life he was in a situation over which he had absolutely no control. She was the most glorious thing he had ever seen in his life, and he could have stayed looking at her until the sun rose in the sky. But instead, perspiring, flustered and slamming the bathroom door shut behind him, he fled.

CHAPTER FIVE

KAYA COULDN'T HIDE in the bedroom for ever, but she wished she could. She was on fire as she got dressed. When she thought of Leo bursting in on her, seeing her naked, her thoughts went into meltdown and she wanted the ground to open up and swallow her whole.

Mortification, blind fury, horrifying self-consciousness: she honestly didn't know which was the strongest emotion. What had gone through his head when he had seen her? She tried to recapture what she'd seen on his face and the only thing she could come up with was... shock.

But then what had he expected when he'd decided to waltz into her bedroom uninvited and then, to top it off, enter the bathroom, knowing that she would be in it?

She looked at her reflection in the mirror and what stared back at her was a woman whose colour was so high and whose eyes were glittering so brightly that she seemed on the point of combusting. She had thrown on her jeans and several layers and had managed to put on socks, even though her ankle was still sore and tender. With her emotions running high, though, it was very easy to overlook her twisted ankle.

She made it very slowly down the stairs, clutching the banister, and with each passing step her fury increased.

By the time she finally made it to the kitchen, she was bolstered by self-righteous anger, which had the great advantage of diminishing her excoriating embarrassment.

She pushed open the kitchen door and the first thing she saw was Leo at the kitchen table. He looked up as soon as she entered.

His computer was open on the table—the Wi-Fi had been restored at some point during the day—but she could tell that he hadn't been working. His eyes were brooding, intense, and she noted the dark flush that spread across his sharp cheekbones as their gaze held and kept holding for what seemed like an eternity.

'How *dare* you?'

Fired up, Kaya hobbled into the kitchen and, when he half-rose to help her to a chair, she glared at him.

'Kaya, I'm sorry if I busted in on you while you were—'

'Don't even say it!'

The last thing she needed was to be reminded of her nudity when he had barged into the bathroom unannounced.

She was burning up. How could he sit there, as cool as a cucumber, while she was *burning up*? And how could her body be so *aware* of him even though her head was fuming, hating him and going over what had happened in those brief *seconds* in torturous detail?

Her brain was being sensible and giving her the ammunition to rage, but her body…that was a different matter. She thought of his eyes resting on her, *seeing* her the way no man had ever seen her before, and something tingled between her thighs and made her nipples tighten in crazy awareness, filled her veins with a rush of hot blood.

And her disobedient eyes were trying hard to put him

into perspective, to see him as the stranger who had turned her world upside down by inconsiderately showing up before she'd had time to get her house in order. But instead all she could see was his ridiculously handsome face: the sharp, chiselled features, the thick, sooty lashes and those deep, dark eyes watching her without revealing anything.

'I knocked.'

'That's a lie!'

'Let me get you something to eat…to drink.'

'I'm not hungry!'

'Kaya…'

'You might own this house but that doesn't mean that you can open and shut doors without knocking first.'

'I knocked!' He vaulted to his feet, pausing briefly to stand in front of her and meet her furious eyes head on.

In his head, he saw her naked coming out of that bath, water streaming over her beautiful, supple body. He couldn't get the image out of his mind, and when he next spoke his voice was low and hoarse.

'I knocked, Kaya. I was worried. I left you alone and came down here, and the minutes ticked by, and the next time I looked at the clock nearly an hour had gone by and, damn it, I was worried!'

He stared at her, raked his fingers through his hair and was overwhelmed. Overwhelmed, now that he was verbalising how he'd felt, by astonishment at just how worried he had been that something had happened to her—that she'd fallen, banged her head, knocked herself out, hell, pretty much gone and done anything to herself.

She wasn't his responsibility!

So why had he been worried sick about her?

Worrying sick about anybody just wasn't in his DNA.

He didn't have that gene. He knew what strength and independence felt like and they didn't include vivid scenarios in his head that bore no relation to reality when he sat down and analysed them.

He was way too emotionally detached for any show of weakness along those lines. He wondered whether, in some weird low-level way, he *did* feel responsible for her and decided that, if he did, then it made perfect sense. She was in his house, temporarily displaced because of him, and while she was there then surely he couldn't treat her with the sort of bone-deep detachment with which he treated everybody else?

And then…there was the connection to his mother, the woman he had never known. Kaya had known her. It was a peculiar situation. When he'd arrived here, the last thing he'd expected to find, or perhaps the last thing he'd had any interest in finding, had been connections to the woman who had given him up for adoption.

Yet, he had not been able to escape the slow build-up of a picture he hadn't asked to see. The mere fact that Kaya was who she was, and there was no denying her inherent *goodness*, gave him the sort of insight into the woman who had given birth to him that he hadn't asked for

However hard he subconsciously tried to prevent his thoughts from meandering into areas he knew would always prove futile, he still found himself doing it. He told her that her pleas for him to try and see Julie Anne for the person she had been before she had died were falling on deaf ears, and *of course* they were, but even so…

His imagination had been stirred, much to his annoyance. So it was a complex situation—little wonder his responses weren't in line with what he would have expected them to be!

'I don't need you being worried on my behalf,' Kaya snapped.

'You could have fallen…hurt yourself.'

'And I definitely *don't* need a knight in shining armour to rescue me from an accident that never happened!'

'Trust me,' Leo ground out, 'No one on this planet would ever be tempted to call me a knight in shining armour…'

Their eyes tangled. He moved towards her and pulled a chair so close to her he could see the luminous, satiny smoothness of her skin close up.

'I'll bet,' Kaya returned in a driven undertone, but her heart was beating fast and there was a swooping inside her that made her mouth go dry.

He might not be a knight in shining armour but he had taken care of her after she'd twisted her ankle. It had been a simple accident but she knew that there were guys who, in a similar position, would have seen her as a nuisance, hobbling around and taking up space in a house they had come to sell.

She thought of him carrying her up those stairs, thought of the gentle way he had examined her ankle and the way he had done his utmost to make sure she was relaxed because of how highly strung and sensitive she'd been with him, and she felt a whoosh of shame at her ungracious attack on him now.

He wouldn't have just barged in for the hell of it.

He just wasn't that sort of guy.

'I—I,' she stuttered, blushing. 'I apologise if I sound a little harsh. I guess I didn't hear you knocking. But you didn't knock on the bathroom door. You just pushed it open and stormed inside!'

'I pushed it open because I heard something that sounded like a grunt of pain.'

'I was trying to get out of the bath.' The water had gone cold, which showed just how long she'd been in it. Was it so surprising that he'd wondered what the hell had happened to her?

'I didn't stop to think, Kaya, and I should have—but what if something had happened to you? What if you were lying on the ground in pain?'

Kaya had an uncomfortable image of herself on the tiles in nothing but her birthday suit, being discovered by Leo and carried to the bed, exposed in all her glory.

She blanched at the vividness of the picture in her head and then breathed in sharply as their eyes met. She felt exposed, as if he could read her mind.

'I may have overreacted,' she said stiffly. 'It was the shock, I suppose, of having you…someone, anyone… I didn't expect it. You caught me…'

'I know how I caught you.'

Leo wanted to groan aloud. Did she have any idea what this conversation was doing to his head, never mind his body?

He couldn't help himself. His eyes flickered over her, from her beautiful face to the shape of her under the layers of clothes. In his mind's eye, he could still see those small, high breasts, the brown discs of her nipples, the curve of her spine, the slenderness of her ankles and the dark shadow of her pubic hair…

His breathing slowed and his eyes darkened.

'You're beautiful, Kaya,' he heard himself say, his voice low and husky, and he sat back and pressed his thumbs to his eyes. 'God, I have no idea what possessed me to say that and I apologise.'

He leapt up, prowled through the kitchen, restless in his own body, and then returned to the kitchen table. But he pulled the chair back, close enough so he wouldn't have to shout but not so close that his nervous system would begin misbehaving.

'I've made you feel uncomfortable and for that I can't apologise enough. I…' He sighed, half-closed his eyes and flung his head back for a few seconds, a man in the grip of something strong and elemental. 'I'm going to leave you…head to one of the other rooms to work. Internet's back on. Kaya, I would offer to carry you upstairs, but I'm guessing you'd probably tell me to get lost.'

'I can make my own way up.'

Had he just told her that she was beautiful? It had sounded like a confession ripped from him, and the sincerity of it had gone to the very core of her and opened the lid of a box she'd been struggling to keep tightly locked. It was a box that contained wild ideas and reckless yearnings…things she'd only seen and felt since this man had appeared on the scene.

This was the very thing she had always sworn she would never do. She'd noted the example her mother had set and made a pact with herself that she would never let some guy rule her head, never mind her heart. She would steer clear of the temptation to let anyone dominate her thoughts. She was never going to be the woman sitting by the phone, biting her nails and desperately waiting for it to ring.

She wanted him to carry her up. She wanted to feel his hardness against her. She wanted him to carry on telling her stuff she knew was out of bounds. She wanted to hear him say more—that he fancied her, that he wanted to touch her, kiss her…*make love to her.*

'Look at me like that,' Leo warned in a driven undertone, 'And you might get a little more than you bargained for.'

'Like what?'

'Right now, I want to kiss you so much it's a physical pain. More than just kiss you, Kaya.'

'What? What more?'

'I'm going to go. This is…'

'C-crazy,' she confirmed shakily.

'So you feel it too.'

'It doesn't matter what I feel. Nothing…nothing…is going to happen. It would be madness. I… I could never… You don't make sense, not to me. Not for someone like me.' And she meant it. She didn't understand how this powerful thing had ignited between them—how it had ignited inside *her*, as though she'd just been a bundle of dry tinder waiting for the wrong guy to come along one day with a box of matches to set her alight—but it had.

Which didn't mean she would do anything about it. No way. She wasn't her mother. She wasn't going to get lost in some bad-news guy. She had her head screwed on even if, right now, her body was doing its best to dictate the state of play.

'I get it,' Leo returned roughly.

He looked away but he could feel her eyes on him and he was held captive by something he couldn't identify, something that was doing a damn good job of making him lose all his legendary cool.

Somehow he'd turned into a horny teenager and all he wanted to do was reach out and touch her. The fact that she wanted him just as much as he wanted her was almost too much to take on board. How the hell were they going to make it under the same roof for another day, hour, minute?

'It's late. Sure you don't want me to help you up?' He spread his hands in a gesture of appeasement. 'You have my word that, however much I'm attracted to you, there's no way you need fear that I'll make a play for you. Not now, not while we're under the same roof. You have my word.'

Kaya believed him with every fibre in her being. She told him she was tired, would grab a couple of tablets for the discomfort and make herself a sandwich. That she was fine.

What she wanted to say was *what if she wanted him to make a play for her? What if she wanted this mutual attraction to take them wherever it wanted to take them...?*

'I don't think we should talk about this again.' She cleared her throat and assumed a firm line, drawing a marker in the sand. Because who knew what was going to happen without that marker? And, whatever this was, she intended to fight it. So would he. They were both adults, and she might be inexperienced, but she wasn't a complete idiot.

'Are you saying we pretend this never happened?'

'That's not impossible.'

'No,' Leo said softly. 'It's not.'

And it was exactly what should happen. She was as fresh as dew on a summer's morning. Her world had been turned upside down, so add *vulnerable* on top of everything else. Whatever this crazy force was running between them, he knew that it was up to him to stamp all over it.

But he hesitated. Those eyes, those softly parted lips... His mind was running amok with forbidden images. He could feel the steel of his erection throbbing painfully and the ache of a need he'd never thought possible.

The silence sizzled between them, an electric charge that could deliver a shock Leo knew both of them would regret. He, because he didn't do complicated situations and this turned *complicated* into an understatement. And she, because who knew where that door would lead to if she decided to dump the principles that had guided her life? One of them had to lead by experience, and that was going to be him, whether he liked it or not.

Because one look at those softly parted lips, and the barely concealed desire darkening her eyes, and he knew that whatever caresses he gave her would be returned in full.

But would there be regrets after? Probably. He didn't do post-coital regrets.

'Let me bring you the tablets, Kaya. They'll kick in fast and make it easier for you to move about.'

He didn't give her a choice. He had to escape the drag of wanting something that would do him no good, would do neither of them any good.

He fetched tablets and water for her and had to control a crazy tremor in his hands as he dropped them on the table, before standing back and folding his arms.

'I'll see you in the morning.'

'I'll start my packing. I know you're not going to chuck me out, but the sooner things are finalised here, the better.'

Leo shrugged and left, shutting the door quietly behind him, and it was only when she was alone in the kitchen that Kaya sagged into the chair and closed her eyes.

It wouldn't be mentioned—none of it. That was the thought she hugged to herself an hour and a half later when she finally made it up to bed.

As he had predicted, the painkillers had done their job

and the pain in her ankle had subsided to a dull throb by the time she was under the covers with the bedroom door firmly locked, although she knew that the last thing he would do would be enter without being invited.

The air had been cleared between them. That was a good thing. There had been a dark cloud, heavy with things unsaid, thick with innuendo and slanted, glancing, shivering awareness. She'd thought that she was the only one feeling it, but she hadn't been, and she told herself that there was no harm in secretly admitting that his attraction to her made her feel euphoric and heady.

The guy was sex on legs. What woman wouldn't be flattered to have his attention turned to her?

If this *thing* between them hadn't gone by the time morning came, then surely the fact that they had agreed to pretend nothing had been said would help things along?

And anyway, she thought, coming back down to earth with a bump as sleep finally began to take over, whatever passing attraction he felt for her would be one that had grown from their proximity and from the fact that they were connected by Julie Anne, whether he wanted to admit it or not.

He was an experienced guy, unlike her, and she was sure that, having been turned away, his attitude would be a mental shrug and a 'you win a few, you lose a few' response.

Sleep eventually came but it was fitful. Her ankle felt better but, in the dead of the night, she blamed it for keeping her awake, even though deep down she knew that the thing keeping her alert and aware was happening in her head.

She wasn't sure what she'd hoped the morning would

bring when she went downstairs, but she was on the defensive the second she found him in the kitchen.

If she had appreciated his stunning looks before, nothing could have prepared her for how devastatingly aware she was of him now that they had opened up about their mutual attraction. Just knowing that he found her attractive added an edge to their situation that brought her out in a cold sweat.

His eyes rested on her, dark and brooding, but when he spoke it was to ask her how her ankle was doing.

She'd told him that it would be best for them to pretend that nothing had happened and he was going along with that. It was obvious in his politeness and in the cool remoteness of his expression. He was going to be considerate and courteous until they parted company.

'I've decided that I'm going to head out today,' she said, keeping as cool as he was. She hadn't thought about going out, and had planned to spend the day clearing more of her stuff, but suddenly the thought of them both circling one another in the house and pretending nothing had happened was too much.

'You're heading out?'

Kaya bristled.

Wherever she looked, he seemed to fill her vision. She had surprised him as he was making himself a cup of coffee and, even though he was in some faded track bottoms and an old sweatshirt, he still managed to look unfairly sexy.

She harked back to him telling her that he found her attractive, to the hot urgency of their conversation the evening before, and instantly felt like passing out.

'It's not a crime, is it?' She blushed because she didn't want to sound defensive. 'Snow's clearing up,' she said abruptly. 'I thought I might take the opportunity to head into town, visit the halfway house. I haven't been there for over two months and I miss it.'

'The halfway house...?'

'Yes.'

'Not a good idea.'

'Why not? I was fine driving yesterday when the weather was worse. I'm accustomed to conditions out here.'

'And I'm accustomed to pounding the pavements of Manhattan in winter, but I'd draw the line at doing that with a twisted ankle.'

'My ankle is better.'

'Really? And what if it decides otherwise while you're behind the wheel of your car? Never mind the fact that you could get into an accident and hurt yourself, you could also get into an accident and hurt other people.'

Kaya shot him a fulminating look from under her lashes.

'Well,' she said sweetly, changing tack and taking advantage of the opportunity suddenly provided to her, 'You could always come with me.'

'Why would I want to do that?'

Caught up in the moment of playing it cool and banking down a libido that had suddenly awakened the second she had entered the kitchen, Leo stilled. Hadn't they parked conversations about the inheritance he hadn't asked for? Every time he thought about it—which was too often for his liking—his head was flooded with all sorts of questions.

What had the woman been like? Over time, all thoughts he had had of her—of which none, thankfully, had continued to intrude until now—had solidified into an image of a woman happy to put herself above everything and everyone. Someone grasping, selfish and unpleasant. Those were impressions he had never had any trouble dealing with.

But, now that he was here, he hated the fact that those impressions had become out of focus. Kaya had clearly loved the woman, and certainly it would seem that she had done many things that were commendable, if Kaya was to be believed.

So who had she been?

Leo loathed the curiosity that kept raising its head because he knew the question about *why* she had dumped him would remain a mystery, whatever had happened thereafter.

And underneath that corrosive curiosity was the simple, jarring hurt of knowing that the love that he had missed out on had been lavished on Kaya. He didn't resent that but it was still something else he found himself dealing with.

The last thing he needed was Kaya taking a few more pot shots at him, although grudgingly he had to commend her for her tenacity, if nothing else.

But, then again, wasn't that one of the things that made her so appealing—the strength he sensed underneath the innocence? He guessed she could be as stubborn as a mule, and outspoken with it, and those were qualities in short supply when it came to the women he had always dated. He frowned impatiently but without much surprise when she continued, with gathering momentum.

'Because if you're that concerned about me making it there in one piece without laying waste to myself, not to mention everyone in my path when my ankle suddenly decides to hit the accelerator by accident, then you don't have an option. You come with me and take the wheel, or I go on my own.'

It was a bluff. She hadn't thought about what might happen if her foot did slip. There was no way she would endanger anyone by doing anything irresponsible, but this seemed a great way of forcing his hand.

What was the worst that could happen? He could refuse, yell at her, tell her to mind her own business. He could storm out of the kitchen in a rage because she'd pulled the dragon's tail.

She realised that anything would be better than the polite treatment he had been giving her. Having laid down ground rules, she was now discovering that she didn't much like them being adhered to.

He was being the perfect gentleman and she didn't want a perfect gentleman. Whatever he had released, whatever temptation he had dangled in front of her, she now had a taste for it. She liked the thrill of seduction.

She'd never felt anything like it and she wondered whether this was what her mother had felt time and time again. But no... When Kaya took a step back and looked at this situation rationally, she knew that it was nothing like what her mother had succumbed to over and over. This wasn't a reckless search for love, clinging to crumbs thrown at her, desperate for the comfort of settling down and finding stability.

She wasn't her mother.

She knew the score even though she wasn't experienced when it came to sex. She knew what to avoid and she knew that, when it came to anything long-term, Leo was definitely not made of the right material.

When she thought like that, she felt a disturbing sliver of excitement race through her.

Who needed the right material all the time? Had that been a mistake—to put all her eggs in one basket? To think that, if she couldn't have it all—the complete fairy-tale, happy-ever-after ending—then it was better to have nothing at all?

He was looking at her in guarded silence and Kaya side-stepped all those unsettling thoughts. She couldn't afford to go there. Could she?

'It's up to you,' she said with a casual shrug, rising to her feet and then over-egging the pudding by wincing, a reminder that the sore ankle—which actually felt as good as new—could hive off at any given moment while she was driving and do its own thing.

'You win.' Leo growled, standing up to glare at her. 'Give me ten minutes. And in case you're wondering…' He reached to where she kept her car keys on a hook by the kitchen door and slipped them into his pocket with a grin. 'We'll take my car.'

CHAPTER SIX

'HOW DID YOU get involved with this place? Now that we're heading there, you might just as well fill me in.'

Leo slanted a sideways glance at the woman sitting next to him, staring through the window with just the smallest of smiles on her face.

He fancied he could detect triumph there. There was no point agitating for an argument about this trip to a place he had no interest in seeing. Truth was, her ankle appeared to be fine, judging from her easy walk to the car. She'd made a show of limping around the kitchen but had obviously forgotten to prolong the act once she'd managed to get him on board for a visit to the halfway house.

'Where to start?' Kaya murmured.

'Perhaps not at the very beginning,' Leo suggested politely. 'A brief summing up might be the best idea.'

Kaya glanced across. She'd felt his eyes on her but now he was staring straight ahead, concentrating on the road. Although the snow had stopped falling, there was still sufficient banked to the side to make driving conditions hazardous.

It was a beautiful morning: bright-blue skies and everything in sharp relief, from the silhouettes of the wintry trees with their naked branches to the crisp colours of the occasional farm house they passed, burrowed far from the road, just about visible across snow-covered fields.

Cities might hold the buzz of excitement but nothing could really beat the peace of a place like this, where people had time to appreciate the small details that nature gave them, from the grass growing in summer, to the leaves falling in autumn and the wondrous vastness of the open, uncluttered skies.

'I'll try but the beginning is a long time ago, when my mother first moved here from Alaska. I know you don't want to talk about Julie Anne...'

'Don't worry yourself about me. Trust me, my sensibilities are remarkably resilient. A few facts and figures might prepare me for what I'm going to find, so you can stick to that brief.'

Kaya had no intention of throwing him a few facts and figures or sticking to any such brief. She had a suspicion as to what he meant by 'sticking to the facts and figures'. A profit-and-loss column so that he could work out how much he could get for the place when the time came for him to fire-sell it, along with everything else.

Hadn't she already tried to appeal to his better nature? Sexy as hell he might be, but when it came to the properties that were now his, the very properties he had ordered her not to bother talking about, any sign of a better nature was not in evidence.

It would take them the better part of forty-five minutes to get to the halfway house. On a clear day and a good run, it could be done in half that time from the house, but the going was slow in these conditions. She had every intention of laying it on thick, because this would be her one and only chance to have her say.

'Julie Anne wasn't living in the town when my mother

lived here. I know that because she told me when we headed south from Alaska. A lot of her friends had left the place but some had stayed, had kids. My mum found out fast enough that Julie Anne had become something of a pillar of the community when she moved here.'

'A pillar of the community. Touching.'

Kaya didn't say anything but she could see from the clench of his jaw and the narrowing of his mouth that this was painful, and her heart went out to him. He was as tough as steel but underneath that armour there was more. She knew it. She'd seen it in the way he had been so gentle with her when she'd twisted her ankle.

His reaction gave her hope that maybe all wasn't lost, at least not as lost as she'd thought.

'My mum made friends with her quickly. We had a tiny little rented place in the centre above a shop. Julie Anne used to come to the shop quite a bit to buy stuff for the halfway house, odd bits and pieces. She and mum struck up a friendship of sorts. They reached an arrangement—I'm not sure how that came about but my mum… could be very persuasive. I ended up getting a babysitter without mum having to shell out. She could do her job and have her fun and there would be back-up when she wasn't around.'

'Very persuasive indeed. Is that why you go out of your way to be the opposite?'

But Kaya heard the teasing smile in his voice and, instead of bristling with offence, she felt a rush of warmth that made her skin prickle. She relaxed into her narrative. She'd never been this open before when it came to revealing her thoughts. She retraced her childhood, took side turns to describe stuff she'd kept to herself and built up a picture of the woman who had become so influential in her life.

Leo listened. In many ways, her childhood had been as tough as his. From everything she said, it seemed she'd skipped the business of having fun and had gone straight into the hard work of looking out for a mother who had been young, irresponsible and scattered when it came to men. She went for the wrong kind... She involved her daughter in the ups and downs of an erratic love life... She'd lost her husband, who had been the great love of her life, and had then proceeded to throw herself into years of futile distraction tactics in a vain attempt to replace him.

He'd gleaned the basics of her story before but, as they drove slowly towards the halfway house, those basics became fleshed out, building a picture of a girl who had been forced to grow up way before her time.

'So that's pretty much what's leading me to my involvement with the halfway house.' Kaya blushed.

'Ah, we get there at last.'

'You're laughing at me.'

'I enjoyed the story-telling.' He glanced across to her and, for a couple of seconds, his dark eyes remained fixed on her pink cheeks. 'And I'm not laughing at you. I had gathered things were difficult for you growing up, but the picture you paint fills in all the blank spaces. You must have been overjoyed when your mother met the guy who eventually became your stepfather.'

'I was,' Kaya admitted. 'I didn't see it coming and it took a while. My mother had become so accustomed to falling for the wrong guy that when the right guy made it on the scene she didn't see him at first for the great person he was.' She smiled. 'She got the ending she wanted. It just took a while and a lot of wrong turns to get there.'

Leo didn't say anything. Was this the girl who believed that love stories really did come true? An alarm bell sounded, a distant one. One that made him say, thoughtfully, 'I suppose that's a road that plays out for some people—the wrong turns and the happy ending.'

'But not for you?'

'Never for me.'

Well, if she were to be silly enough to entertain any ideas about a proper relationship with this guy, then he'd as good as told her not to bother. Had he been warning her off him? Or had that just been a natural response to what she had said?

'Up ahead, around that bend—the halfway house is there. It's a little way out of the town. I think Julie Anne must have located it there so that none of the locals could lodge any complaints although, after all this time, they're very kindly disposed to the girls who come and go. Once a year, there's a fundraiser, and the proceeds go to maintenance of the place.'

Her thoughts were buzzing in her head as his flash car pulled into the courtyard outside the house. There were eight other cars parked in front, all in a neat row to the side where an attempt had been made to define some parking bays.

For a few seconds after she got out, Kaya stood by the side of the car and gazed at the building she hadn't been near in months. When she looked at Leo, it was to see him doing exactly the same thing, looking at it.

It was large, a large, grey square with evenly spaced windows, and surrounded by trees. In summer, it was striking. Now, in winter, it looked bleak and a little run-down.

Leo had moved to stand next to her and for a few seconds he took in the sight of the place his mother had founded, his saintly mother who had been a pillar of the community, doing so much for so many, having abandoned one.

His mouth thinned.

He'd long ago trained himself never to dwell on things that couldn't be changed, but now he could feel a groundswell of confusion and bitterness.

Next to him, Kaya resumed chatting, walking towards the house, her voice high and excited, her hands shoved into the pockets of her windcheater.

He followed. He was already regretting the impulse that had brought him here. He should have called her bluff with the ankle story, for there were no signs of any twisted ankle now. Instead, here he was, forced to accept that the woman who had given him up for adoption had managed to find it in herself to lavish her dedication on complete strangers.

And, once inside the house, nothing changed his mind. It was roomy and bustling, a mixture of offices, rooms for relaxing in, bedrooms and a kitchen that had been fashioned out of two spacious rooms knocked into one. The kitchen was big enough to sit at least a couple of dozen people at the extended pine table.

There were people everywhere. In one of the rooms, there was a table-tennis table, a cinema-sized television and pockets of deep, comfortable chairs in which young women, most either pregnant or holding tiny babies, were sitting and chatting.

Everyone knew Kaya.

From behind her, Leo watched.

She introduced him to several of the employees but she

was completely absorbed in the place, laughing, chatting and glancing into rooms.

With every passing step, Leo was reminded of the life his mother had managed to build in the aftermath of walking away from him. He couldn't wait to leave and yet…he could see the details of a life Kaya didn't want to see erased.

It was shortly before one by the time they were heading back to the house and for a few moments, as he manoeuvred out of the courtyard and away from the halfway house, there was silence.

Leo expected that she was thinking about where they'd been. It was obvious that everyone there absolutely adored her. They had flocked around her and she had been in her element, her interest and delight shining in her eyes and in her responses.

He picked up speed. There was no need for her to give him directions. He knew the way back.

'The place is falling apart at the seams,' he snapped into the silence and didn't look at her, although her lack of response said it all.

'Is that all you noticed?'

The sudden tension in her voice relaxed him. Why, he didn't know.

'I'm trained to notice details like that, especially in places I happen to own.'

Kaya forced herself to count to ten and to squash the tide of disappointment flooding her. 'Aside from that, what did you think?'

'What do you want me to say to that?'

'I want you to say that you were…impressed by what you found! I want you to say that you looked at all those young women, looked at the advantages the place has given them, and liked what you saw!'

Leo gritted his teeth, took a corner a little too sharply and slowed for a bit, but then picked up speed, heading back to the house with his emotions all over the place.

Silence seemed the best option when it came to getting his self-control back on track. Yet that very silence made him feel exposed and vulnerable, allowing insight into emotions he didn't want to put on display yet found impossible to keep concealed.

'Surely you can see that?'

'That *what*, Kaya?'

'You can see the woman Julie Anne was? She devoted her life to that place. Knew and took an interest in all the girls personally.'

'I'm sure she did.'

'So...'

'The place needs a whole lot of money pouring into it, Kaya. I'm guessing that, in between the fun and the laughter and the caring and the sharing, no one has taken the time to make a note of the beams that have woodworm, or the cracks in the ceiling, or the suspicious signs of damp in the kitchen?'

They were back at the house in record time. If the trip out had taken forty minutes at a leisurely pace, the trip back had taken half the time.

Leo leapt from the driver's seat at the same time as Kaya jumped out from her side, making sure to land on one foot, protecting her ankle just in case.

'Yes, everyone knows that there's work to be done on the place, Leo!' She wanted to reach out and hold him, but her hand dropped to her side before she could rest it on his arm. She watched as he inserted the key and noted how he fumbled for a bit before pushing open the door and standing back to allow her past him.

He spun round to look at her, raked his fingers through his hair and then stripped off his jacket, watching as she did the same, following him in getting rid of the layers, including the winter boots.

They stood facing one another.

'I didn't come here to pour money into one of Julie Anne's schemes,' he said in a driven undertone. 'Have you any idea how much it would cost to salvage that place before it starts collapsing?'

'There were plans…costings done…before Julie Anne died.'

'And you're trying to persuade me that I should pick up the slack?' He shrugged but there was a sour taste in his mouth, a feeling of loss that made him angry and belligerent. 'As the good Samaritan I've never been? I don't believe the woman was much of a Samaritan thirty-odd years ago, do you?'

'Leo, I'm sorry.'

Kaya's voice was low and quiet. She had manipulated him in visiting the shelter, and now was torn apart by the notion that she might have done the wrong thing, might have opened up wounds that had been better left alone.

'She tried to atone, you know? That's what I truly believe. I don't know why…why she did what she did all that time ago. I don't have answers any more than you do, but why not judge her on what happened next in her story?'

Leo stared at her, at her beautiful, open face pleading with him to find a heart where there was none.

Although, he'd seen the good the woman had done, had been moved by what he had seen.

At odds with himself, restless in his own skin, all he

could see was Kaya in front of him. Her delicate floral scent filled his nostrils. He scowled, moved closer and groaned as he pulled her towards him. He couldn't resist and he didn't understand why. There was a lot he felt he didn't understand at that moment.

'What is this thing you do to me?' he whispered huskily. He detached, breathing in deeply. He was about to apologise and turn away, thoroughly ashamed that he hadn't been able to fight an urge that was bigger than him, but she pulled him back, drew him down and kissed him.

Leo held her and kissed her back, sliding his tongue into her mouth, meshing it against hers, barely able to contain his desire.

Kaya's lips parted and her eyes were heavy. So were her limbs, all of her heavy as lead, as if suddenly she could only move in slow motion, yet inside was fizzing with excitement.

'Are you sure about this?' Leo groaned against her mouth.

'I'm sure,' Kaya replied, her voice husky with desire. 'I've wanted this. You do things to me too, and I don't understand.'

'Upstairs, Kaya, or else it'll have to be right here.'

Kaya stood shakily and he swept her off her feet and carried her, moving fast, breathing hard.

They got to the top of the stairs and he stopped, leant against the wall and swivelled her so that she was straddling him, and he kissed her, long, hard and urgently. Her fingers were wild in his hair, pulling him into her as close as he could get, so that there wasn't even an inch between them. She was shaking when they broke contact, and he was as well, shaking and barely holding on to control.

He pushed himself from the wall, still holding her.

She knew the house inside out, of course, but it still felt strange to be in his bedroom and to find herself in his bed.

Her head swam with images of them together on it, a swirling kaleidoscope of bodies moving as one, hot, sweaty and coming together.

Sex. The thing she'd always linked to *love*, the thing that had no place in her life unless there was affection, commitment, a future planned... All this time waiting, dreaming her dreams and making her plans, and here she was—sex was all she could think about, all she *wanted*.

Without making any conscious decision, Kaya knew that she wasn't going to breathe a word about her virginity. He'd run a mile if he knew that he was her first and the last thing she wanted this big, powerful man to do was run a mile.

He switched on the lamp by the bed and it cast a mellow glow through the room.

'I want to see you,' he said with a low, husky, shaky growl. 'You don't seem to have any idea how beautiful you are.'

He began undressing and she stared. The body underneath the clothing was so much more spectacular than all her fantasies put together: lean, muscular; he was the alpha male at the very peak of physical fitness. Even in the dim light she could make out the ripple of muscle and the tautness of his sinewy arms. He flung his clothes as he shed them on the ground, only extracting his wallet, which he dumped on the table by the bed.

'You're staring and I like it. Although not as much as I'd like to see you without anything on. But no, wait— allow me...'

Kaya swallowed hard as the reality of her inexperience

hit her full-on. Any man who didn't do commitment and warned women not to expect anything from him was not a man who would jump for joy at the prospect of sleeping with a virgin.

She swept aside that momentary thought and abandoned herself to the glide of his hands as he sank onto the mattress with her. He was still in his boxers but she could see the impressive bulge of his erection. His fingers on her bare skin as he began easing clothes off her had her gritting her teeth for fear of crying out loud with pleasure.

With erotic mastery, he nuzzled her thighs, his tongue licking while his teeth grazed the tender, sensitive skin. She was still wearing her cotton undies and he delicately eased the crotch to one side so that he could burrow into the soft down between her legs.

Kaya sank into the caress with a guttural moan of pure pleasure and weaved her fingers into his hair at the same time, parting her legs so that he could deepen his gentle touch.

He did. He pushed his hands, stretching the underwear under them and pulled it off her.

Cool air hit her but she felt as if she was on fire.

Fierce desire devoured her. Her breathing was rapid and thick and she could barely think straight. How could she, when this man was making her feel things she'd never dreamed possible? How could something that had nothing to do with love feel so good?

She let herself get swept along on a tide of passion. She arched back as he followed the contours of her long, slender body with his tongue, from the delicate hollow of her belly button to the soft outline of her ribs, until that devastating trail ended with her breasts, with her nipples. Somewhere along the line she had kicked off the underwear and ditched her bra, but she wasn't quite sure when, because she was in a hot daze.

'Please,' she begged. Her eyes were dark and drowsy when they met his and he smiled at her.

'I want to enjoy you,' Leo murmured huskily.

But how much longer could he withstand the onslaught on his senses? he wondered. She was driving him crazy. The complexity of this situation…the confusion of a pursuit he had never experienced and hadn't expected…made the taste of her, now that she was lying naked in his bed, all the sweeter.

His prized self-control had vanished in a puff and now, touching her… The feel of her moving under him and against him…

He'd died and gone to heaven.

He nuzzled her breasts and suckled on her brown nipples, and couldn't seem to get enough. Her skin was warm and, as he touched, she wriggled, moaning and sighing, her body slippery and supple under his hands.

The guy who had always prided himself on his artistry when it came to the pleasurable business of having sex was shaking, and in danger of losing his grip and coming before he could sink into her, which was where he wanted to be—deep inside her, filling her up.

Every little whimper of pleasure leaving her lips took him closer and closer to the edge. He cupped the dampness between her thighs with his big hand and inserted his fingers into her, stroking slowly, and loving her wetness.

'I'm not sure how much longer I can hold on, my darling…'

'I need you too,' Kaya whispered.

And she did. Oh, how she wanted his man to fill to her

and take her, soaring away to places she'd never imagined.

She'd never done this before.

The technicalities presented themselves, a wash of reality penetrating the hot haze of lust.

He was impressively built.

Kaya took deep breaths and forced herself to relax back into his caress. She sensed the urgency in him, felt its palpable weight nudging between her legs, and closed her eyes.

She knew that he was reaching for the wallet he had earlier dumped on the bedside table, and heard the tearing of the foil and then his brief withdrawal as he eased on protection.

A man who took no chances.

He entered her, long, hard and deep, and she cried out and flinched back. It was an automatic reaction. It lasted seconds but during that time she heard his exclamation of shock and then his instant withdrawal and soft cursing under his breath. When she peeked through half-closed eyes, it was to see that he was ditching the condom that had slid off during that moment when he had found out… what she'd been so desperate to keep under wraps.

'Kaya!'

'What?' Kaya wriggled up a little but she just couldn't meet his darkly demanding gaze.

'You know what. Why didn't you tell me? You should have told me.'

The last thing he'd expected had been this. A virgin!

And there was more. A tumult of chaotic thoughts rumbled around in his head as he realised that in his shock, God only knew, but the condom had not done what it should have done. Had it torn? He'd felt his own liquid all over his hands as he'd pulled out of her. He couldn't dwell on that. He wouldn't. His eyes were hot and dark as jet as he watched her looking at him. He really *did* forget everything because, damn it, *a virgin*. It was a shot of adrenaline. He breathed in deeply, head thrown back, overcome by something that felt like...*possessiveness*.

He should be worried sick about the consequences of the unforeseen. He wasn't. He was on a high.

'Sorry,' Kaya apologised in an agonised whisper. 'I should have. You're right. I didn't want to because... Okay, I'll go. I understand.'

'No chance,' Leo ground out, already rising to the occasion.

'What do you mean?'

'It's a turn-on, okay? Stay, Kaya. I... I'll be gentle. I can do things to you that don't involve penetration and you can do the same for me.' He shot her a crooked smile. He felt her relax, and the rush of triumph, satisfaction and pleasure that filled him made him light-headed for a couple of seconds. 'Sex can wait for...later.'

'Okay...'

Kaya smiled back and pulled him towards her.

Kaya looked at Leo. He was standing by the window, his back to her, staring out at a day that was only just waking up. They hadn't drawn the curtains and she could glimpse the rosy hue of winter in the skies, a mix of greys and blues and tinges of pink and orange.

He was naked. Naked and perfect: broad shoulders, a narrow waist and long, muscular legs liberally sprinkled with dark hair, just like his chest. All man.

He turned round and smiled slowly as their eyes met. He walked towards her and Kaya adjusted her position on the bed, eyes irresistibly drawn to the hang of his penis and its urgent swelling as he drew closer to her until, as he stood by the side of the bed, it was throbbing and hard.

In the space of four days—lazy days passed in a blur of bed, sex and some food grabbed in between—she had lost all the inhibitions that had kicked in that very first time.

He had taught her and he had taught her well. He had opened her up to a world where only touching existed and she had learned to enjoy it.

'Lick me,' he commanded huskily, and Kaya knelt on the bed, steadying herself, and took him in her mouth.

Leo looked down at her, at her head moving, her hair streaming around her.

He couldn't stop wanting her. Every time they'd made love it had been with the same driving, blind passion with which they'd made love that very first time...fully, tenderly and completely, after the mishap with the condom.

He entered her gently, nudging until she was ready to open for him. On the brink of coming as she weaved her magic with her hand and her mouth, he pulled back and joined her on the bed, first holding her close so that he could feel her heart beating against his chest and then, with some reluctance, angling her so that he could pleasure her lazily...no rush whatsoever...because work had been on hold for days, so why not a few more hours? He went between her legs and settled there, tasting her with his tongue, flicking and rousing against the stiffened nub of her clitoris and loving her increasing demands for fulfilment.

Their bodies had learnt to move in tune with one another, and when eventually he entered her she was as ready for him as he was for her.

They came, and Leo felt the soaring inside him as

he arched back, something raw, powerful and...*dangerously unsettling*.

She nestled against him, sated.

'We should think about getting some work done.' He half-yawned, because it wasn't yet six-thirty and he was discovering that early-morning sex could do that to a guy, even one who was used to getting up at five, raring to go.

'Guess so. I've barely glanced at my emails for the past few days.'

'Really meant with the house.'

Manhattan, Kaya thought, *is beckoning*. Reality might have taken a break, but all breaks had to come to an end. And what happened next...for them? For her?

Had she imagined that they would live in this exciting bubble for ever? Or maybe just until he got around to thinking that he might want more than a few days of stolen pleasure?

Because the rules of the game had changed for her. She'd known him for the guy he was. He didn't want involvement, not even in the heat of the moment when people were wont to say stuff from the heart and not the head. He wasn't on the market for a relationship but *she* was.

She had feelings for this man and not just uncomplicated, superficial feelings—she had deep feelings, feelings of love, affection and tenderness. All those crazy, crazy feelings she'd been so sure she could avoid because she'd told herself that he really wasn't her type.

She had sleepwalked into a situation and it was a catastrophe. He'd woken up now—time to get going—but her? She was lost in a different place. She'd foolishly nodded off and woken up in a different world.

Heart beating fast, she edged back.

She laughed thinly. 'You're right. Can't put off the inevitable for ever!' She turned to stare at the ceiling but all she could see was his beautiful, dear face that she knew so well now. 'Julie Anne's room will take time. I'll start…today.'

Leo felt the shift of her weight away from him. He wanted to draw her back against him, and the very fact that he couldn't be bothered to get out of bed and address work concerns was worrying.

Likewise, he made some space between them. 'Excellent idea,' he murmured. 'Can't postpone what needs to be done, however seductive it is to pretend that we can.'

Two hours later, Kaya was outside the room Leo had adopted as his makeshift office. The door was shut. After so many days of feeling as one with him, waking in his arms and opening herself to him in all sorts of ways, she was now hesitant and weak with nerves.

She had to force herself to knock, push the door open and then stand in front of him as if she were suddenly at an interview waiting to be invited to have a seat.

She looked scrappy in her oldest jogging bottoms, a faded sweatshirt, hair scraped back because it had been getting in her eyes, and she was pale. She could feel it. She'd gone to Julie Anne's room to lose herself in nostalgia and sort stuff out, but she hadn't been able to run away from the chain of thought that had begun in the bedroom when he'd told her that it was time for them to start picking up the pieces of daily reality.

She wasn't going to break down, because she only had herself to blame for falling for the guy, but she'd barely been able to focus on sifting out the million and one things in the room, from paperwork and souvenirs, to clothes, shoes, favourite books and magazines with some article or other she'd thought might come in useful.

And then, at the back of the wardrobe, wedged so far in the corner than it hadn't been visible, she'd found a box. Treasured possessions: a lock of hair, some faded photos, letters…and a journal. Not for her eyes. She had clocked that within a page of reading it.

'I have something for you.' She held out the box and saw him glance at it and stiffen.

'What the hell is that?' Leo snapped.

'I found it in your mother's wardrobe, stuffed at the back. I think you should look at it. There's a journal. You need to read it.'

'What the heck for?'

Their eyes clashed.

He'd been thinking of Kaya solidly. He hadn't managed to get a scrap of work done, not an email sent, and now here she was, handing him something, and he could feel a knot of tension tighten inside him.

'I'll leave it, shall I?'

'Or you could dump it somewhere, shut the door behind you and come and let me make love to you,' Leo drawled, relaxing back in the chair, legs stretched out, hands clasped behind his head.

Arrogant, Kaya thought with helpless fascination, cocky and…*scared*.

'Read it, Leo,' she said gruffly. 'I'll be in the kitchen if you…want to talk.'

Kaya waited over an hour. She made coffee, wondered what was happening with Leo, tipped out the coffee undrunk, made some more and did the same.

She'd opened that box, expecting the usual—some

trinkets, maybe some photos or else just the usual assort-
ment of sentimental bits and pieces which Julie Anne had
been fond of keeping.

The last thing she'd expected was that journal and,
the second she had flipped it open and begun reading,
she'd known that it was a story Leo would have to read,
whatever the contents.

For it had been written by a seventeen-year-old Julie
Anne, living with her parents and pregnant.

*I can't believe what Mama and Papa want me to do.
This is the worst day of my life. I hate them, I hate them,
I hate them. Diego and I are going to run away. We can't
think of anything else to do.*

That had been the opening entry. Kaya had snapped
shut the journal and rocked back on her heels, deep in
thought, heart beating fast, knowing that what she held
in her hands would be a story neither she, and more importantly Leo, had ever thought they would get.

Would either of them want to hear this story? Would
it be better left untold? Sometimes the truth was far less
kind than all the wild tricks the imagination could play.

Lost in thought, she was barely aware of his approach
until she glanced up to see him framed in the doorway.

Under the rich bronze of his skin, he was ashen.

'You don't have to talk about it,' she said quickly.

'You should read it.'

'It's…it's none of my business.'

'It's both our business, even if the reasons behind that
aren't the same. Jesus, it's still morning, but if I could,
I'd hit the whisky.'

He looked at her levelly, his dark eyes deep and un-
fathomable, and she wished she knew what he was think-

ing. The chasm that had begun to yawn between them grew bigger.

'That journal…those keepsakes…' He shook his head and prowled through the kitchen, coming to rest in front of her but almost immediately moving to sit. 'A shock.'

'Life's full of them, I've discovered.'

'Yes, you had your share when you found out about me.'

Kaya wanted to ask what happened next but she knew, just as she knew that she wasn't going to hang around and wait for him to deliver the final blow to what they'd enjoyed.

'You need to…think about whatever it is you've learned, and you won't be able to do that while you're here.'

The silence stretched to breaking point, then he said quietly, 'Agreed. I don't… I don't need reminders of a past that's suddenly taken shape and come to life. I see the bigger picture now. I see the canvas that was painted over thirty years ago and…yes… I need to digest that. Away from here.'

'Then go. It's what you need to do.'

'I still want you.'

'That's not how this goes.'

'There's no recipe for how relationships go or how they end. I have a place in the Bahamas. I would have space to think. Read the journal, Kaya, and come with me. We have a connection that can't be replicated with anyone else. And, even though my head's telling me it's time to go, my body is telling me we need to continue this or else we'll both regret cutting it short too soon.'

'I don't think so, Leo.' Kaya barely recognised the tough, hard edge in her voice but she could feel the barriers falling into place. 'It's been fun, and now we need to call it a day.'

'Is that what you really want? You really want us to walk away from one another before this thing has run its course?'

'I prefer to leave things on a high.' She forced a smile. 'Instead of it fizzling away into disappointment and boredom.'

Leo lowered his eyes, shielding his expression, and Kaya could sense his withdrawal. She was already missing him, missing the easy familiarity that had crept up on them from nowhere. How desperately she wanted that back, but for what? A week or two more of falling even deeper and harder for him? She'd learnt too many lessons in disappointment from her mother to go down that road.

'Your choice,' was what he drawled when he raised his eyes to look at her. 'And no need to rush with packing. I can wrap things up here remotely, I imagine.' His expression gentled. 'And, Kaya, the halfway house? You were worried—don't be. It won't be sold. I will hold it in a safe trust and, rest assured, whatever investment is needed to keep it afloat, to expand it, will be undertaken. Whatever has happened in the past, and whatever my feelings about my mother, her legacy there will be protected.'

And that's why I love you. Because you're a decent guy. You're not a rich bastard, you're a decent guy who can never love... And I can't be the one who loves for both of us.

'Thank you.'

CHAPTER SEVEN

LEO HAD BEEN staring out of the window of his magnificent villa in the sunshine for forty minutes…he checked his Rolex: no forty-eight minutes…when his mobile phone pinged.

What the hell was he doing?

He had hit Manhattan two weeks ago, energised with positive thoughts. No Kaya but, then again, for the best—no tears and no pleading were an added bonus. The best break-up a guy could ask for!

And work? So much of it was waiting for him that it made his eyes water when he thought about it. He would lose himself in his work. There were deals to be done, money to be made. It never failed when it came to nailing one hundred percent of his attention.

The business with the journal, the back story to his adoption…how could he not take some comfort from knowing the details? A frightened teenager pregnant and facing the wrath of her wealthy, conservative, well-connected parents… The decision to run away with his father, the Mexican immigrant who had been working on her father's sprawling estate in the Hamptons…

He had opened that journal and been consumed by the journey his mother had made. He had read and re-read about the headlong rush to freedom and the accident that had taken his father, leaving Julie Anne alone with a baby on the way and no choice but to return to the very place she had been trying to escape.

Depressed for years, isolated and at the mercy of decisions made on her behalf, she had handed Leo over, her parents had assured her, to a loving couple who would look after him the way he deserved to be looked after. She had believed them.

He hadn't been abandoned, as he had thought. Questions had been answered.

Fired up to put the business of his fling with Kaya behind him, because life was full of blips—even invigorating ones—he had quickly realised that the blip had taken more of a toll than he'd expected.

He had no idea why returning to his comfort zone had failed to settle his feverish thoughts. So they'd parted company—it wasn't the end of the world! Had she taken up lodgings in his head because he still wanted her, because for the first time in his life he was having to deal with a woman breaking it off when he'd been happy to carry on?

Surely he couldn't be that egotistic?

But he hadn't been able to focus. He'd scrolled through his phone, idly looking at numbers of women who would bite his hand off for a call from him, and had found himself deleting their contact details.

He missed her.

Sitting in his towering offices in the city, staring down at life happening eighteen storeys below, he was suckerpunched by the realisation that *he missed her*. Not just the sex but *her*—all the things that made her, the sum total of all the parts. He missed her smile, her laughter and her annoying habit of arguing with him and just never giving up.

He missed her optimism and the way she had of being supportive without saying anything at all. And he missed the person he'd been with her, as though a weight had been lifted from his shoulders. Laughter had come more easily and so had relaxation.

If she'd felt the same, she would have called.

She hadn't, although he had checked his phone on the hour to see if he'd missed anything. He hadn't. She would have called and the fact that she hadn't made it all the more imperative that he not be the one to crack.

Pride was an ingrained hurdle too vast to overcome and Leo saw no reason why he should try. He never had before. Nothing had changed, not really. Things started and then they ended. That was the way of the world. If there were feelings there, swirling under the surface, then he would get past them.

However, despite every assertive lecture he gave himself, he couldn't really seem to get past the reality of her abrupt absence, and after two weeks here he was, in a villa he rarely visited. From the air-conditioned splendour of the space he had tailor-made for work purposes when he'd first bought the place, he could stare out at glorious blue skies, even more glorious turquoise ocean and the expanse of icing-sugar sand that separated sea from the sloping incline to his property. Directly in front of him was his infinity pool, basking just beyond swaying palm trees.

It was a magnificent view, which Leo barely took in as he stared out, for a few seconds barely registering the beep of his mobile and only picking it up after a couple of minutes. He was pretty certain it was going to be work-related, even though only a select handful of people had this particular number.

Her name… It didn't instantly register. He wondered whether he had seen it at all but, yes, he blinked and there it was: *Kaya*.

And, just like that, the tenor of the morning suddenly changed. He opened the message and read it. She wondered where he was…was he in Manhattan…? She would like to meet, if possible.

Leo smiled a slow, curving smile of utter satisfaction. So, it hadn't just been him. He hadn't been alone in concluding that what they'd had was too good to throw away just yet. He hadn't stopped wanting her and she hadn't stopped wanting him. Why else would she have texted? Why else would she now be desperate to meet up?

He waited a while to reply, giving it an hour, when he strolled outside and admired the scenery he hadn't previously really noticed.

His reply was as brief a communication as hers had been: he was in the Bahamas, as it happened. Sure, if she wanted to meet up, why not? He would ensure arrangements were made and his PA would be in touch with the details…

Two days, was his instruction to his PA in Manhattan—that was how long he was prepared to wait to see Kaya. Long enough to show her that time hadn't stopped still for him…that he was a busy guy as he always had been; that, sure, he could fit her in but clearly not at the drop of a hat…yet not so long that he ran the risk of her changing her mind. That was the last thing he wanted.

Still smiling, Leo realised that it was possible to focus under tropical skies after all…

Buzzing up high in the sky as the helicopter whirred its way to Harbour Island a mere fifty-four hours after she had sent her text to Leo, Kaya closed her eyes and con-templated the prospect ahead of her.

Her head was spinning and her heart, which she had been so determined to put into cold storage, was flutter-ing madly inside her.

This situation had seemed a lot more manageable from the safety of back home, with a vast ocean between her and Leo. It had been easy to be sensible from a distance. Of course, she hadn't known where she would find him when she'd texted him on the number he had given her when life had been all sunshine and laughter between them, and she had been surprised when he had replied that he was at his villa in the Bahamas.

Yes, he'd told her that, but deep down she hadn't quite believed it. Leo chilling out in the sunshine? She hadn't seen it but she'd been wrong.

She hadn't asked why. Hadn't asked how come he wasn't in New York, to where he had bustled off within an hour of reading that journal and deciding that it was time to clear off. Wasn't he the committed workaholic, after all?

There had been no superfluous chit-chat by text, and he hadn't asked why she'd suddenly decided to pay him a visit when, two weeks before, she had turned her back on him.

Of course, Kaya knew the reason for his lack of in-terrogation. He figured she had read the journal, been moved, had re-examined her decision not to sleep with him again...essential, because things had to fizzle out of their own accord...and had decided to make contact.

He had cockily assumed that she just couldn't resist his charm and had had to get in touch, pathetically hop-ing he'd reconsider and carry her back, caveman-style, to his bed.

Leo was in for a shock.

Kaya tried to train herself to think without emotion, because a lack of emotion was what she was going to need, but it was so hard. It was especially hard now that the journey to see him was nearing its end. She didn't feel prepared. At least, not *enough*.

With a hitched sigh, she looked down at a swirling panorama of blue and white: sky and puffy clouds, the sort of to where place people went to relax and have fun.

Not for her.

She didn't quite know when, amongst all of this chaos and unhappiness, she'd suddenly realised that her period was late. And then she quickly realised a few other things as well: the metallic taste in her mouth; the way she'd gone off coffee; those little bouts of nausea...

She had known what the result of that pregnancy test would be before she'd taken it and yet, when it was confirmed, she had still frantically done three more and, with each successive positive, she'd felt a little sicker as her world dismantled in front of her.

And her choices? Few.

Certainly, there was no question that Leo would have to be told—he deserved it.

She had taken a couple of days to come to terms with the *everything*, then she had texted him.

She'd decided clearly on how to handle things. She would be calm, matter-of-fact, reasonable and undemanding.

The one thing she would not do was become emotional, because this situation demanded a cool head.

Yet here she was. The whole cool-headed approach had disappeared roughly when the plane had started climbing for take-off. She surfaced now with the realisation that the helicopter was dipping, swinging in an arc, its rotor blades slowing. When she looked out of the tiny window, it was to find it circling over an illuminated circle, with a giant 'H' marking the spot where it had to land.

Leo's villa. Her mouth went dry.

She steeled herself as the helicopter ground to a complete stop and then there was gradual silence as the blades stopped whirring then, as the door was pushed open, superseded by the call of insects that was nothing like anything she had ever heard before.

For a few seconds, standing in the open air, readying to disembark, Kaya closed her eyes and just listened. Insects called one another, high and shrill, and mingled with the throaty undertone of frogs, all competing with the rustle of warm breeze through lush shrubbery.

And then his voice…low, velvety and darkly, sexily familiar.

Her eyes flew open, adjusted and then there he was, larger than life and a lot more drop-dead gorgeous than she remembered. He was framed in the doorway of a villa that was picture-perfect, from what she could make out in the enveloping darkness, for out here, with only the light from the stars and the moon, it was inky-black.

'So you came…'

There was mild amusement in his drawl and Kaya was galvanised into motion as he strolled towards her.

He was in a pair of loose, draw-string linen trousers, an old tee-shirt and some flip-flops and he looked more eye wateringly gorgeous than he ever had.

Her mouth went dry, her heart sped up and she hurried down the stunted metal steps just in case he decided to help her down. She wasn't sure if she could face the physical contact.

Behind her, the young, enthusiastic pilot, who had done his best to engage her interest on the brief hop to the island, followed with her bag. There was a moment's reprieve while Leo chatted to him, leaving her time to gather her thoughts and pay some attention to her surroundings.

The dark shapes of the bushes, foliage and silhouettes of the tall, gently waving coconut trees were glorious. She glanced at the villa, which wasn't outrageously big, but perfectly proportioned, pink and white with a wide, wooden veranda encircling the entire property like a bracelet. The gardens appeared to be extensive and partially landscaped, and she could smell the salty tang of the sea and hear the rise and fall of waves behind all the other unfamiliar sounds.

There was some laughter and a few more pleasantries between Leo and the pilot, and then the helicopter was weaving its way back up, up, up and away, leaving the two of them together.

The silence was broken by Leo. He didn't move towards her. He kept his distance, leading her into the villa, which was a marvel of tropical architecture. The blonde wooden flooring was interrupted by colourful rugs, and the breeze blowing through the shutters was helped along by ceiling fans.

'So…' he drawled, leading the way towards the kitchen. 'You're here.'

He faced her, his dark eyes skewering her to the spot and, in return, Kaya looked at him and tried not to drink him in, because she'd forgotten how much he meant to her, and how familiar she was with every angle and contour of his handsome face.

'Yes.' The bracing, impersonal speech she had rehearsed—which would have been followed by a swift escape to bed, having confirmed her return flight for Canada the following day—had vanished, leaving her to struggle with the business of actually being in his presence.

'There's no need to look so terrified,' Leo said wryly. 'I happen to be very glad that you changed your mind. You look good, Kaya.' He cleared his throat and briefly looked away before returning his dark gaze to her face. 'Sit. I'll get you a drink.'

'No! No, thank you.'

Leo's eyebrows shot up.

Not the reaction he was expecting. Actually, her visible discomfort was not at all what he'd been expecting. Possibly a bit too soon to fall into each other's arms, all things considered, but he had banked on more enthusiasm. Or perhaps it was his imagination playing tricks on him. After all, she *had* made the first move.

'It'll relax you,' he drawled, but he remained where he was, staring at her from under his lashes. 'I haven't dragged you here, Kaya.'

'I realise that.'

'Do you want me to coax you out of whatever sudden bout of uncertainty you're going through? Want me to tell you how glad I am you're here? Want me to beg you not to have a change of heart?'

'Would you? Beg me to stay? Because I don't remember you doing that when you left.'

Kaya could have kicked herself for having said that, so she tacked on in a harried undertone, 'But, no. I don't want you to do any of those things, as it happens. I'm here of my own volition and I won't be having a change of heart. I'll have some water, please.'

'You read the journal.'

'Yes.' Kaya could relax with this. With this, she could feel her anxiety and trepidation disappear under a wave of extreme sympathy for this wonderful, generous guy with all that baggage that had made him the wary, hands-off man he was. 'I'm sorry, Leo. It must have broken your heart to have read about your mother.'

Leo flushed darkly.

Unaccustomed to sharing anything of himself or his feelings, he opened his mouth to shut down the conversation, but he didn't. He remembered what this was all about, this spell she seemed to have over him. It was still there because he heard himself admit gruffly, 'It was… good to have some answers.'

'And yet you must wonder what might have been if she had sought you out. Or vice versa.'

'Pointless to dwell on something that didn't happen and now never will. But, like I said, it was good to know that…'

'That although you ended up in foster care, it wasn't because Julie Anne had put you there. No, she had been fed a lie by her parents. She had thought you were going to a good home. So really, you weren't dumped, were you? Not really. Not as you described it to me once?'

'Did I?' Leo shrugged.

'You did,' Kaya told him gently. She momentarily left behind the anxiety over her reasons for being here and was caught up in the moment. Her heart swelled with tenderness for him, even though she knew that that very tenderness was a weakness she had to control.

Lord only knew what Leo had felt when he had read what Julie Anne had endured, but he was right—questions had been answered and for him it surely must have been sweet release to know that were it not for tragic circumstances, he would never have been given up for adoption.

And good for him to know that, as atonement for something she'd felt she could never rectify, Julie Anne had moved to the great British Columbian wilderness, disowned her parents—only taking with her the legacy left by her maternal grandmother—and devoted her life to doing good.

True to his word, the halfway house was already in the process of being modernised.

'But we're not here to discuss my past, are we? That's not why you came, is it?'

He strolled across to the imposing American-style fridge to fetch her some water, and Kaya felt her tension levels ratchet up as reality reasserted itself.

No, they weren't here to discuss his past—far from it.

His fingers brushed hers as he handed her the glass, and heat flooded her.

'This is a beautiful place, Leo.'

'Isn't it? My first purchase after my first million. Two important firsts.'

'Lucky you, being able to afford somewhere like this. Do you come here often?' Kaya knew that she was buying time, which was pointless, because there was only so long she could do that.

'When I can. I find that relaxation has never been my thing, having bought somewhere specifically tailored for that very purpose. I over-estimated my need for down time.'

'I was surprised when you told me that you were here. I guess I didn't see you actually going through with that plan. I don't know why.'

'It was a last-minute decision.'

He flushed at the admission because it reminded him of why he was here: too much over-thinking for a guy who preferred action; too much getting lost in a whole lot of memories about what had felt so good, and missing the woman who had done that—the woman sitting in his kitchen, warily watching him as though he might pounce at any minute. And that journal playing on his mind—those little clips of things his mother had secreted away in a box, hiding her past from prying eyes.

He'd left it all behind, and had seen no point in dragging the past into his present, but he had not been able to leave those feelings behind him. He had spent a lifetime bitterly side-lining the woman who had chosen to abandon him, and he had had to revisit those assumptions and make his peace with a completely new image of her.

His life had been put in a spin cycle, and not even the familiarity of the high-octane fast lane waiting for him in New York had been able to clear his head. So he'd come here. Except, he could do without being reminded of that fact, because it signalled a weakness he found hard to accept in himself. It smacked of running away.

This wasn't how he had foreseen their first few hours panning out: Kaya sitting in guarded, monosyllabic wariness at the kitchen table while his mood plummeted ever deeper into incomprehension and impatience.

He smiled slowly, wolfishly, and strolled towards her until he towered over her and she looked up at him. It was there. He could see it—the low, burning flame of desire—and he felt a kick of triumph, because this was what he felt comfortable with. He knew how to deal with this. He could handle the physical a lot better than he could handle the turmoil of emotions. He'd had to deal with an onslaught of emotions recently, and now seemed just about the right time to put such annoyances to bed.

With a good following wind. And *soon*—the sooner the better.

He stroked the side of her face, a lazy trail on her satin-smooth cheek, and his nostrils flared as he saw her eyes wide and her eyelids flutter.

'I don't know how I could have forgotten how beautiful you are, Kaya,' he murmured huskily, moving to pull a chair close, and sitting so that he was more or less straddling her chair, his thighs on the outside of hers, his finger still on her cheek, not breaking that physical connection. He contoured her mouth with his finger, tugged the softness of her lower lip and then let that wandering finger go further, tracing a path along her neck, across her shoulders and then over the tee-shirt that was just about snug enough for him to conjure up the ripeness of her breasts, the way her nipples swelled to his touch.

'Leo…'

'I've missed the way you say my name.' He dipped his hand down, down, down…and pushed it gently underneath the tee-shirt until he was cupping her thin bra… and cursing the fact that she had worn one, because he was so turned on by her that he didn't want the impediment of any restrictive clothing between them.

Kaya heard his words go over her head. Her mind was foggy and all she was conscious of was his touch. The way he made her body feel, the way he could make it sing… Lord, how she'd missed that—missed *him* and missed *that*.

In a trance, her mind emptied and she sighed and tilted her body back in the chair, conscious of him easing down her bra so that it was underneath one breast, pushing it up.

Her eyes were closed and her lips were parted as he rolled up the tee-shirt, taking his time, then closing his mouth over her nipple and flicking his tongue across the sensitive surface as he suckled and pulled it into his mouth.

She was drowning, clutching the seat of the chair until her knuckles were white, and she slid a little lower as he continued to suckle.

In her mind, she pictured the raw beauty of his body, hard for her, throbbing in its need. She half-opened her eyes, saw his dark head moving at her breast and the fog began to clear. Horror replaced pleasure. How could all that tension, anxiety and sickening panic be swept away by one touch?

She froze for a couple of seconds and then wriggled away. When she glanced down, when he detached from her breast, she saw that her nipple was slick with the wetness of his mouth and she dragged her tee-shirt down without bothering with the bra.

'Kaya...' He groaned, flinging himself back into the chair and closing his eyes for a few seconds. When he opened them to look at her, there was naked desire in the slumberous depths of his dark eyes.

'That shouldn't have happened!'

'What are you talking about? I need you. You need me. Let's go to bed. Let's make love.'

'This isn't... Leo...' Kaya swept shaky fingers through her hair. She was appalled by her weakness, appalled by how quickly he had been able to rouse her, appalled by how shamefully eagerly she had succumbed to his caresses.

'What's the matter? You don't know what you're doing to me.'

'You think I've come here to pick up where we left off?'

'Haven't you? Because that's what your body was telling me a minute ago.'

Kaya stared at him in speechless silence. So much for all the mental preparation she'd tried to do. None of it had been worth a penny the second he had decided to touch her.

She edged back as far as she could, terrified that he would reach out again, ninety percent sure she would have the strength to resist, but terrified that there was still that ten percent that would abandon everything just to have him touch her.

But wasn't that what love did—made her weak and helpless? She'd never really believed that until now, until she was in the grip of its power.

'I haven't come for sex, Leo.'

'Why else would you be here, Kaya?' Leo frowned, utterly perplexed and physically aching from his libido having to climb down from its excruciating high.

Kaya breathed in deeply and felt faint. She weakened, luxuriating in the fantasy that he loved her, that this was a normal situation…that they were lovers waking up to the beauty of becoming parents together.

The fantasy didn't last.

'Leo, I know I didn't have to come here to tell you this face to face, but I didn't think it was something I could convey over the phone, or worse, by text…'

Kaya watched the way he went very still and, before he could start guessing games, allowing her unconsciously to dodge the obvious, she said, quietly, 'Leo, I'm pregnant.'

She saw every flicker of emotion he tried to conceal, from puzzlement that he might have misheard what she had said, all the way through to dawning comprehension, shock and then, inevitably, disbelief.

'You're kidding.'

'I've never been more serious. Why would I come all the way over here to spin you a fairy story?'

'But it's not possible!'

'It happened. I'm pregnant, Leo, and, much as I knew that this wasn't going to be what you wanted to hear, I couldn't keep something this big from you.'

'No, you *can't be.*'

Who was he kidding? Leo looked at the gravity of her expression and knew in a heartbeat that she was telling the truth.

She was as straight as an arrow and honest to a fault.

She was pregnant. He was going to be a father and life as he knew it was going to come to an end.

He could continue thinking of various different ways of transmitting his incredulity and shock but what would be the point of that? Reality was going to remain the same, however much he tried to push it aside.

The room suddenly felt too small…the villa felt too small…the world he'd known was closing in on him and he vaulted to his feet, his movements jerky and lacking in their usual grace.

'When did you find out?' He turned to look at her.

'A few days ago.'

'What a mess.' He rubbed his eyes with the pads of his thumbs.

'I'm sorry.' In none of her wildest dreams had Kaya ever contemplated something that could be a joyous event turning out like this. She had always had such regimented plans for her life, plans that would avoid her ending up in a place where she was vulnerable, and yet what had she gone and done? Fallen hard for someone who didn't want her for anything but sex; someone who was incapable of sharing his heart and soul with another person. Someone who could leave that journal behind.

'Why? It takes two to tango, as they say.' Leo vaulted upright and raked his fingers through his hair. 'I think I need something very stiff.'

'Yes,' Kaya murmured, arresting him before he could head off to get the drink he felt he needed. 'A stiff drink is just what you need for the mess you're now in.' She placed her hand protectively on her stomach and banked down the searing hurt inside her.

'My apologies,' Leo muttered. 'This has come as a shock.'

'And a very unpleasant one, from the looks of it,' Kaya said with raw emotion, tilting her chin at a defiant angle. 'You think your life is over. You think… Maybe you think that you won't be the free bachelor you were before. You're wrong. I came here to tell you about the pregnancy because you deserved to know. I didn't come here to try and pin you down or force you to change your lifestyle! I would never do that. I would never be so self-ish, especially when I've known from the beginning that you're not a guy who wants longevity when it comes to relationships.'

She bunched her hands into clenched fists.

'Come again?'

Kaya reddened. He looked utterly shocked at her outburst, but why should she hold back? It was obvious that he didn't want this baby and was appalled at the grenade that had detonated in his carefully ordered life.

And that hurt. It really did.

'You heard me, Leo,' she persisted stubbornly. 'I'm not

asking you to give up anything for me. This isn't about sacrifice for you, this is about you deserving to have a role in your baby's life if that's what you would want.'

He returned to sit opposite her and his dark eyes were as cold as the wintry depths of Siberia. 'If that's your message, you have some serious re-thinking to do on that.'

'What do you mean?'

'Do you honestly imagine that I'm going to deal with this situation by…what? Throwing money at it and walking away, because I don't want my bachelor lifestyle interrupted?'

'I never said that…'

'It's the implication.'

'Of course I don't expect you to walk away. I know, after everything you've been through, Leo, that that's not a route you would want to take. But I'm just giving you the option, just letting you know that I'm not trying to corner you into doing anything you don't want to do…' She breathed in deeply but, when she released her breath, it was on a shudder. 'I would never stop you from visiting your child. If I were that kind of person, then I wouldn't be here in the first place.'

'That's very generous of you, Kaya, but I have a completely different scenario in mind.'

'What's that?'

'Marriage.'

CHAPTER EIGHT

KAYA WAS MOMENTARILY lost for words. Her mouth fell open and she stared at him in shocked, confused consternation.

'Marriage?'

'Correct.'

'Us? Me and you?'

'I'm not seeing anyone else here, are you?' Leo made a show of looking round the room in search of someone lurking behind furniture.

'That's crazy,' Kaya said.

'Why?'

'Because we aren't in a relationship, Leo.'

'What are you talking about?'

'We broke up,' she told him flatly. 'We had a fling and we broke up—or maybe you don't remember that bit. This was never about love and marriage and making a go of things. This was all about the sex and nothing else.' Just verbalising their situation was like swallowing glass. Every word hurt because every word reminded her just how different it was for her. She hated herself for half-hoping that he would contradict what she'd said. She hated herself for clinging to illusions.

'What does that have to do with the fact that you're pregnant? Yes, I know what we had was a fling, Kaya, and I realise it wasn't meant to stay the course—but things change and a pregnancy changes everything.'

'A pregnancy doesn't change the fact that we don't... don't...love one another, Leo.'

'This is no longer about the two of us and what we want or don't want.'

Kaya could feel his eyes on her and she couldn't meet his unflinching gaze because he saw far too much for her liking. And there was no way she wanted him to see into her head, to see the unhappiness wrapped around her, because she loved this man and he didn't love her back.

She didn't want anyone to feel sorry for her, and he would feel sorry for her. He would try and hide his dismay, but of course he would remind her of what she already knew: she had disobeyed the ground rules. He would gently tell her that he didn't return those feelings and never would. It was probable that the horror of attaching himself to a woman who wanted what he couldn't give would have him running for the hills and doing just as she'd anticipated—money without commitment. Shared responsibility but, beyond that, nothing at all. And, every single time she saw him, she would see the pity in his eyes and she would be hurt all over again.

No thanks.

She had her pride, and her heart was beating like a sledgehammer inside her as she tried not to be swept along by logic that worked for him but not for her.

'But it really is, Leo,' she said coolly. 'And it should be. A marriage should never start on the basis of a sacrifice being made, and a child would never benefit, caught between parents shackled together for the wrong reasons.'

'*Shackled?*'

'Isn't that what we would be if we were to marry without love and without shared dreams? When people start off life together with a child at the centre of it, shouldn't there be hope and love? Shouldn't it be an adventure for both of them and, even if the adventure doesn't work out in the end—and often it doesn't—isn't it important that it's at least there at the start?'

'I'm afraid I don't share your romantic dreams,' Leo said coolly.

'They're not romantic dreams.'

Leo clicked his tongue, impatient to hustle the conversation along to where he wanted it to go.

Neither of them had predicted this but a way through the morass would have to be found. He wasn't going to gracefully retire from responsibility because it suited her. She might be in search of the perfect fairy tale but there was no way their child was going to pay the price for her pursuing that particular dream.

But he couldn't force her hand, and neither did he want to. He could think of nothing worse than dragging a reluctant bride to the altar so that she could become a reluctant and resentful parent, waiting for their marriage to implode.

What a mess.

He raked his fingers through his hair and pressed his thumbs against his eyes. When he looked at her once more, there was genuine empathy in her eyes.

'We're on opposite sides of a great divide,' he conceded heavily. 'I know what it's like to grow up without parents, a number in a system. I never thought about having children but, now that I am to be a father, one thing I know is that I intend to give my child everything it is within my power to give.'

'Are you saying that, unless I do as you say, you'd fight me for custody?' Kaya asked sharply.

'You're doing it again.'

'Doing what?'

'Over-dramatising. Kaya. I would never do that but, by hook or by crook, we're going to have to navigate a way through this—one that meets both our needs.' He paused. 'You want to have the perfect life. You want romance and sweet dreams, and a bucket list of other stuff that usually falls by the wayside before the ink on the marriage certificate's had time to dry.'

'That's so cynical!'

'It's realistic.' He waved his hand dismissively, but when he looked at her something inside him twisted, because he was going to have to be the guy who put a torch to those dreams. He remembered the way she'd looked after they'd made love: face open and flushed, her eyes drowsy and tender. He remembered her laughter, the ring of it that always made him smile.

This wasn't about memory lane, he told himself. It wasn't about getting trapped in mushy nonsense. This was about a baby coming and some hard decisions having to be made.

By hook or by crook, using whatever means at his disposal he saw fit.

'You want to go your own way and pursue your game plan to find the perfect guy, but for me the thought of another man having a say in the upbringing of my own flesh and blood is anathema. What about you?'

'What about me…? What does that mean?'

Kaya was diverted by thinking who this other man was likely to be when the only man she wanted was sitting right opposite her.

Would there ever *be* another man—one who didn't end up always being *second best*?

Yet to agree to Leo's proposal risked so much potential for hurt. When she thought about seeing him every day—being near him, living with him and, who knew?, sleeping with him until such time as it all fizzled out—her heart wanted to break into a million pieces because it would be a life of constant pain. The pain of unrequited love.

He was right—it was an almighty mess—and yet, when she thought of the tiny life inside her, she was filled with love, protectiveness and absolute joy.

Caught up in a tangle of thoughts, Kaya surfaced to hear him saying something about marriage.

'I just can't think about marrying you, Leo.'

'So you've already said. I was asking what you thought about the fact that *I*, like you, would eventually marry. It was never on the agenda, like I said, but if I had a child… I would want them to have what I never had and it's called a nuclear family.'

Leo was being honest. He was a guy who had always envisaged himself walking alone through life but, now that fate had thrown a spanner in the works, then marriage and a partner was inevitable. His starting point would just be different from hers: he would be going into it with his eyes wide open.

'You…marry…?'

'Of course. And I imagine it would be sooner rather than later.' His voice was casual but his narrowed eyes were sharp. He picked up the shock in her voice as she was forced to envisage something slightly different from whatever scenario had been playing out in her head. Well…wasn't all fair in love and war? It wasn't as though he was fabricating anything, although it wouldn't hurt to bring the timeline for this sudden marriage-to-a-suitable-woman idea forward by a few years...

'You can't just pluck a candidate from a line-up and put a ring on her finger, Leo.'

'That's not how it would work for *you*, because you would insist on your "ideal, for-ever guy" checklist. For me, take love out of the equation and I'll be perfectly happy to have a partner I get along well enough with, who doesn't expect what can't be given but appreciates what can, and is happy to be a mother to my child. I wouldn't be fussy with the detail and I wouldn't be looking for the impossible.' He smiled to cement his point.

Kaya felt the colour drain from her face. It was a realistic scenario. This was a man who wasn't on the hunt for love and wouldn't see marriage to an amenable and appreciative woman as making do. He would see it as perfectly acceptable.

And when he said sooner rather than later...? She could imagine the queue of woman who would give their eye teeth to have Leo's ring on their finger. She could imagine more than that. She could imagine how it would feel to share custody with him and his newly acquired wife. To know that, as much as he'd said he would hate the thought of another man being involved in the upbringing of his flesh and blood, she too would hate another woman having a say in her child.

'Of course,' Leo resumed briskly, leaving her to stew in the perfectly plausible scenario he had created, 'I would insist on a very generous maintenance package.'

'Of course,' Kaya said faintly.

Which led her down another alley, one that led to their child having to balance extreme privilege—which he or she would encounter on every trip to visit Leo—and a far more modest situation with her because she could never feather her nest at Leo's expense.

And how would their child feel, should he or she ever find out that she had rejected marriage in favour of single-dom? Deprived? Angry? Judgemental? All of the above?

'We can carry on this conversation in the morning,' Leo said helpfully and Kaya blinked.

'I'd actually planned on returning home tomorrow,' she confessed.

'I'm afraid that won't be happening.'

'But I've said everything I came to say.' Had she? Yes, of course she had, although with what he had just said he'd thrown a curve ball, and she was reeling from it.

'In which case, I'll do all the talking.'

He rose to his feet and stood back, a towering and imposing figure, eyes flinty-hard, allowing no argument.

'I hadn't quite foreseen your surprise visit turning out like this,' Leo admitted, flushing and shoving his hands into the pockets of his loose linen trousers. 'But all the bedrooms are prepared. You can choose which you'd like.'

Kaya stood up as well, hot, bothered and in a muddle she should have foreseen but hadn't. She knew what he'd expected, and the thought of them together in bed made her body burn and filled her with a yearning she didn't want or need.

'It's late.' His voice gentled. 'Yes, it's been a shock to me, but I hope I haven't worn you out by insisting on thrashing this…situation…out without you first catching up on your sleep.' He looked at her hesitantly. 'I… You should have something to eat. I expect, er, you must be hungrier than usual…or are you?'

'Hungrier than usual?'

'In your…condition.'

'I'm okay. I… I'll take some water up, please.'

'Tomorrow I'll show you around the island,' he murmured.

'I haven't come to take in the sights.' Kaya dredged up some asperity to remind herself that this was no longer about emotion but about business.

Leo paused to look at her. 'What else do you suggest, Kaya? That we sit in here, working out the complexities of this situation like two business associates thrashing out a thorny deal? We were lovers. We were also, I'd like to think, friends. We can surely communicate whilst having a tour of the island and making an attempt to relax in one another's company?' He remembered how she'd yielded in his arms earlier, her body betraying her, telling him how much she still fancied him.

Kaya nodded.

'Don't worry,' he said without inflection in his voice. 'There's a way forward to be found and, whether we approach the situation as business acquaintances or ex-lovers, that way will be found. I've said what I had to say on the matter of my idea of a solution, which you've refused, so…' he shrugged '…we'll work a way past that to something satisfactory. And then I'll have you delivered back to Nassau for a flight to Vancouver.

'I'll bring your bag up and show you to the bedrooms. Like I said, take your pick.'

Kaya woke the following morning, alert to her surroundings and without the luxury of any temporary amnesia as to where she was and why she was there.

She'd barely taken in her surroundings the evening before but now she did. She slipped off the bed and stared. The bedroom suite was huge. The bed was the size of a football field. The wardrobes were all built-in, indigo-blue and, as with everywhere else in the villa, the floor was a marvel of pale wood.

She strolled to the bank of windows, pulled open the wooden shutters and gazed out at a sprawling panorama of greens in every shade. Manicured lawns undulated to a distant strip of swaying coconut trees and, beyond the trees, she could glimpse a ribbon of blue sea. There was a refreshing coolness to the breeze and a fragrance to it that made her nostrils flare. It was the fragrance of a thousand different kinds of shrub, bush and flower and, across the lawns, she could make out those very flowers and see splashes of vivid colour, oranges, reds and yellows spilling out of giant pots and clambering around the trees.

The veranda, which tempted her to go outside via a door built into an archway next to the windows, was broad and sheltered and there were chairs and low sofas dotted here and there.

It was the stuff that dreams were made of—not appropriate, given the nightmare she had brought to his door.

She thought back to his reaction. He'd been shocked but he had risen to the occasion without blinking an eye. He had proposed marriage—for him a telling sacrifice, something that showed how serious he was about taking responsibility. She had thrown his offer back at him, but he hadn't tried to force her hand, even though she knew that driving him would be his own past experiences of making it on his own without the support of family—a number in an institution going it alone. It had trained him to go it alone for the rest of his life until she'd rocked his world with an unplanned pregnancy.

Her bag looked sad, small and vulnerable sitting on

the ground by the wardrobes. She got dressed quickly. She didn't know what the day held in store. She'd brought precious few clothes with her—a stern reminder that she wasn't off on some kind of exotic tropical holiday—but she was concerned at how sparse her supply was, some underwear and some random light clothes, last worn last summer and various summers before that.

She looked around her as she headed for the kitchen. The villa really was very big. All the rooms were super-sized and the flow of cool, blonde wood, shutters and faded Persian rugs emphasised the space. The art on the walls was all local, colourful and vibrant. For a house that was apparently seldom used, it was comfortable and luxurious at the same time.

She heard Leo before she saw him, hearing the sound of him in the kitchen, the pad of footsteps and the clattering of crockery.

Heart suddenly pounding, Kaya slowed her pace and then, once at the kitchen door, simply stood and looked at him for a few stolen seconds when his back was turned as he busied himself at a high-tech coffee machine on the counter.

He was so beautiful—tall, athletic yet as graceful as a jungle animal. He was in a pair of low-slung khaki shorts and an old tee-shirt. He was barefoot and he looked fabulously, carelessly elegant.

She cleared her throat.

Leo turned. Of course he'd sensed her approach, *sensed* that she was in the kitchen, before she chose to make her presence known. When she had first texted him, told him that she wanted to see him, he had assumed it would be a straightforward case of picking up where they had left off, and he'd been elated at the thought of that. Having spent two weeks asking himself questions he couldn't answer, and feeling things that made no sense, it had been a relief to be presented with what he understood: sex. An affair. Passion.

But then to be told that he was going to be a father... He'd felt shock, the bottom falling out of his world, a future he had never factored into his present and something else: the stirring of masculine pride, a sense of joy and the need for this woman carrying his child to be the one at his side.

He had offered marriage, and he was ashamed to admit that it hadn't occurred to him that she wouldn't accept his offer. Why not? She'd acted as though it was a tawdry business transaction, but it wasn't. They'd been lovers and he still turned her on, and what more glue was there for a relationship than a baby?

But then, how could he have forgotten that she didn't jump to the same tune as all those other women he had dated in the past? She was her own person; she had turned him down flat and there was nothing he could do about it.

She wanted what he was incapable of giving: love. He'd never been taught how to do that, how to love. He'd been taught how to survive, how to conquer and how to be self-reliant.

Yes, that journal had put a completely different spin on things, had made him revise the circumstances of his past, but too much had been etched in stone to be reversed. Abandonment had turned him into a self-contained fortress and that was something he couldn't reverse.

Love wasn't in his remit.

Which didn't mean that he was going to give up on his determination to keep them together as a family. To marry her.

He would just have to adopt a different approach.

If he couldn't explain the advantages of staying together, then he would have to show her. He would have to lead her to the very conclusion he wanted. He would have to entice her to come to him, because he couldn't and would never force her to do anything against her will.

He looked at her, expression shuttered, for a few silent seconds. She was long, brown, slender and stunning in a washed out yellow dress with thin straps that fell shapelessly to her knees. And she was wearing trainers with thin socks. With not much effort, he could have kept staring at her until he embarrassed himself.

'How did you sleep?'

Leo broke eye contact and returned to the coffee, but he was aware of her moving to one of the chairs, and it wasn't difficult to imagine her hesitance and wariness as she sat down. He knew this wasn't what she'd planned, just as her bombshell hadn't been on the cards for him. He'd looked forward to resuming what they'd had but she'd aimed to lob her hand grenade and then disappear once the deed had been done, with consequences to be dealt with at a later date.

'Great. Thank you. The bed was very comfortable.'

Leo turned, brought her some coffee and went through the business of asking her what she wanted to eat. He'd been here off and on over the years but it was a first for him to have a woman in here with him. For him, the villa was a sanctuary from the pace of life he led. He could have afforded to have help—a housekeeper, a chef, whatever the hell he wanted—but he had always chosen not to. He liked the uncluttered business of not having anyone around. He enjoyed the solitude of losing himself in the peace and calm the island afforded.

However, the down side was that now, in these awkward, challenging circumstances, there was no one to break the intimacy between them—because there *was* intimacy. How could there not be?

Whether she cared to admit it or not, they'd been lovers. He'd touched her everywhere, just as she had touched him. Her head might insist on forgetting that little technicality but her body would certainly remember every second of what they'd shared. It had remembered fast enough last night, just something else she wanted to pretend had never happened.

How could she not see all the advantages of the arrangement he had put on the table? How could she not appreciate the importance of providing stability for the child they had created together? It wasn't as though they didn't get along. It wasn't as though they weren't still hot for one another.

Why couldn't she see how superfluous the business of *love* was? That abstract dream that people always seemed to insist on chasing, even though reality always ended up stepping in to remind them that it was a chimera.

How could she not see that all he wanted was for his offspring to have the sort of family life he'd never had? And it would be a good life. No way was he going to let her disappear without some delaying tactics... If he had to buy time, then that was what he was going to do.

They ate a breakfast of local, buttery bread with cheese and fresh orange juice.

Kaya cleared her throat when the last of the breakfast had been eaten. 'I guess we should have this conversation about the way forward you talked about.'

'Not yet.'

'But...'

'Like I said, I want to show you the island. It's hot now. It's going to get hotter still. It'll be pleasant being outside. Did you bring a swimsuit?'

'No!'

'No problem. There are some pretty good shops in the town.'

'Leo, I don't plan on staying long enough to get in the sea.'

Leo shrugged and decided that with a little persuasion she might find herself changing her mind. Dark eyes briefly rested on her with brooding intensity, and he saw the slow curl of colour that spread into her cheeks and the way her eyes skittered away. He noted the jumpiness of a woman who still wanted to touch him, was still attracted to him. She'd eventually pulled back, the evening before when he'd touched her, but only eventually.

'We can spend the day out, have a look around...visit a couple of the beaches. This place is known for its pink sands—something to do with tiny organisms that attach to the coral in the sea. And of course for its architecture— very New England, but with a backdrop of palm trees and flowers you'd never get in New England itself. You'll like it. Have you ever been to this part of the world?'

'Leo...'

'Trust me, there won't be any pressure from me for you to revisit my proposal. This is just an attempt for us to discuss the situation as...friends.'

'Friends...'

'Exactly. You have to admit, we haven't had a problem getting along. Why adopt a hostile stance because of what's happened? Much better to approach this situation amicably.'

'Okay...'

'Excellent!' He dumped the dishes in the sink and then remained there, leaning against the counter with his arms folded. 'I have a couple of things to do on the work front. Should take about an hour. Explore the grounds! And… I'll meet you by the front door in an hour and a half?'

Kaya nodded.

She had the weirdest feeling that she was suddenly trying to balance on quicksand, although she had to admit that he was being as charming, fair and gentlemanly about the whole thing than she could ever have hoped. Even after she'd fallen into his arms the evening before, like a starving person in the presence of food, he had remained amicable and fair and hadn't reminded her of her temporary weakness.

Because he was essentially a great guy… Why else had she fallen for him?

Which made her think of those women who would soon be auditioning for the role of wife.

It was an uneasy thought, and she pushed it away and blinked as he walked her to the kitchen door, smiling and turning down her offer to tidy the kitchen since he had work to do, and instead ushering her to the French doors at the back which led out to the gardens she had enjoyed earlier from her bedroom window.

And then she was left on her own.

'If you need me—' he pointed to a vague point away from the kitchen to the side '—the room I use as my office is there. Feel free to disturb me.'

Then he'd smiled that crooked, sexy smile that did crazy things to her body and headed off, leaving her to her own devices.

Off to start cutting and pasting adverts for a suitable wife, Kaya thought sourly. She'd noticed that marriage chat had hit the buffers. He certainly hadn't spent long pursuing that line.

She explored the grounds and just about managed to cling on to her determination to be detached about what was happening and not be swayed by seductive talk about marriage. There was a pool to the side. It was cleverly done to blend in with the tropical scenery, and at first glance almost seemed to be part of the landscape with its rich overhang of trees, and a rock pool set at just the right height to tumble as a small waterfall into the turquoise depths.

With the sun getting higher and hotter, Kaya longed to dive in. Instead, she took her time exploring everywhere. The enormous lawns with little clusters of seating here and there under shady trees, and then that tantalising glimpse of sea and the faint rumble of waves.

Leo was waiting for her when, at the appointed time, she headed for the front door, much hotter than she had been an hour and a half previously.

He was wearing loafers and looked cool and relaxed, hands shoved into the pockets of loose, cotton trousers and the same tee-shirt he had been wearing earlier.

'You look hot,' was the first thing he murmured as he ushered her through the front door and towards a small four-wheel drive which she hadn't noticed when she'd first arrived. His hand, lightly resting on the small of her back, made her feel even hotter than she already was.

'I...' She ducked quickly into the passenger seat and smoothed her dress down as she waited for him to join her. 'I hadn't realised how hot it would be here. A different kind of heat to summers at home.'

'Yes,' Leo agreed gravely, eyeing her dress, which was sticking to her like glue. 'The heat is a lot less polite over here, although it's alleviated by the ocean breezes. You'll find that when we're at the beach. I've arranged a boat so I can take you away from the main drag to one of the quieter coves only accessible by sea.'

'Have you?'

'Why not?' He glanced sideways at her, making sure to roll the windows up and switch on the air conditioning for her benefit, even though he would have preferred the wind blowing through. 'Like you said, you're in a hurry to head back and, if we're going to have the conversation we need to have, then having it somewhere a little more private than a busy beach makes sense. I've also arranged a picnic for us to take. Food is of the essence, wouldn't you agree, in your condition?'

'I wouldn't say of the *essence*,' Kaya returned faintly as the little car gave a full-throttle growl and kicked into life.

Leo's voice was quiet and serious. 'One thing you've got to understand is, whatever decision is made about this situation, the welfare of our baby is paramount to me. Skipping meals isn't a good idea—nor is over-heating. You look very hot in that dress. Have you got a hat? Something to keep the sun off your face?'

'Leo, I'm not an invalid! I'm pregnant!'

'All the same…' Leo murmured.

Kaya didn't say anything. She hadn't really banked on this level of solicitousness and it made her feel a little guilty. Had she over-simplified what his reaction would be? She'd known that he would never walk away from his responsibility, but she had balanced that against his lack of interest in permanence and the fact that he didn't love her, that they had already broken up.

She hadn't foreseen how passionate and blinkered his reaction would be, and yet why not? How could she not have predicted that his sense of responsibility might actually be *enhanced* by the fact that he had always blamed his own abandonment on irresponsible parents? That story might not have changed with the discovery of Julie Anne's journal.

And how would that feed into a need to create the perfect family unit, the very one he had not had? With or without her.

He was showing, even at this early stage, all the signs of being the perfect father. He was a guy who gave one hundred percent. Would he be the guy who gave one hundred percent to the married life he'd never planned to have? One hundred percent to a woman who wouldn't demand love, romance and promises of a perfect life, but would be more than happy to wear his ring and enjoy all the material advantages that came with it? Like this villa in the Bahamas, for starters.

She looked at the splendid scenery around them as he drove. Swaying coconut trees sprinkled along the coastline; the sky was the colour of purest aquamarine; flowers, bushes, shrubs and foliage bordered the tarmac in Technicolor disarray. And then she fell silent as they entered the town and she saw what he'd meant about the architecture.

The houses were sparkling bright, a million shades of ice-cream pastels, and the neat fences bordering them in perfect formation were diamond-white, gleaming under the sun. The shops, the cafés and the little boutiques were all picture-perfect against the backdrop of palm trees and flowers, and the place was bustling with locals and tourists.

He swerved into a parking space and flung open his door and, when she looked at him in bewilderment, he

gently reminded her, 'Picnic, remember? I have to collect it before we go get the boat and...' He gave her a
friendly once-over. 'Your dress... The trainers... Let's
get you some more appropriate clothes.'

'No! I'm fine!'

'Shorts...a swimsuit...flip flops...'

He refused to take no for an answer. He described what
she needed in words that made her long for the coolness
of a dress that wasn't sticking to her, and trainers that
weren't making her feet sweat.

He held her hand in a helpful, brotherly manner that
made her teeth snap together, even though she couldn't
take issue with him, and it wasn't his fault that he'd
planted ideas in her head that wouldn't go away.

The sun poured down like honey and going into each
air-conditioned shop was bliss. She barely noticed the
things he was buying for her.

'You'll have to get used to this while you're carrying my child,' he murmured when she protested at purchase number one. 'It's important you're comfortable,
and you're not going to be comfortable in what you're
wearing.'

'And what after the baby's born?' Kaya asked.

'Well,' Leo murmured coolly, leaning into her so that
there was no missing the relevance of what he was saying. 'Naturally, you will be taken care of as the mother
of my child. What you choose to do with that money will
be entirely up to you. It will, however, be a slightly different matter should you become involved with another
man and choose to marry.'

In the act of feeling the soft silk of a sarong, Kaya
paused and looked at him.

'You mean...?'

'I mean my child will have everything within my power to give but…and call me old-fashioned…if you meet another man and get married, then it will be up to him to look after you. I would want to see where my money goes—make sure it's going to my child and not feathering another man's nest. This will all be legally sorted.'

He stood back and smiled, and in that moment, Kaya knew that ground rules were being laid down and that the conversation they needed to have, however jolly the atmosphere he was trying to create, had begun.

He was scrupulously fair, and would be incredibly generous, but he was warning her of boundary lines and he would stick to those.

The road she decided to travel down would have consequences and she would have to accept that.

'I would never take money from you to…' Her voice trailed off.

'I know.' Leo soothed her, his voice relaxing into a smile, resetting the tempo of the day. 'But I've never been a man to take unnecessary chances…'

CHAPTER NINE

LEO COULD TELL that the effect of what he had said had made Kaya stop and think. But wasn't that fair enough? He wasn't being unreasonable. He was simply saying it as it was. She wanted to sally forth in search of true love, and that was fine, but there was no way he was going to let her grow into the notion that his money would go towards supporting another man. Indeed, the thought of it made him clench his fists in impotent fury.

She was his woman.

Leo wasn't sure when this idea had taken root, but he didn't question it, because she was pregnant with *his* child. How could it be otherwise?

Competition was staring Leo in the face and it enraged him. A mythical guy yet to appear on the scene… The more he thought about this faceless person, the more determined he was to eliminate the threat.

He'd planted seeds that had to be planted. He had let her know, in no uncertain terms, that what was good for the goose was also good for the gander. If she wanted to pursue love and find the perfect partner, then he would likewise engage in a pursuit of his own. Not love, but suitability. The net result would be the same—a partner.

If she refused to buy into the only sensible solution to

the situation, then she would have to think long and hard about what happened next.

In the meantime, while she was captive on this beautiful island, and without forcing her hand at all, he intended to use every trick in the book to persuade her to see things from his point of view and to accept that there were far more important things in life than the airy-fairy nonsense of *love*.

He had started with the matter-of-fact realities of life for them both as their ways diverged, leaving only the child they had created as the common link.

Would she be able to contemplate another woman having fun with their son or daughter any more easily than he could contemplate another man sharing what would not be theirs to share?

She would have time to think about that one.

Meanwhile...

'There's a lot more to see of the town,' he said, waiting until she had belted up before starting.

They had detoured to collect their picnic from one of the upmarket restaurants. It was beautifully arranged in a wicker hamper, with a cooler box full of various drinks. He dumped it in the boot along with the towels he had brought and the oversized rug to put down on the sand.

When they made it to the cove she would be left speechless and impressed. It was all part of the lifestyle that could be hers, should she so choose. A little quiet temptation could do no harm.

He slid a sideways glance at her. No one could say that he wasn't enjoying the moment, whatever the gravity of the circumstances.

She had changed out of the dress and trainers into some loose shorts and flip-flops, and a delicious expanse of silky-smooth, golden-brown legs was on display. The top was small and loose yet managed to be incredibly sexy.

It was all too easy to recall the feel of that slender body under him: the high, small breasts with their succulent brown nipples; the flat, smooth belly; the jut of her hips and the grind of her body… It was all too easy to remember the taste of her when he had explored every inch of her, taking his time.

And all too easy to think about them being together again, bodies merging, finding pleasure in what had come so naturally.

He could show her that they could be good together. There was nothing wrong in doing that. He could show her that he could be a good father, a thoughtful partner… and an ardent lover.

He could show her that there was no such thing as the *perfect* life but there was such a thing as a perfectly *acceptable* life.

'What I've seen is lovely,' Kaya returned politely.

The car windows were open, at her insistence, and she had tied her hair back. There was a large straw hat for her to wear to protect her from the midday sun when they got to wherever they were going, even though, as she had reminded him, she wasn't a pale blonde who went red at the first hint of heat.

But he had insisted. She had never known anyone be so solicitous with a pregnant partner. It felt good to be looked after. It made her think that she had become too accustomed to being the one who did the looking after and not the other way round, even when her mother no longer needed care-taking. Old habits died hard.

She shivered when she thought that all that instinct to

protect would go to another woman in due course. But time and again she returned to the misery of a life without love, a life in which responsibility became the driving force with the heartache of knowing that, one day, that responsibility would dim and everything would end up crashing and burning.

Was she being too fussy?

She glanced surreptitiously at his strong, tanned thighs and the strong forearms on the steering wheel, and then had a quick drink of his profile and the way the wind blew back his slightly long, dark hair.

They reached the marina and a boat was waiting for them, small and white with a bright-red canvas roof. The motor was an outboard old-fashioned one and an old guy in shorts and a vest was doing a balancing act as the little boat bobbed on the water.

Around them, the promenade was busy with people coming and going. Cafés, with bright-blue-and-red umbrellas sheltering busy outdoor tables, gave people having lunch and drinks a perfect view of the ocean.

Kaya didn't have to look round to know that somebody was bringing all the gear from the car to the boat, jumping to the command of some invisible signal Leo seemed to give. She was starting to understand that, the minute cash was waved, all things became possible.

Leo was taking charge. When he held out his hand to help her into the gently bobbing boat, steadying her as she tottered on, she felt stupidly feminine.

'Okay?'

She nodded as he leant into her, and then they were off, buzzing away from the jetty where the boat had been docked, moving at a snail's pace. Oh, how blissful it was.

There were just so many things she'd never done!

Lying back on a small boat putt-putting across turquoise seas, with the wind in her hair and her thoughts too lazy to do much, was one of those.

And she loved it.

From her vantage point she could appreciate the strong, muscular lines of Leo's body. He had shoved on some ultra-dark sunglasses and he looked every inch the guy people had probably once thought would never amount to much. Trapped in care but too smart, too aggressive and too tenacious ever to be kept down.

Was it any wonder she'd fallen for him?

Leo, glancing back over his shoulder, steering with one hand on the tiller, caught an expression on Kaya's face that struck up in him, a lazy, assessing watchfulness that spoke volumes.

Lounging back on the wooden plank seat of the very basic boat, she was as elegant as an old-fashioned Hollywood movie star, but without the artifice. He wondered whether she thought that the straw hat was blocking her expression, and he hoped she did, because he was enjoying that lazy, lingering look on her face.

He tipped up the sunglasses, noted the way she tried to revert back to the stern, no-nonsense expression she had been cultivating ever since she had arrived and felt a wave of quiet satisfaction She was no more immune to him than he was to her.

'Look over there.' He nodded to a point slightly behind her and she duly turned. 'That's the cove.'

'Wow.'

Leo watched with darkly appreciative eyes as she hoisted herself into an upright position, twisting and holding on to the hat with both hands, drinking in what could only be called absolute tropical perfection.

They had left the crowds behind and had reached the cove, which was utterly private, a huddled bank of pale-pink sand nestled amidst a backdrop of dense foliage, bush and coconut trees. The water rippling up to the shore was so clear that the dart of little silver fish swimming in small schools could be seen, swerving hither and thither.

He anchored the boat, killed the engine and for a moment took in the magnificent scenery, just as Kaya did.

He joined her on the bench and she felt the unsteady dip of the boat under the weight transfer.

'I've only been to this cove a handful of times,' he admitted.

'You're mad.' Kaya turned to find him closer to her than she'd expected, his thighs lightly brushing hers. 'If I had a house on this island, I'd be here every day.'

'That would prove tricky on the work front.' Leo smiled drily, his expression once again hidden behind his sunglasses. 'The Internet connection is non-existent.'

'Still…'

'Have you decided what you'll do when you get back to Canada?'

Kaya licked her lips. She didn't want to think about that but wasn't that why they were here—to discuss the future quietly in a private spot, like two adults about to part ways and head down different roads?

'You *have* remembered that that's why we're here, haven't you?' Leo stood up, balanced and began shoving the stuff they'd brought with them to the side, leaving her to fulminate over his question, to confront her choices.

Staring, Kaya remained open-mouthed for a few seconds then she scrambled behind him, nearly losing her balance. Her heart was racing, and racing even more when he helped her out of the boat into shallow, clear water that was beautifully warm. She had bought a swimsuit and was wearing it under the shorts, an unadventurous black affair that anyone's granny would have been proud to wear.

Had all this frivolous clothes-buying, picnic-gathering and tourist-gawping somehow made her forget the point of her being here in the first place? What had happened to her determination to stay just long enough to break the news face-to-face, before returning to Canada to sort herself out and move on with her new life?

'Of course I've thought about it,' she informed him just as soon as they were both on land and he had heaved their belongings out of the boat, which was now rocking gently to one side while they set up camp further along under the semi-shade of overhanging trees.

'Good!'

Kaya smiled tightly. She watched in silence as he spread the rug, handed her a towel and then stripped down to his swimming trunks, at which point her mouth went dry.

'You should get out of the shorts, Kaya. It's too hot to have anything on but a swimsuit, and I take it you *are* going to go into the sea, aren't you? There's nothing like it, trust me.'

'I will in a minute,' she muttered. She didn't want those dark eyes in her direction, looking at her from behind dark sunglasses, making her feel hot and bothered and reminding her of what she wanted from him but couldn't have. She didn't want her body misbehaving...*again*.

'We need to discuss the business of where you'll live,' Leo murmured, filling the silence.

'What do you mean?'

'I live in Manhattan. Yes, I'm willing to commute, especially in the early stages—possibly buy somewhere in Vancouver as a base—but realistically that wouldn't be a long-term solution.'

'What are you suggesting?'

'You know where I'm going with this.' Leo didn't bother pulling his punches. 'This situation is going to require sacrifices and that's where we're going to have to meet in the middle.'

'I've never lived anywhere but Canada…and of course Alaska, when I was very young, but that doesn't count, not really.'

'Times change. I think twenty miles' distance from one another should do it, don't you agree? I have an office in Boston and would consider relocating there. There are many attractive places in and around that part of the world that will allow joint custody to work very well between us.'

'Joint custody…'

'It *is* what you're after, isn't it? You don't want marriage, so that will have to be the next option.'

'Of course. Yes, that's exactly what I want.'

'Splendid. We can informally agree that, until he or she is one, I will take the brunt of the sacrifice on my shoulders and travel as necessary. We can revisit that arrangement at that point. As far as visiting rights are concerned, nothing has to be put on paper at the beginning, as far as I'm concerned, although that will be open to change.'

'I don't understand…'

'If at some point sticking to a regular, agreed schedule becomes difficult, then naturally lawyers will be involved.'

Kaya paled at the vision being painted in front of her although he made sense. Compromises would have to be made; a life of sharing timetables would have to be worked out.

'In the meantime—' he waved one hand to smooth over the temporary tension '—I will have my PA sort out alternative, suitable accommodation for you wherever you agree to settle. A relocation company would probably work best, and naturally money would be no object. You just need to tell me what sort of place you're after. You can leave the rest to me. A shortlist will be compiled to save you the trouble of taking too many long-distance trips when you'd be better off...getting your affairs in order and, of course, resting.'

'This all feels as though it's moving very fast,' Kaya said a little unsteadily. 'I'm not even three months' pregnant yet!'

Leo looked at her, unsmiling, propping himself up on one hand and removing the sunglasses to stare at her. 'There's a lot to sort out,' he told her, pausing for her to digest that and join the dots to the alternative, which would have been painfully simple in comparison. Joint custody and finding separate properties would not have been a necessary consideration, for starters. 'I don't think that sticking our heads in the sand and waiting until the last minute is going to work, do you?'

'No, but...'

'We can continue this later,' Leo drawled, throwing her a lifebelt, leaving her to mull over what he had said. 'Right now, I'm going to take a dip. Join me?'

'I... Perhaps in a minute...'

Leo shrugged and stood up, a thing of masculine beauty, every muscle honed to perfection. Kaya followed him with her eyes as he strolled down to the sea, waded in and then took the plunge to slice through the blue, blue water, his movements smooth, fast and confident.

Leo disappearing into the distance felt like a telling pointer to the role he would eventually adopt in her life. Someone moving away from her, vanishing to new horizons with someone else but always, painfully, returning because of the child they shared. Always returning to shore but never to be with her in any significant way.

And thinking about that hurt.

She sneakily stripped down to the one-piece and, after a while, when over-heating seemed to be a threat, she headed out to sea.

She had been brought up in snow and was an excellent skier. She loved that wonderful freedom but the confidence she had hurtling down a snowy slope was lacking when it came to water. She'd learnt to swim as an adult, sporadic lessons here and there, teaching her just enough to be safe.

She tentatively waded out. Leo was a speck in the faraway distance. He was lying on his back staring up at the sky, not a care in the world, from the looks of it. Whereas she…felt as though she had been assailed from every possible angle by a bombardment of realities and truths she hadn't banked on.

She had naively come out here to do the decent thing and tell him about the pregnancy face-to-face, expecting to be the one to drop the bomb, the one in ultimate control. She'd had the situation clear in her head. Leo didn't love her and, however decent he was, he had never been interested in a relationship. She'd thought she would be doing them both a favour by giving him options and walking away to let him consider them. So how come she was the one floundering now?

Wrapped up in her thoughts, and becoming increasingly confident in the warm, clear, shallow water, Kaya wasn't expecting the tiny drop in the ocean floor, a shifting of the sand between her toes, and she gave a panicked yelp as she lost her footing.

Fear of drowning overcame the voice in her head telling her that this was not a dangerous situation. Panic made her splash and flounder, surfacing and gasping.

She was choking and gasping, and barely noticed Leo moving as fast as a shark in her direction until she felt his arms around her. She clung and practically sobbed her relief.

'Jesus, Kaya!'

For once, her usual fiery independence deserted her. She was just so grateful to feel safe as he carried her back to shore and laid her on the rug as gently as if she were a piece of porcelain.

'I panicked. I feel like a fool. Thank goodness there's no one here! I... I'm sorry.'

'Why are you apologising?' Leo said roughly. 'You scared the hell out of me.'

'I'm not a strong swimmer,' she confessed in a sheepish whisper. 'I never had lessons when I was a kid and then, as an adult, well, it's different. I can keep myself above water but that's about it. The bank suddenly dropped and I... I panicked and couldn't think straight.'

She drank some water and looked at him, ensnared by his eyes, and she realised in a heartbeat that this was what she would blithely be giving up—this safety with a guy who would always look out for her. Maybe not because he loved her, maybe just because of their child, but she would be safe with him. Her heart might not be safe, but everything else would be, because he would be the guy she could always count on.

Feeling *safe* was a luxury she had not always been able

to count on. Her young, grieving and distracted mother had loved her, and had been fun, but when it had come to providing a safety net... For a long time she had been simply too selfish to pick up that baton.

'Understandable,' Leo murmured.

'What would I have done if you hadn't swum to my rescue?' She shivered when she thought about how cavalier she had been, going into the sea when she was a timid swimmer, when she was *pregnant*, had another *life* to consider...

And then she thought about how cavalier she was being now, waving aside Leo's marriage proposal and everything that came with it, waving aside the security of a united family for the sake of her own self-protection.

If things got truly unbearable wouldn't divorce always be a possibility? Wasn't it worth trying, at the very least?

'You wouldn't have been here in the first place,' Leo pointed out reasonably.

'Thank you.' She smiled.

'For coming to your rescue? You wouldn't have drowned, Kaya. I guarantee that. The drop may have been sudden enough to freak you out but you would have recovered. Nothing would have been lost but a little of your self-aplomb.' He stroked back her wet hair.

In return Kaya hesitantly touched his cheek and felt him still under her hand. His eyes darkened with just the hint of the obvious question in their depths.

'Okay,' she said quietly.

'Okay? What does *okay* mean?'

He'd stepped back, not trying to force her hand, respecting her decision...waiting for her to come to him. Was that what was happening now? Was she coming to him? He was giddy with relief at the thought of that.

He'd swum out there, enjoying the cool peace of the ocean around him, and he'd lain on his back, gently floating and mentally trying to work out whether he'd done the right thing in not pushing her.

It made him sick when he thought about how much was at stake. From never having contemplated the prospect of being a father, he'd been catapulted into a possessiveness that had knocked him for six. He'd gone from the guy who had complete control over every aspect of his life to the guy who had none in these new, unforeseen circumstances.

He'd missed her. He'd never missed anyone in his life before but he'd missed her when he'd returned to New York. He'd ached for her and now, with so much at stake, he could scarcely breathe for expectation.

Inside, emotions swirled, things he'd never felt before just out of reach. He felt vulnerable and bewildered at the same time and keen to find some solid ground.

He had had to grit his teeth to hold on to his game plan but the feel of her hand on his cheek felt almost too good to be true.

If he were to think of this in terms of winning and losing, had he *won*? *Had his patience paid off?* He could think like this. It was easier than getting lost in stuff he didn't understand, in feelings that made him edgy, impatient and nervous.

'Okay,' he quipped unsteadily, 'You believe me when I tell you that drowning was never going to happen?'

'Okay, I'll marry you.' Kaya inhaled deeply, well aware of the enormity of her decision, but determined to pull back from the temptation to let go of all her pride. 'For all the reasons you say, it makes sense.'

'What about love?' Leo asked with a shuttered expression. 'What about your dreams of finding Mr Perfect?'

Kaya lowered her eyes. 'Sometimes it's important to think of the bigger picture.'

Was that the non-answer he was looking for? He was getting what he wanted—a marriage that was necessary, as far as he was concerned, given the circumstances—and yet something inside him twisted because he suddenly wanted more than concerns about the bigger picture.

Still, the main thing was that he was getting what he wanted. She'd made her decision, and it wasn't as though he had levered threats or tried to use his wealth to bribe her into doing what he wanted, what he knew was the only thing to do.

'Look on the bright side,' he murmured, capturing her hand with his and planting a gentle kiss on her wrist, his dark eyes never leaving hers. 'We still have *this*.'

Kaya didn't pretend to misunderstand. Her body agreed with every word of that. They might not have *love*, he was saying, but they had sex.

It would have to do.

She would enjoy it—and what was ever perfect in life, when she thought about it?

She drew him towards her and felt liberated. He kissed her, a gentle, enquiring kiss, a kiss that still tiptoed around the decision she had made. She pulled him into her so that they toppled back, half-laughing, her mouth never leaving his.

No turning back.

They made love surrounded by the sea, the surf and the blue skies above, just the two of them here in this wonderful bubble. For her, it was wonderful, passionate, bitter-sweet love. She enjoyed him in the knowledge that this was all there could ever be and it was going to have to be enough.

'What if someone comes?' she whispered as he slowly tugged down the swimsuit top to expose her breasts. He grinned and propped himself up on his hands to stare down at her.

'No chance. The island is very private, and if anyone approaches by boat we would hear from a distance away. But, trust me, that's not going to happen. What's going to happen, my darling, is this...'

Kaya melted into the tenderness of his love-making. He was the ultimate thoughtful lover, respectful of her pregnancy, even though she told him that there was no need to be. But secretly she adored that respect, adored the way he made her feel, as though she was the most delicate thing on the planet and to be protected at all costs, even when it came to over-frisky love-making.

He suckled on her breasts, cupped them in his hands and told her that he could already feel that they were fuller, riper, her nipples bigger and darker.

'And more sensitive,' Kaya murmured, lying back with shameless abandon as she urged him to suck harder until she was sure she could come just from the wet caress of his mouth on her nipples.

He stripped her and it was glorious, feeling the warm sun on her body and the soft sand between her toes when her feet slid away from the rug.

His erection, freed from the swimming trunks, told her all there was to know, that this man still very much wanted her, but she'd known that all along.

He parted her legs and the breath hitched in her throat as he played with her there, teasing her with his fingers, mouth and tongue, finding her clitoris and stimulating it until she was writhing with pleasure.

She begged him to stop, and begged him not to stop, which made him smile. She was open and ready for him when at last he thrust into her, long and deep, and moving with gentle, persistent rhythm.

He pushed a little deeper every time until she was shuddering into exquisite orgasm, shaking and trembling as she climbed higher and higher, and her fingers clutched and dug into his tightly corded shoulder blades.

Sated, Kaya lay against him and felt complete.

She knew that she would always have to be careful, to make sure that the love she felt wasn't reflected in her face. What would happen if she told him that she'd fallen in love with him? Right now, with no ring on her finger, he would back off. She knew he would. But later, if they were married? Something would be lost. The easy familiarity of friendship which he was willing to extend would seep away, replaced with awkwardness and discomfort until whatever they had, from lust to affection, would wither and die.

She couldn't bear the thought of that.

But what she was signing up to? However tough it felt would be a lot less tough than the alternative, and she basked in that realisation and smiled at him.

'I've missed you,' Leo confessed in a roughened undertone. He stroked back her hair and smiled down at her.

You've missed this, Kaya thought realistically.

'So,' she said softly. 'I guess plans need to be revisited?'

'We can revisit them after we've had a swim, and this time I'm going to be right by your side, so you have nothing to fear. Then we're going to have a long, lazy lunch, and then maybe we can have a bit more fun… And when we're back at the villa we can do the revisiting…'

'Okay.' She began getting to her feet and he gently tugged her back down and tilted her so that they were looking at one another, their faces only inches apart.

Kaya could see every laughter line on his face, every worry line. His dark eyes were deadly serious.

'Sure about this?'

Kaya nodded.

'You were right.' She sighed with heartfelt sincerity. 'We're bringing a child into the world. That child didn't ask to be here but it's important that we both do what's right for him or her. And putting aside…well, the stuff I'd hoped for when it came to marriage and kids…is just something that has to be done.'

She was only saying what he had said to her in the first place. She'd come round to his way of thinking. The *responsible* way of thinking.

'Kaya,' he said huskily, 'I…'

I love you? Leo froze. He didn't know where that had come from. He couldn't love her. He couldn't *love*. His heart thudded, protesting that assumption.

'You what…?'

'You're doing the right thing.'

Love? He found it hard to think straight and he knew he had to get past this crazy nonsense and focus on the here and now. She was going to marry him. They were doing the thing that made sense, the thing that was best for their child. Children didn't ask to be born and should never have to pay the price for mistakes their parents had made.

They would have that thought guiding them and they

would have sex. The physical side of things, he could understand, and that thought calmed him.

'I'm just doing what you're doing, Leo. I'm making sacrifices. You're prepared to move to Boston and I know that'll probably be a huge wrench for you.'

The sun was beating down on them and the rug felt hot, even under the shade of the tree with its low-hanging branches.

The sound of the sea, gentle against the shore, was soporific.

Leo stared into her eyes and had trouble swallowing. She was everything to him. He was the sacrifice she was forced to make. Sex and a baby would be their bond.

He'd lived his life with sex as the only thing he could offer a woman but, now he wanted to offer so much more, he was with a woman who wanted it all but from another man.

She would give everything up, including the place she called home, so that she could do the right thing. And that was what he had persuaded her to do by presenting her with facts, figures and scenarios that he'd known would unsettle her. He'd set his mind on something and had used every trick in the book to get what he'd wanted.

He hadn't bothered to dig deeper into things that should have unsettled *him*: why he'd missed her so much; why his heart turned over when he thought of her; why spending the rest of his life with her had been a decision he'd reached without batting an eye, baby or no baby.

She was talking about Boston, building herself up to a move, and sounding cheerful about it.

He interrupted her mid-sentence. He could take what she was offering, touch her soft mouth, make love to her and feel her body moulding to hers.

'Kaya…'

She smiled but his eyes were grave when he looked at her.

'This time, it's for me to apologise. It's not going to work.'

'What?' She was still smiling.

'Marriage. You were right—it's not for us. Boston, yes, that makes sense. But marriage? No. We have to let that one go.'

CHAPTER TEN

BOSTON…MARRIAGE…THE sort of picture-perfect gin-
gerbread cottage he had always scorned: *that* was what
was on Leo's mind ten days later as he stared out of the
vast expanse of glass that separated him from the busy
Manhattan streets below.

He could have had it all. He could have had the woman
he'd fallen in love with. He could have just accepted that
the circumstances weren't ideal and he was now plagued
by what he had given up.

If things had been bad for him before he'd gone to his
villa in the Bahamas, then they were indescribable now.
He ached from the sorrow of knowing what he couldn't
have and from the vague notion that he had brought the
whole situation about all by himself.

He'd been arrogant and smug. He had slept with Kaya
and managed to convince himself that he was untouchable because he always had been. He'd known the kind
of guy she wanted but, instead of showing her from the
start that he was that guy, when he scraped away the superficial stuff he had glibly shrugged and assumed that
the sort of considerate man she was after, the sort of man
who made dreams come true for women and wanted a
future with them, wasn't him.

He hadn't spotted love for what it was until it was too

late. He couldn't blame himself for that but he did blame himself for misreading the signposts along the way.

Now she was gone. Not to Boston, not to house-hunt with him, even though he had done his best to try and convince her to, but back to Vancouver to think things through.

He hadn't had a leg to stand on so he had been forced to let her go. The last day they'd spent in the Bahamas had been agony for him but he had concealed it well.

And her? She had carried on smiling, not once berating him for stringing her along, and not once implying that she had known best all along. She had been sweet, quiet and well-mannered and, in return, he'd backed away and fought against the pain of watching her and seeing her leave him.

He had no idea what she was thinking about Boston. If she decided to stay put in Vancouver, then there wasn't a thing he could do about it. He couldn't drag her kicking and screaming to some house he'd chosen for her.

And he'd been looking. It was a job he could have farmed out to his PA, but he had spent time looking himself, getting in touch with the biggest relocation company that dealt with that area and outlining the sort of thing he was looking for.

He looked at his mobile phone and, fed up with the business of dealing with his chaotic thoughts, he scrolled, found her number and dialled it.

Kaya was tidying the last of the rooms in the house. It had been a labour of love and a useful way of getting her mind off what was happening in her life.

So he'd changed his mind about marrying her. Was it that surprising? Maybe he'd made love with her that last time and it had dawned on him that sex, for what it was worth, wasn't going to be quite enough to see them through a baby and everything that would come afterwards.

He'd broken it off, she'd looked at him while her world had been falling apart and she'd smiled and kept on smiling, nodding her agreement with his decision for the rest of the short time they'd been at the villa.

She was sure he'd been relieved that she'd had the decency not to kick up a fuss or to tell him that he should have listened to her in the first place. It was hard to tell. When he chose, it was impossible to read what he was thinking.

And, once she'd returned to the house, he had called daily to find out how she was doing. He was solicitous and zealous in his concern for her health, the pregnancy. He asked her questions and she replied, but all the while she wondered what he was doing, what he was getting up to.

Out of sight, out of mind—wasn't that how it went? He'd walked away from her and was living his life as it had been before they'd met. Had he met someone else? Someone to take the sting out of the hand he'd been dealt? Had he idly started casting his eyes around for the women who would step up to the plate, expecting no more than he considered himself capable of giving?

He'd mentioned Boston.

When Kaya thought of going there, of looking around houses knowing that she wouldn't be sharing any of them with him, she chickened out and made excuses for not being ready.

'Still stuff to do here...'

'I have to go to the halfway house and go through the books...'

'I can't spare the time right now to go to the estate agents… Maybe later, maybe next week…or next month…'

'Is there really a rush just yet…?'

Now, sitting back on her haunches with little piles of paraphernalia around her, and the growing emptiness of the house reminding her that decisions couldn't be put off for ever, she looked at her phone and saw his name. He could have phoned her on the hour and, every single time his name flashed up, she'd know that her heart would skip a beat.

'Leo, hi.'

What was she doing…? How much left was there to pack away…? Did she need any assistance? He could have a team assembled within a day to finish everything off for her… She shouldn't be doing anything that required manual effort, not in her condition; it was important she took care of herself…

Kaya stared off into the distance as she heard the dark, velvety smoothness of his voice and listened to his concern, always at the forefront, always reminding her of the kind of guy he was, so much the opposite of what she had originally thought.

'It's good for me, doing this,' she said quietly. 'It's a lot of personal stuff. It wouldn't feel right for a team of people to be here going through it.'

'I get that, but you're pregnant.'

'You worry too much. I'm fine. I… Leo…about Boston…'

'It's actually why I was calling you.'

Down the end of the line, Leo vaulted to his feet and strolled to the bank of windows that overlooked Wall Street. He was going to pin her down. A decision had to be made. His head was exploding from not knowing, from her being so far from him, her voice so distant down the end of an impersonal line.

'I've been working on this and I've found somewhere I think would be suitable.'

'Really? For me, Leo? How do you know what I would find suitable?'

'I'm going on instinct and, as you don't seem that interested in finding anywhere there, it's all I have to go on.'

'I'm sorry. There's been a lot to do here, with the house and everything.'

'Granted, but time won't be standing still.'

'Maybe you could email me the details and I'll let you know what I think of the place, you know? Save all the bother of travelling from Vancouver to Boston.'

Leo gritted his teeth at her airy dismissal.

She couldn't have made it more obvious that the last thing she wanted was to see him. Unfortunately, the more he thought about it—and he'd spent most of the past couple of weeks doing nothing *but* thinking about it—the more his gut told him that, the longer she remained holed up in Vancouver, the less likely it would be that she would consider moving location to fit in with what he wanted.

She would find her comfort zone, the place where she felt she belonged, she would eventually just refuse point-blank to accommodate him and there would be nothing he could do about it.

'You'll be chauffeur-driven to my private jet and met at the airstrip by my PA, Kaya. Trust me, there won't be any bother.'

'Your PA...'

'Would you rather she show you around with the estate agent?' It was a job keeping the edge out of his voice. He couldn't bear the thought of her not wanting to see him. He hated to think that she was toughening up, getting used to not having him anywhere in her life.

'It might be a good idea.' Her voice was cool and reasonable. 'If I have to see a bunch of houses, then I wouldn't want to waste your time by dragging you out every time one comes up on the market. That okay?'

'Fine,' Leo said through gritted teeth, thinking that it was absolutely in no way *okay*. 'No problem at all.'

Kaya was sitting in his private jet less than a day and a half later. She barely noticed the luxury, its leather and walnut perfection. She had had details of her trip texted to her and had realised that she couldn't keep dodging the inevitable for ever.

If she'd wanted to, she could have stayed in Vancouver, made him tailor his busy life to suit her, but that would have been petty and spiteful. The truth was that, as Julie Anne's house had started emptying, its soul had begun to disappear and, as it had disappeared, the little town where she had grown up had begun to feel small and constrained.

Leo, vibrant, dynamic and larger than life, had shown her the incompleteness of the life she'd been living. The prospect of moving to a different place, to open a new chapter in her life, held a certain appeal.

Boston was supposed to be a beautiful city. She would love it. It would be a fresh start and, if Leo was going to be the spoke in the wheel, then she would have to deal with that spoke and get used to it because it wasn't going away any time soon.

Thankfully, she had a reprieve, because he wouldn't be meeting her personally—and why would he, considering she had already been dispatched from his life in terms of marriage material? But she would have to face him sooner rather than later and, when she did, she wasn't going to go to pieces and start getting sentimental.

She wasn't going to think about women he might have been seeing or would be seeing, and she wasn't going to create entire life stories in her head about what might or might not happen in his life over the next few years when it came to finding a partner.

Boston was in the grip of winter cold when she roused herself to notice that the jet was landing. Snow was falling and there was a determined layer of white everywhere, the sort of settled snow that would be around for the long haul.

She would be met at the airport by his car containing his PA, who was called Donna, and she would visit the house he had sourced for her. Everything would go exactly according to plan. Kaya knew that because everything Leo did went just as he wanted it to. She was under no obligation to like the place he had chosen but, unless it was downright objectionable, then what was the point in being fussy?

It wasn't as though this house represented the start of a wonderful life for her with the guy of her dreams. This would be bricks and mortar and, as long as it did the job, then why worry? In time, she would move to a place she would call her own, once she had found her feet and come to terms with her emotions.

It was freezing.

Head down, she rushed towards the long, black car waiting for her.

He saw a slender, graceful figure layered with so much clothing that it was hard to see her shape, and wearing her woolly hat pulled so low down that Leo, waiting behind privacy glass in his chauffeur-driven four-wheel drive, marvelled that she could see anything at all.

He had come. He'd had to come. He couldn't *not*. She'd been holed up in Vancouver and, with each passing minute, the terror of losing her had got more and more acute. Having confronted the thing he'd never dreamt possible, it now had him in its vice-like grip and refused to let him go.

He'd got the message loud and clear that, released from the bind of having to marry him, she was moving out of his orbit. Her disembodied voice down the end of the line had been remote when they had spoken, and she'd shown next to no interest in the various places he had located for her to rent. There was no longer any need for her to grit her teeth, look on the bright side and channel her energies into making the best of the situation, starting with sex.

He thought about her every second of every minute of every day. He adored this woman and, for the first time in his life, he knew what it felt like to be vulnerable and he didn't resent it. He accepted it.

Could he spend the rest of his life like this, tormented? No way.

She pulled open the door, head still down, and it was a couple of seconds before she realised that Leo was in the car, sprawled in the back seat, leaning against the door.

And then she gasped.

What was he doing here?

She looked away quickly. She hadn't had time to rehearse her reaction. She could feel hectic colour flood into her cheeks and she made a business of fussing with her backpack, buckling herself in and slamming the door behind her.

He looked coolly, impossibly sexy in casual black jeans and a tan cashmere jumper, with what looked like a black, long-sleeved, skin-tight tee-shirt underneath.

'I wasn't expecting you.' Kaya schooled her face into a polite smile but her heart was racing, her pulses were pounding and her mouth was dry.

'I know. I…was the trip okay?'

He hated the polite utterance that left his mouth. He wanted to wrap his arms around her, pull her to him and bury his face in her hair. He was afraid. Afraid of a mine-field of exposed feelings lying ahead of him. Afraid of being committed to a course of action that would end up going nowhere. Had his rigidly controlled world begun unravelling when the truth about his past had been re-vealed? Or had he just been waiting for the right woman to come along and break the spell?

Leo didn't know. He stared at her, wishing that he could read what she was thinking.

'Kaya.'

'You said your PA would be showing me the house.'

They spoke at the same time.

Ensnared by the glittering depths of his dark, dark eyes, Kaya could only stare. But then she blinked and re-minded herself that this was the guy who had given her the freedom she had asked for because he had no longer seen the value in marrying her, all things considered. She doubted she would ever be able to do more than specu-late on his reasons for changing his mind.

She would pretend to be happy if it killed her, so she forced a smile and made a something and nothing remark about them talking over one another.

'How do you feel about moving to Boston?' he asked, buying time.

'I think it's going to be great,' Kaya said brightly. 'I mean, I'll be able to carry on working remotely with my clients, and then it'll be exciting getting out there and meeting new people.'

'New people…'

'I suppose I became quite accustomed to small-town living, accustomed to doing the same things all the time with the same people. Course, I plan on returning often to visit my old friends, but it's going to be fantastic expanding my social circle.'

'There's nothing wrong with small-town living.'

'I didn't think that was your thing.'

'It never used to be but times change. I've always been a guy who can adapt.' He inhaled shakily. 'Kaya…this situation between us…'

'We've talked about it enough.'

'There are things I have to say to you.'

'I don't want to hear.'

'And I don't want to say them but I have no choice.' Now he knew what it felt like to look down the side of a precipice, one foot outstretched, hoping to make a safe landing on a wing and a prayer. 'Kaya, the past two weeks have been hell.'

Kaya was utterly thrown by that remark.

'What do you mean? No, I don't want to hear.'

'I know you don't. I know you're where you want to be but please—let me speak. Being apart from you has been unbearable.' He raked his fingers through his hair and realised he was shaking but he didn't care. 'This is maybe not quite the place for a conversation like this but, Kaya, I can't spend this entire trip pretending that everything is okay when nothing is.'

'I have no idea what you're talking about.'

She looked suspicious, bewildered and guarded and for a few seconds Leo wondered whether he had the guts to finish what he'd started, but almost immediately he knew that he had to.

'I've missed you,' he said roughly.

'No!' Her voice was sharp. 'It's not going to work. I'm not going to make the mistake of falling back into bed with you because the sex is good, only to wake up the next day to realise that, in the bigger scheme of things, sex doesn't matter that much. I'm not climbing on a merry-go-round with you, Leo.'

'Is that what you think happened?'

'Like I said, I don't want to talk about this.' She made to look away but he gently caught her chin with his fingers and she froze.

'Tell me why you think I felt I had to…let you walk away from me. From us…from this thing I want more than anything in the world…'

'Because…' Kaya tilted her head defiantly '…you realised that, if you don't have love in a relationship, then it's never going to succeed.' She half-closed her eyes and breathed in deeply, taking the plunge. 'Or, more likely, you had me out there and you realised what you knew all along—lust is something that comes and goes. It went, and being stuck in a relationship without even the benefit of sex was just never going to work out. The best thing you could do would be to call it a day before it went any further. I get it. I really do.'

'Do you?'

'You didn't have to meet me here just to tell me that. I wasn't born yesterday, Leo. I know who you are. You told me at the start, and a leopard never changes its spots. You don't do commitment, and you don't do love, except now commitment has been forced onto you. But that doesn't mean anything else has been. You don't have to explain your decision to me.'

'You've got it all wrong,' Leo said urgently.

'Which bit? The commitment bit? The getting bored bit?'

'The *everything* bit. I used to be that man, Kaya—locked away in my ivory tower, disciplined and unavailable—but then you came along. I'm not sure when it happened but that man began to morph into someone else.'

'Leo, please don't do this.'

'What?'

'Tell me lies you think I want to hear.'

'I've never lied to a woman in my life before,' Leo protested, flushing darkly. 'I've always thought that it's much better to tell the truth, even if the truth is inconvenient.'

'Then what are you saying?' Kaya heard the agonised longing in her voice and hated herself for it, for that horrible weakness she'd tried so hard to put to bed.

'I'm saying that I love you, Kaya, and that's why I let you go.'

'You love me? You want me to believe that you suddenly love me?' she said angrily.

'I don't blame you for being sceptical. I never thought it would happen, that I would find myself so deeply in love with a woman that I would relinquish everything to do what was right for her. But that's the guy I am now, and that's why I'm here, throwing caution to the winds. I love you. I knew that in your heart you wanted to find your dream, and marrying me, doing what I wanted, would have stood in the way of that dream. I wasn't going to let that happen and so I let you go. I'm telling you this,

Kaya, because I couldn't *not*. It's…bigger than me…and if it had never found a voice, if you had walked away without at least knowing how I felt, I would have lived a life of regret for ever.'

'How can I believe you? How?'

'I would never lie to you and I would never lie about this thing I'm feeling. I adore you, Kaya.'

'You never said…'

'I didn't know. I just knew life was empty without you in it.'

'I wish you'd said.'

'Would you have come flying back into my arms?'

'Yes!' Kaya smiled then laughed, swept away on a wave of happiness that was tentative to start with but then gathered momentum, growing bigger and bigger until all her doubts and unhappiness disappeared under its force. 'I've loved you for so long, but I knew that I couldn't say anything because you'd been so adamant that you weren't interested in all that fairy-tale nonsense.'

She reached for him and stroked his cheek. 'I'm so glad you've told me now, so glad you couldn't wait. I love you, my dearest Leo, and I'm never going to stop.'

Leo had wanted them to be married sooner rather than later. At the time, it had been a case of 'why wait?' but then, sooner rather than later, it had become an urgency to have this woman be his wife, wear his ring on her finger.

He ditched the separate Boston townhouse and moved into the cottage with her, the very cottage he had found and she had loved. They had seen it and walked around it, holding hands, dreaming of a future, and everything had been right in the world.

Leo still sometimes stopped to think how much he

had changed and how unimaginable the joys were of not being a slave to making money, of burying himself in the cold world of finance because it was safe.

Having turned his back on his emotions his whole life, he now succumbed to them with equal single-minded-ness, because he could think of nothing else he wanted to be than the guy who devoted himself to the woman he loved.

They were married when Kaya was six months' preg-nant. The cottage had gone from walls, rooms and empty spaces to a home filled with things she treasured and, here and there, were memories of Julie Anne—whose place in Leo's life was now a peaceful one. Thoughts were treasured of a mother who had loved him and would have kept him close, had fate not got in the way.

'Spending time in my New York penthouse is going to be a culture shock,' he'd said to her, dropping a kiss on her head that first day when they had declared their love and had strolled around the sprawling cottage. They'd discussed what they would do with some of the rooms, before going outside to inspect the generous wild, luxu-riant grounds waiting to be turned into all sorts of things that Kaya had already been excited about: an orchard… somewhere for vegetables…a play area…a pond where wildlife would flourish.

'Why?' Kaya had looked at him and smiled but she'd known. This big, powerful man, once so invincible, was the guy who had fallen in love with her and couldn't bear the thought of them being apart.

And, as he never tired of telling her over the weeks and months to come, he had never had a home before he'd met her. He'd only ever had very, very expensive houses.

It was a quiet wedding, with only a handful of close

friends there, including some of Julie Anne's, who had countless stories to tell about her and her legendary generosity. And of course her mother and her stepfather, who had travelled from New Zealand and were staying on for a couple of weeks.

They would go and visit, Kaya promised, just as soon as the baby was born and things had settled a bit.

She knew their ranch couldn't be left for too long and it was incredible that they were staying for as long as they were.

Life was so full and so busy that the months crept upon them with the stealth of a thief in the night, and suddenly brought them a baby girl. Isabella Julie was born at a little after dawn on a crisp autumn morning. As brown as a berry and with a mop of dark curls, she arrived without fuss and was the apple of Leo's eye.

With every smile and every look, Kaya could see just how much he adored his daughter, and just how much he adored *her*.

The guy who had sworn himself off love had come full circle…and for her? Not a second passed by when she wasn't grateful for the love that had found her, the love that had disobeyed both of their red lines and found a way to settle between them until nothing else in the world mattered.

* * * * *

ONE FORBIDDEN NIGHT IN PARADISE

LOUISE FULLER

MILLS & BOON

CHAPTER ONE

JEMIMA FRIDAY STEPPED off the plane at L. F. Wade International Airport in Bermuda into air that was as warm and soft as sun-dried bedsheets.

It was only seven hours and seventeen minutes since she'd left Heathrow Airport, but it felt as if she had arrived not just in a different country but on a different planet. Gone was the abrasive, cold grey London sky and in its place was a cloudless canopy of perfect aquamarine. Better still, the sun was shining.

But it wasn't just the sky that was lighter and brighter. Everyone making their way across the runway to the arrivals terminal was dressed in pastel colours, and they were smiling.

Her heart gave a wobble. She was a little low on smiles right now. She'd had to extend her overdraft again. Her PhD on 'accidental' reefs had lost its way and, to top it all, last week she came home to find her boyfriend, Nick, in bed with another woman.

She was still more than a little apprehensive about this, her first solo holiday. But despite her nervousness she had to admit that it wasn't a completely crazy idea to get away from the scene of the crime and go somewhere the sun was shining and people smiled without a reason. Maybe she might even find a reason to smile, she thought as she made her way to passport control. That holiday fling her sister Holly was so certain would happen.

Although given her track record with men it seemed highly improbable.

It felt like a hundred years since Holly and Ed had suggested that she take a holiday but in fact it was two days. At first she had been too stunned to react, but as it sank in, she was appalled.

'I can't just up sticks and fly to the other side of the world,' she'd protested when her siblings had turned up at her cottage with a takeaway and tub of ice cream...

'Why not? And Bermuda isn't the other side of the world. It's only seven hours away. That's about the same time it would take to get to Inverness.' Ed had flopped down on the sofa, then frowned. 'Did that bastard take the TV?'

'What?' She had glanced across the room at the holes in the wall where Nick had unscrewed the TV bracket. It wasn't just the TV that had disappeared. Other things were missing too. Nick's ratty bathrobe no longer hung from the bedroom door and she didn't keep tripping over his guitars. And there was a hollowed-out ache inside in her chest, although she could still feel her heart beating, which surprised her as the rest of her felt numb with shock and shame.

Her ribs seemed suddenly too tight.

Had she thought Nick was different from the other men she had dated? In appearance maybe, but pretty much the first time they met she knew he was a mess. He was in a band but got paid in pints and he slept on other people's sofas. Only instead of running a mile she had started seeing him.

Holly and Ed had been appalled, of course, then resigned. He was, they agreed, exactly her type. Handsome, damaged, and destined to break her heart. But even though she knew they were right, she had wanted him. Or rather she had wanted to do what she had failed to do for her father. To fix him, to save him from himself.

Her breath caught in her throat as she pictured her father stumbling out of the pub, staring at her blearily as if she were a stranger and not his fifteen-year-old daughter. But you couldn't fix someone who didn't want to be fixed. It had taken a long time for that message to sink in, and finally she was done trying.

Done with tortured, unfixable men.

Done with men, full stop.

'Don't change the subject,' she had said, more to stop her brother railing against Nick's perfidious behaviour than because she wanted to discuss the twins' hare-brained scheme. Ed had already been eloquent on the matter and she didn't need to be reminded again of her ex's flaws or her stupidity in ignoring them. 'And it's obvious why not. I'm supposed to be finishing my PhD, not gallivanting off on holiday. Look, it's a lovely idea and I love you both for thinking of it, but I can't possibly—'

'But that's the thing—you can't not. You see, it's not an idea...' Holly had given her a sheepish grin. 'It's a fact. We booked the flight.'

'And sorted out the accommodation,' Ed had added. 'You leave the day after tomorrow and, yes, I know it's short notice—' he had raised his hand up like a traffic policeman to stop the flow of her objections '—and, yes, we should have talked to you first but we knew if we gave you time to think you'd never do it.'

Holly had grabbed her hand and pulled her onto the sofa. 'I know you're worried about your PhD but you've been working on it for ten months now. Ten days isn't going to make a difference one way or another. Besides, you've always wanted to go to Bermuda and it's the perfect place to work.'

'If I'm going to work then I don't need to fly to Bermuda. Besides, they probably don't even have the Internet.'

Sensing weakness, Holly had grinned. 'Of course they do, Jem. I checked. And as you already know, they have over four hundred wrecks off the coast. So if you find some sexy sailor to take you out on his boat you can write it off as fieldwork.'

'And,' her brother had chipped in, 'you haven't had a holiday in years. Everyone needs a holiday, Jem, even you.'

A holiday.

The word had tasted like sherbet on her tongue and as expected she'd capitulated. When the twins stuck together they were almost impossible to unstick, and although the idea of travelling on her own to a distant and mysterious island made her pulse beat out of time, a part of her had felt almost relieved that she would be somewhere other than the cottage.

'Please, Jem. You need this. Just promise me that you'll go all in.' Reaching out, Holly had touched the blonde hair scraped into an unforgiving bun at the back of her head. 'Promise me that you'll let this down for once. And wear your contacts.'

'Okay, okay, I promise I'll let my hair down.'

'And have some fun.' Holly's blue eyes had gleamed. 'Have a fling. You're not just swapping homes, you're swapping lives.'

'You don't know anything about her. She could be a social outcast.'

'Then be someone else. It's just ten days, Jem. You can be anyone you want.'

And that was the difference between them. The twins

were like their father. She was like hers. When life gave them lemons, they made lemonade. She never got that far because she was too busy worrying about the ratio of sugar and water. Or whether the lemons were ripe enough.

You can be anyone you want.

She glanced over at the luggage carousel, Holly's words replaying inside her head. Right now she'd settle for being that lucky person whose bag was the first to appear.

Incredibly, her suitcase was the first to appear. So far, so smooth, but she still had to find her way to Joan's beach house and she headed towards the exit, her nerves popping as she stepped into the sunlight again.

It was still strange to think that she would be living in someone else's house. Almost as strange as the idea of Joan living at Snowdrop Cottage. She bit into her lip. She'd only had one, snatched conversation with Joan Santos and she seemed fun and friendly, and Holly said she would drop round and say 'hi'. So stop worrying, she told herself. But that was easy to say, almost impossible to do. Worrying came as naturally to her as breathing. And taking an impromptu holiday on her own was well out of her comfort zone.

Only it was too late to think about that now.

There was a line of taxis waiting outside the airport and she approached the first in the queue trying to channel her younger sister's charm and her brother's unflappable calm.

'Where to?' the driver asked as he slid her bags into the boot of the car.

'Farrar's Cove, please. Do you know it?'

He nodded. 'Oh, I know it.' Slamming the boot, he grinned. 'Don't look so worried. It's beautiful. Very private and quiet. You pretty much got a whole beach to yourself. But if you get tired of quiet, just walk right on up the beach to the Green Door and you can dance until the sunrise.'

She leaned forward. 'The Green Door.'

'It's a bar.' His grin widened. 'It's raw Bermuda; you won't find many tourists but it's the best bar on the island. Best rum. Best music. And not just because my sister owns it.' She saw the driver grin in the rear-view mirror. 'Just ask for Aliana. She'll look after you. Tell her Sam sent you. That's me.'

'Nice to meet you, Sam, I'm Jemima, but most people call me Jem.' She smiled. It was kind of Sam to look out for her but bars weren't her thing. She didn't drink, and as for dancing. Reaching up, she touched her bun. Letting her hair down was not something she did naturally.

Settling back against the warm leather upholstery, Jem stared through the window at the passing streets. Aside from the legendary triangle, and the namesake shorts, all she knew about Bermuda was that it was supposed to be the inspiration for the island in Shakespeare's *The Tempest*. But as they drove through the main town of Hamilton, she was more than a little surprised.

It was a pastel paradise. Everything was painted in soft pinks and yellows and blues. But mostly pink. It couldn't be any more different from England's grey cities and yet strangely there were old-fashioned British telephone boxes.

Just like the one Nick had pulled her into that first night they met when it was raining so hard. She had thought it was so romantic. A week later he'd told he was in love with her and moved into the cottage.

There had been no signs, nothing amiss when she let herself back into the cottage early. Music, some indie band that Nick loved and she tolerated, was playing loudly. And the cottage was swelteringly hot; she could remember feeling that familiar tic of irritation that Nick, who paid no bills, had no qualms about turning up the heating while she wore a coat and fingerless gloves and sat with a hot-water bottle to stop her body from cramping as she hunched over her laptop.

She hadn't called out his name. She had wanted to surprise him.

And she had.

A shiver of misery and humiliation pulsed across her skin as she remembered the moment when she stepped into the bedroom. At first, she hadn't quite taken it in, almost as if her brain was trying to protect her from what her eyes were seeing, only she couldn't not see it. See them. Nick, his handsome features blunted with desire; the woman's mouth an O of shock, their bodies shining with sweat in the pale afternoon light.

The woman had fled. Nick stayed. At first he was sulky and defensive, then accusatory, listing her faults, then finally he told her he was leaving. And that was that. Another failed relationship, another reminder of how she had failed to save her father from his demons.

For a moment, the shadows of the past seemed to creep into the taxi, and with an effort she pushed them away. While she was here in the sunshine, she was going to take a holiday from all the memories and regrets that crouched in the shadows.

Away from the town, the countryside was gentle but she kept getting tiny, teasing glimpses of pink sand and a sea that looked like blue glass. As he drove, Sam chatted about Bermy, as he called Bermuda, and by the time she felt the car slow, most of her nerves had faded away.

They had left the main road some five minutes earlier and now the road surface was getting rougher, and then the dunes parted and she felt her breath catch in her throat and before the car had even come to a stop she was opening the door and running towards a tiny pale green painted cottage.

When Joan had said it was 'compact' she hadn't been joking. But the sand touched the steps leading up to the veranda, and it was pink.

She blinked. There were palm trees too.

It could have come straight from the pages of *Robinson Crusoe*. It was perfect and she took a photo and sent it to Holly and Ed.

Inside was as tiny as it looked. Tinier even than her cottage at home. Just a bedroom, a miniature bathroom and living room with a kitchen at one end. There was a bowl of exotic-looking fruit on a doll's-house-sized table and tucked underneath was a piece of paper with her name on it.

Hi Jem,
Welcome to my home! Use whatever you want. I made up the bed fresh and the towels are brand new.
    Just a heads-up, my axe packed up yesterday and I didn't have time to get it fixed but you can hire one in Hamilton.
Have fun,
Joan x

Joan sounded so nice, she thought, staring wistfully down at the note. It was a pity she was never going to meet her. She frowned. Why would she need an axe though? And why would she need to hire one? She turned towards where Sam was putting her bags by the door.

'Sam, do I have to chop wood for something? Only Joan says the axe is broken.'

He laughed. 'Axe is slang. She means her moped. That how you planning on getting around?'

Truthfully she hadn't got that far. It was one of the many

things she hadn't had time to plan for. 'I suppose so. But don't I need to have a licence?'

He shook his head. 'Not if you're hiring one. The Cycle Shack is the place to go. It's down by the harbour. I'll drop you there on my way back to the airport.'

The Cycle Shack clearly did a whole lot more than hire out bikes and mopeds. It also sold hardware, fresh coffees and acted as a collection and drop-off point for post and parcels. And judging by the people milling around chatting and greeting one another, it was also a popular place just to hang out.

There was a meandering queue weaving round the store. Finally she reached the front. The woman behind the counter smiled. 'Good morning, how can I help you today?'

'I need to hire a moped. Or at least I think I do. I should probably try one first.'

'Okay. Let me get someone to come and help you.'

As she disappeared out the back, still smiling, Jem heard her phone ping and, pulling it out of her bag, she saw that in response to her photo Holly had sent her a GIF of a coconut falling on someone's head.

Predictably, Ed had left her unread.

Sighing, she looked up just as a man wearing a red baseball cap wandered into the room, clutching a cardboard box. He slid the box onto the counter, glanced up briefly, just long enough for her to catch a flash of green as her eyes bumped into his, and then picked up a clipboard and turned away.

Her pulse twitched, and she felt heat spill over her face. He had clearly seen her, and she waited for him to look up and greet her, noticing in the meantime and almost against her will how his white T-shirt clung to the contoured muscles of his shoulders, but he didn't turn and finally she cleared her throat.

He still didn't turn, and she felt a flicker of irritation. 'Excuse me. Do you think you could help me?'

Now he turned and straightened up, and she felt her pulse jerk forward as eyes the colour of uncut emeralds met hers. Beneath the cap, he was astonishingly, shockingly beautiful. Hard, high cheekbones; a straight jaw and a curving, sensuous mouth that was edged by a dusting of stubble. He might not have noticed her but his looks and height basically commanded attention. 'Help you?' His voice was deep and husky. She liked it.

And she was not the only one, she realised, as the woman standing behind her murmured, 'You sure can, baby.'

A smile tugged at his mouth as his gaze flickered towards the woman, and then he was moving towards Jem with the careless grace of a pirate swaggering across the deck of his ship.

The careless what?

Slightly disconcerted by that mental image, and hoping her face wasn't as hot-looking as it felt, she nodded stiffly. 'Yes, please. If you're not too busy.'

Oh, great. For some reason she couldn't explain, she was using what Holly and Ed called her 'headmistress' voice.

As he came to a stop directly in front of her, her stomach tightened and she felt a prickle beneath her skin like pins and needles.

'How can I be of help?' he said softly.

Her ribs squeezed around her lungs. Up close his eyes were not just green. There were flecks of blue and brown and gold so that it was like looking into a kaleidoscope. And yet there was something raw about him, something irrefutably male that didn't go with those rainbow eyes.

It was impossible to look away.

He knew it too. But then on an island this small he probably had the pick of the women.

'I need some way to get around the island,' she began a little breathlessly, 'so if I could get some advice...'

She felt his narrowed gaze make a slow, assessing sweep of her face.

'From me?' He stared at her for a moment as if he was making a decision. 'Okay, then, let's go out front,' he said finally.

Outside, the smell of oil mingled with the sea air as she followed him to where two lines of mopeds sat on their stands in the sun. Behind them was another line of bicycles. The man stopped and turned to face her and she swallowed hard. She had thought that maybe in daylight he would look more ordinary but if anything the sunlight seemed to accentuate the miraculous lines of his face.

Wishing she still had the buffer of the counter between them, she said quickly, 'So what are my options?'

'You have three. These are the basic ones.' He gestured towards the line of black mopeds. 'They're practical, they do the job, but they're not going to turn heads. Then we have these.' His hand rested lightly on a pistachio-coloured scooter with cream upholstery and a wicker basket. 'They are Italian. A little bit faster, a little bit more stylish.'

'And what's the third? You said there were three.'

Squinting up at the sun, he pulled off his cap and tucked it into his back pocket. 'A good old-fashioned pushbike.' He turned away from the line of mopeds. 'That's probably your best bet. It's what I'd recommend for those of a more cautious disposition.'

She felt anger twitch through her. What did he know about her disposition? 'I don't bet,' she said crisply.

'Exactly. You don't like going outside of your comfort zone.'

Her eyes narrowed. 'Actually I prefer the Italian one.'

'Really?' He seemed amused. 'Ever ridden one before?'

She glared at him. 'No, but my brother has a motorbike.'

'Good for him, but it's you I'm interested in.' His gaze rested on her face and she felt her cheeks grow warm. He meant as a customer, she told herself quickly, but the raw sexual challenge in his green gaze took her breath away.

She watched, panic and anger and something she didn't want to identify fluttering in her throat as he pulled the nearest moped off its stand. 'Then you better give it a test drive but before you do that—' he picked up the helmet that was hooked over the handlebar '—you need to put this on.'

She took the helmet from his hand. Feeling all fingers and thumbs beneath his gaze, she tried to fit it over her head but her bun was too rigid. 'Here, let me—'

Before she could protest, he reached up and heat exploded inside her as his hand grazed her neck and she felt her hair tumble to her shoulders. 'Now try.'

It was a whisper of a touch but as he took a step back she had to force herself to ignore how it had blazed through her, swift and hot like a flame.

This time the helmet went on easily though.

'Right.' He gripped the handlebar. 'This left side is the front brake. The right side is the rear brake and the throttle. Here—' he pointed to some switches '—you have lights, indicator and the horn. Bermudans love their horns.' He gave her the same flicker of a smile as he had to the woman in the store.

'So to start, you turn the key, squeeze the brake, any brake, and then press the ignition. Voila,' he said softly as the engine started. He switched it off. 'Your turn.'

She sat down on the seat and repeated everything he had just shown her.

'Good. Just get used to the throttle. You'll want to keep your feet close to the ground. Now give it a bit of acceleration.'

The moped started to move. Her heart bumped upwards. 'Nice and slow.' His green eyes were watching her intently and the slow burn of his gaze made her skin feel hot and tight. 'Slow and straight. Now see if you can take it round the car park.'

Jem felt a rush of exhilaration as she navigated the parked cars. She could probably run faster than she was moving but being on the moped made her feel like a character in a black and white film. If only Holly were here to see her.

As she came to a stop, she glanced over triumphantly to where the man was standing, but he was gone. Switching off the ignition, she pulled the moped backwards onto its stand, her elation of moments earlier slipping away. But perhaps he'd gone back into the store to do the paperwork, she thought, tugging off the helmet and resting it on the seat.

'Hey there.' She turned, her heart lurching, but a different man was walking towards her, smiling warmly. 'I'm George. How can I help you today?'

'It's okay, someone's already helping me…only I don't know where he went. He was just here…' Her voice faltered as her gaze snagged on a familiar red cap. She frowned. The man was walking along the jetty. 'Where's he going?'

'Who?' George glanced over to where she was looking. 'You mean Chase. Probably out on his boat.'

'You mean he's a fisherman.' Her stomach felt as if it were in free fall. 'But I thought he worked here?'

George shook his head, grinning. 'No, Chase don't work for me.'

Jem stared after the retreating figure, her cheeks burning with shock and confusion.

In the end she put the Italian moped back and rented one of the bicycles. She knew it was ridiculous to let the actions of a stranger, however handsome, affect her decision but Chase's deception had left her feeling off balance and out of depth.

Her throat tightened.

So many people had lied to her already about what they had or hadn't done and what they would do in the future if she'd only give them another chance and she was sick of it. But after Sam's kindness, and with the beach house and the Bermuda sun putting her in a holiday mood, she'd actually started to think that Holly and Ed were right. She could be someone different here. Someone edgy and adventurous and sexy.

Only then Chase Whatever-His-Name-Was had tricked her into thinking he worked at the Cycle Shack. Worse, he had clearly seen her for the sensible, 'put money aside for the bills' kind of woman she was, and after that it was impossible to picture herself riding around on anything other than a pushbike.

But probably it wasn't just that electric, unsettling interaction with Chase that had flattened her mood. It had been a long day. As she let herself into the beach house, her phone pinged and, pulling it out of her bag, she saw that it was a message from her brother.

Skinny dip? Go on, I dare you!

She stared down at the message and then laughed out loud. Except she knew Ed wasn't joking. She glanced at the gently rippling blue sea. He would be the first one in. Nothing ever fazed him. He was up for anything.

Whereas she was always the one who had to do a forfeit. Sometimes her whole life felt like a forfeit.

Raising her arm, she squinted up, then down the beach. It was completely empty as far as the eye could see. Almost as if she were marooned on a desert island.

Go on, I dare you!

Her heart skipped a beat. Could she do it? Could she swim naked in the sea? She had a bikini but Holly had chosen it, which meant that it was so small she might as well not bother wearing it.

So don't? Biting her lip, she glanced up the beach, trembling with excitement. There was nobody around.

Go on, I dare you!

Ignoring the butterflies spiralling up in her stomach, she ran back into the house, tossed her glasses on the table, grabbed a towel from the bathroom, and then quickly, before she could change her mind, she stripped off her clothes and wrapped the towel round her waist.

At the shoreline, she took one last look and then dropped the towel onto the pink sand and waded into the water. It felt lovely, and unlike the sea at home it was completely transparent. I did it, she thought, a pulse of triumph beating across her skin.

What was that?

She froze, her body electric with panic. But probably she was imagining it. Only then she heard it again. Somewhere nearby, someone was whistling. She spun round towards the shore but there was nobody on the beach. Her eyes narrowed on where the bay curved into the sea, and then, heart thumping out of time, she stumbled out of the water. She snatched up her towel and scampered back into the beach house like a startled rabbit, closing the door behind her.

Clutching the towel around her trembling body, she squeezed up against the window frame. But there was nobody there.

And then she saw him, standing upright on a paddle board, drawing the blade through the water with smooth, effortless strokes. Her glasses were still sitting on the table but she didn't need to be wearing them to know who he was. She had only met one person in her life who moved with such careless grace.

She licked her lips. The man she knew only as Chase looked exactly as he had at the harbour.

Except now he was shirtless.

Her breath bottled in her throat. He had looked good in a T-shirt, but there was no superlative that could adequately describe what he looked like without one. Her eyes hovered greedily on his biceps, then locked onto his chest. He was all smooth golden skin and primed muscle. A light scattering of golden hair cut a line into the muscle of his washboard abs, thickening as it disappeared beneath his low-slung board shorts.

She squeezed back into the house. Her mouth was dry and her skin felt as if it were on fire and beneath her skin, there was chaos. Breathing out unsteadily, she reached up to touch the nape of her neck where she could still feel the imprint of his hand from earlier.

At that exact instant, he looked over at the beach house almost as if he could feel it too and a jolt of electricity crackled down her spine.

But of course he couldn't feel it. Whatever she had imagined at the Cycle Shack had been just that. A figment of her imagination. And for him it had been a game.

He was out of sight now and she slid down against the wall, her cheeks tingling, the sharp tang of shame rising in her throat.

Coming here was a mistake. She wasn't brave enough to be someone else. So even though it would mean breaking her promise, *again*, tomorrow she was going to change her ticket and go back home.

She stayed there for a long time until the sun slipped beneath the horizon and then, still clutching the towel, she climbed into Joan's bed. There was nothing for her here, she thought, gazing through the window at a star-studded night sky. But as her eyes slid shut it seemed as if the stars weren't white, but a dark, glittering green.

CHAPTER TWO

DAMN IT!

Wincing, Chase Farrar held up his hand and stared at the staple he had just embedded into his finger.

He glared accusingly at the stapler. How the hell had that happened? He gave the staple an experimental wiggle but it didn't move. Which meant he would need some tweezers. And he should probably wash it first. It would help loosen it.

Yanking open the door to his office, he stalked down the corridor, nodding at Callum, one of the twenty-member crew of the *Umbra*. There was a medical kit in the sick bay, and at other points dotted around the boat.

He stopped, frowning, a memory of the day before replaying jerkily inside his head.

The medical supplies.

He had left them sitting on the counter at the Cycle Shack. He swore again, this time audibly and with less restraint. He didn't forget things. Back in New York, his PA had once joked that he should be her PA.

'Everything okay, boss?'

Callum had stopped in his tracks, and was staring at him inquiringly, and briefly he wondered what the crewman would say if he told him the truth. That a pair of grey eyes had thrown him off track and had him pretending to hire out mopeds for a living. But instead he nodded. 'Everything's fine. I just need to get some tweezers.' He held up his hand. 'Speaking of which, I forgot to pick up the medical supplies from town.'

There were other things he'd prefer to have forgotten, like how the woman had raised her chin and not just met his eyes but inspected him, briefly and coolly.

Even before she told him she was on holiday he had known she was a tourist, that much was obvious from her clothes. A teacher, maybe, he thought, hearing the put-down in her husky voice. Although not an experienced one. She was in her mid twenties at most although she was trying her best to look older with those glasses and the way she did her hair.

He made a fist with the hand; the same hand that had brushed against the nape of her neck as he loosened her hair. A pulse of heat danced across his skin in time to the throb in his finger.

Not married either. He could spot 'married' a mile off, with or without a ring. But why did he care either way?

His eyes narrowed.

He didn't.

Forcing himself to focus on the package he had left back at the harbour, he locked eyes with the crewman. 'I need someone to go collect them from the Cycle Shack. Can I leave that with you?'

'Yes, sir.' Callum nodded.

He turned and made his way to the sick bay. He washed his hand, and eased the staple out of his skin with the tweezers. The kit was low on quite a few items and he felt another stab of irritation at his forgetfulness.

This was his boat. The crew was his responsibility, and he took their health and safety seriously. Obviously, accidents happened. He knew that better than anyone but that didn't stop most being avoidable. He was just lucky they were close to shore. Only he didn't like relying on luck.

Snapping the medical kit shut, he hung it back on the wall.

It had been a long time since any woman had got under his skin like that.

For years now, his life had been clearly compartmentalised. In New York, he ran Monmouth Rock, one of the biggest insurance businesses in the world, and when he wasn't working, he worked out and slept. Sometimes he dated. Friends of friends. People in his circle. But he made his intentions—or perhaps a better word would be his limitations—clear right from the start and he never allowed things to get serious.

After everything he'd experienced in his thirty-seven years, casual, short-term, contained was all he could contemplate when it came to relationships. And there was no shortage of women who were happy to play by his rules.

Down here in Bermuda, things were even more clear cut. Instead of work, he used his focus and energy and his immense wealth to look for sunken ships. So all in all, life was good. Simple.

But the blonde at the Cycle Shack had made everything feel a whole lot more complicated.

She had some kind of physical effect on him, made him lose his balance, tangled up his thoughts. He had been so distracted—no, fascinated—by the molten shimmer of her gaze that he had forgotten all about the medical supplies. Truthfully, he would have struggled to remember his own name.

His chest tightened as he remembered how she had blushed when he'd taken off her glasses. Watching the slow flush of pink colour her cheeks, he'd been stunned, enchanted, amazed that there was still someone in the world who would respond like that. And for some reason that had made his libido not just sit up straight but fight to slip its leash.

She had felt it too. He could almost see the tension coming off her frame in waves as she fought against it.

Suddenly needing air, he made his way outside. As he took a few deep breaths, his gaze flickered across the deck to the busy harbour, automatically searching for a glimpse of fluttering blonde hair.

It meant nothing, he thought, turning deliberately to stare at the open sea. She had caught him off guard too, that was all. It was always the same at this time of year.

Maybe he should give Emma a call. She would distract him. Emma was one of the women he hooked up with when he needed a date for an event or to feel skin against skin. She was beautiful and smart and he enjoyed her company in and out of bed. He could fly her down from New York. She would be here in two hours.

Only it was not something he'd ever done before. What if she got the wrong idea?

He frowned. This was her fault. That nameless woman who had somehow managed momentarily to make him forget the past. It was her fault that he needed a distraction.

But it wouldn't happen again. There was no reason for their paths to cross during her holiday so he could forget about that brief flicker of attraction that had passed between them like electricity.

And even if she had been moving here for good, it wouldn't change anything. He wasn't looking for a relationship with someone who still blushed when she talked to a man. Because he wasn't looking for a relationship at all.

Pressing the plunger down on the cafetière, Jem poured herself a cup of coffee and stepped out onto the deck of the beach house.

She had woken late, for her anyway. Holly and Ed were still at that point where they found it a struggle to wake before noon but she had always been a poor sleeper. But last night, lulled by the sound of the waves, she had fallen asleep instantly and woken as sunlight flooded the room.

The same sunlight that was now warming her skin.

She padded down the steps and wriggled her toes in the sand. It was just too perfect, almost as if she were in a film set on a beach. But maybe all holidays felt like this.

Her eyes narrowed into the sunlight. Truthfully she could barely remember her last holiday. Or perhaps it was another of those things she wanted to forget. She glanced back at the turquoise-coloured ocean. Either way, this was the real deal. Her toes twitched against the pale pink sand. Why, then, was she thinking of leaving?

Not just thinking. Her bag was zipped up, ready to go. She had packed it this morning after showering, scampering around the tiny house, snatching up books and shoes and sunblock, feeling not like the guest she was, but an imposter.

But why?

Green eyes holding hers steady, captive. *Chase.*

She steadied herself, but her breath kept jerking in her throat as she pictured him standing on the paddle board, his clean profile cutting a line across the crisp blue sky. She hadn't chased him but she had done the next best thing, riding in circles even though the moped she'd been sitting on wasn't his to rent.

And now the memory of that moment was chasing her away.

It crushed her to know that. To be such a coward. To not even be able to count how many other times she had let her fear of failure or of being a disappointment get in the way of living her life. There had been that job in Costa Rica restoring the coral reef. She was shortlisted but, having read up on the charity's founders, she had dropped out of the running. They were clever, important people doing important work and she was struggling to finish her thesis so of course she had to withdraw her application. It was one thing to let yourself down but to let down other people would be unforgivable.

She bit into her lip. She wasn't just scared of letting people down. She was scared of confronting them too. Look at how many confrontations she'd failed to have with Nick over his drinking. Only at the back of her mind, she was always terrified of what the consequences might be.

But if she left now, she would have to break her promise to Holly. *Another promise.* Neither of the twins understood why she felt so compelled to date such damaged men. To them it was just a baffling pattern of behaviour that needed to stop. They didn't know it was a form of atonement, and how could she explain that without telling them what she was atoning for?

How each time she failed to save her current boyfriend there was more to atone for, and so it carried on.

It was almost a year since she'd ended things with Frank and sworn to her sister that she wouldn't get so involved next time. That she would keep things casual. Only then she'd met Nick.

When she found him in bed with that woman, nobody said *I told you so*, except Ed, but she knew how upset both he and Holly were, and this holiday was their treat. Could she really let a complete stranger chase her away from this paradise? Bermuda might be small but the chances of her bumping into Chase again were surely remote.

And Holly was right. This wasn't just about having a holiday, it was about rebooting her life, tearing up the rules. Maybe not play with fire but why not strike a few sparks? For starters, she could take back the bike and swap it for one of those ice-cream-coloured mopeds, and later she would check out what was behind the Green Door.

But first she was going to unpack.

After returning the bike, she rode back to the beach house on the pistachio-coloured moped she had tried out with Chase, the wind whipping at the ends of her hair, feeling uncharacteristically cool and sophisticated.

He wasn't all that. Probably if she met him again he would be underwhelming.

If only she knew where he was she could have ridden past him with her nose in the air but instead she spent the rest of the day on the beach, eating the fruit that Joan had left and swimming, this time wearing her bikini. She had also emailed Joan to ask her where she could go diving.

The diving course had been her last birthday present from her father. She didn't count the cottage. You couldn't include something you got left in a will. But other than a few dives off Cornwall she'd never really had a chance to test her skills in real life. That would be tomorrow's challenge. Tonight she was going to go dancing.

Having washed her hair and left it to dry in the warm air, she pulled on a lightweight cream wrap dress and some tan sandals and, remembering Holly's directive, she put in her contact lenses and then added some make-up.

Joan's mirror was as tiny as everything else so all she could look at were sections of herself. But she was surprised to find that she liked what she saw. She dithered momentarily about whether to walk along the beach but in the end she decided to take the moped.

Had Sam not given her directions, she would never have found the Green Door. There was no sign but the door was green and she could hear the music jumping through the evening air even before she switched off the engine. As she pulled off her helmet, her eyes widened. The pubs at home got crowded but this was like a New Year's Eve party. There were people spilling onto the beach, drinking and laughing under a canopy of lights and flowers, and everyone seemed to be smiling.

Inside, it was difficult to see the bar itself. Finally, she managed to get to the front. There were several people working behind the bar. Three men and one very beautiful woman in a clinging red dress. One of the barmen leaned forward. 'What can I get you, baby?'

'Lime and soda, please?' she said quickly. It was her drink of choice at home. It looked enough like alcohol that she didn't stand out in the pub. Her family and friends knew that she didn't drink but she had discovered that it was easier on nights out to pretend she did than be obviously teetotal.

'You must be Jem.'

She glanced up, startled.

'I'm Aliana.' The beautiful woman behind the bar smiled at her. 'Sam told me you might be dropping in.'

'But how did you know who I was?'

Aliana laughed. 'We don't get many tourists out here. Look, I gotta go back to work, but I'll keep my eye on you. Enjoy the vibe.'

She managed to find a table in the back room, and to her surprise it was easier than she expected to follow Aliana's advice. Normally on nights out, she was so tense, so on edge; she always felt like the 'grown-up' in the room. But here, she wasn't responsible for anyone. She could just sit and watch. As her eyes moved across the room, the crowds parted and she caught a glimpse of a pool table. A game was in progress. One man was standing at the side, his cue upright in his hand like a staff. But it was the other man, the one bent over the table, who caught her attention.

She couldn't see his face but she could almost feel his concentration.

Although how he could concentrate with so much going on around him was anyone's guess, she thought as he potted the ball with an audible crack.

The final ball, apparently. There was applause and cheering and she found herself smiling but as he straightened up she felt her body still. There was something familiar about that back.

At that moment he turned towards her and she felt her face dissolve in shock. Around her, everyone else in the room seemed to fade away. It was him. The man from the Cycle Shack.

Chase.

What was he doing here? Her heart raced at the sight of him. For a moment she just stared, her glass frozen mid-air. Earlier she had imagined herself on the moped, glancing at him with cool confidence, but now that he was standing in front of her she just wanted to run. But it was too late. As if feeling her scrutiny, he looked over and his gaze collided with hers.

Suddenly she was aware of nothing except the dark, uneven thud of her heart.

And his eyes, clear, green, steady on her face.

Her fingers tightened around the glass as a group of women stumbled in front of him, laughing and clutching at one another, and he disappeared from view, and for a moment she thought she might have imagined him, but then the crowd parted and she saw him again, weaving his way through the crowd towards her.

Leave, she told herself fiercely, but she was rooted to the wooden bench. Her stomach clenched as he stopped in front of the table, that same flickering smile pulling at his mouth.

'Hello again.' He paused and she felt her stomach somersault as his green eyes locked with hers. 'How's the moped? Let me guess, you swapped it for the bike, didn't you?'

'I did swap it for the bike. But then I swapped it back,' she added, giving him a small, challenging smile.

'Is that right?'

She nodded. 'I didn't get very good advice.' Lifting her chin, she cleared her throat. 'Apparently the man who helped me didn't actually work at the Cycle Shack.'

His smile widened and she felt her pulse accelerate. 'I spend enough time there it feels like I do.'

'But you don't.'

'No, I don't,' he agreed.

'Well, don't let me keep you from your game, Mr…?' Lifting her drink, she looked pointedly past his shoulder.

'Just call me Chase.'

'Is that your name?' she replied tartly, although she knew it was. 'Or are you just trying it out for tonight?'

He laughed softly. 'It's definitely mine although when I was a kid I used to wish it wasn't. Having a stand-out name at school seemed to get me into more trouble than my friends.' He shrugged. 'But it's a family name.'

He was trouble, all right, she thought, with or without the name, but it suited him. *Chase.* It was what predators did, she thought, her brain spinning like a top. And this man was an apex predator.

He held out his hand and, caught off guard by this sudden formality, she took it. Like everything else about him, his handshake was confident, masculine, firm. Although his mouth looked as if it would soften to kiss a woman.

Her pulse twitched madly as he released his grip, and

she flexed her fingers beneath the table to try and shake off the tingling imprint of his touch.

'And you are...?'

'Jemima,' she said stiffly. 'Jemima Friday.'

'Really?' In the pulsing light, his eyes glittered like emeralds. 'Interesting name for a stranger on an island.'

Her mouth was suddenly dry, her throat too tight. 'And you get one Robinson Crusoe joke, so use it wisely.'

He nodded slowly. 'I'll bear that in mind.' Somebody shouted his name and he glanced over his shoulder but he didn't leave. He just stood there looking at her, his green eyes searching her face as if he was making a decision about something.

'Look, about before, I was out of order at the Cycle Shack. I shouldn't have done what I did and I'm sorry.' His eyes dropped to the empty glass in her hand. 'Why don't you let me buy you a drink, to apologise?'

'You don't need to do that.'

'I'd like to. Please, what are you drinking?'

Her insides tightened as he stared down at her. She had told herself that he wasn't that beautiful. That if she met him again she would be underwhelmed. But she had been wrong. Beneath the soft pulsing lights his face was shockingly, arrestingly beautiful.

And she wasn't the only one to notice. Theoretically it was so crowded in the bar that it should be impossible to pick a face from the crowd but Chase was not just inconspicuous, he seemed to exert a gravitational force over the room, judging by how many women were glancing over at him with surreptitious and not so surreptitious glances.

'It's just lime and soda.'

She half expected him to protest, to insist that she have something more exciting from the list on the chalkboard, but he simply nodded. And it was then, watching his shoulders as he made his way to the bar, that she realised he was making the crowd part, he was responsible for the ebb and flow she had seen earlier.

Her heart thudded against her ribs. This was madness. *It's just a drink,* she heard Holly's voice inside her head. *Just enjoy the vibe.*

More than anything she wanted to watch him walk towards her again, but she knew that seeing him move towards her with that tantalising, casual grace would undo her completely. Instead she forced herself to stare across the room at the photos on the wall. They were different sizes and some were curling at the edges with age but the thing they had in common was that they all seemed to picture grinning men standing beside giant suspended fish.

'Are you interested?'

Her pulse jolted forward as Chase appeared beside her. 'In what?' She stared at him in confusion.

'Fishing.' He was holding two glasses of lime and soda, and as he dropped down onto the chair opposite, he slid hers across the table. 'You know, sport fishing. Wahoos, tuna, marlin. The whole Hemingway schtick. Not that he came to Bermuda. He was out in Bimini and the Keys, but sport fishing is a big part of the tourist industry here too.'

He'd read Hemingway. That was a surprise. But why? Fishermen read books too.

She shook her head. 'No, sorry. Is that what you do on your boat? Take tourists out fishing?'

His mouth ticked up at one corner. 'No, I fish for myself.' His green eyes narrowed and she felt his gaze rake over her again.

'So why have you come to Bermuda, then?'

It was a simple enough question but the answer was anything but. Then again, Chase didn't need to know anything but the basics.

She shrugged. 'I just needed a holiday. And I've wanted to visit Bermuda since we did *The Tempest* at school.'

Really? She winced inwardly, hearing the twins' groan of despair inside her head. Had she actually said that out loud? But it was true. Ever since that term when she studied the play she'd been fascinated by shipwrecks and Bermuda was the shipwreck capital of the world.

'And now you are,' he said softly.

Her heart thudded. The table suddenly felt too small. Or maybe they were sitting too close. She felt something stir inside her as his eyes met hers. He was a stranger and yet no one had ever looked at her so intently as if they were trying to reach inside her. It felt oddly intimate.

Too intimate.

And far too soon. There was still some of Nick's stuff at the cottage.

He leaned forward. 'So what do you think of the "still vex'd Bermoothes"?' She felt another jolt of surprise. Not many people had read *The Tempest*, let alone could quote from it.

'I think it's beautiful,' she said simply.

'So can I tempt you into trying your hand at fishing?' Chase said. His gaze was lazy and yet intent at the same time, like a cat watching a mousehole.

She felt her face grow warm. She had no doubt that there were any number of things Chase could tempt a woman into doing.

'Maybe another time. What I really want to do is go diving.'

He raised an eyebrow. 'You dive?'

His obvious astonishment made her eyes narrow. 'Yes,

I dive. Not snorkel. Dive.' She pulled out her phone. 'Here. That's my PADI certification.'

'Okay, okay.' He held up his hands, laughing. 'My bad. It's just you don't seem like an outdoorsy kind of a girl.'

'That's because I'm not a girl. I'm a woman with a PADI certificate for open water and enriched air. I just haven't done it in a while. I've been busy with work.' Not true. 'Busy with life.' Also not true.

He stared at her for a long moment and she held his gaze, her pulse jackhammering in her throat. How could a look make her feel like this? He hadn't even touched her and yet there was something in his eyes that made her feel naked and exposed. She could feel it moving through her, not playfully or gently, but fiercely like lava.

Without warning, he shifted back in his seat and got to his feet and she felt a sharp nip of disappointment, pain almost. So that was that, then.

'Dance with me.'

His words, somewhere between an order and an invitation, were so direct, so at odds with what she was expecting him to say that she stared at him in shock, her breath fluttering in her throat as he held out his hand again.

Back in England Holly and Ed both danced with a complete lack of self-consciousness that she admired but had never managed to emulate. But this wasn't really dancing, she realised as he led her onto the dance floor and the shifting crowd swallowed them up. There was not enough room to dance. Instead, people were clutching each other, grinding rhythmically, their closely packed bodies radiating sweat and heat.

As Chase turned to face her, he leaned closer and she felt his warm breath against her ear. 'Is this too much for you?'

Her stomach knotted fiercely. He was too much for

her. Intoxicating like moonshine, she thought as the lights caught the curve of his cheekbone.

Reaching up, she curled her arms around his neck. 'It's not enough,' she said, and his pupils flared and he moved nearer, his hands gripping her waist, anchoring her to him so that she could feel every detail of his body, feel the heat of his skin, the flex of his fingers. Mouth dry, she stared up at him, feeling the air leave her body. She had danced with other men but she had never looked so closely into their eyes, so intently, so intimately. It was fascinating and terrifying in equal measure and she was suddenly desperate to feel his mouth on hers.

They stayed like that for a long time. Finally, the music started to slow and she felt him draw back. 'Let's get some air.'

Outside, the moon was high and silvery in the sky and the cool air made her head and senses swim. It was Chase who broke the silence. 'I'll get Aliana to call you a taxi to take you back to your hotel.'

That was a good idea. Very sensible, she thought. Except she didn't want to be sensible.

You can be anyone you want.

That was what Holly had said, and for one night only she wanted to be wild and passionate and demanding. She wanted to throw caution to the wind. Only if she left now, if she walked away from this beautiful, sexy stranger, she would be just Jemima. Sensible, sedate, sober. Stuck in a rut of failed relationships.

But she didn't want a relationship with this man, she thought dazedly. She wanted sex. Just sweet, mindless sex. Sex without any ties or burdens, without explanations or any kind of data sharing.

Sex. The word fizzed on her tongue. Sex with Chase. Her

heart was hammering in her ears. And why not just sex? Nick might have trampled on her heart but she still had a heartbeat and she wanted it to pound tonight.

She cleared her throat. 'Is that what you want?'

He flexed the fingers of his right hand. For a split second she saw his profile dark against the sky. 'I want what you want.'

'And what do I want?' she said huskily.

His green eyes were almost black in the darkness, and he wasn't smiling. A finger of anticipation and excitement tiptoed down her neck.

'I don't want to put words in your mouth. You have to say it,' he said, the roughness in his voice scraping against her skin. 'You have to make it clear what you want.'

For a moment, neither of them spoke. The music was reverberating through her body. She could feel it low in her belly, joining a different, heavier pulse that was impossible to ignore.

She took a step towards him; in doing so she was saying yes. But it wasn't enough. He was right: she had to say it out loud.

'Okay, then. No questions. No conversation. You don't need to know anything about me and I don't want to know anything about you. All I'm looking for is a one-night stand.' It was what she had promised to do back in England. But she wasn't just doing it for Holly. Now that she was here with this beautiful, sexy stranger, she was doing it for herself. 'I want to get naked with you, now, tonight. Is that clear enough?'

The words sounded so blunt, so explicit. She had never spoken like that to anyone in her life and his slow, hot glance trapped her breath in her throat.

There was a hair's breadth of space between them. Tip-ping back her chin, he stared into her eyes and then his head dipped, his mouth grazed hers and yet there was something fierce beneath it, something hot and dangerous, something that made her melt on the inside. And then he fitted his lips to hers, kissing her hard, a searing kiss, open-mouthed, urgent; a kiss that stole her breath, robbed her of reason, rendered her helpless as he slid one hand around her waist, the other through her hair, his lips and tongue urgent now, his body a hard press against hers.

She arched against him, her hips meeting his, wanting more, skin tingling, blood pulsing hot and fast.

He made her want so much. She could have been anywhere in the world. Truthfully, she could be out in space, drifting among the stars. As soon as his lips had met hers, she was aware of nothing but his kiss.

Pinpricks of light exploded like sparklers inside her head. His desire was so raw, so unfiltered it knocked her off balance, and yet she wanted it all. She wanted him.

His hand dropped from her hair to her collarbone, fingers slipping beneath the dress to find hot, bare skin, making a shivery, tortuous pleasure spiral up inside her. Lips parting, she moaned against his mouth.

He wrenched his mouth from hers, his hands gripping her elbows as she swayed forward. For a moment, he seemed to hesitate, and something rippled over his face—shock, confusion—as when a breeze lifted the surface of a lake, and then it was gone as quickly as it came.

'Let's get out of here,' he said hoarsely.

'And go where?' she whispered, panic mingling with desire.

'Your place. Or mine.'

Her place? She tried to picture Chase in Joan Santos's tiny house. And then there was the morning. How did that work?

'It's probably easier to go to yours.'

He leaned forward and his mouth covered hers again. His eyes were dark, his expression intense. 'My place it is, then.'

He had a motorbike. Of course, he did, she thought as he buckled up her helmet. Leaning onto his strong back, her arms wrapped around his waist, she felt as if she were floating. Blood was beating in her ears and the air streamed past her, dark and cool like water.

His place turned out to be a boat. She waited as he unlocked the gate to the private jetty, and then he took her hand and helped her on board.

Inside, moonlight was streaming through the windows of his cabin. A book lay on the bed, its cover arching up like the roof on a house, and she felt a pinprick of shame at her earlier prejudice, and then she felt his hand in her hair, lifting it away from her neck, and a wall of need slammed through her as his lips found the pulse beating frantically behind her ear.

Dragging in a breath, she turned to face him and kissed him hungrily, her desire making her confident as she realised that with anonymity came mind-blowing freedom.

This was right. This was what she wanted. He was what she wanted. There were no promises to break; no hopes to dash. There was nothing but need—her need for his hard body inside her. A need she saw reflected in those dazzling green eyes.

She ran her hands over his chest, loving the feel of the hard smooth muscles, awed by the difference between them. She could see the hunger in his eyes, the dark flush on his cheekbones. Excitement surged through her and she tugged his shirt over his head, swallowing hard as she saw his bare chest, and the outline of his erection pressing against the fabric of his shorts.

Her mouth was dry; breath trapped in her throat.

She was so ready to start that she was shaking with desire and, hooking her fingers into the waistband of his shorts, she slid them down over his hips.

He sucked in a breath, muscles tensing and, head spinning, she stared at him in silence.

Oh, my goodness.

He was big and hard…very hard.

'Take your clothes off,' he said softly. 'I want to see you naked.'

It was a command, not a request, and the heat in his voice licked at her skin like flame. With hands that shook slightly she undid the belt of her dress and let it slide from her shoulders. His pupils flared but he didn't look away from her face and she kept her eyes trained on his.

Now she undid her bra and dropped it to the floor.

'Stop,' he said hoarsely, and she stood there, her nipples tightening, breasts aching. For a second he stared at her, breathing unsteadily, eyes glittering in the moonlight, face taut with concentration, saying nothing. Just waiting, the electricity between them tangible.

And then she saw his control snap, and he pulled her into his arms, hands palming the swell of her breasts, grazing her taut, aching nipples as he kissed her deeply, thoroughly. She moved against him, arching into the hard press of his erection.

'Yes,' she whispered into his mouth. 'Yes,' she said again as his hands slid down to cup her bottom.

Lifting her slightly, he backed her onto the bed and knelt in front of her. She shivered all the way through as he slid her panties down her thighs. The air was cool against her skin and she felt so bare and her hand moved instinctively to cover herself but he batted it away, his head dipping between her legs.

A moan of pleasure escaped her lips as she felt the tip of his tongue flick against the swollen bud of her clitoris, sending shock waves through her. She shuddered, arching against him, pressing herself closer, wanting more, wanting to answer the seductive, head-spinning ache.

She took a strangled breath, trying to clear her head, to shake the dizziness away, but she was melting into a pool of need. She had never felt anything like this before.

Her head fell back and she clutched at the sheets, her belly clenching, tight and hot. He was teasing her. The tantalising rhythm of his tongue made her think of his body on hers, and in her, and she let go of the sheets and gripped his shoulders, hips arching, a flickering, sharp current of heat surging through her, flooding her limbs.

She felt him move up the bed and then his mouth was hot and damp against hers as he lowered his hips against her pelvis. The press of his erection took her breath away and a shiver of excitement ran through her.

'I want you.' Her fingers wrapped around him and she opened her legs wider.

He grunted. 'Wait—'

He reached past her and yanked open a drawer by the bed. 'Condom,' he said, tearing open the wrapper and sliding it on. Raising himself up, he rubbed the blunt tip between her thighs, stroking back and forth, and then he pushed into her and began to move, slow at first then faster, teasing her still quivering body back to life.

She squirmed against him, not bothering to hold back the moan climbing in her throat, dazzled by the pressure and size of him, muscles tightening on the inside, trying to grip him as he moved against her, his body driving deeper and harder and harder and deeper and then a fierce white heat exploded and she shuddered helplessly beneath him and she felt him tense, his lips brush hers as he groaned her name against her mouth, jerking forward, hips arching as he thrust inside her.

CHAPTER THREE

BLINKING DROWSILY, Jem fluttered her eyes open. It was the light that had woken her, pressing against her eyelids and pulling her from the darkness of sleep. Light from a pale, soft-edged sun, although she had fallen asleep with moonlight streaming through the same window.

She glanced round the boat, body stiffening as her brain tried to make sense of its surroundings, and then she remembered everything. The impossible pressure of Chase's body on her, and how she had shaken with need and eagerness as his hands, his tongue unravelled her into a shuddering, breathless frenzy.

Her face felt warm.

All was calm now.

And she didn't need to remember the impossible pressure of Chase's body because he was there beside her, his arm heavy across her waist. He was still sleeping, his chest and stomach curved around her back, his unshaven cheek nestling against her shoulder.

Chase what?

Her breath caught as she realised that she didn't even know his surname. But then why did she need to know it? She wasn't taking a register. For what she wanted, she didn't need to know his full name.

And it wasn't just his name she didn't know. There were

no words to explain how he had made her feel last night. But it was enough to have done this; to know how his body felt on hers and inside her. To have stretched out beneath his glittering, green gaze, stripped not just of clothes but all inhibition and restraint, with his pulse beating through her.

She felt her body ripple to life and for a fraction of a second she considered rolling over and reaching for him as they had done over and over again in the moonlight, but if she did that then he would wake up and then what?

Her heart began beating a little faster. She had no idea what the etiquette was for the morning after the night before. Should she stay and say goodbye? Was that what people did?

Maybe.

Or maybe there were different rules on holiday. Surely most people got up and left because, like her, they weren't looking for conversation and commitment. She stared out of the window at the steadily rising sun. After all, wasn't that the point of a one-night stand? There was no second act. No finding your true love. Like the fairy godmother's spell, the magic wore off, if not at midnight then soon after. Footmen became mice again. And in this case, a lover would simply turn back into a handsome stranger with whom she had nothing in common except a desire for one passionate encounter.

Her chest was suddenly tight around her heart. In the story, not all the magic wore off: true love triumphed and Cinderella found her happy ever after. But that was just a story, she thought, glancing round the neat but shabby cabin. And Chase was a fisherman, not a prince. As for happy ever afters, maybe they did exist outside fairy tales; for other people, maybe, just not for her.

The sharp cry of a bird outside brought her back to the here and now and she felt a sudden rush of panic. Shifting noiselessly onto her side, she gazed over at the man beside her.

Chase was still asleep, one arm thrown across the pillow, his face in shadow, but there wasn't much time. It was seven-fifteen according to the old-fashioned alarm clock on the bedside table, but in another few minutes the sun would creep across those movie-star features and then he would be rubbing his face and sitting up, his hair ruffled, his green eyes half open and soft.

Her breath caught in her throat, and suddenly she was fighting the wild beating of her heart. He really was a fantasy come to life, and what they had shared had felt like a fantasy too because it was. What made it so intensely erotic was the fact that there was no need for any jarring return to reality. No morning after. No uncomfortable sharing of space. No awkward conversation.

Reaching out, she brushed a strand of hair away from his forehead.

He'd been so generous and she'd felt so alive, so free, so completely without inhibition. She didn't want to ruin the memory of all that by letting reality intrude.

So there's your answer, she told herself. *It's time to leave.*

It was harder than she thought to extract herself from Chase's arm, to abandon the delicious warmth of his body. She dressed, holding her breath, her heart beating in her mouth as Chase shifted in his sleep. Picking up her sandals, she tiptoed to the door, then turned back to the bed.

She was never going to see him again. And yet she would never forget him either. But then she knew that right from the start. She hesitated, torn between panic and her need to be polite. There was an envelope on the bedside table and a pen. She hesitated again, then began writing. Leaning forward, she rested the note on the bedside table and then she turned and crept back out of the cabin and into the pale dawn light.

* * *

'Excuse me, boss.'

Chase swung round, his forehead creasing. 'What is it?'

His first officer, Alex, was standing at his elbow. 'We just got an update on that depression. It looks like it's getting bigger, and it's going to come pretty close.'

'So?' He frowned, his eyes narrowing with poorly concealed irritation. 'We've had closer and bigger storms.'

'Yes, sir.' Alex paused. 'Thank you, sir.'

He felt rather than saw Alex retreat. Behind his back, he could sense the other crew members on the bridge catching each other's eyes and that only added to an irritation he knew was both unfair and disproportionate.

But then he had been tetchy since he stepped foot on the bridge. Not because of the storm. Storms he could handle. What had made him so testy was waking this morning to find his bed empty even though Jemima Friday should never have been in his bed in the first place. Mouth twisting, he replayed the events of the night before. He shouldn't have gone over to talk to her at the Green Door. That was his first mistake. No, his second, he corrected himself. His first was pretending he worked at the Cycle Shack.

He scowled down at the electronic charting display screen, his jaw tightening. So many mistakes, all equally out of character. He didn't sleep with women he met in bars. And the one and only time he'd had one-night stands was right at the very beginning after Frida's death when his grief and guilt were so agonising that it hurt to breathe. He couldn't have coped with affection or intimacy then. He had simply wanted oblivion and the easiest way to achieve that goal was to self-medicate with alcohol. Lots of it. And, to wash it all down, meaningless sex with strangers.

Outside the window, a gull was soaring through the sky.

He had read somewhere that a gull's wing was about as near as nature got to perfection. Hard to disagree with that, he thought as he watched it drift effortlessly on the thermals, noting the more rounded shape of its silver-grey wings. Wings that were almost the same colour as Jemima's eyes.

The gull wheeled away, and he stared at the empty sky.

There had been nothing meaningless about sex with Jemima. On the contrary, even now, hours after he was inside her body, his own body was still twitching with the memory of their fever dream of a sexual encounter.

And hard and aching for a round two that wasn't going to happen.

Only apparently the memo from his brain detailing the one-night status of last night had gone missing en route to his groin.

His fingers twitched against the screen. What the hell had he been thinking? He hadn't needed to approach her at the bar. He could have ignored her.

Should have ignored her and he definitely should never have asked her to dance. And when they went outside, he should have got Aliana to call a cab and sent her back to her hotel. But he hadn't done any of those things.

Instead, he had taken her back to the boat. Not the *Miranda*. At least he hadn't lost his mind completely. For some reason, Jemima thought he was a fisherman and he had seen no reason to disabuse her of that fact, so he'd taken her to the boat he kept down by the shoreline.

He had bought the boat as a favour. It was not worth fixing but he liked to spend a few hours whenever he was on the island just tinkering with it. Or sometimes he would stay up and fish on those nights when he couldn't sleep.

The tension in his body spilled over his shoulders. He hadn't slept much last night. Waking, he had almost thought he had dreamt what happened but then he'd seen the note. It took every ounce of willpower he had not to reach into the pocket of his shorts and pull it out. Not that he needed to. He could remember every word.

Thanks for a wonderful night. Tight lines. J.

Tight lines. He chewed on the words angrily.

He knew the phrase. It was something a fisherman might say to a mate instead of wishing him good luck.

His lip curled as he remembered her insistence that last night be a one-night-only thing. Coupled with her unannounced and unexpectedly precipitous departure this morning, it was clear that Jemima Friday had friend-zoned him. And he didn't know why it should be getting under his skin, but every time he replayed those words inside his head a fresh surge of fury would rise up inside him.

When even was the last time a woman had given him the brush off? He was more accustomed to his dates trying to make what amounted to friends with benefits into something more serious.

Not Jemima.

And much as he disliked admitting it, that annoyed him. She had been so eager and responsive last night. Then again, when they had first met at the Cycle Shack he'd had her down as the shy, sensible type. Only how did that square with the woman he'd met at the Green Door who said she wanted to get naked with him? Heart accelerating, he wondered which Jemima was the real one.

He felt a tic of irritation pulse across his skin.

The only correct answer to that question was who cared? And yet, frustratingly, he found that he did care.

And what made it doubly baffling and frustrating was that she had made him remember how good sex was.

Obviously he'd had sex. It had been eight years since the

accident and he wasn't a monk. But after Frida, sex had been simply an itch to scratch. It was pleasurable, for both parties, but not personal. And yet somehow this woman, this stranger, had changed that, made him want her.

Probably because she had upped and left like Cinderella running from the ball. Only instead of leaving a shoe, she had left that note. Now he reached into his pocket, and he felt his temper stir again as his fingers brushed against it. He knew that if he had woken to find Jemima still in his bed, he would have been desperate to get rid of her. That was how it worked. In the cold light of day, the magic of the previous night faded abruptly. Everything lost its sparkle.

But when he woke she wasn't still in his bed. At some point between when he had pulled her against his drowsy body and the sun rousing him from sleep, she had sneaked out on him, which meant there had been no jolt back to reality.

So now she was stuck in his head, her naked body bathed in moonlight, skin gleaming with perspiration, blonde hair spilling over her shoulders.

His phone vibrated in his other pocket and, grateful for the distraction, he retrieved it and pressed his thumb against the sensor. Reading the text, he felt some of the tension ease from his shoulders. Marcus was not the most eloquent of communicators but at least some things were happening the way they were supposed to. All he needed to do was concentrate on those and soon enough Jemima Friday would turn into Jemima Last Week.

Stepping out of the boutique, Jem slid her sunglasses on and glanced cautiously down the street. But there was no sign of any broad-shouldered man in a red cap.

She hadn't planned to come into Hamilton.

After leaving Chase's boat, she had made her way to the road and had been on the verge of calling Sam to pick her up when a bus arrived. To her astonishment, the driver had been willing to drop her off some two hundred metres from the Green Door. Perhaps it was his unhesitating and cheerful flexibility or maybe it was the infusion of post-orgasm endorphins in her body but, having collected her moped, instead of returning to the beach house she had found herself heading towards the capital.

She glanced down at the glossy rope-handled bag dangling from her hand. She hadn't planned on buying the dress either.

Clothes shopping was something she did under duress. Holly was the shopaholic in the family, but then she had been walking past one of the boutiques on Front Street and she had seen it in the window.

It was not something she would buy ordinarily. For starters it was yellow. And it was short, too boho, and definitely too expensive, but the Jem who had woken that morning was looking for something to match her mood. Something casual and confident. And buying a beautiful dress on a whim was exactly what casual, confident Jem would do.

Feeling unshakeable, she'd walked straight into the shop and asked to try it on and everything had been going fine until it was time to pay and she had started chatting to the woman running the store.

'So how long are you staying in Bermy?'

'Just another week.' She'd smiled. 'Are you a local?'

The woman had nodded. 'Lived here all my life.'

'Any tips for a first-time visitor?'

She had many. Don't buy fruit from the last stall in the marketplace. Church Bay was the best spot for snorkelling. And the best breakfast in town was at Bocado.

'I mean saltfish and banana, not bacon and egg. But you need to jet down there now before the men get back off the boats.'

She had smiled again and thanked the woman but, at the mention of men getting 'back off the boats', casual, confident Jem had melted away like ice cream in direct sunlight.

Feeling nervous and breathless, she walked quickly across the square to where her moped was sitting on its stand. With hands that trembled slightly she packed her shopping into the wicker flower basket. There was no real reason to panic, she told herself. Although Hamilton was not big, the chances of her running into Chase Whatever-His-Name-Was in town had to be slim at best.

But even the possibility of it made her whole body feel taut and achy and restless, as if she had ants under her skin.

By the time she reached the turn-off that led to the beach house some of her panic had subsided and she was calm enough to slow down as she went round the corners. Not that it was necessary. Since arriving she hadn't seen cars.

Her eyes widened with surprise. There were not one, but two pick-ups parked on the edge of the track, the kind driven by builders. She stared at them uncertainly. There were no other houses on this stretch of beach. Maybe they were working further up the beach. But as she approached the house, she saw the door was open and through it she could hear the sound of vigorous hammering. Stepping inside, she almost dropped her bags.

The kitchen was in disarray. The fridge was standing forlornly on the deck next to the old sink. A new sink, still shrink-wrapped in bluish plastic, sat next to it like the before and after shot in a fashion magazine.

'What do you think you're doing?'

The men turned towards her in unison. The surprise and

confusion on their faces were not reassuring. Still clutching her bags, she took a step closer. 'Who are you, and what are you doing in my house?'

The man standing nearest cleared his throat. 'We work for Mr Farrar, ma'am. We're here to do the refurbishment.' He gave her a mollifying smile. 'It's all arranged.'

She shook her head. 'Not with me, it wasn't.'

Reaching into his back pocket, the same man pulled out his phone and scrolled down the screen. 'It's all here. Kitchen and bathroom refurbishment, starting today.'

Bathroom.

She swung round, mouth dropping as she stared into the bathroom or what was left of it. Everything was gone. The sink. The toilet. The shower. All that remained were some pipes sticking forlornly out of the wall.

Breathing shakily, she leaned against the doorframe to steady herself. How was this happening? Not just happening, it had already happened, she thought, her eyes darting around the devastated bathroom again. 'How long will it take to make it good again?'

The man rubbed his hand across his jaw. 'About a week. It's not just the fixtures. A lot of the pipes need replacing.'

'A week.' Jem stared at him in horror. 'And what am I supposed to do?' Her gaze swung back to the bathroom, panic swamping her. She couldn't stay here without a toilet or running water, but she didn't have the money to stay in a hotel or a B & B.

'No, that isn't going to work for me. Look, you're going to have to put it back,' she said firmly.

'Put it back?'

As three men stood and stared at her with a mixture of disbelief and bemusement, the last of her endorphins drained away and she felt suddenly exhausted and exasperated. This was her holiday. She hadn't asked to have the beach house refurbished so why was it suddenly her problem to solve?

'Yes, put it back,' she repeated.

One of the other men shook his head. 'Boss ain't going to like this,' he muttered.

'I don't care what your boss likes or doesn't like,' she said stiffly. 'He is irrelevant.'

'I'm not sure that's either fair or true but I've been called worse.' A deep, oddly familiar voice resonated around the tiny house and they all turned as one towards its owner.

A man was standing in the doorway, sunlight framing his muscular body as if he were some celestial deity come to earth to intervene in mortal matters. *No*, not just a man, Jem thought, shock pounding through her in a clattering drum roll. It was Chase.

She suddenly couldn't breathe. But what was he doing here? She watched dazedly as he shook hands with each of the men before turning towards her. 'Chase Farrar,' he said, his green eyes flicking to her face as if he'd heard her question even though she hadn't asked it. 'I'm the irrelevant boss and your proxy landlord.'

Her heart was banging like a gong. *Farrar*. She'd heard that name before. Her brain lit up like a fruit machine hitting the jackpot. This was Farrar's Cove. But surely it was just a coincidence.

'I don't understand,' she said slowly. 'What does that mean?'

'It means what it says. I'm the landlord, so, as you can see, I am perhaps a little more relevant than you thought.'

There was a slight edge to his voice. But why? He wasn't the one who had come back to find his house being ripped apart by strangers.

She gestured towards the wreckage of the bathroom. 'I can't live like this—'

'Of course not,' he cut her off smoothly. 'But as far as I was aware Ms Santos had made arrangements to stay somewhere else while the work was being done. I only found out she had someone staying here when I emailed her this morning to confirm the schedule of work and she said you were doing a house swap with her.' His eyes locked with hers and her heart thudded hard and she felt something stir inside her, her body betraying her. 'I thought I'd better come over and see how things were going.'

'Well, I don't have a bathroom or a kitchen so I would say they were going badly.' Her voice sounded shrill and she knew that it was revealing more than she wanted about how she was feeling, but she couldn't seem to do anything about it.

She felt a prickle of frustration. It was bad enough that her holiday home was now a building site, but that she had to be dealing with the one man on the island she most wanted to avoid seemed just too unfair, not to say unbelievable, to be true.

And yet here he was.

'I would have to agree with you.'

Chase was staring down at her, his green eyes steady on her face, that mouth of his flickering at one corner. And just like that she remembered how he had kissed her, remembered the feel of his lips on her and the rough urgency of his hands.

Her pulse leaped in her veins and, terrified that he might be able to read her mind, she batted away the memory and lifted her chin. 'Good, then it seems like we're all in agreement.'

The man who had spoken to her before cleared his throat. 'The lady wants us to put it all back, boss.'

She watched as Chase turned towards him and smiled. 'Thanks, Marcus, but I think I can take it from here. Why don't you and the guys take an early lunch while I sort things out with Ms Friday?'

He phrased it as a question, as if it were optional, but there was no mistaking the commanding note in his voice. What had possessed her to think that this man was a simple fisherman? Jem thought as the men shuffled out of the door. As she stood here in the shell of the beach-house kitchen it felt utterly obvious that Chase Farrar was not simply a fisherman. It wasn't just his manner. Now that she looked more closely, she could tell that his boat shoes were not the kind you picked up at the local sailing outfitters. Only she had ignored the signs because that was what she always did.

Like with Nick.

She knew that, beneath his charm and good looks, he was flaky and weak and damaged. But she didn't date regular men who got paid and remembered your birthday and told you the truth about where they'd been.

And in the same way she had sensed that Chase was more than he appeared to be. To anyone else—her sister, for example—that would be a red flag, but she couldn't help herself. The louder the alarm bells, the more she wanted to stay and make things right.

And yet she still felt played. Stupid. Small. Just hours ago it had felt as if she had unlocked a different side of herself with this man. And it had all seemed so real, but just like at the harbour he had been pretending to be someone he wasn't. Her arms tightened around the bags she was holding. Their night together wasn't a moment of truth. It was all a hoax, and now she felt like a fraud.

But she wasn't about to tell Chase that. She had already

shared too much of herself with this man. She wasn't going to let him have anything else.

'Sort things out? And how exactly are you going to do that?' she said sharply. 'Or are you a plumber as well as everything else?'

She was using that voice again, Chase thought, his eyes resting on Jemima's face. The one that reminded him of the principal at his high school. Few, if any, people spoke to him in that way. It was one of the consequences of being a high-net-worth individual: people tended to fawn over him. They certainly didn't use that dismissive tone or look at him as if he were some stray dog who had followed them home.

'I can put you up in a hotel for however long it takes. You don't believe me?' he said coolly as her lip curled.

'The first time we met you pretended to be working at the Cycle Shack, and last night you let me think you were a fisherman, so forgive me if I'm not inclined to believe anything you say.'

Reaching out, he took the bags from her arms and dumped them on what remained of the kitchen counter. 'I fish.'

Her eyes flashed, the grey swallowing up her pupils. 'But you're not a fisherman.'

'And you're not staying in a hotel,' he countered.

Her face stilled. 'I didn't say I was.'

'No, but you let me think you were.'

'That's different.'

He heard the catch in her voice. It was. But it also wasn't.

'Was that even your boat?' she said quietly after a moment of silence.

He frowned. 'Of course it was.'

'There's no "of course" about it.' She glanced past him,

her lip trembling. 'You know what, don't worry about it. I don't need your help. I can sort things out myself. And you, you can go back to living your "lives".' And before he had a chance to open his mouth, she had turned and stalked out of the door.

Staring after her, he felt a ripple of irritation. He wasn't to blame for any of this. In fact, if she'd told him where she was staying he would have been able to postpone the work—again—and then none of this would be happening.

But it was, and somehow he was tangled up in it, tangled up with her.

His heart beat jarringly inside his chest. This wasn't who he was. When it came to dealing with women he never crossed any lines, but Jemima and Joan had made it so that the lines were not just blurred but overlapping. He gritted his teeth. He wasn't responsible.

Or perhaps, in a way, he was. He had seen Jemima in the bar but he could have left her alone. But he hadn't, and one thing had led to another and he'd kissed her. And he could have, should have left it at that, only then she'd kissed him back and he'd been derailed, hot and horny as a teenage boy.

He found her down by the shoreline. She wasn't crying but she was close. He could tell by the set of her shoulders and the way she was staring fixedly out to sea, her phone clutched in her hand. And he didn't like how that made him feel.

But then he didn't like feeling anything at all. For him, feelings, caring for someone, about someone, were in the past. Aside from the most impersonal version of lust, those feelings, like certain kinds of caresses, were something that were off the menu when it came to his interactions with women. He'd shut that part of himself down; he'd had to. He didn't have it in him to take on someone else in that way. Only there was something about Jemima, a wariness in those beautiful grey eyes that he understood. As if she was expecting the ceiling to crack apart and fall on her head. Because it had already done so.

He knew that feeling well.

'Who are you calling?' he said gruffly.

'A hotel. They don't have any rooms.' She breathed out shakily. 'She said that it will be really difficult to find a room because of the boat parade.'

He swore silently. Of course. He'd forgotten it was this weekend. There would be twenty thousand extra visitors on the island.

'So what are you going to do, then?'

She glanced up at him. ''I'm going to do what I should have done in the first place. I'm going to go to the airport and change my ticket and get the first flight back home that I can.'

He frowned. She was leaving?

'You don't need to do that.'

She was shaking her head. 'I knew it was a mistake coming here. This isn't who I am. I should have never let them talk me into it.'

'Hey…' Reaching out, he caught her shoulders and turned her to face him. 'Slow down. Who talked you into what?'

Her lips quivered. 'My brother and sister. They booked this holiday for me as a treat and now it's all ruined.'

The gentlest of breezes was catching her hair and lifting it away from her face and as he studied her profile he felt himself responding, just as he had at the harbour and then again at the bar. He gritted his teeth. But he didn't have to sort this out personally. He had people on the island who could deal with it. He had people all around the globe to deal with the slightest hiccup in his life, and yet…

'It's not ruined, and you shouldn't go back home. You'll regret it if you do and there's no reason for you to do so.'

She sniffed. 'That's easy for you to say. You're not living on a building site.'

'And you won't be either. Look, this is just one of those things that happen sometimes. But it's my builders who ripped a hole in your beach house and your holiday.'

He hesitated. 'So let me help you.'

'Help me how?'

'I have a house here. Not on the main island, on one of the smaller ones.' She stared up at him, her eyes wide with shock and confusion as if she couldn't believe what he was saying, and that made two of them because he couldn't quite believe it either. But now that he had said it, he felt a complete and total conviction that it was the only option.

'I know what you're thinking but you don't need to worry about me being there. I'm taking the boat out tonight and I won't be back for a good few days, so you can stay there until the work is done.'

Her belly clenched as he stared down into her pale, wary face. 'Unless that's going to cause a problem with your boyfriend.'

'I don't have a boyfriend.' She glanced past him to where the waves were rolling against the sand. 'I don't do relationships.'

He stared at her profile, saying nothing, wondering why that statement both pleased and agitated him. 'I don't do them either so go and get your bag packed because you're coming with me,' he said finally. 'And I'm not taking no for an answer.'

CHAPTER FOUR

DUSK WAS FALLING.

Eyes narrowing, Jemima gazed across the water. It wasn't just the sky that was darkening, the sea was now the colour of new denim except where a dark orange line bled into the horizon.

The speedboat was hugging the coastline of the island, which she had since learned was not an island at all but an archipelago made up of around one hundred and twenty islands. The main island itself was actually eight smaller islands linked by bridges.

But then in her experience things were so rarely what they seemed. Situations, actions and people could all confuse and deceive.

Her pulse darted forward in time to the slap of the waves against the hull. Take Chase Farrar, for example. He was a man who fished but most definitely wasn't a fisherman. And yet this was his glossy, high-spec speedboat that was scudding across the waves with smooth, expensive purpose. His hands were calloused and rough like a working man's but he had that backbeat of authority in his voice that made people stand up straighter and listen.

And apparently he owned an island. Her gaze fixed on the fast-approaching curve of pink sand that was just about visible in the fading light. This island: Bowen's Cay.

Her throat tightened. He had told her that as she got into the speedboat and she still couldn't quite believe it. But maybe land was cheaper out here.

Flashes of panic at the prospect of staying in Chase's house made her skin shiver. Although given that he wasn't going to be staying, this was probably the riskiest part of their time together. Which was why she was keeping her gaze firmly averted from the man driving the speedboat.

Unfortunately she didn't need to see Chase to be aware of him. She was unnecessarily attuned to his every move. Sometimes she got so distracted she forgot to breathe.

A light offshore breeze was whipping through her hair and she was grateful for the additional oxygen as she wondered, not for the first time, if she'd made the right decision agreeing to stay in his home.

Should she have kept trying to find alternative accommodation? Maybe. But she could tell from the receptionist's voice that she was highly unlikely to find a room at such short notice. She could have listened to her gut and seen it as a sign that she wasn't meant to be here at all. And a part of her had really wanted to scuttle back to England to the safety of her own, tiny cottage.

Only then she had looked up into his eyes and remembered how she had scuttled back into the beach house when he'd interrupted her skinny dip and she'd felt ashamed of herself, of her fear and her timidity.

And in that moment she had known that if she went back to England she would always be that timid, fearful person.

Besides, going back to England would mean having to see Holly's disappointed face and Ed's despairing one. In comparison, Chase's offer seemed like a blissfully straightforward solution to her problem, a problem that was at least some of his making. After all, it was his men who had turned her idyllic holiday home into a building site.

Her heart thumped against her ribs. This wasn't some Faustian pact. And it would only be for a week at most and it wasn't as if he were even going to be there.

She felt the boat slow and glanced up, her throat tightening as Chase switched off the engine. A tall man wearing Bermuda shorts and a polo shirt stepped forward and deftly caught the prow of the boat. A slim, dark-haired woman in similar clothes stood beside him, smiling.

'Good evening, Mr Farrar. Welcome home.'

She watched Chase step onto the jetty with the same casual grace with which he did everything and then nearly jumped out of her skin as his hand clamped around her elbow. 'Here, let me help you.'

He was just being polite, she told herself, but as he released his grip, she took a quick step sideways, her hands curling into fists to stop herself from rubbing the place where his fingers touched her skin.

'This is Ms Friday. She'll be staying at the house. Jemima, this is Robyn and Troy. They will be looking after you.'

'A pleasure to meet you, Ms Friday.' Troy smiled. 'I hope you enjoy your stay.'

'Thank you.'

Troy glanced up at the sky.

'It's going to be a close thing tonight, boss.'

Chase nodded. 'I reckon so.'

'The house is just up here.' As they walked along the path it lit up ahead of them like a landing strip. Which was both impressive and lucky, she thought, glancing up at the sky. It must be cloudy because there were no stars tonight. It made the sky feel closer somehow, the sea too.

She shivered, the butterflies back in her stomach again,

and then quite suddenly the house appeared out of the lush tropical vegetation. It was, she decided, more a hideaway than a house. A piece of treasure plucked from the seabed cupped in a hand.

There were a couple of steps leading up to a wide wooden veranda and Jemima followed him cautiously inside. 'I'll give you a quick tour of the house,' he said, turning to give her one of those blink-and-you-miss-it smiles.

He wasn't kidding, she thought as Chase walked swiftly through the house, opening doors and rattling off the names of the rooms. There was an urgency to the tour, as if he had somewhere he'd rather be, which he did, she reminded herself. But it was the coolness of his manner that was getting under her skin.

Irritated by the sheer stupidity of that thought, she turned her attention to the house.

Here, unlike on the main island, there were no pastels, no eye-popping candy colour. Instead, the decor was understated and masculine, a luxurious mix of wooden floors, pale walls and architectural-looking furniture. The lighting was soft and unobtrusive like a harvest moon.

'And this will be your room,' he said abruptly as she followed him upstairs and through yet another door.

'It's lovely,' she said, because it was. Her eyes moved appreciatively from the curved rattan bed with its white voile curtains to a vase of delicate pale green orchids.

'There's a dressing room through there.' He indicated another door. 'For when you want to unpack.'

She glanced back over to where her bags were sitting neatly by the bed.

The bed.

It had been turned down, one corner of the duvet folded back invitingly to reveal a smooth white sheet, and her cheeks grew warm as she remembered the tangle of sheets on the bed on Chase's boat and the contours of his body as they melted into one another.

She could feel his level gaze raking her face, and, needing to get away from him and the bed, she turned towards a second door and said quickly, 'What's in here?'

It was the bathroom. A very beautiful bathroom with a free-standing marble bath and a walk-in shower that could happily fit a football team. There was a selection of toiletries in matt, metallic tins and she picked one up, her eyes widening as she read the list of ingredients. White clay. *Camu-camu*—whatever that was. Orange flower water. Vetiver and passion-fruit oils.

'It's there to be used, so help yourself to anything you want.'

Her chin jerked upwards, and she blinked. Chase was standing behind her, his gaze resting on her reflection. In this light, the irises were the colour of the pine forests at home and she felt a mix of hunger and homesickness so intense that her belly clenched painfully.

'Thank you.' Dropping her gaze, she put the tin down carefully as if it were a newly laid egg. He was so close she could feel the warmth of his body, and the scent of his skin, his scent, enveloped her. As she breathed it in, her eyes met his reflection again and she felt fingers of heat low in her belly, impossible to ignore.

He was doing this to her, she thought, fighting panic. He was making her feel all hot and confused and on edge. But how? They barely knew each other. And yet with him, she felt she knew herself better. Which was crazy and utterly illogical.

'Are you hungry?' he asked, breaking the taut silence.

Yes: but not for food.

The knots inside her tightened. It was a small consolation that she hadn't said it out loud but something in his eyes made her think that he had heard her unspoken thoughts.

She shook her head. 'No, I'm actually quite tired. It's been a long day. I might call it a night.'

Night.

The word whispered between them, conjuring up darkness and the white heat of his skin in the moonlight, and for a moment neither of them spoke, and then he nodded. 'Good idea. I need to speak to Robyn and then I'll be heading back to the boat. Enjoy the rest of your holiday. I'll get someone to let you know when you can get back into the beach house.' He hesitated, a muscle flickering in his jaw, and she felt a tremor ripple through her as his green gaze roamed her face.

'Get some sleep, Jemima,' he said softly, and then he turned and strode back the way they had come.

Was that it?

She stared around the empty bathroom feeling oddly disappointed by his sudden departure. Which was ridiculous as she'd not even said goodbye to him this morning.

Her heartbeat stalled against her ribs. Was it only this morning? It felt like a lifetime ago. No wonder she was feeling so thrown. But it wasn't just the timescale that was messing with her head. Less than twenty-four hours ago they had been tearing each other's clothes off in a frenzy of passion and need. Now he was talking to her as if she were a guest at his hotel. The distance between them was putting her teeth on edge.

In the bathroom, she glanced at the bath, then the shower. But she could wait until tomorrow. For some reason she felt oddly shy about getting undressed when Chase was in the house, which was also ridiculous given that he had already seen her naked. And not just seen her. He had touched her too.

She screwed up her face, irritated to find Chase Farrar back in her head again. He wasn't supposed to be there but, probably because she was in his house, every thought she had seemed to lead inexorably to him.

But only if you let it, she told herself crossly. She brushed her teeth without looking in the mirror and then forced herself to undress slowly. Pulling on an oversized T-shirt, she climbed into bed.

It was like climbing onto a cloud. Or what she imagined it might feel like climbing onto a cloud. Soft and cocooning yet also inexplicably light. And yet she couldn't fall asleep.

Shifting onto her side, she shivered all the way through. She knew why. Being here in Chase's house was obviously going to be unsettling. But if she wasn't going to let him back into bed with her, she was damned if she was going to let him back into her head. It must be the waves keeping her awake, she told herself firmly. She could hear them through the window and they sounded louder than last night, heavier almost. But perhaps this particular island was more exposed.

She must have fallen asleep at some point because she woke with a jolt, her heart hammering against her ribs. Rolling over, she found her phone and clicked on the screen. It was not even ten o'clock. She lay there in the darkness for a few moments, but this had happened so many times in the past she knew there was no point in just lying there.

It was better to get up and get a cup of camomile tea and read a book than watch the clock mark the hour and half-hour until dawn. And if Robyn wasn't up, she could easily sort herself out.

The house itself was silent but the sound of the wind and the waves accompanied her as she made her way downstairs. She was using the torch on her phone to guide her but everything felt different in the darkness and the sound of her feet moving lightly across the smooth floorboards made her feel like an intruder, not a guest.

Wishing she could switch on the lights, she tiptoed into the living room only to realise that it wasn't necessary. Eyes widening, she stopped to gaze through the huge floor-to-ceiling windows that covered three sides of the room.

There was a storm out at sea. High above the white-capped waves the lightning was criss-crossing the night sky, flickering between the dark, scudding clouds like a strobe light at a rock concert.

'Impressive, isn't it?'

The voice caught her by surprise, and, startled, she spun round. Her stomach did a tiny, clumsy somersault. Chase was sprawled out on the sofa, his green eyes gleaming cat-like in the shadows, a laptop half open on the coffee table beside him.

'It's amazing,' she agreed, pressing her hand against a nearby armchair to steady herself. What was he doing up? Why did he have to be here now?

His gaze skimmed lightly across her oversized T-shirt, and her body reacted, the hair on her arms prickling to attention, her breasts suddenly heavy against the light cotton fabric. He had changed clothes too. Now he was wearing grey sweatpants and a black T-shirt, and his hair looked tousled as if he'd been sleeping. Actually he looked like an invitation to sin, she thought, her heart jumping in her throat as he sat up and stretched, his T-shirt tightening around his contoured chest.

But just because she'd played with fire and not got burnt, didn't mean that she should stir the embers, and, hoping that none of what she was thinking was visible on her face, she said, 'I thought you were going back to your boat.'

He shrugged. 'Storm came in bigger and closer and faster than predicted so I decided to wait until morning and catch up on my emails instead.' He gestured towards the laptop. 'That's the great thing about the modern world: someone's always at work somewhere.'

His green eyes found hers and, needing distance from that too intense gaze, she took a step backwards. 'I'm sorry, I didn't mean to disturb you.'

Chase stared at Jemima in silence, his whole body tensing.

It was a bit late for that, he thought. The storm might have stopped him from getting back to the *Miranda*, but Jemima was the reason he was wide awake, lying on this sofa, pretending to read his emails. Apparently knowing that she was lying in bed in the same house as him was a green light for his imagination so that his head was full to bursting with feverish images of her.

And that was before she'd come tiptoeing into the living room wearing nothing but a T-shirt. It was shapeless and so oversized that it would be impossible to guess at what lay beneath. Unfortunately, he didn't need to guess.

'You didn't.'

Although she had. 'I was just watching the fireworks.' He gestured towards where lightning was still forking through the clouds accompanied by a distant growl of thunder. 'Did they wake you?'

She shook her head. 'I don't think so. I think it's just being in another different bed.' There was a short silence as her eyes juddered across the space between them to meet his, then flicked away, and he noticed a blush creeping up her neck and into her cheeks.

And just like before, he found that he couldn't look away. He cleared his throat.

'No, it's fine,' she said quickly. 'I just thought I might make myself a cup of herbal tea but it's really not that important.'

'Help yourself. The kitchen's through there.'

Leaning forward, Chase reached for his laptop. 'Or I could just show you,' he said, shutting it firmly even though he had definitely been intending to check the weather forecasts again when he'd picked it up.

And yet here he was standing up and walking into the kitchen because he wasn't sure if she would take him up on his offer and then she would leave, and he didn't think he wanted that. Although it was difficult to know why he wanted her to stay, but, truthfully, wanting someone, wanting her, was such a rarity for him at this point in his life that he was as fascinated by it as he had been by that blush.

In the kitchen, he dumped his laptop on the counter and switched on the lights. 'Take a seat,' he said, directing her to the stools nestling around the breakfast bar, and stared assessingly at the bank of pale oak cupboards.

'What would you like?' He pulled open a cupboard, stared at the contents and then tried another. Then another, and another.

'Do you want me to help?'

'No…actually, yes, I have no idea where anything is,' he admitted, opening another cupboard and staring at the jars of various kinds of rice. 'Mostly Robyn fixes things for me.'

He caught a flash of grey as her eyes clashed momentarily with his and then she leaned forward to open one of the drawers and he forgot all about her eyes as the hem of her T-shirt hitched up to reveal the backs of her thighs.

His body stilled.

It was all too easy to remember those same thighs wrapped around his hips in the moonlight as she lifted her body to meet his. That night that had ended too soon, only now she was here. In his house. In that T-shirt that wasn't designed to arouse in any way. And yet...

He clenched his hands tight, then tighter still so that he had something to focus on other than the ache in his groin, and, back in control, he turned and yanked open another drawer. Thank goodness! 'Here we go.' He stared down with relief at the carefully organised rows of tea. 'We have peppermint, ginger and turmeric, camomile, lavender and valerian root. I'm going to keep going until you pick one.'

She cleared her throat. 'Camomile would be lovely.'

During the time it took to fill the teapot with boiling water, she watched him while appearing not to, in the same way that an antelope would watch a dozing leopard.

'Are you not having one?' she said as he put the teapot on the breakfast bar and handed her a cup and saucer.

He shook his head. 'I'm not a fan. But I might grab something to eat. Why don't you join me?' Without asking, he picked up the teapot and filled her cup. He didn't know if she wanted to drink it now but it was something to do while he waited for his brain to offer up an explanation as to why that was a good idea.

It was just politeness, he reassured himself. But his invitation echoed inside his head just like at the beach when he had asked her, in a roundabout way, if she had a boyfriend.

He couldn't remember the last time he'd blushed but he felt his skin grow warm now. Jemima's life back in England was none of his business and yet, inexplicably, he had wanted to be sure she was single.

She was shaking her head. 'I'm not hungry.' But as she spoke, her stomach gave an audible rumble and she bit into her lip, and as their eyes met he felt a rush of triumph as she tried and failed to stop her mouth curving at the corners.

'Well, maybe I am a little bit,' she conceded.

'You're in luck,' he said, opening the huge larder fridge. 'This is one of Robyn's specialities.'

'What is it?' She looked down at the bowl he had put in front of her.

'It's a *poke* bowl.'

Watching the flicker of curiosity in her grey eyes reminded him of the clear waters of Lake Superior where he grew up. Of fishing with his father and cook-outs with his cousins. Back then he had been a different person. Back then he hadn't known what the world had in store for him. He was young and naive. He didn't know how quickly things could end or how badly. He didn't know then that there was a pain that could drag you down and leave you gasping for breath beyond the reach of the sun.

His chest tightened. Over time, the scars had healed, hardened and now he didn't have to worry about feeling pain. He didn't have to worry about feeling anything. Nothing except basic needs. Thirst. Hunger. Desire. But they could all be contained.

'Robyn comes from Hawaii. *Poke* is practically the national dish out there. Basically it's meat and fish and vegetables and fruit chopped up into tiny pieces. That's what *poke* means in Hawaiian—to chop up.'

She stared down at the neatly chopped rainbow arrangement of rice, beetroot, edamame and avocado. 'It's so pretty.'

'And delicious.' He held out a fork. 'Here, eat.' She did, and he watched with some amusement as she sampled each of the various components.

'Good?'

She nodded. 'The flavours are incredible.'

They were. And he'd thought he was hungry, but weirdly

he found that his appetite seemed to have disappeared, so that it was a struggle to even lift the fork to his mouth.

'So do you come from Hawaii too?'

He glanced across the table, momentarily caught off guard, not so much by her actual question but by her sudden trespass into the personal. Most of the women he knew didn't ask him much about himself. But then most of the women knew all they needed to know.

'No, I come from Minnesota, from a small town near Lake Superior. And you?'

She hesitated. 'A village in the Peak District.'

Shifting back on the stool, he held her gaze. 'We have something in common,' he said softly. 'Except I left and you stayed.'

Now she frowned. 'I didn't come from Edale. I was born in Sweden, and then I lived in Ireland. I didn't move to England until I was four.'

'Why Sweden?'

She shrugged. 'My mother is Swedish.'

That explained the colour of her hair. As his gaze touched her head, he remembered how the silken strands had felt in his hands.

'And what about your dad?'

'English.'

She didn't blush this time, but she glanced away as if she didn't want him to see her eyes and he knew that she was hiding something. Holding something back. He couldn't see the barricades she'd raised between them, but he could sense them. So that was another thing they had in common.

He watched her chew on her lip. He shouldn't care, and yet he found himself wanting to prise her apart like an oyster.

'You didn't say what you do back in England, job-wise I

mean,' he said at last. But then the last time they met, neither of them had been interested in small talk. There was a silence as both of them separately acknowledged that fact.

She cleared her throat. 'It didn't come up.'

He met her gaze. 'No, I suppose it didn't,' he said softly.

A faint flush suffused her cheeks. For a few seconds, she didn't reply and then finally she put down her fork. 'I don't really have a job. I help out in the university bookshop and sometimes I do a bit of tutoring but I'm actually working on my PhD.' She looked up at him almost defiantly as if he might challenge her. 'It's on "accidental" reefs.'

The phrase was familiar but not in any detail. 'And what does that mean, exactly?' He was interested.

Jemima hesitated. 'I suppose in layman's terms it's when a wreck becomes a reef. Basically from the moment a vessel sinks the ocean takes over. It starts to form a new underwater habitat. Over time, fish colonise the wreck. Algae and corals grow on the surface and the currents draw in clouds of plankton, which attract fish, which in turn entice sharks and other larger predators. Eels and groupers move into the darker spaces. The wreck creates a whole new ecosystem.'

He stared over at her, captivated by the light in her eyes. 'Why "accidental reefs"?'

'I did a degree and a masters in ecology, and one of my lecturers had a lot of bottom time. He got me interested but it was my sister who badgered me into doing the PhD.' She gave him a small, careful smile. 'She's a force of nature. My brother is too.'

It was a habit of hers, he'd noticed, to introduce her siblings into the conversation when things got too personal and he found himself wondering why she used them as a shield.

'I thought the general consensus was that wrecks are a menace, even some of the older ones.'

He was interested enough in the topic but it was Jemima herself who was holding his attention. She listened, an unusual enough quality in itself. But she was also assessing and evaluating what he said, whereas most people tended to value only their own viewpoint. No wonder she was doing a PhD.

'There's been a lot of research done on the negative impacts,' she admitted. 'You know, pollution from leaking fuel and rust particles. But wrecks exist. It's important to find a way to live with the negative.'

'Don't make perfect the enemy of the good,' he said softly.

Another blush. 'Exactly. You can't change the past, you have to improve on it. That's why I'm interested in the positives.'

'Which are?'

Watching her forehead crease, he found himself fighting the urge to reach over and smooth her forehead with his thumb.

'For starters, it protects the natural reefs from divers, particularly where tourism relies on diving trips.'

He nodded, and as he did so he realised something. He had been tense for weeks. It was always like that in the run-up to the anniversary of his wife's death. His body seemed to clench in on itself. He lost his appetite and his nights were interrupted with tangled, febrile dreams, but, listening to Jemima talk, he felt as if she had laid a cool hand against his forehead.

'And in the future as ocean temperatures rise, artificial reefs can help certain marine species migrate towards more suitable habitats nearer the poles. Anyway—' she cleared her throat '—that's enough about me, what about you? What's your job?'

His eyes held hers. 'Is that how this works? You show me yours and I'll show you mine?'

A drop of pink spread slowly across her cheekbones. 'It seems only fair.'

Fair. Shifting in his chair, he felt his throat tighten. That she still wanted, expected things to be fair made him feel suddenly protective of her. And grateful that she had never experienced the loss and loneliness and grief that he had.

'I'm in insurance. Reinsurance, mostly.'

'Is that a joke?' She stared at him, her grey eyes narrowing in disbelief.

'No. I set up my own business about ten years ago.' Holding her gaze, he smiled. 'Although I do know some pretty good insurance jokes if you're interested. The one involving an actuary and the magic lamp is my favourite.'

'Maybe another time.' She gave him another of those measured stares. 'So your boat is just for leisure?'

He felt his ego protest at that assessment. 'Not leisure, sweetheart,' he said, shaking his head. 'Treasure.'

'Treasure?' she echoed softly, and, watching her lips soften around the word, he had a near ungovernable desire to lean forward and taste her surprise.

'When I want to relax I come down to Bermuda and look for treasure.' Turning round, he reached for his laptop. 'I start by looking for shipwrecks. That's why I have a house here.'

It wasn't quite as simple as that.

After the accident, he had wanted to stay down in the void that was his pain. It had felt as if there were nothing else. His parents, his friends had all tried to help him with his grief, but he hadn't wanted their help. He had wanted to be alone. It was what he deserved and so he had hired a boat from Beaufort in North Carolina and taken it out in bad weather that got worse. Got dangerous.

He had grown up on the shores of the biggest lake in North America. Sailing was not just a hobby, it was part of everyday life, like cereal for breakfast, so that he couldn't remember ever learning how to sail. It was just something he did, like walking. And he was a good sailor, but that day was the closest he ever came to losing control of a boat.

He spent two days wrestling with the sea, barely sleeping, raging at the wind and the waves. On the morning of the third day, the storm blew out. Checking his phone, he read through the increasingly panicky texts from what looked like his entire contacts list. And in that moment of exhaustion and reprieve, he realised that he couldn't just give up. That he had no choice but to keep moving forward. That if he gave up then he would pass the baton of misery on to them.

As the sun had risen and flooded the sky with a thin golden light he had seen Bermuda for the first time, and he had felt a kind of kinship with the island. Like him, it weathered the storms of life, and like Bermuda he would have to be separate and alone.

It had to be that way. He wouldn't, he couldn't do it again. He couldn't care, feel, need…

Opposite him, Jemima tucked a strand of hair behind her ear and he remembered its glossy weight and how it had suggested all manner of possibilities to him.

Impossibilities, he told himself firmly, flipping open his laptop.

'Because Bermuda has more shipwrecks per square mile than any other place on the planet,' she said slowly.

He nodded. 'That's what they say.'

'And you look for them.'

Tapping the keyboard, he nodded. 'That's exactly what I do. Whenever I can, I come down to Bermy and go looking for wrecks. Like this one.'

She glanced at the screen, her eyes widening.

'That was our last big find. It's a Spanish boat, from a convoy that sank in October 1715.' He clicked through the photos, talking her through the artefacts, but instead of looking at the screen, he found himself watching Jemima's face. She listened with her whole body, he thought, and, gazing down at the curve of her breasts, he felt his own body harden, and for a few pulsing seconds he considered pushing the laptop off the breakfast bar and lifting her onto it and seeing what happened.

'Doesn't it damage the wreck?'

She was looking straight into his eyes, and, caught off balance between the eager, responsive woman in his head and the reality frowning up at him, he was harsher than he intended to be. 'It's a wreck, Jemima. The clue's in the name.'

'Yes, but there's a whole community of marine life there.' She pointed at the screen and the disappointment in her voice snagged on his skin. Most women purred with excitement when they found out he looked for treasure, but Jemima was making him feel like a jerk.

'And we work around it. Look, I've done it all. Base jumping. Free climbing. White-water rafting. This is the biggest rush.'

'So that's all it is for you? An adrenaline rush.'

Watching her mouth flatten, he felt the starkness of her words stick in his throat as he shrugged. 'Adrenaline is good for you. It can block pain. Help you breathe. Improve your sight, boost your immune system.' Intensify your pleasure, he thought silently as she stared up at him.

'But there's so much more to it than that,' she said quietly.

For the second time in as many less than five minutes, his ego rebelled against her dismissive tone. He could have told her that he employed a team of marine archaeologists, and that Farrar Exploration was committed to displaying the finds in museums. He could have told that, after years of working punishing hours to build a global business worth billions, he had earned the right to take three months off every year to comb the ocean for its secrets. But why should he have to defend himself to some snarky little student eco-warrior? This wasn't some college debate.

'More than what?'

'Short-term pleasure.'

'There's nothing wrong with short-term pleasure,' he said softly.

He watched, waited and, sure enough, her cheeks turned pink.

'I didn't say there was,' she said stiffly. 'I just don't think that the ocean is there to be plundered for thrills.'

'Thrills make money. And money makes the world go round.'

'You're very cynical.'

'And you're very naive.'

'I'm not naive.' Outrage shone out of her eyes. 'I just think it would be so much better if we all concentrated our efforts on something other than satisfying our own transitory, selfish agendas. Because the world is doing its best to sustain us, but it needs our help.'

Her face was flushed and she looked a little stunned by her outburst, and he felt ashamed suddenly of how jaded he must seem and he might have even told her so if she hadn't suddenly slid off the stool. 'Thank you for the food. I'll be sure to tell Robyn how delicious it was. I'll let you get back to your emails.'

'I'll see you at breakfast.' He got to his feet too and suddenly they were both standing, and close enough that he could see her pulse beating in her throat. For a moment, they stared at one another, and then she blinked.

'I don't really eat breakfast.'

'That's a shame. Robyn does the most fantastic croissants.'

He thought for a moment that she was going to tell him where to put his croissants, but instead, she said, 'Goodnight,' in that absurdly stiff principal's voice and stalked out of the kitchen.

The sudden silence in the empty kitchen made his shoulders tighten and he put his hand over his heart, feeling it beating out of time. Watching her face light up with that flare of passion reminded him of how she had caught fire in his arms. She might have left that morning, but he hadn't been able to forget that night, and now he pictured her mouth, pink and swollen from his kisses, her blonde hair tangled against the pillow.

The air twitched around him. In that moment they had felt so close, so connected, but that was the trick sex played on people. Away from the unravelling heat of the bedroom, he and Jemima were not just different, they were poles apart. She thought the world was benign and that you could work with it to make things better, whereas he knew that life was dangerous and cruel and random, and you had to be constantly vigilant to counteract that threat.

In other words, he and Jemima had nothing to offer one another except on one level. But he could resist her. After what he'd been through, he had no doubt of that.

The trouble was he wasn't sure he wanted to.

CHAPTER FIVE

OPENING HER EYES, Jemima stared confusedly around the darkened bedroom. But then it wasn't that surprising to feel a little disoriented given that she was waking in her third different bed in as many nights.

And she hadn't slept well mainly because despite having said goodnight to Chase Farrar in the kitchen, he had stayed stubbornly inside her head. Only in her head, she had kept her cool instead of blushing and getting all worked up.

She bit into her lip. She never should have said anything. It was none of her business what he did or why he did it. But watching his eyes narrow on some unseen prize at the bottom of the ocean had made her realise that the only difference between Chase and all the other men she'd ever dated was that, rather than needing alcohol or gambling, he was a thrill-seeker, a man addicted to the adrenaline rush of diving for treasure.

In other words, instead of breaking the bad habits of the past as she'd promised, she was simply repeating them.

That was why she had reacted as she had. It was a shock hearing him talk in that way because she had thought he was different from all the other men she had fallen for. But it turned out that she had simply proved her sister's theory that she was only attracted to sexy but ultimately unreliable addicts.

Feeling a rush of exasperation with both the old and the new Jemima, she rolled out of bed and padded into the bathroom. What she needed was a shower and, peeling off her T-shirt, she stepped under the water, turning the temperature up until it was punchingly hot.

Closing her eyes, she tipped back her head so that the water ran down her back, turning slowly on the spot. It felt good. Fight fire with fire, she told herself as the heat pierced her skin. And that was what she needed to do now: fight this crazy pull of attraction she felt for Chase.

Her skin was tingling now and she switched off the water and wrapped herself in a cloud-soft white towel, and then, bending over, she wrapped another towel around her wet hair to form a turban. Straightening, she stared at her reflection in the mirror, her pulse shivering as she remembered his green eyes, that flicker of heat.

She had felt it again last night in the kitchen. Low in her belly, impossible to ignore.

Her fingers trembled against the towel. It was crazy to feel like this about someone she hardly knew. What was even crazier was how close she had come to kissing him again last night. She looked at her reflection again, depressed by the colour in her cheeks and the glitter in her eyes. But there was no point in pretending. She had wanted him.

Wanted to touch him and be touched. Wanted his hands to slide over her body.

And then what?

She stared at her reflection angrily. Did she really want to have sex with Chase Farrar again?

Her body felt suddenly hot and tight. Yes, she thought, remembering the friction of his skin against hers. A thousand times yes. But things were already way more complicated than they were supposed to be. And it didn't matter that his touch had melted her with its heat. In fact that by itself was a reason to keep her distance. Chase was a fantasy. Or rather the man who had ordered her to strip naked, the man who made her body feel like a living work of art, was a fantasy. The reality was that he was as addicted to 'thrills' as Nick was to alcohol.

Not that it mattered because she was done with men like him. Done with obsessing about how to decipher their complicated, conflicted lives.

It was better that he stayed as a beautiful memory, she told herself. Only it was difficult when she was living under his roof, sharing a meal with him.

Walking back into the bedroom, she opened the curtains. Her eyes widened. The sky was the warm gold of a ripe peach. The storm had gone. And soon Chase would be gone too. All she had to do was stay strong until then.

There was nobody in the kitchen but she could smell the warm scent of freshly cooked pastry. Outside, she found the source of the smell. A plate of croissants, steam spiralling up from their crisp golden outer shells. Beside them sat another plate of beautifully sliced fresh fruit and a bowl of what looked like Bircher muesli. But it wasn't just the food that looked so appetising. The table was set with a creaseless white tablecloth and fine, white china.

It looked nothing like her own table at home with its circular stains from Ed's coffee mugs and all her mismatched crockery. Fantasy versus reality, she thought, walking away from the table to the Perspex balustrade that edged the deck, her eyes leapfrogging across the curve of pink sand to the shimmering turquoise water.

Slipping off her glasses, she rubbed them against the hem of her blouse but there was no sign of last night's storm. If she hadn't seen it with her own eyes she might have thought that it was just a dream. Only a slight ripple on the surface of the ocean.

What the...?

She blinked as Chase emerged from the waves, rearing up like some kind of mythical sea god, his blond hair slicked back against his skull. He had his back to her and she stared at the water trickling down his shoulders, her heart pounding inside her chest.

It was one thing having dinner in her T-shirt... It was another to eat breakfast sitting opposite that. She took an unsteady step backwards.

There was an audible crash as her leg collided with the table, the sound snapping around the quiet cove like a gunshot, and she froze as Chase's chin jerked up and he spun round to face her. He'd said he was in insurance, she thought, her mouth drying as his eyes locked onto her with the precision of a sniper. She couldn't imagine why he would lie about that, and to be fair she hadn't met that many insurance brokers, but it was hard to imagine any of them looking like the man standing in the sea like a temptingly masculine riposte to Botticelli's *The Birth of Venus*.

For a moment they just stared at one another and then he started to wade back through the water with slow, strong strides.

But not slow enough, she thought as he came to a stop in front of her moments later. 'Good morning,' he said softly. 'I didn't know you were up.'

'Good morning.' She gave him a small, tight smile, keeping her gaze firmly locked on his face as he pulled a T-shirt over his head. 'I think breakfast is ready,' she said unnecessarily as he could see the table too. But there was something about this man that made her say stupid, unnecessary things.

And made her act on impulses she didn't even know she had.

It was easier once they were both seated and he was no longer shirtless to eat and talk. Their conversation was insubstantial, partly because Robyn appeared at intervals to replenish her coffee and clear away their plates, but also because after last night it seemed wiser to stick to banalities. It also gave her a chance to admire the house.

The design was less colonial than the typical Bermudian house. Instead it seemed to take its cue from one of those hill towns in Italy. The large deck where they were sitting acted as a kind of piazza, with the living area housed in an adjacent bungalow. Two separate bungalows perched above it, angled away from one another to create privacy and provide access to views.

'What are your plans for today?'

Chase's voice pulled her back into the moment and she turned, smiling stiffly. 'I don't know. I haven't really thought about it but don't let me keep you.'

There was a beat of silence and he leaned back in his chair, his eyes narrowing against the sunlight. 'I'm taking the boats out into open water. The ocean opens up its secrets after a big storm so it's a good time to go hunting.'

She nodded. 'So I've heard.'

When she was about four years old her parents had moved to the west of Ireland. After a storm, people used to go down to the beach at Streedagh to look for gold because rumour had it that when the Spanish Armada retreated, some of the boats got separated from the fleet and they ended up being smashed on the rocks off the coast there.

They hadn't lived there long. The lure of the pub had caused the rows between her parents to become even more frequent and explosive and they had moved back to England after just a few months.

Chase was watching her idly but something in his gaze made her feel like a bird with a cat's paw on its tail. 'Why hear it from other people? Come and see for yourself.'

'What? Go with you, you mean? No, I don't think that's a good idea,' she protested. More time with Chase? After what had so nearly happened last night? No. Definitely not.

'Why not? It's just a regular day trip but without all the hassle.'

Why not?

She stared at him in silence, a roaring noise in her ears as she replayed that moment in the kitchen when they stood staring at one another with the tension between them pulled to snapping point.

He leaned forward and she suddenly got a glimpse of that authority she'd seen at the beach house. 'You said you wanted to dive.'

'I do.'

'But what? You'd rather be doing easy duck dives with a bunch of clueless tourists?'

She felt her temper flare. 'I didn't say that. But I don't have any equipment.'

'But I do. Come on, Jemima.' His use of her name made her stomach flip over. 'You want to dive, so let's go take a look at your "reefs".'

The glitter in his green eyes made her want to reach out and touch his face and some of her anger dissipated. It would be madness to agree but, then again, surely there was no real risk of anything happening with the two of them wearing wetsuits and fins.

'Okay, then,' she said slowly.

'Great.' Pushing back his chair, he got to his feet.

'What are you doing?'

He grinned then, one of those slow, curling smiles that wrapped around her throat so that it was difficult to catch her breath. 'Going fishing! Come on.' And as he pulled her to her feet she felt a sudden rush of excitement just as if she were standing like a surfer on the shifting edge of a wave, her body quivering with tension and anticipation.

In less than ten minutes, Chase had chivvied her out of the house with an even more streamlined set of belongings and into a dune buggy and then they were bumping across a track towards what he called the dock. She was expecting some kind of basic jetty but as they turned a corner her mouth dropped open.

There were not one but six jetties and everything looked custom-made. That thought was confirmed a moment later when Chase said, 'We only finished the construction work on the floating decks two months ago. They're state of the art, designed to handle a storm surge of ten feet.'

She nodded but she wasn't looking at the jetties. Her eyes were fixed on the boats moored beside them on the turquoise water, in particular the largest one, a stunning white yacht, actually make that a superyacht, she thought, breath catching, as her eyes travelled the length of the boat from the stern to the bow. 'That's the *Miranda*,' Chase said softly as he slowed the buggy to a stop and switched off the engine.

She felt her pulse miss a beat. 'After *The Tempest*?'

He nodded. 'Seemed appropriate.'

Their eyes met and she felt a flutter of happiness rise up inside her. Then feeling suddenly exposed, she glanced back to the gleaming white yacht.

'She's beautiful.'

'I think so.' He seemed pleased. 'And that one is the *Umbra*. She's the support vessel, the workhorse. Not as pretty but her beauty lies in her functionality. That's where we keep the dive store and all the tools—you know, the DPVs, the submersibles, the amphibious plane. Oh, and there are some of the usual toys for just letting off steam: jet skis, hydrofoil boards.'

The submersibles? An amphibious plane?

The words were still echoing inside her head as they made their way through the yacht. She smiled politely as various crew members were introduced. Her head was bursting with all this new information, and most, if not all of it, seemed to contradict her first impression of the man she'd met at the harbour. A man she had thought was just some local fisherman who now turned out to be the owner of a fleet of boats as well as an island.

How had she got Chase so wrong?

Because he led you to believe he was something he wasn't. Her shoulders bowed a little as Holly's voice popped into her head.

And you didn't ask him the right questions, Ed chimed in. *You never do because if you did, you couldn't in all conscience date most of the idiots you end up with.*

That's not fair, she countered angrily. *You were the ones telling me to let my hair down. So I did, I had a one-night stand. Surely the point of casual sex is that it's casual. You don't need or want to know anything.*

And she hadn't: not even his surname.

Exactly. She could practically see Holly rolling her eyes. *And nothing's changed. He's still a one-night stand. He just happens to be a one-night stand who owns an island and a yacht.*

And an amphibious plane, Ed added. *Which is awesome,*

*by the way, but doesn't alter the fact that you're on holiday
and this is about having fun, remember?*

I am having fun, she protested.

But Holly and Ed had disappeared, probably in disgust
that she had travelled thousands of miles simply to miss
the point.

'You can use this room.' Chase swung open a door.
'I'll get someone to bring you a wetsuit and you can get
changed.' Stepping into the cabin, she nodded mutely. The
decor was similar to the interior of the house. There was rattan furniture, pale walls and eau-de-nil furnishings and all
of it hinted at a scale of wealth where money was no object.

'Is everything okay?'

Chase's voice, cool and deep like the ocean, made her
turn round. 'Yes.' She nodded. 'But what was the name of
your insurance company again?'

He hadn't told her, and she knew from the tiny pause before he answered that he was trying to work something out
in his head before he did. 'Monmouth Rock,' he said at last.

She stared at him, her heart jumping in her throat. She
knew next to nothing about insurance, but there couldn't
be many people on the planet who didn't know that name.
She could even picture the logo: the towering dark rock
rising out of the foam-topped waves. It was on the front of
that football shirt she had bought for her brother's birthday.

'You own Monmouth Rock.'

It was a statement, not a question, but he nodded anyway.

'I'm the majority shareholder.' His green eyes were
opaque, impossible to read. Gazing up at him, she felt the
jumble of pieces inside her head that hadn't seemed to fit
together suddenly slotting together to make a picture. Chase
Farrar was one of the super-rich, those mythical creatures

for whom ordinary problems like paying the mortgage were mere pinpricks.

And what about pleasure?

Her skin felt suddenly hot and tight. If you could do anything, go anywhere; if nothing was beyond your reach then no doubt ordinary pleasures would seem just that. Ordinary. Dull. Uninspiring.

No wonder he was here chasing treasure.

'I see.'

His shoulders shifted. 'It didn't seem important when we met.' He meant important enough to share with someone he was simply having sex with. And he was right, she thought, mentally listing the many things she could have told Chase, but had chosen not to, for exactly the same reason.

'I suppose not.'

He stared at her for a few seconds, his green gaze burning into hers, and she held her breath, aware that they were alone, and terrified suddenly that he would want something in return. A kiss, a secret.

You show me yours... I show you mine...

'Come up on deck when you're ready,' he said curtly and then he turned and stalked out of the room, closing the door behind him.

As promised, one of the crew members brought her a wetsuit, and she stripped down to her bikini. The wetsuit fitted like a glove, as it should, and she felt another flicker of excitement as she made her way to the deck.

Five people were already suited up, including Chase. As he walked towards her with that familiar lazy, dangerous ease she felt her stomach quiver. That five-millimetre neoprene was hugging his body in all the right places.

'It's a good fit,' he said, his gaze moving critically over

her in a way that made the wetsuit feel as if it were dissolving into her skin.

'Okay then, time to swap onto the dive boat.'

'We're diving here?' She had expected them to go further out to sea.

'That's the thing about Bermy. You only have to go a couple of hundred metres from shore and it gets deep real quick. That's why it's so popular with divers.'

The dive boat was a lot smaller than the *Miranda*, but it was still spacious enough for six divers and two other crew members to stand in a semicircle around Chase.

'So, there's going to be six of us diving.' His gaze moved slowly round the semicircle. 'Billy, Dale, Jonah, Linda, me and Ms Friday, who will be joining us today. Ms Friday is doing research for her PhD.' The crew either smiled or raised their hand in acknowledgement and then their gazes snapped back to Chase and she wondered again why she had ever thought this man hired out cycles and mopeds for a living.

'We should be able to fit in three separate dives today. Dive site is eighty feet down. Water visibility is coming in just under two hundred feet so bottles on and then we'll do a buddy check.'

A buddy check was a standard procedure on every dive she had ever done. Basically it was a pre-dive safety checklist. And a buddy, well, it was exactly what it sounded like. A diving partner who kept an eye on you under the water.

Jemima swallowed. 'Who's my buddy?' She said it quickly to get it out of the way, but she knew what his answer was going to be even before he answered.

'I am, of course. We're probably not quite matched in experience but we have a connection.'

Her heart lurched and a trickle of excitement that had

nothing to do with the dive wove through her, picking up speed as it travelled as his eyes rested on her face, green and steady and unblinking.

'Don't worry, I know it's been a while, but I'll be right beside you,' he said softly.

They ran through the checks and she was surprised and relieved at how much she remembered. Finally, the last check was complete.

The sunlight on the water was dazzling.

She felt Chase's hand on her shoulder. As she turned to face him, he gave her the thumbs up, and she returned the gesture and then they both took a giant stride away from the boat.

How could she have left it so long? That was her first thought as she entered the water.

It was like jumping into another world. Or into a living work of art. A pristine watercolour as mesmerising as any Monet only down here the colour was not static like on a canvas. It was constantly changing, darkening or growing brighter, shifting in the rippling forks of sunlight.

That she had forgotten.

Chase was right, she thought, with a pulse of excitement. The visibility was incredible. It was like looking through glass. Around her technicolour fish were darting jerkily in every direction, apparently unfazed by the gleaming grey sharks and rays that moved lazily through them in over-lapping ellipses. And there, covered in shivering sponges and lurid pink and orange coral that looked too garish to be real, lay the wreck.

Turning, she tapped Chase on the arm and he nodded and they swam down lower. The boat was on its side. Some parts had disintegrated but the shape of the hull was clearly visible and fish were flitting in and out of the shadowy interior.

She swam towards a pair of angelfish, then got distracted by a bright yellow trumpet fish moving vertically through the water. And all the time Chase was there, keeping pace with her.

Within what felt like no time at all, it was time to surface.

Back on the boat, she was elated.

'That was amazing,' she said, pulling off her mask and blinking into the sunlight. She turned to Chase and, without thinking, she grabbed his hands and squeezed them with excitement. 'I've seen footage on the Internet but that was so much more incredible than I could have imagined. There were so many species.' She knew she was babbling but she couldn't stop the spate of words. 'Imagine if more people knew about this.' Her smile faded. 'Oh, but I forgot to take any photos.'

'It's fine, we've got another two dives, remember? These guys are going to move on after lunch.' He jerked his head towards the other divers. 'But I can take you down this afternoon.'

His words made her blink and, suddenly aware of the press of his fingers, she let go of his hands. 'I thought this was your dive site.'

Shaking his head, he gave her one of those quick, devastating smiles. 'We don't dive until we have a reason to, and so far I haven't had a reason. As for this site, locals stripped this wreck bare years ago. I just thought it would be good for your research.'

Her pulse was jerking against the skin of her throat. 'You did that for me?' she said slowly.

He frowned. 'You sound surprised.'

Probably because she was, but why? Okay, Chase was cocky and hedonistic and he wanted different things in life from her, but he was letting her stay in his house, and taking her diving. And in bed he had been more than considerate. He had been generous, fierce, tender, using his hands, his mouth, his tongue, his body to unravel and transform her.

She felt his gaze on the side of her face, and, blanking her mind to that memory, she shook her head. 'I suppose I am a little. After what you said yesterday evening, I thought you'd want to get on with your treasure hunt.'

Her pulse thudded at her temples as his eyes rested on her face. 'I don't mind waiting for something if it's worth it. In fact, I'm a big fan of delayed gratification.'

He wasn't talking about the wreck. She knew that and he knew that, and for a second they stared at one another in silence and then she cleared her throat. 'Well, thank you for that. It was really kind of you.'

'It was my pleasure.' He held her gaze. 'So are you interested in going back down?'

It was a bad idea. Clearly it would be better, safer, to refuse, which meant there was only one possible response to that question. She took a deep breath. 'Yes,' she said.

After lunch on the yacht, it was time to dive again. This time, she remembered to take some photographs. Thank goodness for digital cameras, she thought as she zoomed in on the coral stretching over the wreck's hull. Swapping to the video camera, she felt her heartbeat slow. It was so calm down here away from dry land. So easy to forget that the real world even existed.

Chase tapped her on the arm, and, putting down the camera, she glanced round and saw that he was pointing to a striped sergeant major snuffling along the seabed. She started to follow him and then out of the corner of her mask, she saw it. A turtle propelling itself forward into the wreck using its paddle like flippers. She twisted in the water to watch it and then kicked forward. She had to get a picture.

A hand clamped around her arm. Chase was beside her, his eyes narrow beneath the mask. She pointed at the turtle but, shaking his head, he jerked his thumb towards the surface. She frowned, then reluctantly returned the signal and, still holding her arm, he guided her back up to the boat. As she climbed back on deck, he ripped off his mask and turned to face her.

'What the hell do you think you're playing at?' His deep voice was soft but there was a dangerous undertone that made the two remaining crew members scuttle to the other end of the boat. Gone was the easy intimacy and teasing smile of earlier, now his expression was as hard and inaccessible as the rock on his company's logo.

'You should have let me know if you wanted to go look at something, or do you not understand the meaning of dive buddy?'

He was talking about the turtle. 'Yes, of course I do,' she protested.

'Really?' The ice in his voice made her flinch inwardly. 'Because, for me, every dive is a contract, a duty of care for your buddy's safety.'

'I agree.'

'So, what, you just forgot?' His lip curled. 'Or were all the pretty fish too distracting for you?'

'No.' She was shaking her head. 'That's not how it was.' Fighting to keep her voice steady, she started to explain what had happened but he cut across her.

'It's exactly how it was.' And nothing was going to persuade him otherwise. She could see that in his eyes, in the hard, uncompromising set of his jaw. 'You're my buddy. You say you know what that means but it was just words because you didn't follow through.' She felt a prickling heat spread over her face as his eyes narrowed on her.

'You know, this isn't some dive pool, Jemima. This is the ocean and I don't dip my toe in it with anyone who isn't on the same page as me when it comes to understanding what they are responsible for. You can't just opt out when you feel like it. You made a commitment—' He broke off, his hand tightening around his mask.

Pain, a pain that had nothing to do with him, an old pain that was never far from the surface, fuelled her anger.

'You didn't give me a chance to—'

'To what? Prove me wrong? And what if you hadn't? What if I was right?' His voice was still fierce, but beneath the anger there was a rawness and a depth of passion that shocked her. 'Then it would all be too little too late.' He stopped, his beautiful mouth taut against his teeth. 'Do you know exactly how very little it takes to lose everything? No, of course, you don't. You're just a child, a stupid, thoughtless child.'

She stared at him, her heart sliding free of its moorings, stunned by the intensity of his fury. Even though the sun was hot on her back she felt cold inside her wetsuit. 'I'm not a child, and I do understand, and next time—'

'There's not going to be a next time.' A muscle jumped in his jaw. 'I don't do second chances because I spend every working day calculating risk, Jemima, and what you call second chances I call preventable accidents. And the consequences of those accidents are far reaching and devastating in ways I hope you never have to experience.'

His words hit her straight in the solar plexus like the kick of a horse, and there were tears in her eyes quite suddenly. It was a decade ago now but she could still remember sitting in that small, stifling room in the courthouse when the coroner had read out the verdict of accidental death. This, though, was a more accurate verdict because her father's death had been preventable.

By her.

Only she hadn't followed through then either. She had given up, walked away—no, make that crept away. And afterwards, she had only seen him that one last time.

She was suddenly afraid she would be sick.

'This was a mistake.' His face was shuttered, voice expressionless. 'My mistake. I thought you understood what was at stake but you don't, and I don't have people around me who don't understand the consequences of their actions. Particularly in the ocean.'

There was a long silence.

'I'm going to finish up here.' Chase glanced over his shoulder to where the crew were staring pointedly out to sea. 'I'll get someone to drop you back at the house.'

She stared after him, her chest splitting with a pain that had everything to do with him and nothing to do with him, a pain she would always have to shoulder because once again she had failed to follow through.

Back on the *Miranda*, Chase stalked into his cabin and slammed the door shut. He tossed his phone onto the bed and sat down, and then almost immediately got to his feet and began pacing round the room, his heart pounding out a drum roll of frustration and disbelief.

He kept a dry boat. Alcohol and diving were not just incompatible, they were a dangerous combination and he made no apologies about mandatory drug testing for the crew. Right now, though, he could have done with a glass of whisky. Or maybe a bottle, just something that would take the edge off his tension.

His jaw tightened.

It was her fault that he was feeling like this. Jemima had broken the rules. Worse, he had broken his own rules, inviting her out for a day of diving for no other reason than because he wanted to. Just as he had wanted to stay sitting there with her at breakfast. Talking. Eating. Catching her eye. Because it reminded him of all the things he had forced himself to forget. The kind of intimacies that went further than sex.

Catching sight of his reflection in the mirror, he stopped pacing. For a moment, he stood there, breathing unsteadily, replaying the moment when he had checked her buoyancy vest. It had taken every ounce of willpower he had not to lean in and press his lips against the soft hairs at the nape of her neck.

He jerked his head back, his gaze darting to the mirror. But it wasn't his reflection looking back at him now. It was Jemima, her grey eyes wide, not with hunger, but shock and misery.

Swearing softly, he turned away.

She was soft and sweetly serious, he thought, remembering her slightly incoherent outburst the night before. It wasn't so much what she'd said that had surprised and unsettled him. It was because he sensed that she wasn't just talking about the wider world but something deeper, something intrinsically personal to her. He had seen it in that quiver to her mouth. Something, most likely someone, had hurt her. Was that why she was here, thousands of miles from home? Was she running away from the hurt?

There was no point in running, he wanted to tell her. Pain was like your shadow. You could never escape it. You could lose yourself in drink or drugs temporarily, but to have any kind of life the only solution was to shut the door on your feelings. All of them.

That was the price you had to pay.

But that wasn't right for someone like Jemima, he thought, picturing her small, tense face, hearing the emotion in her voice as she talked about saving the world. He didn't know how old she was but in that moment she had seemed young, too young to be around someone as jaded as him.

She was also not his problem.

Not his problem, he repeated. What he needed was some fresh air to clear his head. Maybe stretch his legs. Which was how, an hour later, he found himself standing outside her cabin.

Of course, he'd told himself he was just going to say goodbye and no hard feelings, act like a grown-up, right up until he stopped in front of her door, but now that he was here he felt as if every second since he'd walked into Joan Santos's house had been leading up to this moment.

He took a slow breath, then tightened his hand into a fist and rapped his knuckles against the wood.

CHAPTER SIX

'JUST A MINUTE.'

He heard movement inside the room and then the door opened and Jemima was there. She had changed out of the wetsuit and her body looked stiff beneath the blouse and shorts. Behind her glasses, her eyes looked suspiciously bright. His stomach twisted. As if she'd been crying. Over her shoulder, he could see her bag at the end of the bed.

'I'm nearly ready,' she said quickly. Her voice was strained. It betrayed too much, and he felt something claw at him inside. 'I just need to grab a few last things.'

Chase stared at her, his pulse beating a drum roll through his limbs. If he had any sense he would say goodbye right about now and walk away, but...

A memory of Jemima, standing naked in front of him, quivering like a wildflower in the moonlight, slid into his head overlaid with that flush of rose pink that stained her cheeks wherever she met his gaze. Instantly, any sense he had was forgotten.

'That's not why I'm here.' He hesitated. It had been a long time since he'd had to explain his behaviour to anyone. Who would he explain himself to? Robyn. His COO. But also there was nothing to explain because he had made sure that he always did the right thing.

Only he hadn't done the right thing with Jemima. In fact

he had done the very opposite, letting his imagination over-ride what was actually happening.

'About earlier, on the dive boat. I might have overre-acted.' He frowned, remembering how, in the moment, panic had put an aggressive edge on his voice. 'Actually, I know I did. It's what I do. My business is all about worst-case scenarios and any dive is chock-full of those.'

And not just dives. Life was dangerous and unpredict-able and unfair and devastatingly cruel. Heart contracting, he thought back to the face of the police officer who had told him about the crash. She had been so young; around Jemima's age probably. He could remember the tremor in her voice and how she couldn't meet his gaze. Her eyes kept flickering away from his face as if it hurt to look at him.

He could feel Jemima's gaze on his face now.

'It happens all the time. Just last month I came across this boat, anchored up, guys on deck leaning over the sides. We got closer and it turned out they'd lost a couple of divers.'

His pulse slipped sideways, pulled on an unseen current. Of all the possible explanations, why had he picked that one to share? But it was too late to backtrack.

'Apparently it was supposed to be a short, deep dive and the guys who went down were very experienced. Only they hadn't resurfaced. The skipper went to take a look but there was no sign of them. It was only when he got back up they noticed that neither of the divers had taken their digital compasses.'

He could tell from the look on her face that Jemima un-derstood the significance of that fact. How without a com-pass it would be near impossible to reorient yourself to the position of the dive boat.

'All of us were just staring at the water and then one of my crew spotted this tiny glint of silver way, way off in the distance. It was a good kilometre from the dive boat but we went to investigate and there they were. One of them was wearing a watch. He was aiming it at the sun. That's what we saw.'

'Were they okay?'

'They were a bit shaken. But they were fine.'

She bit into her lip, her face suddenly taut. 'How did you know they were in trouble? The people on the boat.'

Because he was looking for it. His ribs squeezed around his lungs so that it was suddenly hard to catch his breath. It was the least he could do after having failed so devastatingly to see what was going on right in front of him.

He shrugged. 'Something felt off, you know?'

'And you were right,' she said quietly. 'You were right about earlier too. I did get distracted. I didn't follow through.' Her mouth quivered. 'I should finish packing.' He felt a spasm of panic and pain as she started to close the door.

'No, that's not why I told you that story.' He took a step forward. 'I was trying to explain why I overreacted.' Although that barely scratched the surface. 'But the fact is that anyone can get distracted.'

'Not you.'

'Yes, of course me. I went down to the harbour to collect medical supplies and instead I ended up trying to rent you a bike.' He thought that might make her smile but instead she wrapped her arms around her torso as if she was cold. It made him want to reach out and hold her. But what right did he have to touch her now? And she would be leaving soon. Dive or no dive, that was the plan. Only did it have to stay the plan?

'Jemima, please.' He took a deep breath. 'Look, I shouldn't have spoken to you like that. I guess I was worried because you're my guest and I feel responsible for you.'

'Well, you're not.' Her mouth quivered. 'We barely know each other.'

His fingers flexed. But he wanted to know her. And he didn't want her to leave. 'I came down to say goodbye when what I should be saying is sorry. And I am. Sorry. For what I said. For how I said it.' He took another step towards her. 'Please, I'd like you to stay.'

He watched her bite down on the inside of her lip. 'I thought you didn't do second chances.'

His chest tightened. Earlier, with panic and anger blazing through him, that had been true. Now though, staring down into her wide grey gaze, he was willing to make an exception.

'I don't do one-night stands either. But I couldn't walk away from you that night.'

There was a moment of heavy silence, the kind that smothered all sound.

He could see her pulse beating in her throat. 'I didn't want you to walk away.' Her voice brushed against his cheek like the wing of a gull and he stared at her, rooted to the spot by the storm in her eyes.

'And now,' he said hoarsely. 'Do you want me to walk away now?'

He held his breath as she reached up and rested her hand against his chest. 'No.'

Chase stared down into Jemima's face, his pulse leaping through his ribs to where her hand rested against his shirt, shivery pleasure dancing across his skin. He held his breath as she touched his cheek, her fingers grazing the stubble along his jaw, conscious only of the hammering of his heart and of his need, a need he saw reflected in her glazed grey eyes.

This was madness, he thought, distant alarms sounding in the margins of his brain. This could only make everything more complicated than he wanted it to be. But he couldn't move; couldn't look away.

And then she clasped his face in her hands in a jerky movement, and as her mouth found his he knew that only she could quiet this humming in his veins and he reached for her, locking his hand in her hair, pressing the other against the indent on her back, urging her closer.

He felt her breath shudder against his mouth and she moved against him, pressing her pelvis against his groin.

From somewhere on the boat, there was the sound of voices, a shout of confirmation. Her startled eyes met his and he saw her confidence falter and he stood there, not moving, not breathing, awash with panic and fear lest she call a halt.

His body was shaking inside, clamouring for her from head to toe but he waited, and he would walk away if he had to, but a second passed and then another, and then she stood on tiptoe to reach closer, hands fluttering to his shoulders, fingers biting into the muscles, kissing him blindly, greedily.

The walls swam around him as she started to pull him into the bedroom.

'Wait,' he muttered against her mouth, turning to kick the door shut, and then she was pulling him close again.

His need for her swelled up inside him. He wanted her, wanted her so badly, had been wanting her again from the moment he woke to find her gone. And now she was here, in his arms, her soft mouth working on his already over-heated senses.

'I've been thinking about this for days,' he murmured against her mouth, 'thinking about you.'

'I've been thinking about you too,' she said hoarsely. His teeth clenched as she slid her hands down over his body, down to where his erection was pushing against his shorts. As she cupped the weight of him, he sucked in a sharp breath.

It would all be over far too soon if he let her keep touching him like that.

Batting away her hand, and driven by the hunger uncoiling in the pit of his stomach, he scooped her up into his arms and carried her over to the bed.

He reached down and touched the swell of her breasts, feeling the taut nipples, his hands trembling and clumsy with a hunger he had never experienced. He felt feverish, drunk almost with lust and relief that it was happening. Leaning forward, he kissed her again, slowly, deeply, tasting her excitement, her nerves, her need.

'I want you,' he whispered.

Her eyes met his and he could see the glitter in them, see the flush of heat in her cheeks. She touched his face, his mouth, her trembling fingers hot against his skin.

'Then take me,' she said, and the need in her voice was like a flint to the steel in his shorts.

Blood pounding like a wrecking ball inside his head, he stripped off his top and threw it onto the floor and then pushed his shorts down past his straining erection. Her eyes widened, the pupils dilating; he could see her pulse leaping at him through the delicate skin of her throat, and, holding his gaze, she reached down and began to unbutton her blouse.

Still holding his gaze, she let it slide from her shoulders. He stared down at her breasts, his body hardening, hypnotised by the taut, quivering nipples, and then he leaned forward and licked first one swollen tip, and then the other.

Her fingers bit into his haunches. 'Chase...' She made his name last three syllables as he licked a path up the curve of her neck to her pink, parted lips.

'Jemima...'

Desire drowning him, he lowered his mouth and kissed

her again, pushing her back onto the bed. He tugged off her shorts, taking her panties with them, then took a step backwards, the cool air between them just enough to keep things from ending much too quickly.

She was naked now except for her glasses and, staring down at her, he gritted his teeth. She was beautiful. And she was his. To touch. To stroke. To taste.

Sliding his hands beneath her bottom, he pulled her closer, parting her thighs so that he could settle between them. For a moment, he breathed in her scent, his thumbs caressing her silken skin, and then he tilted her so that she was more open to him and traced a line with his tongue between her legs.

She jerked forward, lifting her hips, and he felt her fingers tangle in his hair as she moaned softly, shivers of pleasure or excitement or passion scudding across her skin in time to the sweep of his tongue.

A grating sound rose in the back of his throat. He loved the taste of her. Loved the noises she was making as she started to move against him, arching upwards, her body spasming and twisting frantically like a puppet on a string, hands flexing against his shoulders.

She cried out, and he felt her shudder, and shudder and shudder.

He shifted up the bed, his mouth finding hers, and she gripped his arm weakly, her fingers closing around the hard length of him, guiding him inside her.

Heat roared through him. He was so close now; his body tensed, the fog of unfocused thoughts that might loosely be described as his brain suddenly clearing, and he pulled back and out.

'I don't have any protection on me.'

She stared at him, her grey eyes wide and unfocused. 'I don't have any either.' Her breathing was still ragged.

'They're in my cabin, I'll go and—'

But she was shaking her head, pulling him closer, and now it was too late to stop, he didn't want to stop, he couldn't stop. He was so desperate for release, but he didn't ever take risks when it came to sex, and, reaching up, he pulled Jemima underneath him so that the hard length of his erection was pressing into the softness of her belly.

'Yes,' he muttered as she wrapped her legs tightly around his waist and then he was moving against her in an ever quickening, mindless rhythm and the friction kept building, growing stronger and sharper.

He lunged forward and, groaning, he juddered against her with convulsive liquid force.

For a moment he couldn't move. He just lay there, listening to the slap of the waves against the side of the boat, his heart pounding, his breath tearing his throat, her breath hot against his chest. Beneath him, he could feel the aftershocks of her orgasm still pulsing through her in waves and, shifting his weight off her body, he rolled onto his side, drawing her into his arms, aware of the slick wetness on her skin and his.

'I'm sorry,' she said after a moment.

Her face was pressed into his chest but he heard the catch in her voice and he turned so that he was on his side facing her. He could see the pulse at the base of her neck beating wildly. 'For what?'

But he knew what. He knew that she was remembering the moment when she had guided him into her body without protection. There was a stretch of silence and then she looked up at him. 'I don't know what I was thinking.'

'Thinking?' He ran his hands over her body, leaning back

slightly so he could admire her small breasts. 'I don't think either of us were thinking.' That was certainly true for him. His body, his brain, his whole being had been consumed with one *un*thinking purpose.

He placed his open palm against her face. 'We weren't prepared. Either of us.' That was an understatement, he thought, gazing down at her flushed face.

She bit her lip. 'It shouldn't have happened. I shouldn't have let it happen. But I don't regret it.' She seemed genuinely confused by that statement and he laughed softly.

'I don't regret it either.' He pulled her closer and felt her body shudder as her nipples brushed against his chest.

'Are you sure? I mean, you didn't…it wasn't—'

'It was.' Although it had happened faster than anticipated, a sudden, unstoppable quickening of his, like a seam tearing. He couldn't have held back another second. He hadn't lost it like that in years, possibly ever. No matter how good the sex had been in his previous relationships, he'd always managed to pace himself so that there was time to put on a condom. But he had lost control with Jemima.

And yet he hadn't been lying when he said he didn't have any regrets.

Then again…

His gaze slid hungrily along the curve of her bottom. He'd had sex with her, twice now, so why did he still feel hungry? It made no sense.

Or perhaps it made a kind of limited sense. *Yes*, thanks to this encounter, one night had turned into one night plus, but it all felt a little rushed; tantalising rather than satisfying. Like being invited back to a banquet only to have all the delectable dishes whisked away after just a few mouthfuls.

And before he got a chance to sample the dessert menu. His gaze travelled over her body to where her nipple was playing peekaboo beneath the hair that had fallen forward across her breast. Next time, he'd make sure they made it to desserts.

Next time?

Confused by the tangle of emotion that thought produced, he leaned forward and kissed her lightly on the shoulder, and then, loosening his arms, he shifted to the edge of the bed.

'Are you hungry? Because I'm starving.'

Hungry.

Jemima stared at Chase dazedly as he stood up. Her whole body was still quivering inside, tingling from the aftershocks of her orgasm and the stunned realisation that she and Chase had gone from a one-night stand to whatever it was called when you hooked up for the second time, only now he was talking about food.

As he turned towards her she had to force herself not to stare at his beautiful, naked body.

'I don't know.' Frankly, she didn't care, but Chase was already reaching down to pick up his clothes.

'Pick something.' The coolness in his voice scraped against her skin. 'Gianluca and his staff are all cordon-bleu-trained so they can pretty much knock up anything you want. I'm thinking steak and chips.'

Her head was spinning. She had no idea what was happening. In the past, with her boyfriends, sex had always happened after a couple of dates, more than a couple in some cases. With Chase sex had been the endgame, the finishing line. Only now they'd had sex again.

But what did that mean? Did it mean anything?

She didn't know the answer to either of those questions. She just knew that the whole point of a one-night stand was that it only happened once and she had messed that up. Just as she always seemed to mess up everything to do with men and relationships. And now she was in a no-man's-land. Except there was a man and he was half naked.

'I'll go tell the galley.'

'No, I don't think that's a good idea.' She sat up and his gaze flattened into a slant of green. For a split second she stared at him in silence, trying to clear her head, trying to understand the look in his eye. A look that didn't seem to match the coolness in his voice. It was as if he wanted her but didn't want her.

He raised an eyebrow. 'So not steak and chips?'

She felt a tremor of panic. The cabin felt suddenly tiny and claustrophobic and her throat felt suddenly too tight so that it was hard to catch her breath.

This was exactly why she had left last time. The confusion and awkwardness of post-coital interaction. This not being sure what he was thinking. Not being sure what she was even thinking.

'I don't care about the steak and chips. I'm talking about this.' Conscious of her naked body in comparison to his semi-clothed one, she bent down and began picking up her clothes from the floor. 'You and me. Look, just because we slept together—'

'Twice,' he interrupted her quietly.

Her fingers curled into fists. 'Just because we slept together again doesn't mean I want to have dinner with you.'

'You did last night.'

'That was different. It wasn't planned,' she protested.

'And this was?' He glanced back at the bed.

'No.' She blinked. It wasn't planned, and yet it had felt inevitable, inescapable, necessary. She felt exhaustion pressing down on her, heavy and stifling like a storm about to break. 'I don't want to talk about it.'

'Oh, that's right. I'd forgotten. No questions. No conversation.' His face was expressionless, but there was an edge to his voice. 'That's why you did a runner last time. But we're on a boat in the middle of the ocean so that's going to be a little harder to pull off, don't you think, Jemima?'

'Not as hard as you think,' she snapped. Hating that she couldn't keep the shake out of her voice, she snatched up the remainder of her clothes and walked stiffly towards the bathroom and shut, then locked the door.

As solutions went it wasn't particularly effective, she realised a moment later. She couldn't stay in the bathroom for ever, but neither did she want to keep having that horrible conversation with Chase.

It was all such a mess, she thought as she buttoned up her blouse.

And it was her fault. She had drawn a clear line in the pink sand the morning after the night before but then she had to go and blur the boundaries between them by staying in his house and going diving with him. It had been a stupid thing to do but then, when it came to men, she was stupid, and weak.

Look at how she'd let Nick treat her. And he wasn't the first.

Her throat tightened and she felt suddenly close to tears. The whole point of coming to Bermuda was to do things differently. To be different. And with Chase, that had happened. She had felt an intense physical attraction to him and acted on it without thought of even the immediate future.

Without any kind of thinking at all.

And it had been scary, but also empowering, only now she was back where she started. Letting herself be buffeted along by stronger currents like those two divers. Repeating the mistakes of the past when what she should be doing was breaking free of them. She pictured her father's face, the skin red and flaky, his bony cheeks covered in patchy grey stubble. Only that would mean facing up to who she was, and what she'd done.

There was no sound on the other side of the door and she unlocked it cautiously, but the bedroom was empty. She felt both relief and a disappointment that made her heart feel as if it were being squeezed hard by a huge fist. And the irrationality and hypocrisy of that made her want to scream.

She was losing her mind. She needed to get off this boat and as far away from Chase Farrar as possible. Grabbing her bag, she yanked open the door—and stopped.

Chase was sitting on the floor opposite the cabin.

Her stomach twisted with shock and another kind of relief entirely. The stupid kind that made her whole body fill with light, and made her thoughts spiral towards the impossible.

'What are you doing?'

'Waiting for you.' The huskiness in his voice brought a rush of heat to her cheeks. 'I was worried but—' glancing at her bag, he got to his feet '—I see I didn't need to be.' Eyes narrowing, he stalked past her into the bedroom. 'What? No note? How disappointing.'

As she watched him turn, her heart began to pound fiercely. 'Why are you bringing that up?'

'Because that's what you do, isn't it?'

'And now you can see why,' she countered. 'It's a whole lot easier than trying to talk to you.'

'Oh, now you want to talk. Because earlier you preferred to sulk in the bathroom.'

As he stalked towards her, she felt her whole body

tighten. Twenty minutes ago their bodies had collided on that bed, driven by a mutual hunger that was as intense as the storm that hit the island last night. Now that storm was blowing in a completely different direction. 'I wasn't sulking. I was upset.'

Jaw tightening, his gaze held hers. 'Yeah, because we had sex again.' His voice was so cold that for a moment it seemed to freeze her brain and she couldn't take in what he was saying. And then she did.

'No, that's not why I was upset.' Except it was, in part, and, looking into his eyes, seeing the emotion smouldering there, she knew that he had heard it in her voice.

His gaze burned into her face. 'I'm sorry to disappoint you, Ms Friday.'

'And, of course, this is only about you.' Now she felt a flicker of anger. Not just with Chase but with herself for thinking that a one-night stand might change the essential dynamic between her and every man she had ever met, except her brother. 'You know, I don't know why I thought this would be any different. Why you'd be different.' Her voice came out scratchy.

Why I'd be any different, she might have said.

Chase frowned, his gaze suddenly intent on her face. 'Different from what?'

Feeling trapped, she looked away, a lump forming in her throat.

'Different from what?' he said again.

He was standing too close, his hard, muscular body radiating power and authority, and something that felt oddly like concern. 'It's complicated.' She wished he would leave but he just stood there, waiting, his body blocking her in, and she knew that he wasn't about to let her go this time. Not without her answering his question first.

'This is why I wrote that note,' she said finally, avoiding his eyes. 'Because I don't know how to do this. I thought I did but I don't. You see, I lied to you. Before. I told you I didn't do relationships. That wasn't true.'

She felt his green gaze narrow on her face. 'You have a boyfriend.'

'No.' Finally she looked up at him. 'Not any more. But I did. His name is Nick. He cheated on me. That's why I came to Bermuda. Why I'm having this holiday. My brother and sister thought I should get away. Go somewhere new. Be someone different. Let my hair down. They sorted it all out, and I went along with it because—'

'They're a force of nature.' He finished the sentence for her.

'Yes, but then I met you.' Her pulse skipped forward as she remembered that moment at the harbour when he had swaggered out from behind the counter. 'And I wanted you, and you made me want to be this cool, impulsive, wild woman so I let you think that was who I was.'

He said nothing, just stared at her, waiting.

'It all seemed so easy in the moonlight but then when I woke up I panicked.' Had she been the expert she claimed to be, she would have casually informed him the night before that she had an early start. Instead she had ended up creeping around in the dawn-lit cabin, terrified that he would wake at any moment and the spell would be broken, and that night of fantasy would be lost and forgotten among the awkward goodbyes.

'I know I acted like it was something I do all the time, but I've never had a one-night stand and I didn't know how it worked.' She swallowed. 'It was so perfect, I didn't want to ruin it, so I got up and left. And it would have been fine if we never met again.'

She saw him swallow, saw a muscle tighten in his jaw.

'Only we did. And it was too late to tell you that I'd never done anything like that before. But then you knocked on my door and I realised that it didn't matter what I told you because I knew the truth. I knew that it wasn't fine. That I still wanted you, and I don't want to feel like this, but I can't seem to stop myself.'

But she did stop now. Lowering her face, she breathed out unsteadily. She had never admitted half as much to anyone but then she had never felt so physically connected to any man.

'And I feel the same.' Pulse trembling, she looked up to see his pupils flare. 'So why run from it?' he said hoarsely.

Her belly clenched, his question stabbing at her, slicing through her defences.

'I don't.'

'Yes, you do. It's like you said. You know the truth. We both do.' His green gaze burned into hers. 'So what's the point of running? Or hiding? Or pretending that you don't want this?'

Heart thudding, she gazed up into his beautiful, sculpted face, her insides tightening, her body betraying her, the raw, sexual challenge of his words pounding through her like a drum roll. For a moment neither of them spoke or moved, and then he reached out, tugged gently at the band in her hair, and she stared at him transfixed, unable to move, helpless, fascinated by his touch.

'You came to let this down.'

As her hair tumbled loose, he twisted the blonde strands, winding them into a rope as Rapunzel had done so that the prince could climb up the tower to rescue her. But instead he used it as a pulley to draw her closer to him. 'To have fun, and go diving. And I get that this is all new to you.

But that's not a reason to leave. So why not stay here with me on the *Miranda*? Just until the beach house is fixed? I have an event in New York coming up but other than that I'm all yours.'

It was just a phrase, she told herself, but his words made her body ache.

He untwisted her hair and let it hang loose. 'I can make all those things you want happen.'

A moment earlier she had wanted him to leave. Now her heart was beating against her ribs, his suggestion catching the sunlight like the divers' watches, pulling her in. This was only supposed to be a day trip. But then this was only supposed to be a one-night stand and what he was suggesting would mean being here on the *Miranda* for several days. The thought sent a fast twitch down her spine. Was that wise? She had already let it go further than she'd planned.

Then again there was still an end date, and it wasn't as if Chase were proposing marriage. Like her, he wanted to have fun. A pulse of heat pirouetted across her skin. So why walk away now? Why not have fun with him? And if she spent a little longer having fun out here with Chase, then maybe back in England she would be less likely to return to her old, bad habits.

'Is that what you want?'

She could see the dark flush in his cheekbones and his eyes were full of heat, but she needed to hear him say it.

'Yes,' he said simply, and he took the bag from her hand, tossed it onto the floor. She didn't say anything. She just stared at him, her heart pounding, and then she sidestepped past him and shut the door. As she turned to face him, he crossed the room in two strides and kissed her hungrily, his mouth drawing the heat from hers, his hands gripping her waist and pulling her back towards the bed.

CHAPTER SEVEN

PRESSING HER FACE against the submersible window, Jemima was lost for words, her mind empty, the questions and uncertainties of the last few days soothed away by the view through the glass. Only this time it wasn't just the sea life that was mesmerising but the water itself, she thought as the sunlight slipped away and the colour palette moved through a light curaçao to a bruised blue.

'What do you think?' Chase's voice made her jump and she turned to find him watching her, his green gaze shimmering as it met hers.

'I think it's very cool,' she said carefully.

He tipped his beautiful head back and laughed. 'I know, it's a bit of a toy, but it does serve a purpose. It means we can check out deeper sites without having to send divers down. Although, to be honest, we probably wouldn't even use the submersible until we locate a suitable wreck.'

'But how do you know it's suitable if you haven't taken a look?'

He turned towards her and she found herself trying to take in his expression, his features, just as she had been doing ever since she had agreed to this fling. Because it didn't matter that some things had the feel of a relationship—the shared breakfasts, the long afternoons spent in bed, that intense pull of attraction that shimmered around them like a heat haze. None of it was heading anywhere. None of it was permanent.

The snatch of a song about summer flings echoed inside her head, and she glanced up through the glass bubble, her gaze following a school of silvery Bermuda chub.

It wasn't summer but fling was the best word to describe her 'relationship status' with Chase. She liked the idea that she was jumping into something new, or diving, even. And as with diving there was that shock of entering another state of being. But it was a good shock. Better than good, it was perfect for her life right now. She had promised Holly and Ed that she would have fun and she was having fun.

Although being the nerd she was, she had done a little covert research on the Internet just to reassure herself and it turned out that there were rules about holiday flings; thankfully she was following most of them.

She knew why she wanted to have a fling. She and Chase were on the same page. Plus there was zero chance of them dating long-term under different circumstances so there were already natural boundaries in place. And, finally, they were practising safe sex. Her face grew warm as she remembered how close she had come to letting him stay inside her that first day on the *Miranda*.

Safe in some ways.

The obvious ways.

But there were other hazards and unforeseen consequences that no condom could protect against.

Like having to accept the unlikelihood of her ever finding a man who liked pleasing his partner sexually as much as Chase did. A man who was happy to take the lead, to be guided, to wait, to celebrate her hunger while satisfying his own.

A beat of heat danced over her skin. She'd had sex with

her previous boyfriends but mostly she had been too worried about their pleasure to think about her own. She was too shy to say what she wanted, what she liked. Truthfully, she hadn't known what she liked.

Until now.

With Chase.

And now she knew the difference between having sex and having good sex. No, make that sublime sex. A lick of heat flickered up inside her at the memory of his hands moving urgently across her body and his hardness clamped between her thighs. No one had ever touched her like that or made her feel so helpless, so hungry.

Locking her knees, she was suddenly aware that Chase was saying something to her. Hoping that the shifting light would hide the colour in her cheeks, she said quickly, 'Sorry, I missed that.'

'I was just saying that we have other equipment we can use before we send down the sub.'

'What kind of equipment?'

'That depends on the depth of the water. The deeper you go, the more pressure there is and in those cases we use a remotely operated vehicle. They can be operated from the surface and you can add in manipulator arms, high-res cameras, viewing monitors. Then there's metal detectors, light systems. It just means that we can check out the sites with as little interference as possible,' he added. 'That way we can minimise the impact on the marine life.'

Their eyes met and she remembered that argument they'd had in the kitchen what felt like a lifetime ago—although it was just a matter of days, she realised with shock. But then time seemed to work differently here in Bermuda. Or maybe it was him, she thought as his gaze moved over her.

He had tipped her life upside down so why not time?

'How did you get into this? Looking for treasure, I mean.'

There was a beat of silence and then he shrugged. 'I grew up near a lake that's basically the size of a sea. We had a boat—not like the *Miranda*, more of a dinghy, really. But we spent a lot of time on the water and you end up diving wrecks and I guess it fired my imagination. I've always had a very vigorous imagination,' he added softly.

His eyes rested on her face and she felt her mouth dry. She knew all about his imagination.

She nodded. 'Down here is like another world. I can see why being able to think creatively would be helpful.'

He smiled. 'Nice divert,' he said softly. 'But you're right. We come up against challenges all the time that you just don't get on land. We've even had to design equipment for specific problems, and that's exciting in another way. Here, take a look at this,' he said, shifting the joystick minutely, then holding it steady. Glancing down, she saw that they were floating directly above a vivid orange coral colony.

Her pulse quivered with excitement. There had to be at least thirty, maybe forty different species of coral down there.

She leaned forward, her gaze travelling along the wreck where it crouched on the seafloor like a huge, sleeping animal. It was the *San Amunia*, a Spanish galleon that had been caught in a hurricane off the coast of Bermuda in 1654 and sank with no survivors. The ship had been picked over by salvage teams and amateur hunters, but it was now serving a second purpose as a home for hundreds of different species.

Reaching up, she touched the glass. Privately she had been a little dismissive about the sub. Surely nothing could beat the immediacy of diving. But now that she was here, she could see that, although it was less hands-on, the bubble allowed for a three-hundred-and-sixty-degree experience so that you could see how the marine life interacted with each other rather than having a viewpoint that was limited by the size of your mask.

'It's really incredible. Thank you for taking me out.'

'I'm glad you're enjoying it. I only got it about a month ago so I haven't had much of a chance to use it, you know, with the weather and—'

A shadow moved over the bubble of glass and they both glanced up to watch a spotted eagle ray swooping smoothly through the water, more like a bird than a fish, its great fins rising and falling like wings, the tail spine trailing after it like a kind of reverse antenna.

'They look like they're flying,' she said softly.

'They do fly. Most rays do, I think. They launch themselves about six feet into the air. If I hadn't seen it I would never have believed it…it was astonishing.' He checked himself. 'There's footage on the Internet, if you're interested.'

He glanced away towards where the rays were foraging around the bottom of the wreck and her eyes fixed on the fine, pale hairs at the nape of his neck, a pulse beating high in her throat. Why had he swerved the conversation away from the personal to the generic? It was so swift and subtle she doubted most people would have noticed, but she did a similar thing when she didn't want to give something of herself away. Only she talked about her siblings. But what could Chase possibly want to keep to himself about spotted eagle rays?

She cleared her throat. 'Why do they do it? Why do they jump?'

'For fun.' He grinned. 'Or because they're trying to shake off the parasites that live in their gills.'

'Like chickens having a mud bath.'

Glancing over, he laughed softly and she felt the sound move through her, tangling inside, unravelling her. 'I'm not that familiar with chickens but it sounds feasible. I've heard lots of different theories. Some people think that the males do it during mating season. To get noticed by the females.'

She heard the inflection in his voice and a flicker of sensation skated across her skin, hot and sharp like a flame. Chase didn't need to do anything to get noticed. Even today, in faded shorts and with his hair falling across his forehead, his was the kind of beauty that made people forget what they were saying when they saw him.

And it wasn't just women. Men responded to it too; or maybe they simply responded to the intangible but unmistakable leader-of-the-pack aura of authority that was as much a part of him as those glittering green eyes.

Outside the bubble, the rays had disappeared from view, and she leaned forward to see if she could see another.

'He'll be back. That wreck is like an all-you-can-eat buffet.' He hesitated, then tapped the joystick. 'Would you like to have a go?'

'Me?' She frowned.

His eyes gleamed. 'Yes, you—unless there's a very tiny stowaway in here that I don't know about.'

She laughed then. 'Okay, yes. I would like that.' Her eyes darted around the cabin with its state-of-the-art dashboard. He might think of it as a 'toy' but just thinking about how much it cost made her nervous. 'But do you trust me?'

'I could ask you the same question.' His gaze held hers, steady and direct. 'I mean, just getting into a submersible involves a substantial amount of trust.'

Did she trust him? She thought back to how he had gone through the safety measures in place in case of an emergency: the four days' worth of air, extra food and water, the rescue sub at the ready. She knew Chase would never put her in danger, but then she realised with a jolt that she trusted him in other ways too. Which was a first with anyone she'd been intimate with. Aways before she'd felt that betrayal and hurt were inevitable just as a spinning coin must eventually fall on its side. But probably because theirs was a physical relationship with a limited shelf life, she felt as if there was not the same risk of hurt or disappointment.

A gear shifted inside her head, reversing her back to when they'd argued after having sex again and he had waited outside the cabin to see that she was all right. It was a moment of care that went outside the boundaries of the physical.

'I do trust you,' she said quietly.

He didn't react but the sudden intensity of his gaze made her feel something a lot more complicated than nervous.

'Then it's very simple—there are four thrusters that allow the sub to move in any direction. This is up, this is down, left and right. Now you try.' He lifted his hand and she took hold of the joystick. The leather was still warm from his grip and for a moment she lost concentration, imagining that same hand warming her body. Very specific parts of her body.

The sub jerked forward, and now his hand covered hers. 'You're doing fine. Just ease into it. Like this. See? Good.'

'And how do you stop it?'

'That's a good question.' She felt his fingers splay over hers and the submersible stilled, hovering gently. 'Not one I would have thought of asking.'

'You wouldn't?' It seemed obvious to her.

He moved closer, his eyes resting on her face, the green layered with a dark heat she could feel inside her.

'Because when I'm with you, stopping is the last thing

on my mind,' he said, his voice daring her in that dark, soft-edged way that made heat dance along her limbs and her skin prickle with a mix of panic and desire.

For a moment she couldn't breathe. Dizzily she stared up at him and then impulsively she leaned forward and kissed him, moaning softly as he kissed her back, his lips moving across hers, slowly, deliberately, tongue parting her lips in a sensual exploration that made her belly feel hot and tight with need.

She really was dizzy now. Her head was spinning. She blinked, bracing herself against the sea. No, actually, it was the submersible.

'Chase.'

He jerked backwards and Jemima's eyes met his, the pupils flaring with shock and a hunger that matched the need galloping through his body. Which would be fine except that they were five hundred feet under water in a bubble of air. Breathing out shakily, he moved the joystick fractionally and the sub slowed, then came to a quivering stop.

There was a flush of pink along her cheekbones. 'I don't remember anything about that in the safety protocol talk.'

He shook his head. 'No, I'm pretty sure kissing your co-pilot is not standard procedure.'

His heart thudded as she reached out and pressed her hand flat against the front of his shorts, feeling the hard length of him. 'I think it might be time to go back up to the boat.'

'I think so too,' he said hoarsely.

They made it to the cabin. Just.

They didn't take off their clothes. As he opened the door to her cabin, she grabbed his hand and pulled him inside and he caught her by the waist, spinning her round and back against the door, bringing his mouth down on hers with a hunger that made her gasp. And then he was pushing her dress above her waist, sliding on a condom and thrusting into her, both of them still standing. It was fast and hard. Sex at its most basic and her climax was so intense that he had to hold her against him to keep her upright.

It was natural to feel this desperate, he told himself as he watched her sleep. There was a clock ticking. The credits were going to roll on this episode with Jemima as soon as the beach house was fixed. And she was feeling it too; that was why there was this tension between them and why he had snapped at her. So although it felt as if her talking about her ex had changed things between them, it was just that this wanting Jemima, wanting someone specific, hadn't happened in such a long time and it was knocking him off balance.

Why else would he have ended up telling her about those divers?

His spine tightened as he imagined their shock and terror as they broke through the surface. It made him remember Frida and his own shock and the agony of understanding that she was gone and that he was alone too. Only for him it was an aloneness that would last for ever.

And yet, being with Jemima in the sub all those metres below the surface he'd felt, not alone, but connected so that he had thought about telling her the truth. But then he had come to his senses.

She had got upset, and in the moment she had needed to share something about herself, and that was fine but there was no need to reciprocate.

Not outside bed anyway.

They spent the rest of the day relaxing. Or rather she relaxed on a sunlounger and Chase joined other members of the crew to hop the waves on his custom-built jet ski. Watching him perform a series of faultless back flips and barrel rolls, Jemima wondered drowsily if he ever ran out of energy. He seemed to have endless stamina.

Her eyes fixed on where he sat on the jet ski, his hair salt-tangled and bright in the sun's dazzle of clear gold, water trickling down his muscular torso. It didn't seem possible but she wanted him again, wanted him now.

Just as if he could hear her thoughts, Chase looked up at the yacht, his green gaze tearing into her, and she felt an excruciating, irresistible tug low in her pelvis. She could imagine his hands on her stomach, her hips, between her thighs.

Watching him turn the jet ski towards the *Miranda*, she felt her pulse leap in her veins. Soon she wouldn't have to use her imagination. That was the upside of this arrangement.

And the downside?

She bit into her lip. She wasn't allowing herself to think about that right now. She was living for the present. Enjoying every moment while she could. And there was a lot to enjoy, she thought, her stomach cartwheeling as Chase walked out onto the owner's deck.

'I thought we might head out to deeper water tomorrow.'

Looking up at him, Jemima frowned. 'I thought the sub only went down two hundred metres.'

They were lying in each other's arms, bodies twitching and spent.

When they'd returned to the cabin earlier, they had stripped and showered and she had taken him in her mouth with the water cascading down her back. Finally they'd made it to the bed. Capturing her wrists, he had lowered himself between her legs, taking his time, making her wait, waiting for her to beg.

And she had begged, crying out his name, rocking against his mouth, her body losing shape, weightless suddenly and adrift, thighs shaking as her orgasm hit.

'So you were listening to me earlier.' Lifting her chin, Chase kissed the corner of her mouth and worked his way to the other side. 'You're right, it does, but the *Eurybia* can go another three hundred metres.'

Five hundred metres. That was deep. Even just thinking about it made her feel breathless. Then again, she was still trying to catch her breath from before, she thought, nestling in closer to Chase. His name suited him. With his latent muscularity and smooth, tanned skin, there was something of a hunter about him.

Although she was as greedy for him as he was for her.

She had no words to describe what it was like to explore his beautiful body with such unthinking freedom, or how his touch made her feel, just that she felt happier than she could ever remember feeling, calmer too. And safe. Her heart slipped sideways a little. She had never felt safe before with any of the men she'd dated. She had always been on edge, waiting like Chicken Little for the sky to fall on her head. Except that made it sound as though her life was filled with drama.

And sometimes it was, but mostly it was less attention-grabbing, more quietly exhausting. A kind of slow-motion panicky treading of water to keep from going under, and a feeling of being incredibly alone.

Her throat tightened and she remembered Chase talking about the divers. Picturing the two men bobbing in a wide expanse of blue, that random glint of silver, she shivered.

'What's up?'

As Chase pulled her closer, she tilted her head back to meet his gaze. 'Nothing.'

He raised an eyebrow. 'I lost you there. Where'd you go?'

She reached up to touch his face, marvelling at the perfection of his bone structure and the smoothness of his skin.

'I was just thinking about those two divers you told me about. They were so lucky.'

Something flickered across his eyes like water moving beneath ice. 'What they were was arrogant and careless. They thought they were different. That those bad things they saw on the news only happened to other people. Bad things can happen to anyone given the right set of the wrong conditions.'

Like alcoholism crossed with pneumonia and a sudden, unseasonal but vicious drop in temperature, she thought, no longer on a superyacht but standing on a rainy London street near Piccadilly Circus where the lights were always on and you felt as if you were walking through a dream. But it was real. All of it was real.

Her chest tightened. Her father was a careless drunk. He forgot to eat. He had fallen and hurt himself multiple times. On one terrible occasion he had been beaten up and robbed on his way home.

And yet his death had been avoidable.

'You disagree?'

'No, you're right,' she said slowly. 'Bad things can happen to anyone, anywhere.' Especially when you did nothing to stop them from happening.

Glancing up, she found Chase watching her closely, his beautiful green eyes narrowed on her face as if he was trying to see inside her head. And she felt a sudden overwhelming urge to tell him the truth, to lay out her secrets before him, which wasn't just a bad idea, it basically was the very essence of a bad idea.

It was true that, since she had agreed to stay, they had

talked about lots of things. But it was as if there were an electric fence humming between them. Aside from her telling him about her exes, any time anything got too deep or personal, they both backed away. And it didn't get any deeper or more personal than telling someone how you walked out on your alcoholic father. It was certainly too deep and personal for a holiday romance.

'Was it near here?' she said quietly. 'Where you found them?'

She felt the muscles in his arms tense and he stared down at her blankly, almost as if he were surprised to see her there, and then he shook his head. 'You don't need to worry. A lot of the crew are locals. They know where most of the strong currents are.' He said it casually, but there was an edge to his voice and she knew that as far as he was concerned the conversation was over even before he lowered his mouth to hers.

His hands were moving across her hips, now they were slipping between her thighs, his touch light, teasing, persuasive. In a moment, her skin would grow warm and she would start to melt, to dissolve into pure need.

Maybe she was reading too much into it. Maybe it was just that brush with almost-tragedy that had caught him off guard and reminded him of the power and unpredictability of the sea; the way a flat, calm surface could hide a riptide.

She caught his fingers, twisting them around her own. 'But shouldn't I know?'

There was a small, taut pause. His eyes narrowed a fraction. 'I thought you said you trusted me.'

'I do, but—'

'So trust me when I say that we won't be diving anywhere close to that site.'

He was right; she could trust him. *So row back,* she told herself. And yet—

Trust me.

She'd lost count of the number of times people had said that to her, and always they'd been lying. And with all those other people, it had mattered. The whole point of this fling with Chase was that it didn't need to matter. It was different. She was supposed to be different with him.

But this was her being different.

The old Jemima, the one she'd left back in England, would never be thinking like this. She would have looked the other way, and kept looking until she found her boyfriend having sex with a stranger in their bed.

Behind him, she could see the ocean rippling in the sunlight. It all looked so calm and welcoming, but sometimes the currents pulled you into dangerous waters anyway.

'It must have been horrible,' she said slowly. 'Stumbling across something like that.'

'Like what?' But he knew what. There was a wariness in his voice that hadn't been there before, the same rigidity in his body.

'Divers lost at sea. I can't stop thinking about it and I wasn't even there.'

He rolled over, taking her with him so quickly that she was on top of him before she had a chance to blink. 'I was just happy to help,' he said, and now he was moving his hands lightly down her back to the curve of her bottom, his touch making heat blossom deep inside her.

In another moment, she would lose the power to think, much less speak. It was something that had happened before, she realised, this reaching for one another. It was as if they had an unspoken agreement whenever there was a need to move away from tricky or unnecessarily personal topics of conversation. But why would he want to stop talking about those divers? Or the rays in the sub?

Gritting her teeth, she wriggled free and sat up. 'But it must have been upsetting,' she persisted.

'For them, sure.' His green eyes were dark with passion but as he reached up to cup her breasts with his hands, she could feel the tension in his body.

But why? She swallowed.

'So it wasn't your boat? Your divers?'

This time, he didn't move a muscle. She knew because she was watching him so closely she could see him breathing. But his expression hardened minutely.

'No, it wasn't my boat or my divers. Why would you ask me that?'

Staring up at him, she felt a tingly shiver dart down her spine. He was telling the truth. But he was also holding something back. That was the thing about dating so-called 'recovering' addicts: you got pretty good at being able to separate out all the strands; you could pick out the lies of omission from the distortions of the truth; the half-truths from the lies they had told themselves so often it felt as though they were real.

And all of it was tangled up with their shame and your guilt for having failed them. She felt suddenly exhausted, just as she used to feel when her dad was trying desperately to hide the truth from her, from himself.

'Because you seem so tense about it. I thought maybe—'

'If I'm tense, Jemima, it's because you're putting two and two together and making five.'

He tipped her off his lap and shifted to the edge of the bed and she stared at his back, her heart beating shakily. Blaming the other person was something else addicts did when they were trying to cover their tracks.

'That's not what I'm doing—' she protested.

But he cut her off. 'Then maybe you should rewind what

you just said, because it sure sounded like that to me. I think I'm going to hit the gym. While I'm gone you might want to brush up on your pillow talk.'

'Pillow talk?' she echoed.

He was yanking on his clothes. 'Yeah, you know, the stuff people say to each other in bed in between having sex.'

People? Was that what she was to him? One of many. Faceless and interchangeable. The brusqueness of his words was like a slap to the face. 'I know what pillow talk is, Chase.'

'Apparently not. Or do you think all this is somehow going to make me horny?'

'What are you? Fifteen? I don't care if you're horny or not,' she said, grabbing at a T-shirt and yanking it over her head, her anger nudging past her shock at the sudden change in his mood. She felt as if she were driving a getaway car down a motorway. Her heart was ricocheting off her ribs, hands clenching so tightly that she thought the bones might shatter.

He stared down at her; the angles of his beautiful face looked as if they were cut from stone. There was a tiny, taut twist to one corner of his mouth. 'Lucky for you. Because you throwing accusations around—'

'I wasn't throwing accusations around. I was trying to understand you.'

'Then clearly you've missed the point of our arrangement, because I don't want to understand you and I sure as hell don't need you to understand me. Just to make things clear, this is about sex.'

The room went silent and still and for a second or two, Jemima just stared at him, her breath churning in her throat, his words echoing inside her head. She couldn't feel her hands, her body. It was the first time he had made her feel like that, like her other boyfriends had made her feel. Diminished and stupid. But unlike with them, she felt no sense of failure. Just a sudden, fierce anger that left her breathless.

'Yes, it is.' She rose from the bed like Venus rising from the waves. 'But you're the one who's missing the point if you don't also know that it's also about respect.'

There was a silence punctured only by the splintered sound of their breathing. She couldn't remember ever speaking to anyone like that. For a moment, she just sat there on her bed, listening to her heart banging in her chest.

'Mexico.'

His voice made her jump and she glanced over at where Chase stood facing her. There was no mistaking the tension in his body now. He looked as if he were bracing himself against the impact of some unseen, outsized wave.

'What about Mexico?'

Another silence, longer this time.

'You asked me where those divers got lost.' The anger was gone. In fact, his voice was wiped of all emotion. 'It was off the coast of Mexico.'

Staring across the room at Jemima, Chase felt his chest tighten.

'Why didn't you just tell me that?' Her grey eyes found his, clear, puzzled, the anger that had lit them up moments earlier fading.

Because of this. Because in answering one question he had unleashed a wave of others. Only they were harder to answer. And each one would be more painful than the last.

'I didn't think you needed to know. I thought it would make things complicated. I knew you didn't want that. Neither of us did.'

He heard her breath quicken. 'Why would you being in Mexico complicate things?'

His head shuddered like a building in an earthquake. 'Because I was with my parents-in-law.'

Her face seemed to shrink. She sank back down on the bed and he could see that her legs were shaking. 'You're married?'

He shook his head. 'Not any more.' He could hear the finality in his words; she heard it too. He could tell from the way her body seemed to lose shape.

'What was her name?' she said quietly.

'Frida. I didn't tell you about her because—' His head was spinning, there were so many reasons, and yet weirdly he couldn't think of one.

'You don't have to explain. We don't have to talk. We can just sit here.' Jemima's voice cut across the panicky swirl of his thoughts and instantly he felt calmer. She was right. He didn't have to tell her anything, but for some reason he wanted to.

'She was their only child. They miss her especially around the anniversary of her—' The word stuck in his throat.

'When did it…? When did she…?'

'Eight years ago.' His chest tightened. He had never talked to anyone about the accident. Had never wanted to, but then this was the first time he had spoken Frida's name aloud to anyone outside his family and it seemed to loosen something inside him so that before he understood that he was doing it, he began talking about a past he had buried along with his wife.

'We met at college. When I dropped out, she still married me. For our honeymoon, we hired a yacht. Not like the

Miranda. It was smaller but we both loved sailing. That's when we saw the rays.'

He hesitated, then cleared his throat.

'She got her law degree, joined a firm while I messed around on more boats. Then my dad got ill and I went to help out at his insurance firm, and I liked it. But I wanted to do things my way so I set up Monmouth Rock.'

Something strange was happening to his voice. It sounded different, almost as though it were being artificially generated.

'We started trying for a baby and she got pregnant really quickly. But then we lost the baby early before the first scan. And we were upset but we tried again, and she got pregnant again. And she miscarried. It kept happening. The doctors were doing all these tests and we talked about surrogacy but Frida wanted to keep trying.'

It had been the hardest thing that had never happened.

'By then the business was global and I was flying all over the world and it was hard for both of us. She was struggling. Not sleeping. She blamed herself even though it wasn't her fault. And then one day she told me she couldn't do it any more. She couldn't keep trying.'

It had been the worst moment of his life watching her despair. Or so he had thought then.

'So we stopped trying for about a year. She went on the pill. She changed her diet, started doing yoga and painting and we agreed that we would use a surrogate. We were looking into it when she got this bug and she was sick for days. It must have messed up the pill because about a month later she found out she was pregnant. And this time it stuck, and she was so happy. I was too.'

His chest tightened. There was no easy way to say what happened next. In fact, he'd always thought he didn't have the words, but glancing over to where Jemima sat clutching the sheet around her body, her gaze still, steady, unwavering, he said quietly, 'She was five months pregnant when she lost that baby.' There was a tiny silence. 'It was a girl.'

He felt as shocked now as he was then. Shocked too that he was telling Jemima.

'I'm so sorry, Chase.'

Her voice was so soft he wished he could just wrap himself in it. But he didn't deserve to be comforted. He didn't deserve her sympathy.

'I had some time off but then I had to go back to work.' He frowned. 'I wanted to go back to work because I thought that if things got back to normal it would help. But it didn't. She was hardly eating. She'd stopped seeing her friends. I took her to the doctors and she was given anti-depressants but they made her drowsy. In the end I decided to take some more time off work. We had a house in upstate New York. I thought we could spend some time there, together. I was going to drive her, but I had to hand over things at work and it all took longer than I thought it would.'

He felt as if he were underwater. Every breath was being torn from his lungs. 'I was still at work when the police came to find me. Her car had spun off the road and hit a bunch of trees. She was killed instantly.'

For several seconds, every part of Jemima's mind was narrowed in on finding words that could take the pain out of Chase's voice and then she was unfolding her legs and moving towards him. She slid her arms around his body, feeling his grief, his loss bleed through her.

Seconds later, she felt his arms tighten around her.

'I'm so sorry,' she whispered against his chest. It wasn't enough, but it was what she was feeling and she wanted to give him her truth. That was her job as a 'witness' to that most private of emotions: grief.

'I'm so sorry that happened to you.'

She heard him swallow. 'It's not just me it happened to. Her parents are still so devastated.'

'And you're there for them.'

'And you think that makes me some kind of saint?' He loosened his grip; his beautiful face was taut. 'It's the least I could do after what I let happen to their daughter.'

'You didn't let anything happen,' she protested. 'It was an accident.'

'An accident is just what people say so that they don't have to feel responsible.'

Except he did feel responsible. Which was why he had reacted so strongly when she had swum after that turtle. The whole experience of losing his baby and wife in short succession had made him want to save people from themselves as fervently as she wanted to save the planet. She caught his hands. 'You weren't responsible. How could you be? You weren't even there.'

He was shaking his head. 'But I should have been. I should have stopped her from driving. I should have come home but I didn't. Even though I knew it was raining hard. And that she hadn't been sleeping. Hadn't been out of the house for weeks. I cut corners like those divers.'

'You did everything you could. You took time off work. You took her to the doctor.'

'I know, but what she wanted, what she needed was time to grieve, time to heal, only I couldn't bear seeing her suffer so I just kept looking for solutions, trying to fix her.'

'You were trying to help her, to look after her because you loved her.' She felt her throat tighten as she thought about her father, about how hard it was to reach someone when they were lost in the shadows.

'I didn't do enough. She was my wife and I was like a bystander.'

'Because it was happening to you too. You were in shock,' she said gently.

'No, you don't understand. I didn't see what was happening.' The pain in his face made her want to cry. 'When the business started to grow, I found it really difficult to fall asleep, so I got some pills to help. She'd been taking them. That's why she'd been so drowsy. I didn't even realise until after the autopsy.'

Her heart lurched at the guilt in his voice. Chase was right. Grief was about time passing but guilt was different. It had to be cut back by someone who knew what they were looking for like a gardener separating bindweed from morning glory.

'People hide things when they're hurting, Chase. And sometimes what they hide hurts them the most, hurts them more than the original pain, whatever that is. But seeing, understanding that is only possible if you're not in pain too. And you were in pain.'

He didn't reply but she felt some of the tension in his body soften.

'I'm sorry,' he said finally. 'You shouldn't have to be dealing with this.'

'It's fine. You needed to talk. I was here.'

His eyes found hers, and he reached up and stroked her face. 'I always felt that telling someone would make it seem like I was wanting to share things, share my life, but it's not like that with you. We have this beautiful understanding of what we are, what this is. Maybe that's why I can talk to you, because you get it. You get that it doesn't change anything.'

It shouldn't hurt so much hearing him describe their relationship like that, but it did. Maybe because it was making her think about her own loss. But her pain was irrelevant right now.

Reaching up, she stroked his face. 'One day, you'll find someone who makes you want to change things.'

He shook his head. 'That part of my life is over. I know what it feels like to love someone and lose them and I will never go through that again.' He slid his hand through her hair. 'Right now, all I want is here with you.'

It was what she wanted too, and it scared her how much she wanted it, wanted him, and she knew that she was at risk of letting it get muddled up with other feelings.

Her pulse stuttered. Who was she trying to kid? It was already muddled. She wanted more than this. More than they had agreed to, and if she didn't act to subdue the way she felt about Chase she would be heading for another emotional disaster.

But she would deal with that later, she thought as he pulled her closer. And, closing her eyes, she arched against him hungrily.

CHAPTER EIGHT

THE NEXT DAY they didn't go back out in the submersible again. Instead they chilled on the yacht, which was very easy to do. As well as a swimming pool and a gym, the *Miranda* had a steam room, a sauna, a cinema, a basketball court and, best of all, a library.

Gazing up at the bookshelves, Jemima remembered her surprise when Chase had mentioned Hemingway at the bar. There were so many things she had got wrong about him. Like when he had got so angry with her on the dive. He was angry because he was scared. For her. Worried. About her.

She replayed the pain in his voice as he told her about his wife's accident, and her chest tightened. The thing she needed to remember was that his concern wasn't personal to her. Because of what happened, Chase felt responsible for people, even random divers.

'Pick one. I know you want to.'

Her body stilled. Chase was standing behind her. He was so close she could feel the heat from his body. His scent, that impossible to replicate mix of clean skin and maleness and sandalwood, enveloped her as his arms slid round her waist.

'There's no real order, I'm afraid, but I know the Hemingways are over there on the second shelf.' She could hear the smile in his voice, and she groaned softly. So he had noticed her reaction. Now that she knew him better, it was hard to imagine why she'd thought he had never read a book back then.

'Okay, I may have been a little judgey at the bar,' she admitted. 'It's just that most men I know only read the sports section of the paper.'

She felt his lips find the pulse below her ear. 'And am I like every man you know?' His voice was a hot whisper against her skin.

No, she thought, picturing him that night, how he parted the crowds as he moved. 'You were wearing a baseball cap that first day at the Cycle Shack and then you asked me about fishing so I made an assumption. The wrong assumption. But that's why I was surprised.'

Her heart quivered against her ribs. He was the surprise. Every day, she found out something new, something unexpected, something that made her want to know more, to know everything.

'Pleasantly, I hope.' His warm breath was tickling her skin, teasing her, making her belly clench and unclench, then clench again.

'Of course,' she said hoarsely. 'I like it that you read books.' There was so much more to him than simply thrill seeking, she thought, remembering how carefully he had manoeuvred the sub around the wreck. He was good company too, with views not just on sport as she'd assumed but literature, politics, music.

'That doesn't surprise me in the slightest. You know, I had you down as a teacher when we met at the harbour.'

'Why? Because I was wearing glasses?'

'That, and you used this voice when you spoke to me. Kind of strict and snippy. Pretty sexy actually.'

She laughed. 'You have a one-track mind.'

'Not true.' His voice softened and she felt it like a flame

inside her. And she was melting on the inside. It was that easy, that swift. 'I don't just want your body, I want your mind, Dr Friday.'

Something inside her twisted Chase wanting her mind didn't sound like something that should happen in a fling and she wished that Holly were there so that she could ask if he was just flirting. Or if it meant that he wanted more. The possibility of that pulled at a thread inside her so that when she spoke, her voice sounded scratchy and tight.

'I'm not a doctor yet.' And she probably never would be, she thought, her mood dropping a notch as it seemed to do whenever she thought about her life back in England. But that was the downside of a holiday. At some point you had to go back home and face up to all those things you had put on hold.

'It's just a matter of time.'

'And effort,' she said quietly. 'I do have to write it.'

'And you will.' He turned her to face him. 'Are you worried about it?'

Yes, she wanted to say. And not just about her PhD. She felt overwhelmed and yet also depressingly underwhelmed by her life. Here in Bermuda and with time on her hands, it was easy to see the choices she'd made in the round, and the far-reaching consequences of those choices. How she had stalled somewhere between adolescence and adulthood. A student homeowner who dated boys in bands and still borrowed money off her mum.

But after everything Chase had told her last night, she wasn't about to host a public pity party. It would be crass to think his revelations had given her the green light to raise her own woes. That wasn't what this was about. Last night had been the exception, not the rule.

'No, not really. It's just been a bit of a slog. But I should have expected that. I mean, when you have to write upwards of sixty thousand words you're going to hit the occasional stumbling block.'

'But he's not in your life any more.'

'Who?' She stared at him blankly.

'The stumbling block. Your ex.' His lip curled. 'Who is he anyway?'

The directness of his question caught her off balance, mainly because she had, to her astonishment, stopped thinking about Nick. And now that she was having to, it was as if she were remembering him from long ago and far away. He was just a blurred, indistinct shape, almost as if she were standing on the seabed staring up at him through the water.

'He's a singer in a band. He plays the guitar too.'

'Is that your thing?'

Jemima blinked. 'My thing? You mean am I some kind of groupie?'

He shrugged. 'Plenty of women like pouty guys with guitars. That's probably why so many men play them,' he added drily.

'No, that's not what it was about.' She was shaking her head without even realising that she was doing so. 'I didn't even really like his music.'

She felt Chase's narrowed gaze slowly inspect her.

'So why did you date him?'

Because he was a mess, and I thought I could fix him.

For a moment, she imagined saying that sentence out loud but surely that came under the heading of Too Much Information, for a fling anyway. And yet as she looked up, it felt almost as if he knew what she was thinking.

'Was he rich?'

Frowning, she shook her head again. 'The opposite. He was always skint.'

'*Skint?*'

'It means having no money. But it wouldn't have mattered if he was rich. I wouldn't date someone because of their money.' Quite the opposite, in fact. The more impoverished, the more hopeless they were, the better, she thought, thinking about exes. That was what they had in common.

He stared down at her, and there was no reason why she should blush at that moment, but she did anyway.

'So what, then?' She saw him swallow, saw his jaw tighten. 'Is he good-looking?'

Objectively he was, despite what Holly and Ed said. And yet when she pictured Nick's face, the face she'd once thought so mesmerisingly handsome, she could only see the weak chin and his perpetually sulky expression. 'I thought he was,' she admitted.

The sunlight was behind him so that his face was in shadow. After a moment, he reached out and touched her cheek, lightly. 'You deserve better.'

But I don't, she wanted to tell him. She didn't deserve to find love and happiness.

And yet, she did feel happy. Here. With him.

But of course that was the inherent paradox of the holiday fling. There was this outside-the-lines recklessness to the whole thing that was incredibly exciting and sexy. And because you were on holiday from the usual rigmarole of your day-to-day life you felt calmer, more in control.

Closer.

But a holiday fling was expressly finite. Keyword: holiday.

It didn't matter what happened in the movies, in real life holiday romances came with a built-in expiry date. There was no point in blurring lines between the now and the future. If it worked on the beach, it almost certainly wouldn't work in real life; Holly and Ed had drilled that into her back in England.

And having heard Chase talk about his marriage last night, she had realised something about herself. That whatever it was she had felt for her exes, it was certainly not the kind of love he had described to her. She wasn't sure she knew how to love like that.

Or if she ever would.

She blinked. 'I agree. But I'm not looking for anything serious.' Reaching up, she pulled a book off the shelf. 'Right now I'm happy with Mr Rochester.'

Not as happy as she usually was, she thought an hour later as she shifted position on the sunlounger. That was no reflection on the book. She loved *Jane Eyre*, both the character and the plot. Charlotte Brontë's story of an ordinary woman overcoming the obstacles in her life to find love and lasting happiness with the man she loved was a classic for so many reasons and she had read it countless times, but today she couldn't seem to follow the words.

Telling herself that the sun was too dazzling to read, she shut the book. But it wasn't the sun that was making it difficult to concentrate, it was him.

She glanced over to where Chase lay beside her, his muscular body gleaming in the sunlight. Unlike her, he wasn't attempting to read. Instead, his eyes were closed and she gazed at him greedily, grateful for the opportunity to just stare and stare.

That was what she needed to focus on. His beauty. His skills as a lover. But it was hard not to think about everything he had told her. Everything that had happened to him. Losing his baby. Losing his wife. They were huge life-transforming events and now that she had heard the pain in his voice, she couldn't unhear it. On the contrary, she could feel it reaching out to her.

But she was going to resist it.

Chase Farrar might be the most beautiful man she had ever met, possibly the most damaged. But he wasn't hers to fix for that very reason. She was here for fun, not to dole out therapy, and it didn't matter that she felt so close to him. In fact, that was a reason not to get any closer. Getting closer would increase the risk of him finding out who she was and what she'd done, and she knew how he'd react. Even just thinking about his face changing made her hands shake so much she nearly dropped the book.

No, this needed to stay simple. She needed to sideline everything she was feeling for him, and just embrace the physical need they felt for one another.

They ate lunch on the deck. It was the most perfect of days, she thought, gazing across the deck. The sea stretched away from the boat in every direction, gleaming blue beneath the hazy sun. As for the meal...

Today's menu was the most wonderful food she'd ever eaten. Lobster salad with mango puree and tempura followed by a chocolate and hazelnut eclair with banana ice cream and salted praline.

'Do you like it?'

She glanced up. Chase was watching her, his green gaze resting on her face. He was dressed casually, his feet bare, blond hair still damp from the pool, and just looking at him made her palms itch to touch him.

'It's delicious, but I don't understand how Gianluca does it. How does he come up with these flavour combinations?'

'It's what he's trained to do.' His eyes held hers steady and before she even realised what he was about to do, he reached over and picked up one of the shards of praline and bit into it.

'Hey, hands off.' She pulled her plate closer. 'I was saving that till last.' But her mouth was pulling at the corners.

'I'm not that patient. I can't wait until the end for the best bits. I want it at the beginning. And also in the middle. Especially when I'm with you,' he added softly.

She laughed. 'Don't try to distract me.' Picking up the last shard of praline, she took a deliberately tiny bite.

He rolled his eyes. 'I bet you're one of those people who unwrap presents really slowly so as not to tear the paper.'

'There's nothing wrong with that. In fact, it's the correct way to do it because then you can reuse it, which is better for the environment. Although personally I'm not a fan of wrapping paper.'

'Really? I thought you'd be all about curling ribbons and tying little bows.'

She held his gaze. 'You'd be surprised at how few things merit a bow. But as it happens I use *furoshiki*, you know, those Japanese fabric wraps.'

He nodded slowly. 'I've heard about those. Can you use any fabric? Like a sheet maybe.'

She frowned. 'I don't see why not.'

His dark green gaze simmered as it met hers. 'Good. Because I can think of nothing I'd like to do more than spend the afternoon in bed, unwrapping you.'

Heart thudding, she stared at him, mute and undone. Impatient. Lost somewhere between the hunger in his eyes and the heat building low in her pelvis.

She cleared her throat. 'Shall we skip coffee?'

He nodded. 'Let's do that.' Leaning forward, he fitted his mouth against hers and kissed her, his hand sliding through her hair, tilting her face so that he could deepen the kiss.

It took both of them a few seconds to register that his phone was ringing. He made a rough sound in his throat and pulled back. Eyes still fixed to her face, he yanked the phone from his pocket, frowning down at the screen. 'I better take this,' he said, getting to his feet and walking towards the pool.

'Would you like me to bring out some tea and coffee, Ms Friday?' Peter, one of the stewards, had come to clear the plates.

She glanced over to where Chase was still on the phone. It was impossible to read his expression, but he seemed to be listening intently, one hand jammed into the pocket of his shorts. 'No, thank you, Peter. I think we're good.' Shifting back in her seat, she stared out across the ocean, which was now a couple of shades darker than the sky. She knew Chase kept in contact with his New York office but he left the day-to-day running of his business to his C-suite. It must be something important for him to pick up.

'Sorry about that.'

He was back. He had only been gone a few minutes but her heart flipped over as he sat down, as golden and beautiful as any of the treasures he brought up from the ocean.

'Everything okay?' she asked, more out of politeness than because she expected him to share the details of his call.

'Everything's good,' he said slowly. His eyes switched to her face. 'That was Marcus. He wanted to let me know that they're just tidying up at the beach house. You can move back in whenever you're ready.'

She stared at him blankly, his words buzzing in her head like a sudden, unexpected swarm of bees. This was always going to happen. Only despite knowing that right from the start she hadn't seen it coming. She'd just let the days bleed into one another beneath the brilliant blue of the sky and got lost in Chase's glittering green gaze.

And now it was over.

'That's great,' she managed. Her voice hardly sounded like hers, but he didn't seem to notice.

'Yeah, he sent photos.' He held out his phone and she took it, and scrolled through the pictures, feeling giddy and faintly sick. 'It looks amazing. Joan will be thrilled. They must have worked really hard to get it all done so quickly.'

'They work fast but they do a good job.' He hesitated. 'So when do you want to be dropped back?'

It was a question that needed answering but her head was still full of how he had just reached across the table and kissed her. Hungrily. Deeply. It was a kiss that made the world tilt sideways and yet it was also a kiss that meant nothing.

Nothing in the sense of feelings and permanence, because this relationship was always going to end when the builders finished at the beach house. Only now that moment was here, it was hard to imagine leaving him. Harder still to picture waking up the next day without Chase beside her.

She felt an ache in her chest but ignored it. That was what they'd agreed and it was what she wanted, she told herself. There was no point in being disappointed. No point in pretending this was more important than it could ever be.

'Whenever is easiest for you.' She fought to keep her voice light and careless, balling her hands, trying to keep the emotion inside her. 'I'll work around your schedule. Are you thinking now or tomorrow?'

'I have that engagement I told you about in New York tomorrow evening.' His face was completely expressionless as he looked across the table, but there was a note in his voice she couldn't place. 'Have you ever been?'

She had forgotten about his trip to New York. Not that it mattered now.

'To New York?' She shook her head. 'No, this is my first time abroad.'

There was a long silence. 'Why not come with me, then? Get your first bite of the Big Apple.'

Jemima stared at him. Was he being serious? It seemed like a step away from the 'just sex' rules of their fling.

'I know that's not what we agreed,' he said as if he'd read her mind. 'But I feel like yesterday things changed. I changed them.' As a gull wheeled across the sky, he glanced upwards, his jaw tightening. 'This is your holiday. I promised you fun, and diving.'

'And you kept your promise,' she protested, and she was shocked to realise that out of all the men in her life, aside from her brother, Chase was the only man ever to do that. 'Lots of people make promises, Chase. Like my exes. They were great at promising all kinds of things. But there's a difference between saying you're going to do something and actually doing it.' Beneath the table, her fingers knotted. 'I've had a lot of fun.'

'Not last night, you didn't. You had to sit and listen to me unpack a load of emotional baggage and I shouldn't have done that. It wasn't fair. You didn't sign up for that. But I thought maybe a trip to New York might go some way to making it up to you. I have this event, but aside from that my time is my own. I could show you around.'

As she pictured the gleaming skyscrapers and the Statue of Liberty, and Chase's hand wrapped around hers, her limbs felt as if they were filling with light.

It was so, so tempting, but... 'You've already done so much for me. You don't need to do that.'

'I want to do it,' he said softly. 'I want to show you where I live.'

She stared at him dazedly. An impromptu trip to New York was the kind of thing couples did. Only they weren't a couple. They were lovers who weren't in love. Friends with benefits who'd only met a week ago and would go back to being strangers when she left Bermuda.

Her nails were cutting into her hands now. The thought of leaving Bermuda, of leaving Chase, made her feel as if she were drowning and, taking a deep breath, she counted to ten inside her head. 'Then yes, I'd love to go to New York with you.'

It was breaking all the rules. But this was her holiday, her rules, she thought defiantly, and she leaned in and kissed him because kissing was so much easier than trying to address any of the conflicting and contradictory emotions squeezing her heart.

At some point she was going to have to say goodbye, but not yet. Not until after New York.

New York. New York. So good they named it twice. Maybe that was why his heart felt as if it were beating at twice its normal rate, Chase thought, gazing down at Central Park from the window of his penthouse triplex apartment.

They had flown up late at night, arriving in darkness and to a flurry of seasonal snowflakes. His gaze drifted back down to the lights below. When he couldn't sleep he often stood here watching the traffic, taking comfort from the fact that he wasn't alone.

But he wasn't alone any more, he thought, glancing over his shoulder to where Jemima lay sleeping, her blonde hair splayed across the pillow, her naked body silvery in the moonlight.

He felt his own body harden, and his pulse gave a betraying twitch.

It wasn't the city that was making his heart beat at twice its normal rate. It was her, because, despite having told Jemima, told *himself*, that this arrangement was just a mutual interlude of pleasure and satisfaction, when he had heard Marcus say that the beach house was ready for her to move back in, he had been so paralysed with panic it had felt as if his spine had turned to ice.

It was understandable, of course. He and Jemima had hardly spent a moment apart since that day when he'd gone to her cabin to confront her, and it had been a long time since he'd spent the night with anyone, much less shared so much of his life.

Including the moment when it had imploded.

His chest tightened. For the best part of a decade he'd held it all together, pushed the grief and chaos and despair to the farthest, deepest parts of his mind. And then Jemima had called him out, demanded a respect that he should have given her automatically, and it had shocked him that he had become a man like that. A man who had to hurt others to hide his own pain.

It had shocked him into speaking. And once he started he couldn't stop, the barriers inside him that had cracked and given way like a dam breaking, releasing a flood of trapped memories.

And it had been hard and painful. Just like when he'd dislocated his shoulder last year during a storm and the *Miranda*'s medic had to rotate the joint until it went back into the socket. But now, although it still ached, it was a different kind of pain. The kind you knew would fade rather than need constant managing.

Was sharing his past the reason why he was finding it hard to imagine Jemima returning to the beach house?

The answer to that question, and to why he responded to her with such intensity, were not something he wanted to examine right now.

And he didn't need to. As he'd told her two days ago, that was the beauty of their relationship. It was about living in the moment. There was no need to give yesterday any more thought than tomorrow.

It was enough that she was here.

Except it wasn't.

The ice in his spine was back. He had told himself that he had invited her to New York on a whim, but the truth was that leaving her behind in Bermuda was not an option. Not when they had so little time together remaining. Now the panic was back too, sliding over his skin smoothly so that he couldn't get a grip of it.

'Chase.'

He turned. Jemima was half sitting up in bed, her eyes drowsy with sleep and something else, something that made hunger ripple through his body in a wave that almost knocked him off his feet.

'Chase.' She said his name again but he was already walking back to the bed and as his mouth found her, she took a quick breath like a gasp. 'I missed you.'

'I missed you too,' he said, pulling her against him, with an urgency that was not just simple desire any longer but a need to hold her close while he still could.

They woke late and ate a leisurely breakfast in bed, watching the sun catch the corners of Manhattan's skyscrapers.

'What do you think of it?' he said softly as her gaze returned to his face.

'I think it's amazing. I feel like I'm in a film.' Her mouth curved into one of those tiny smiles that made him want to kiss the corners and work his way inwards. 'I don't know how you get any work done though. I think I'd just spend my whole time staring out of the window.'

'I'm used to it.' Leaning forward, he ran his fingers over the curve of her hip. 'But there are other things I prefer to stare at.'

And touch. Caress. Lick.

His body pulsed its approval of that idea but, behind her, the New York skyline beckoned in the distance. Only that wasn't why she was here. He'd invited her because he had to. Because the idea of returning to New York alone had made him feel as if gravity had stopped working and he were breaking apart. Because he had suddenly realised how much he enjoyed her company.

He stared across the room to the view of the city that had been his home for over a decade now. This apartment had been his home too with his wife. After Frida's death, he'd clawed his way out of the darkness and found purpose through expanding his business and looking for shipwrecks, but at the heart of his life there was a void.

Now for the first time he could see how lonely he'd been.

How lonely he would be without Jemima.

With an effort, he lifted his hand from her hip. 'Right, you need to get dressed because we're going to go sight-seeing.'

Their eyes met, hers shining, and then the shine faded. 'I don't really have any warm clothes. Do you think I could borrow a coat?'

'Not necessary.' Still holding her hand, he slid off the bed and led her into the dressing room, watching her face as she stared at the selection of outfits his housekeeper had collected from his PA and which were now hanging from the rails. Beneath them several pairs of glossy leather boots and shoes were arranged neatly on the shelves.

'I can't accept this,' Jemima said, reaching out to touch a glossy white puffy coat. 'Any of these.' Her fingers trembled against a pale blue satin slip dress.

'Really?' He leaned back languidly against the door. 'You're quite welcome to walk down Fifth Avenue in that bikini you were wearing in Bermy but I'm warning you, you'll either get arrested or get frostbite.'

'I'll pay you back.' Her cheeks were pink again and she sounded flustered.

'There's no need. You're my guest and, besides, you being here is helping me. So think of it as a clothing allowance.'

'Me being here is helping you,' she repeated slowly.

'I need a plus one for this event.'

'Is that what I am?' She glanced up at him, her grey eyes wide and soft in the light spilling in through the window.

He thought about all the other plus ones he'd taken to similar events. In one sense, yes, and yet all of those women had been interchangeable. If one wasn't available he simply took another. But he couldn't imagine taking anyone other than Jemima.

As promised, they spent the day sightseeing. Jemima was sweetly excited by all the famous monuments. He watched her eyes widen as they walked towards the Empire State Building, and the decade between them seemed to be, not just about age, but experience. Grief had built an armour between him and the world, but she made him notice things that he took for granted. Like the yellow taxis and the screens in Times Square.

'What's this building?' she asked as they stepped through the revolving door into another huge glass tower.

'It's my office,' he said coolly. 'Hi, Mike,' he greeted the doorman, his heart pounding as he guided her through security to his private elevator.

'If you have some work to do, I can—' she began, but as the lift doors closed he pulled her against him and kissed her fiercely. 'I don't. I brought you here because the only way to truly see the city is from above.' Taking her hand, he led her onto the rooftop towards the helicopter that was squatting there like a dark, metallic insect.

'We're going in a helicopter.' Her voice was a squeak of disbelief.

Nodding, he pulled her closer, wrapping his arms around her as a cold breeze lifted her hair. 'Now aren't you glad you're not wearing a bikini?'

It really was the best way to see any city. At around a thousand feet up in the air, you got the kind of view usually reserved for postcards. As they followed the curve of the Hudson, he pointed out various landmarks. 'That's where we're going tonight,' he said, pointing down to the American Museum of Natural History. She glanced over at him, the smile that had been there a moment earlier faltering. 'Are you sure you want me to come with you?'

'Completely. Look, it's just an exhibition. We don't need to stay long. Just show our faces.'

'Your face, you mean,' she said quietly.

Time was supposed to fly when you were having fun so he must have been having a lot of fun, he thought later as he sat waiting in the open-plan living room for Jemima to get ready. One moment they had been gazing down at the Chrysler Building, the next he was changing into a suit and tie and texting his driver to tell him to bring the car round.

He felt rather than saw movement behind him and, turning, he forgot about the passing of time. Forgot almost to breathe. He was conscious only of the hammering of his heart.

Jemima was standing halfway down the stairs, her hair in some kind of loose chignon. She was wearing a cropped white silk shirt and a silver skirt that shimmered beneath the overhead lights. Her nude painted lips offset the smoky eyeshadow beneath her glasses.

'You look beautiful.'

He glanced at the strip of taut stomach, then wished he hadn't as his body tightened painfully in response. 'What is it?' he said as she bit into her lip.

'I've been trying to get these contacts in only I'm so nervous, my hands are shaking too much.'

'Don't be nervous, and don't worry about wearing contacts.'

Her eyes flicked up to his face. 'I wouldn't wear them either, but I honestly can't see anything.'

He crossed the room and took the stairs two at a time until his eyes were level with hers. 'Keep them on.' But take everything else off, he thought, his gaze dropping to the band of smooth skin. 'I mean it. I like that nobody else gets to see your eyes without them the way I do.'

The pulse at the base of her throat jerked forward and heat rushed through him, his body responding, growing hard, and he kissed her softly on the mouth, then drew back, groaning. 'Okay, I think it's time to leave, otherwise I'm going to have too many reasons to stay.'

CHAPTER NINE

HE WAS GLAD he had returned for the exhibition. It wasn't just that it was interesting, he liked watching Jemima. In fact, that was turning into a whole new distraction for him.

And he liked her company. Her laugh. Her curiosity. Her intelligence. After so many solitary years spent turning his back on anything more than sex with the occasional benefit, Jemima made him feel happy and whole in ways that he had not just forgotten but never experienced. It was both daunting and thrilling.

'So this is something your team found.' They were looking at a heavy gold chain that looked perfect despite having been immersed in water for nearly three hundred years.

'We found it in a wreck off the Bahamas.'

She frowned. 'The Bahamas?'

'I went down to help transport food and water after Hurricane Tana hit three years ago.' He saw that she was staring at him uncertainly, as if she wasn't sure if he was joking or not. 'It's not all about the adrenaline,' he said quietly.

'I know that.' Leaning forward, she touched the tiny Monmouth Rock logo on the explainer next to the glass display case. 'Is that why you support the trust?'

She had noticed. He felt a small prickle of surprise. Not many people bothered to look at the small print, let alone details like business logos. But then Jemima looked closer than most people. Saw more. Cared more.

'They do good work.' The International Marine Conservation Trust was one of many charities Monmouth Rock supported. 'I like that it's a joint initiative with marine archaeologists and biologists.'

They spent about an hour admiring the exhibits. Or rather Jemima did. He went back to admiring her. 'Have you had enough?' he said finally as they drifted slowly back through the gallery. 'Or do you want to go to the after party?'

'There's an after party?' she said, and he could see the excitement in her eyes at such a novelty.

'Not officially, but this is New York, New York, baby. You're in the city that never sleeps.' He sang the words softly then spun her round, dipping her in his arms. 'There's always an after party.'

After the cool serenity of the museum, Le Bomb was packed and deafeningly loud so that you could feel the music move through your body. It reminded him of that first night in the Green Door, and he found himself wishing that he could reset time and start again. Instead, he pulled her against him. If they could just keep dancing then maybe the night would never end.

But it did. Finally at around three o'clock in the morning, he felt her start to flag.

'Let's go home,' he whispered. As they walked through the foyer, he felt Jemima's hand tighten around his arm. 'What is it?'

'There's something wrong with that woman.' He turned. A woman with dark hair was slumped on one of the velvet couches in the foyer. Her friends were patting her back, giggling.

Chase stepped closer. 'Is she okay?'

'She's just been sick. She'll be fine.'

'Can she sit up?' Jemima sidestepped past him. Squinting down at her friend uncertainly, one of the women shook her head. 'I don't think so.'

'What's her name?'

'Shannon.'

'Hey, Shannon. Can you hear me?' He watched Jemima crouch down next to her. 'Can you hear me?' As the woman groaned, she turned towards him. 'Can I borrow your jacket? And could you call an ambulance? Her breathing is wrong. I think she has alcohol poisoning.'

They waited until the ambulance arrived. On the ride back to the apartment, Jemima was quiet. Remembering how upset she'd got about the divers, he squeezed her hand. 'She'll be okay.'

But Jemima didn't look okay. She looked pale and her skin looked taut around her eyes and mouth and he knew that she wasn't just thinking about the woman. That it was something to do with whatever it was that she had been holding back.

She nodded. 'Hopefully.'

'Well, she's got a better chance of being okay than if you hadn't been there.'

Her face stilled. 'I saw her earlier. In the bar. I should have done something then.'

'Done what?' He frowned. 'Look, you noticed her, which is more than most people did, and you called the ambulance. You did everything right.'

'You don't know that.' She was shaking her head.

'I know what I saw, Jemima.'

'I'm not talking about tonight,' she said shakily. 'And you don't know what I did.'

Chase was so stunned by her words that he didn't feel the limousine slowing in front of his apartment building.

'Jemima?'

He reached out to touch her, wanting, needing to reassure himself as much as her. What could she have done? But she was already out of the car, walking so fast that he had to run to catch up with her.

They were standing in the lobby. As the lift doors opened, she stepped inside and flattened herself against the side as if he were dangerous. Or she were.

'I don't understand what's happening here.'

It was more than that. He was sideswiped by what Jemima had said in the car, and by the sudden, violent change to the mood of the evening. She had not just withdrawn, she was in full-scale retreat, he thought, watching her eyes do a jerky circuit around the lift.

'You don't need to.' He winced inside, hearing the echo of what he'd said to her on the *Miranda*: that their relationship was just about sex. Only it wasn't true then, and it felt even less true now.

As the doors opened, he stepped aside to let her pass, scared that if he didn't, that if he left first, she would take the lift back down and flee into the night. Because he had seen that look before. That need to hide away with your pain. Although Frida hadn't fled so much as sleepwalked.

But back then he had been a different man. A man who was incapable and unwilling to see what was in front of him. He wasn't that man any more. In large part thanks to the woman he was following into the living room.

'I want to.'

'Well, I don't.'

Her eyes were huge and dark as if he was hurting her just by being there and that hurt more than he could have imagined. Hurt enough that he had to press his feet into the quarter sawn white oak flooring to steady himself.

Behind her, he could see a thin, pale line along the horizon and he knew that if he walked to the window and looked down, the city would look like one of those snow globes they sold for tourists. But up here it felt as though everything were still shaking.

'This was a mistake,' she said hoarsely. 'All of it. It was supposed to be a one-night stand. I should have gone to a hotel. I should never have let you talk me into it.'

'You think I talked you into this?' He was shocked, appalled.

'I wish I had been thinking, but I was busy pretending this was who I am, but it's not.'

He stared at her, his heart ricocheting against his ribs. He couldn't believe that she was the same woman who had reached for him in the moonlight. He could remember the heat in her eyes, that fierce glitter of desire. They had been lovers. Now she was looking at him as if he were her enemy.

No, not her enemy, he thought with a jolt. Her executioner.

'Look, I get that you're upset about what happened in the club. I am too, so maybe it would help to talk about it,' he said, and he was surprised and relieved to hear how calm his voice sounded. But that was what she needed him to be because she was in shock, he just hadn't realised it earlier because she had seemed so cool-headed and efficient.

'I don't want to talk.' She looked away to the far side of the room and he saw a flash of something like fear cross her face. 'I want to go to bed. On my own.' Her voice was edged with hysteria and he could see that she was close to tears. Could almost hear her desperation to escape hammering through her veins as she toed off her shoes and edged towards the stairs. And then she was running up them lightly, disappearing into the darkness. He heard a door slam, the slight click of a lock.

He stared down at her shoes, his heart pounding. He felt suddenly exhausted, and cold, as if the falling snow had leached into his bones. But he couldn't risk going to bed in case she sneaked out as she had before. Only this time there would be no note.

Keeping one eye on the staircase, he made his way to the kitchen. Aside from coffee he wasn't a big fan of hot drinks, but he needed something to bring warmth back to his limbs. He made a pot of tea, remembering as he did so that night on the island when she'd found him watching the storm.

It was nature at its most explosive. Stunning and terrifying, even more so when you were out on the ocean, and yet he was more scared now than he had been that night.

He made his way back into the living room and sat down on the sofa. His eyelids felt heavy and, picking up a cushion, he hugged it closer, letting his body go limp. Except it wasn't a cushion, it was Jemima. His arms tightened and he pulled her against him, her heartbeat washing through him, steadily like waves hitting the shoreline.

His eyes snapped open.

'Jemima.'

The cushion was on the floor but she was standing there at the end of the sofa, still in her shimmering skirt and blouse. In the half-light, her face was pale and blurred at the edges, her pupils, saucer wide. 'I'm sorry for what I said. You didn't talk me into doing anything. I wanted it, wanted you, and I don't think it was a mistake. I just wanted you to know that I didn't mean what I said.'

'I do know…' He hesitated. 'And I know that after everything I told you the other night you have no reason to think I could help.'

She was shaking her head. 'I don't think that.'

'I wouldn't blame you if you did,' he said quietly. Now that she was here, he was desperate not to scare her away.

And she was scared as well as being upset, he realised suddenly, remembering how her eyes had darted round the room.

His feet braced against the floor.

No questions. No conversation. You don't need to know anything about me and I don't want to know anything about you... I want to get naked with you, now, tonight.

He could hear Jemima's voice in his head, could still feel his reaction; that moment of wordless shock followed by a heart-pounding affirmation. Yes, and yes, and yes again.

And for a light-headed second, part of him wanted to pull her closer, kiss away the ache in her voice, but he couldn't do that, not before he knew what or who had made Jemima both fear and seek the shadows. Not before he knew for certain that he wasn't the reason.

'What scared you?'

She didn't react; it looked as though she wasn't even breathing. He only realised he was the one holding his breath when she sat down on the other sofa.

'This. Having this conversation...' Her voice trailed off and she made a small, helpless gesture. 'I never have. People don't know. I didn't want you to know.'

Her eyes drifted down to where her hands were clenched in her lap.

'But you knew anyway,' she whispered.

'Knew what?'

She was shaking her head. 'Remember that first day we went diving?'

His eyes narrowed. 'I remember that I was irrational and unfair.'

'You told me that I didn't follow, though, and you were right. Maybe not about that dive. But about me. The one time it mattered I didn't follow through. I did the opposite, I gave up. Even though he had nobody else I left him. I left him to die.'

Chase stared at her in silence. His heart felt as if it were trying to break through the bars of his ribcage. Whatever he had been expecting her to say, it wasn't that.

'Left who?' he said finally.

'My father.' She sounded breathless, as if she'd been running and maybe she had. Fleeing from the past, the memories, the pain. It was so hard to keep out of reach. Harder still to turn and face them. He stared at her in silence, remembering how it had felt telling her about Frida. But this was her story, he could only prompt her to tell it.

'How did he die?'

'He got hypothermia. He'd been trying to get into his flat, but he was always losing his key and nobody was there to let him in. The police thought he decided to sleep in the porch.'

She was shaking now as if she was cold too.

'Why didn't he go to a friend's house or a hotel?'

'He didn't have any friends. He didn't have anyone. He had people he drank with, but they were like him.'

'Like him?'

'He was an alcoholic. I don't know exactly when it started but by the time I came along it had gone from him liking a drink to needing one. And then another, and another.'

The exhaustion in her voice came from another time.

'That must have been hard.'

She bit her lip. 'It was. Particularly for my mum. She loved him so much.'

'How did they meet?'

'They worked at the same university. He was a professor of political science but he also wrote columns in various newspapers. He had this beautiful voice. My mum used to call him the "snake charmer" because he could get politicians to say things that nobody else could. When he wasn't drinking he could be sweet and funny but alcohol made him nasty, and he kept losing jobs. They got divorced and a couple of years later my mum got remarried to this really nice man called Adam, and then Holly and Ed were born.'

Which explained why the twins were so different from her, he thought, gazing over at her small, pale face.

'Adam's lovely.' Some of the tension in her voice eased a fraction. 'He's so solid and kind. I think him being like that was one of the reasons why I decided to go and live with my dad. Because I knew Adam would look after everyone. And my dad needed looking after.'

'How old were you?' he said quietly.

'Thirteen, nearly fourteen. It wasn't that I didn't see him. I did. I saw him every weekend but I hated leaving him, and it didn't feel fair for him to be alone.' There was a shake in her voice now. 'And I thought, I actually believed that I understood him better. That I could help him. But it was so hard.'

As she pressed her hand against her mouth, his throat felt so tight it ached even to breathe.

'There was never any food. He kept forgetting to buy it, so I got him to put money aside but when he needed alcohol he'd just take it. Sometimes he'd fall over and hurt himself. One time, he collapsed and he got taken to hospital but he discharged himself. Another time he got mugged and he came home covered in blood, but I didn't want to tell anyone because it felt like I'd be betraying him.'

Chase felt his heart squeeze tight. He understood what it was like to feel both helpless and responsible, but he had been an adult. At thirteen, Jemima was little more than a child.

'Had he been drinking that night?' he said gently.

She nodded. 'He drank every night. I'd lie awake at night worrying about where he could be, terrified something had happened to him, imagining all these awful scenarios. But at the same time I'd dread him coming back. He'd just sit there and cry.' There was a tight twist to the corner of her mouth. 'I was tired and stressed all the time, and I was missing school so that I could look after him.'

He saw her bite down on the inside of her lip. 'And then one of my teachers asked me to stay behind. She told me that they were worried about me. About my grades, and I think I'd been waiting for someone to tell me that because I went home and I packed my stuff. I waited until he got back from the pub and I knew he was safe and then I left.'

Her eyes skidded away towards the window.

'I didn't go and see him for a couple of weeks. I was ashamed and I thought he'd be angry but then one day, about three weeks after I moved out, I was coming back from school and he came out of this pub.'

She was still staring across the room, but she was blinking now, trying to keep the tears back.

'It wasn't one he went to regularly, and I didn't recognise him at first. He looked so thin and his face was all red and blotchy, and he had this terrible cough.'

For years now he had fought to keep his own pain at bay but, listening to Jemima work to get each word out, he wished he could take her distress and make it his burden.

'I was scared that he was going to have a go at me, but he didn't. He asked me about school, and Mum, and he told me that he didn't blame her or me for leaving.' Her voice looped higher. 'He said he'd heard me leave but that he hadn't tried to stop me because he had nothing to make me stay. It was the last time I saw him alive.'

Her face quivered and then she was crying, pressing her hand against her mouth to stifle her sobs. He got to his feet and was beside her in two strides, pulling her against him. He felt her stiffen and then her body seemed to lose shape and he lifted her onto his lap and let her cry against his shoulder.

'I should have stayed with him.

He stroked her face. 'You were a child.'

'I left him.' Tears were spilling down her cheeks. 'He had no one in his life but me, and I knew that, and I still left him.'

'Say you'd stayed? Then what?'

'He'd be alive. I would have been there to let him in.' She cried again then and he held her close. Finally as the sky began to lighten, he got to his feet and carried her upstairs and laid her on the bed, peeled off her clothes and his and then pulled the covers around them both.

She fell asleep almost immediately, curling her body around his just as she had so many times before. Why then did it feel different? Was it the way her head was resting on his chest? Or the jerkiness of her breathing?

His heart contracted. It wasn't anything Jemima was doing. It was him. He was the reason it felt different. Because despite his believing that it wasn't possible for him to love again, the impossible had happened. He had fallen in love with Jemima. Fallen in love with the woman at the harbour who had asked for his help in that ridiculously over-polite tone and then turned to quicksilver in his hands back on his boat. The same woman who had shucked open the hard shell he had built around himself, letting the light in on the darkness he'd held so close for so long.

He breathed out shakily. She had made love not just possible but inescapable, necessary. And now that he knew that, he wanted to tell her how he felt. Tell her that things were different. Roar his love from the Manhattan rooftops. This love that had given his life a meaning it had lost when Frida died. A love that would outlive this holiday. A forever kind of love. The kind that needed and deserved to be witnessed and sanctioned.

But having told her that part of his life was over, how could he persuade her that he had changed his mind? More importantly, having agreed that this was a holiday fling, how could he persuade Jemima to change hers?

CHAPTER TEN

BREATHING OUT SLOWLY, Jemima gazed up at the ceiling
of the sauna, blinking hard. They had woken late, reaching for each other in the midday sun, and as he'd slid into
her body she had been intensely grateful for the heat that
rushed through her, a heat that blotted out everything but
the pleasures of the flesh, his and hers.

Maybe that was why when he'd suggested that they have
a swim and take a sauna she had so readily agreed. But this
was a different heat and unfortunately it didn't seem to be
offering the same level of oblivion.

It was too late to take back her words, but she doubted she
could even have done that at the time. Something had happened when she saw that woman at the club. It had tapped
into her memory, pressed against some invisible crack and
within seconds, the crack had widened and everything she
had tried so hard to hold in had started spilling out, and
that was that.

She glanced up through her lashes to where Chase lay
on his back at a right angle to her. That he was keeping his
distance a little was hardly surprising. It was a lot to deal
with, and she still wasn't entirely sure why she had felt so
compelled to tell him everything.

Not quite everything. She hadn't told him how much she

was dreading the end of their affair or how impossible it would be to live without him.

There was a tiny, almost inaudible beep. 'That's fifteen minutes.' Her pulse jerked forward as his deep voice filled the room.

The sauna was one hundred and eighty metres above ground and it had a triple-glazed high efficiency annealed window that allowed you to stare at the Empire State Building while you relaxed. The fact that she had barely looked at the view said a lot about the man who had just rolled languidly onto his side to face her.

Not just his looks. It was how he had acted in the early hours of this morning. It was fair to say that nothing had ever meant more to her than his calm, measured attention and lack of judgement, except perhaps how he had pulled her into his arms and held her, his body warm and solid against hers.

'You don't have to get into the pool now. I know you can stay in longer than me,' she said quickly.

'No, I'm hot enough.' But as he held the door open for her, he caught her hand.

'Let's skip the pool. I have a better idea.' As she hesitated, he smiled down at her, just a slight, teasing curve of his lips. 'Come with me. I think you'll like it. Here, put this on—' he handed her a robe and some flip-flops '—and these. You can't go in barefoot.'

He led her along the side of the pool and opened a door into what she had assumed was a changing room. It wasn't. She stared in amazement. It looked almost like the sauna except that, instead of wood, the walls were clad in stone and everything was covered in what looked like...

'Is this snow?'

Shutting the door, he nodded. 'I was doing business in Dubai, and they had one of these in the hotel.'

'This is completely wild. Is this actual snow?' She stared up dazedly at the ceiling, blinking into the tiny white crystals dropping onto her face.

'It snows all day every day if you want it to. Solar power, before you ask, and, while I remember, the jet we flew here on is powered by sustainable fuel.'

She smiled. 'I'm impressed, but I'm also curious as to why you want it to snow every day.'

'It's supposed to be good for you. Mainly though it's because it only snows about twelve days a year in New York and I miss the snow back home.' His green eyes locked onto hers. 'I thought you might be missing it too. Home, not the snow. Or maybe that as well.'

There were snowflakes on the end of his eyelashes. For a moment she couldn't speak; her breath was knotted in her throat.

'Because of last night,' he said softly. He reached over and touched her cheek and it was impossible not to lean into the warmth of his hand. 'Look, I know you probably feel weird, but you don't need to. We both had things we'd been holding onto a long time. I'm just glad to have been of some help.'

For a moment she thought he was going to say something else but then he reached out and took her hands and pulled her against him, his green eyes resting on her face as he rubbed his nose against hers.

'And because we have this trust thing I'm going to let you into a secret. The real reason I have this room is so I can build snow people.'

She felt a tug of heat low down as he caught her smile. And relief that she hadn't wrecked these last days together.

'You should just come to Edale if you want to do that.' Realising the implications of her words, she said quickly, 'We get masses of snow where I live. It's beautiful, like something from *The Snow Queen*.'

His eyes were steady and unblinking on her face. 'Maybe I could drop by next time I'm in London.'

She felt a rush of something that she knew to be happiness, which was ridiculous because another part of her knew that it would never happen. Should never happen, according to the rules of the holiday fling. Only this didn't feel like a fling any more. For either of them.

But then again she knew only too well how attracted she was to the dark and unpredictable and there was no point in trying to ignore that fact or the disastrous consequences of ignoring it.

'It's not exactly drop-by-able but I'd like that,' she said carefully. 'But first I'd really like to go back to Bermuda. To the beach house. I don't feel like I've spent nearly enough time there and it's nearly time for me to go home.' She knew that, of course, but saying it out loud made it suddenly, painfully real. Her heart punched upwards into her throat as she tried to picture the blank space where Chase would have stood, the silence of her world without his voice.

No, not yet.

She took a breath. 'And I'd really like you to come with me.'

He touched her cheek, brushed his thumb over her bottom lip and then tilted her head up to meet his. 'I'd like that too,' he said softly.

It was better that they had talked, Jemima thought as she stared through the window of Chase's private jet at the brilliant blue sky. Aside from inviting him to build snow people in Edale, of course.

It was noticeably easier to breathe and her body felt looser and lighter now, as if a burden had been lifted from her shoulders. And really that was exactly what had happened. Before today, talking about her father, his life, his death had been out of bounds and impassable for so long, like those terrible war zones where landmines were still waiting to be cleared.

It hadn't been painless to say what had to be said, but with Chase's arms wrapped around her the flame had been pure and contained like a votive candle. It was a flame that would never go out, but it would never hurt her any more either.

And now she could see how much of her life had been dictated by her guilt and her grief. How it had cast a shadow over her like a mourning veil. But Chase had lifted the veil, and she had let him because she knew he understood what she was feeling. He had felt it himself, and been as trapped.

With hindsight, it was obvious that they'd had that in common all along, which was no doubt why it had been so easy to leapfrog from one-night stand to holiday fling, and now to this understanding that she had never had with anyone before, not even the twins.

There was still an irrevocable sadness that her father hadn't been able to cope with life without a drink, but she had accepted that dating damaged men would never fix the past. Things felt clearer now, and not just the past.

She could picture the title of her thesis, the chaotic pages of notes, only now patterns were forming, sentences shifting into focus. Blinking into the sunlight, she turned her head, and felt her pulse jerk as she found Chase looking at her as if he'd been waiting for her to turn or perhaps to say something. For a moment, all she could do was gaze at him.

He was so beautiful, but he was so much more than that. He was a good boss and he cared about people, the planet… Her breath caught. He cared about her.

'What is it?' he said softly.

'Could I borrow your laptop? I left mine on the *Miranda*. Would you mind?'

'Of course not. Help yourself.' He handed it to her, and in answer to the curiosity in his green eyes, she said quietly, 'I just need to write a few notes for my thesis.'

She wrote solidly for the remaining two hours of the flight time. Wrote more in those two hours than she had written in the previous six months. It wasn't finished but she had a title that was worthy of the word-count, and a structure.

'Is it going well?'

Looking up, she found Chase watching her again, and she nodded slowly. 'I don't know why but I think I know what I'm doing.'

'Of course you do. You're going to save the world. You've already saved me.'

I have?

The question formed in her mouth but before she had a chance to ask it, his phone buzzed, and as he glanced down at the screen she forgot about what his answer might be. His eyes were suddenly blazing green.

'What is it?'

'It's Billy. The lab results have come back.' There was a shake to his voice. 'That cooking pot they found near that partial wreck off the south-eastern reef, it looks like it might come from the Portuguese fleet that disappeared in 1594.'

She squeezed his hand. 'That's incredible.' But looking

up at Chase's face, she felt her chest tighten and her excitement ooze away. She had seen that look so many times in her life. It was the look of an addict getting their fix: Part relief, part panic that it might not be real. Only she had chosen to ignore it because she had wanted him to be different. Because she had wanted their truths to mean something. And they did, but not enough.

It was never enough.

'You must be so pleased.'

He looked up from the screen, his face blank, as if what she had said made no sense, as if he had forgotten she was even there. The thought winded her. But, of course, she could never compete.

'I just needed proof,' he said slowly. 'Now I know it's out there.' Only that wasn't all he needed, she thought, forcing her mouth into what she hoped was a smile. There would always be the next fix, and then the next.

After the apartment, Joan's house felt even more like a doll's house. As Chase had promised, his builders had done a good job. So good, she wished they could come and renovate the cottage.

The next two days were bittersweet.

Outwardly everything was perfect. That first evening, they made love and they talked, sitting on the sand, some part of them always touching the other. He was everything she wanted in the world right there. He made her world complete.

And she allowed herself that one night, but the next morning and with every passing hour she tried to pull back a little. To not take his hand quite so quickly or lean in so eagerly for a kiss because it was going to stop soon enough and she had to wean herself off him because time wouldn't stop. But even if she could stop it, it wouldn't change anything. It wouldn't change all the ways that Chase was wrong for her.

'What's up?'

She glanced up at him, her head still reeling from the impossibility and rightness of that statement.

'Nothing, why?'

They were sitting on the porch watching the tide turn.

'You're frowning.' He reached out and smoothed her forehead. As always, his touch made her shiver inside.

'I just realised I need to check in.' Because tonight was her last night in Bermuda. The thought made everything inside her roll sideways like a boat about to capsize.

'In fact I should probably start packing.' She started to get to her feet. 'It's a really early flight.'

He angled his head back, his green eyes holding her so that she sat back down. 'So leave later.'

'I can't. There's no more flights tomorrow.' She had checked.

'Then why don't I take you?'

For a moment she just stared at him. Maybe she had misunderstood. 'You want to take me back to England?' she said, finally.

His fingers tiptoed over the curve of her hip. 'I have some business in London next week, but I can just go earlier. You could show me your cottage. We could build some snow people in your garden,' he said softly.

A honeyed sweet lightness was spreading through her limbs. Chase in England, in her cottage. She could see him, crouching on the lawn behind the cottage shaping snow, his green eyes dark like the mistletoe that grew around the oak trees.

'I don't want this to end, Jemima, and I don't think you

do either.' There was an edge to his voice, like an actor who wasn't quite sure of his lines. 'So why don't we just carry on like this?'

'Like this,' she repeated slowly. 'So it would be like another holiday.' Although she would have to go to work.

'Why does it have to be a holiday?' His gaze was dark and intent on her face. 'It could be like this every day.'

She stared at him in confusion. 'How could that happen?'

'It's very simple. I love you and I think you love me.'

Jemima stared at him, mute with shock. Her heart had stopped beating. Chase loved her. He loved her. She could feel her world rearranging itself into a place of yearned-for possibilities, a blurring, swirling carousel of lights and bright colours, and it was so beautiful and she wanted it so badly that she could hardly bear to look.

Her heart jerked inside her chest, making her jump.

I love you and I think you love me.

His words rolled queasily around her head. Every man she had ever dated had said a version of that sentence. And at the time they'd thought they meant it, and probably Chase thought he meant it now and maybe he did. Maybe it could work. She loved him and he was amazing in bed, and he was kind. Considerate. Sweet. She thought back to how he had taken her out in the submersible and then to New York. No one had ever done anything like that for her before. He had wanted to make her smile but he had also held her while she cried.

She stopped herself, pinching off the flow of hope.

Of course, he didn't love her. They had met nine days ago. And yes, a lot had happened in that time but it didn't mean any of this flame and hunger would work in real life. She glanced past his shoulder at the shimmering curve of water and the looping sunlight, watching it break into pieces and fly away like petals. In its place she could see the wet streets of England and cold grey reality.

'But I don't. I don't love you,' she lied. 'And I doubt that you love me. It just feels like love because we're here in paradise and it's all so perfect, but this isn't my life.'

'It could be.'

Could it? Her throat tightened. The desire to agree with him, to pull him closer and tell him that he was right was nearly impossible to resist, but the very fact that she could think that way was a reason not to. Wanting something to be true didn't make it so. She had come here to learn that lesson and, thanks to Chase, she had.

'Please don't do this. Please don't make this any harder than it is.'

'You're the one that's making it hard, Jemima. I'm saying it's simple.'

She got to her feet, shaking her head. 'Yes, you're saying it. But saying and doing are two different things.'

His face hardened. 'And I know that. I'm not one of your ex-boyfriends. I'm not your father. You know who I am. You know I'm not going to break my promises. You can trust me and I know I can trust you because you've made me remember the good things about loving someone, not just the risk.'

She thought about the snow room, and the yachts, and she remembered how his eyes had blazed when Billy had texted him about the bowl. Yes, she knew who he was. She knew he was addicted to the adrenaline rush of diving for treasure. She also knew who she was to him. She was a novelty right now. Like the beach house. And he was excited by the idea of playing with her in the snow in her garden. But Chase was a man who had a room in his penthouse where it snowed three hundred and sixty-five days a year on command. His command. How long before his attention would waver and be drawn to the glittering prizes waiting to be discovered beneath that endless blue ocean?

The idea of those green eyes drifting away made her feel suddenly sick.

'I do know who you are, Chase,' she said quietly. 'You're a billionaire who looks for treasure in his spare time.'

'And that's a problem?' Now he was on his feet. 'You said you didn't care about money. Except you do if there's too much of it.'

'I care about honesty and right now you're not being honest with me or yourself. I saw how you reacted to that text message from Billy.'

'Yeah, I was excited. It was exciting.'

'You weren't excited, Chase, you were transfixed. You didn't even know I was there.'

'That's not true.'

'I know what I saw. And I saw how much it mattered to you.'

'You matter to me.'

'But I won't. As soon as we leave here, it won't feel the same. It can't because none of this is real, you know that. You just don't want to admit it.'

'I'm real.' He held out his hand. 'We're real, Jemima.'

She stumbled backwards, needing distance between them. If only she could cover her ears too. That way she wouldn't have to listen to his words and be tempted into doing what she always did. What she wanted to do now, which was let herself be talked round.

'No, what we have is special. It's special and unique and I've loved every moment of it but it's like you said before— the reason it's special is because it's not meant to last. It's a world within a world that has nothing to do with real life.'

'Jemima...'

'I'm sorry, but I can't.'

He stared at her for what felt like a lifetime. She could feel herself crumbling inside. She wanted him to stay so badly but she would simply be postponing the agony.

'This was only ever meant to be a one-night stand.'

'And it didn't stay one for a reason.' His voice sounded raw, as if it were scraping over a wound.

'Yes. Sex.'

As his eyes narrowed on her face, her heart felt as if it were going to burst. 'You're a remarkable woman. Smart and sexy and strong and beautiful. And I thought you were brave. But you're a coward.'

'Please, just go.' It hurt to speak, to breathe.

He walked away. Or she assumed he had. She was crying so much she couldn't see. And now, standing alone in paradise, she admitted to herself what she couldn't admit to him. That he was right. She loved him.

Only she had pushed him away. She had pushed him out of paradise.

CHAPTER ELEVEN

GAZING UP FROM the screen of his phone, Chase felt his chest tighten. The sky was changing, growing lighter by the moment. Ten minutes ago it had been the same colour as the lead ballast bars down below in the *Miranda*'s hull. Now it was the same soft grey as Jemima's eyes.

In another hour it would shift and lighten into a faded blue, and by then she would be gone.

Heart pounding, he glanced back down at his phone. He'd lost count of the number of times he'd checked for messages. Enough to know that Jemima had meant what she said at the beach house. And he could hardly blame her, he thought, replaying the moment when he had told her that he had wanted to carry on seeing her.

As if they were teenagers who had just hooked up at a party.

Unable to sit with that cramping sense of loss and cowardice, he got to his feet and walked across the deck. Leaning against the handrail, he gazed down into the shifting blue waves, remembering how she had swum by his side on that first dive, communicating simply with hand signals, every movement synchronised to his.

He loved her then, this beautiful woman who wanted to save the world.

Had been in love with her since that moment when she

summoned him to talk to her about hiring a bike in that crisp, precise English voice. But after so many years of not allowing himself to feel anything, he hadn't recognised what he was feeling. Hadn't wanted to recognise it until that night in New York. Holding her close, feeling the rigidity melt from her body, he had felt not trapped, but freed.

And what had he done with that love?

His hands trembled against the railing. He had waited, waited too long, only acting when she began checking in to her flight. And he should have told her earlier, told her better, but instead he had left it to the last moment. And instead of explaining to her how he felt and why, he'd made it sound simply as if he wanted to keep on sleeping with her, tossing in his love almost as an afterthought.

And now she was leaving Bermuda.

Above him, a lone gull was beating towards the ocean and he stared up at it, seeing instead a plane, her plane moving inexorably into the distance, into an unknown future.

He glanced around the silent deck. Only for him, a future without Jemima was no future.

The sound of the alarm was surprisingly loud in the quiet of the beach house. Not that she needed help waking up, Jemima thought, glancing at the flashing numerals on her phone. She had seen every half-hour and hour since she had woken at three o'clock from a dream that had jerked her awake and left her shaking in the darkness. In her dream, the *Miranda* was disappearing from view and she was in the water, holding up her arm, waving and crying, but the yacht kept moving further and further away until she was alone in the vast blue ocean.

And she was alone now. As she gazed round the empty beach house, the absence of Chase was unbearable. He had made her laugh, made her feel sexy and strong. He had held her while she cried and in his arms she had felt herself healing.

Only she had been too scared to admit her love to him. Too scared to admit his love might be real. Now it was too late.

Picking up her phone, she saw a text from her sister.

Can't wait to see you. The new and the old you. The unstoppable Jemima Friday. xxx

Her heart cartwheeled in her chest. She had told herself that she and Chase couldn't survive in real life but now here was Holly telling her that she was unstoppable. And she was. But she wanted Chase there by her side.

She felt her eyes blur with tears. Experience had taught her to assume that she was only capable of loving irreparably damaged men, and so she had simply refused to accept that loving Chase was an option. That he was different and she was different with him. She had held onto her first impressions like a dog with a bone and it didn't matter that she had lost him and pushed him away, she knew that her love for him was never going anywhere.

Except love wasn't a big enough word for the feeling that now overwhelmed her. A feeling that made everything she had ever called love before feel insipid and colourless in comparison because loving Chase was not a feeling. It was an imperative. He was up there with oxygen and water and food and shelter.

Without him she couldn't survive.

Only she had been so scared that it might not work that she had sabotaged it intentionally.

Her phone alarm chimed again, and, looking down at

the time on the screen, she felt her pulse quicken. How could it be so late? Her flight was in less than an hour. She swiped onto her list of contacts, and scrolled down, picked a number.

Somewhere on the island, a phone was ringing. Her breath caught as a man's voice answered.

'Sam,' she said quickly. 'It's Jemima. Jemima Friday— you gave me a lift from the airport. I was wondering if you could come and pick me up. I'm in a bit of a hurry.'

Waiting for Sam to arrive was agonising. She couldn't stay still and in the end she had to leave the house and walk up and down the beach to stop herself from screaming. Finally she heard the sound of his car.

She ran back to the house, darting into her bedroom to get her shoes.

The door was open but Sam knocked on it anyway and she felt a rush of relief that he was there.

'I'll be there in two seconds. I know that there's a speed limit on the island but I really need you to drive as fast as you can because I need to get to the harbour.'

'Why do you need to go there?'

She froze, then turned, her heart in her mouth. It wasn't Sam standing in the doorway, but Chase.

Blood was rushing to her head. She felt as if she were floating. 'What are you doing here? I thought you were on the boat.'

'I was. We found a cannon yesterday just before the light went. It's beautiful, hardly a nick on it. They're going back down this morning.'

'Why aren't you with them?'

Chase stared at her, his heart filling his throat.

'Because I didn't want to be there. Not without you.' Beneath her glasses, her grey eyes were wide and stunned. 'I know you don't believe me.' He took a deep breath. 'And I know you don't love me and you think I don't love you and I can understand why you would think that. Why you would think it was just words. But it's not.'

He gritted his teeth against the tears building in his throat. 'After Frida, I was so scared of loving again, that's why I didn't accept what I was feeling. But I love you, Jemima. That's why I want to come to England with you. Why I had to come here today. I don't want to be anywhere you're not and I know I didn't make that clear yesterday. I said too little, and I know it's too late but I'm not your father. I couldn't just let you leave. I had to come after you.'

Jemima felt as if her heart were about to burst. 'It's not late.' She was shaking her head. 'Not for me. Yesterday, I panicked. I've made so many mistakes in my life and I couldn't bear for you to be one of them. I thought that it would be better to remember all this, remember you, like a beautiful dream rather than try and make it real. But then you went and I couldn't breathe.'

They both moved as one, reaching for another, hands touching, gripping, tightening around each other. She felt Chase pull her closer. 'I shouldn't have left.'

Her hands tightened in his shirt. 'I shouldn't have pushed you away. I was just so scared of losing you.'

Leaning forward, he rested his forehead against hers. 'That doesn't make any sense.'

'I know.' She started to laugh, and then, quite suddenly, she was crying.

'We make sense, Jemima. You and me,' he said softly.

She reached up and touched his face. 'Perfect sense.'

Heart pounding with relief and gratitude, he lowered his mouth and kissed her. Finally, they broke apart. 'Why were you going to the harbour?'

Her face softened and he watched with delight as a blush spread across her cheeks. 'I was going to hire a boat so that I could go and look for you.'

He frowned. 'But you don't know where we're diving.'

'I would have found it because you were there, and I wouldn't have stopped until I found you. X marks the spot.' Standing on tiptoe, she brushed her lips against his.

She felt his hand still in her hair. 'You're my treasure.'

'And you're mine,' she whispered. They stood like that for a long time, just holding each other, their hearts beating in time to the waves falling onto the beach behind them. Finally Chase cleared his throat. 'Talking of treasure, I found this yesterday on the dive. Ordinarily I'd give it to a museum but then I thought of a better use for it.'

Jemima stared at the ring with its tiny blinking emerald. She was lost for words.

'I know it's a little tarnished…'

'It's beautiful,' she whispered.

'I was hoping you might wear it on this finger.' She watched him slide the ring onto the third finger of her left hand, her heart beating wildly, terrified to move in case she woke up from what must surely be a dream.

'I know this was supposed to be a one-night stand…' Chase hesitated. Not because he had doubts but because he had none and he wanted to savour that feeling of absolute rightness for just a second longer.

'It was,' Jemima said hoarsely. 'But then it became two nights, and now I don't even know how many it is.'

He nodded. 'I was wondering how you feel about for ever?'

Jemima blinked. 'Are you asking me to marry you?'

His green eyes were clear and unfaltering and as he nodded, she felt a happiness so pure it felt as though she were filling with sunlight.

'Yes.' Her eyes filled with tears. 'Yes, yes, yes…'

He pulled her against him and she felt his breath shudder against her cheek.

'Jemima Farrar,' she whispered. 'It works.'

'Of course.' He looked down into her beautiful grey eyes, feeling at ease with the world, and with himself, and so in love that he found that he was smiling. 'Or I could be Chase Friday if you prefer.'

'Really? Interesting name.'

'Yeah, I've heard you get one Robinson Crusoe joke, so use it wisely.'

She laughed and he started laughing too and then they kissed, holding each other close, then closer still as the sun rose above the beach and the waves fell against the sand.

* * * * *

COMING SOON!

We really hope you enjoyed reading this book.
If you're looking for more romance
be sure to head to the shops when
new books are available on

Thursday 4th
January

To see which titles are coming soon, please visit
millsandboon.co.uk/nextmonth

MILLS & BOON

Introducing our newest series, Afterglow.

From showing up to glowing up, Afterglow characters are on the path to leading their best lives and finding romance along the way – with a dash of sizzling spice!

Follow characters from all walks of life as they chase their dreams and find that true love is only the beginning...

Two stories published every month. Launching January 2024

millsandboon.co.uk

MILLS & BOON®

Coming next month

THE BUMP IN THEIR FORBIDDEN REUNION
Amanda Cinelli

'Sir, you can't just–' The nurse visibly fawned as she tried to remain stern, her voice high with excitement and nerves as she continued.

'She knows me.' The man stepped into the room, his dark gaze instantly landing on her. 'Don't you, Isabel?'

Izzy froze at the sound of her name on Elite One racing legend Grayson Koh's perfectly chiselled lips. For the briefest moment she felt the ridiculous urge to run to him, but then she remembered that while they may technically know one another, they had never been friends.

It had been two years since Grayson had told her she should never have married his best friend, right before he'd offered her money to stay away from the Liang family entirely.

She instantly felt her blood pressure rise.

True to form, Grayson ignored everyone and remained singularly focused upon where she sat frozen on the edge of the exam table.

When he spoke, his voice was a dry rasp. 'Am I too late…have you already done it?'

Continue reading
THE BUMP IN THEIR FORBIDDEN REUNION
Amanda Cinelli

Available next month
millsandboon.co.uk

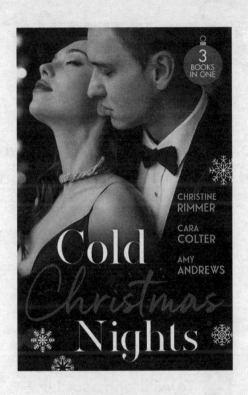

LET'S TALK

Romance

For exclusive extracts, competitions and special offers, find us online:

- **f** MillsandBoon
- **X** @MillsandBoon
- **⦿** @MillsandBoonUK
- **♪** @MillsandBoonUK

Get in touch on 01413 063 232